'Highly evocative, ...ric..
and entirely convincing'
William Boyd

'Beautifully detailed and encompassing the vagaries
of Maugham's life, the contours of
his creativity and the personal and
political tensions covertly quivering through
the sultry colony around him'
Sunday Times

'A book that believes instinctively in the
beauty of language, in the ability of
the sentence to transport us; we get
to luxuriate in every description, live inside
every image'
Andrew McMillan

'Historical fiction at its best . . .
immersive, transporting, and exquisitely crafted'
Cristina Henríquez

'An undeniably compelling tale . . .
complex and beguiling'
Big Issue

'Expertly constructed, tightly plotted and
richly atmospheric'
Financial Times

The House *of* Doors

TAN TWAN ENG

CANONGATE

To A. J. Buys

&

To the memory of my father
Tan Ghin Hai (1937–2013)

This paperback edition published in Great Britain in 2024 by Canongate Books

First published in Great Britain in 2023
by Canongate Books Ltd, 14 High Street, Edinburgh EH1 1TE

canongate.co.uk

3

Interview with Tan Twan Eng and Tom Sutcliffe on *Front Row* 15 May 2023
reproduced with permission of the BBC

The right of Tan Twan Eng to be identified as the
author of this work has been asserted by him in accordance
with the Copyright, Designs and Patents Act 1988

Excerpt from *The Summing Up* by William Somerset Maugham
© The Royal Literary Fund. Reproduced by permission of United Agents LLP
(unitedagents.co.uk) on behalf of The Royal Literary Fund.

British Library Cataloguing-in-Publication Data
A catalogue record for this book is available on
request from the British Library

ISBN 978 1 83885 833 9

Typeset in Bembo by Palimpsest Book Production Ltd,
Falkirk, Stirlingshire

Printed and bound by CPI (UK) Ltd, Croydon CR0 4YY

'Fact and fiction are so intermingled in my work that now, looking back on it, I can hardly distinguish one from the other.'
Somerset Maugham, *The Summing Up*

BOOK ONE

Prologue

Lesley
Doornfontein, South Africa, 1947

A story, like a bird of the mountain, can carry a name beyond the clouds, beyond even time itself. Willie Maugham said that to me, many years ago.

He has not appeared in my thoughts in a long time, but as I gaze at the mountains from my stoep on this autumn morning I can hear his thin, dry voice, his diction precise, correct, like everything else about him. In my memory I see him again, on his last night in our old house on the other side of the world, the two of us on the verandah behind the house, talking quietly, the full moon a coracle of light adrift above the sea. Everyone else in the house had already retired to bed. When morning came he sailed from Penang, and I never saw him again.

Ten thousand days and nights have drifted down the endless river since that evening. I live on the shores of a different sea now, a sea of silent stone and sand.

Half an hour earlier I was finishing my breakfast on the stoep when I noticed, on the ridge below, a familiar figure pedalling up the steep and dusty dirt road. I followed him with my eyes as he came over the rise and coasted down the short, poplar-lined driveway. Reaching the stoep he dismounted from his bicycle and propped it against its kickstand.

'Goeie more, Mrs Hamlyn,' he called out.

'Morning, Johan.'

He took out a parcel from his saddlebag, came onto the stoep and handed it to me. The parcel was wrapped in heavy brown paper and secured with two loops of twine, but I could tell that it was a book. Robert had been dead nearly six years now, but his post – catalogues and gifts of books from antiquarian booksellers in London, newsletters from his clubs – continued to trickle its way here long after I had informed the senders of his death.

'It's not for Mr Hamlyn,' said Johan. 'It's for you.'

'Oh?' I patted around my pockets for my reading glasses, put them on and squinted at the name typed on the parcel: Mrs Lesley C. Hamlyn.

For a moment or two I continued to stare at my own name. Except for the monthly letter from my son in London, I couldn't remember when last I had received any post addressed to me.

Johan pointed to the stamps. 'Funny-looking bird.'

'It's a hornbill,' I said. The bird's large, curved beak and heavy, bony quiff gave it a comical appearance. It perched on a branch above the words 'B.M.A. MALAYA'.

'Keep them for me?'

I blinked at him. 'What? Oh. Yes, of course.' I put the package down on the table. 'Cup of tea, Johan?'

He shook his head. 'Full bag of mail today.' He turned to go, but I stopped him. 'Wait, Johan.' I hurried inside the house and returned a moment later with a small paper bag. 'Some koeksisters for you.'

'Baie dankie! Yours are the best, even better than Tannie Elsie's.'

'You'd better not let her hear that.'

'Ja, she's still sore you won best melktert at the kerk basaar. She told my mother you shouldn't even be allowed to enter the competition.'

Even after twenty-five years there were still some people in the district who saw me as an outsider.

Johan was looking at me, a slightly worried expression on his face. He nodded at the package he had brought me. 'I hope it's not bad news?'

I did not answer him. I watched him as he pedalled away and disappeared down the road. Returning to the table, I sat down, drew the parcel towards me and examined it. There was no return address, but the postmarks, smudged like aged tattoos, told me that it had been mailed from Penang sometime in September 1946. The tangle of overlapping addresses by different hands had somehow managed to pick up my wind-blown spoor: the package had been sent to Robert's old chambers in London, before being forwarded to our solicitor in Cape Town and, almost half a year after it had been posted from Penang, it had found me on this sheep farm fifteen miles outside Beaufort West.

I cut the twine with my fruit knife, inserted its tip into a fold of the wrapping and with two or three brisk strokes filleted the package open. The corner of a book appeared. I peeled away the wrapping until the title revealed itself: *The Casuarina Tree* by W. Somerset Maugham.

There was nothing else in the package – no letter, no note. I turned the book over in my hands. Robert collected first editions, and he had all of Willie Maugham's books – his novels and his short-story anthologies, the plays and the essays. It crossed my mind that this volume in my hands was a first edition too, the colours of the tropical trees and the blue sky on its dustjacket already faded.

The table of contents listed half a dozen stories. I thumbed the pages to the last one. Murmuring the story's opening paragraph under my breath, I found myself instantly transported back to Malaya. I felt a heavy tropical heat smothering me, thick and steamy, and the pungent, salty tang of the mudflats at low tide clogged my nostrils.

I checked the title page, but there was no inscription, nor a signature. Printed underneath the title was the arcane-looking glyph Maugham placed in all of his books. This particular one, however, was slightly different: some unknown hand had drawn a thin, black vertical rectangle around the symbol, enclosing it in the centre. Running from top to bottom was another straight black line, bisecting the frame precisely in the middle.

I frowned, puzzled.

An instant later I saw it, I understood what the lines were telling me. Carefully, as though fearful that any sudden movement would dislodge the rectangle around the symbol, I set the book down on the table. The open page arched slightly in a passing breeze, then flattened out again. I leaned back in my chair, my gaze fastened on the glyph, this anchor embedded in the paper.

Robert and I had uprooted ourselves from Penang at the end of 1922, sailing on a P&O liner to Cape Town. We stayed a pleasant fortnight in a hotel by the sea before taking the train to Beaufort West, a little town three hundred or so miles to the northeast. Bernard, Robert's cousin, was a sheep farmer, and he had built us a modest bungalow on his land. The bungalow, whitewashed and capped with a corrugated tin roof painted a dark green, stood on a high broad ridge. From the deep and shady verandah – I would never get used to the locals calling it a 'stoep', I told myself – we had an unbroken vista of the mountains to the north. These mountains had been formed by the dying ripples of the earth's upheavals an eternity ago, upheavals that had begun far to the south at the very tip of the continent.

It was high summer when we arrived, the sun smiting the earth. Everything was so bleak – the parchment landscape, the faces of the people, even the light itself. How I ached for the monsoon skies of the equator, for the ever-changing tints of its chameleon sea.

A week after we had settled into our new home we were invited to the farmhouse for dinner. The sun was just burrowing into the mountains when we walked the half-mile there from our bungalow. We had to stop a few times along the way for Robert to catch his breath. Bernard Presgrave was thirty-eight, twelve years Robert's junior. Robust and ruddy-faced, he reminded me of Robert when I first married him. His farm was called Doornfontein, the Fountain of Thorns, the kind of inauspicious name that would have set my old amah Ah Peng muttering darkly, 'Asking for trouble only.' But Bernard and his wife Helena, a placid and dull girl from the Cape, appeared to be prospering.

The other guests – farmers and their wives from around the area – were already gathered in the straggly garden behind the farmhouse when we arrived. We joined them in a circle beneath a camelthorn tree, its bare branches spiked with thin white thorns as long as my little finger. The laughter and shrieks of the children playing at the bottom of the garden rang across the evening air. A pair of oil drums, cut open in half, rested on trestles, wood fire lapping away at their insides. Lamb chops and coils of sausages were smoking away on the grill. The farmers were Boers, blunt-faced and blunt-spoken, but affable once we got to know them. The meat of the gossip that evening – and chewed over and over into gristle throughout the district that summer, I would discover – concerned a wealthy middle-aged Englishman and his beautiful young wife who had moved to Beaufort West from London the previous summer.

'His doctor advised him that the air here would be good for her,' said Bernard, keeping one eye on the lamb chops on the grill. 'Graham – the husband – bought a piece of land on Jannie van der Walt's farm and built their new home on it, a great big house. We'll take you out there one of these days to take a gander at it.' Bernard went to the oil drums and flipped the lamb chops over; fat dripped onto the fire, sending clouds of maddened smoke hissing into the air. 'The wife's health improved,' he resumed when he sat down again, 'but one morning, about three weeks ago, she walked out on him. Left him when he was still snoring away in his bed.'

'She took all her jewels,' Helena picked up the tale, 'but she didn't leave a letter for Graham, the poor man, not even a note.'

Bernard chuckled. 'Knowing Graham, that deplorable lack of manners probably enraged him more than anything else.'

'Ai, that's not funny, Bernard,' his wife said.

'Coincidentally, our GP in the dorp disappeared that same morning,' Bernard continued. 'Left his wife behind. Neither hair nor hide of him has ever been seen again.'

I glanced over to Robert sitting opposite me; our eyes met. 'Just the sort of tale Willie would have relished,' he said.

'Willie?' asked Bernard.

'Somerset Maugham,' said Robert.

'Who's he?' one of the guests asked.

'A writer,' Robert said. 'A very famous one. An old friend, actually. He stayed with us in Penang. He's promised to visit us here. We'll introduce you to him when he comes.'

'I liked some of his stories,' said Helena. 'But "Rain"' – she made a face – 'I'll never forget that one.'

'Is dit 'n lekker spook storie?' one of the men asked, rubbing his hands together with relish.

'No,' replied Helena. 'It's about a . . . a woman.' Her face flushed; she smoothed the folds of her skirt around her knees. 'Oh, I'll lend you the book, Gert – you can read it yourself.'

'Ag, who has time to read?'

Bernard grinned at me. 'Did he put you two in his stories?'

Twilight was dissolving the mountains. I pulled my shawl closer around my shoulders. 'He probably found us,' I said, giving just the briefest of glances at Robert, 'to be the most boring married couple he'd ever met.'

Life here for us was not much different from our old one in Penang. Robert and I had our own bedrooms, and every morning we would meet for breakfast on the verandah. Afterwards he would adjourn to his study to work on his memoirs — he had begun writing them shortly after we moved here. There was not much to keep me busy around the house. Liesbet, the wife of one of the Coloured farm workers, cooked and cleaned for us. She was a few years older than me, a fat woman with broad flanks and a round smiling face which reminded me of the Malays in Penang. To fill my days I decided to create a garden in front of the house. The soil was as dry as the powder in my compact, but with the help of Liesbet's son Pietman, I persevered with it.

In the evenings Robert and I would relax on the verandah with our whisky stengahs and gin pahits and watch another day slip away behind the mountains. And later, before we retired to our bedrooms, I would play my piano for a while. Robert would sit in his armchair, sipping his favourite pu'er tea, his eyes closed as he drifted away to the music.

On the large map pinned up in his study the lower shores of the Great Karoo lie about a hundred and fifty miles to the north of Doornfontein. But there were days when I felt it was much closer, and I was convinced I could sense its timeless silence reaching out from the deepest heart of the desert — its stillness, its infinite emptiness. It called to my mind a story I had once heard: a pair of explorers, husband and wife, had got lost during an expedition across the Gobi Desert. To hide their growing despair and feelings of hopelessness as they wandered deeper and deeper into the desert, they stopped talking to each other. I often wondered which of the two was more oppressive: the silence of the desert, or the silence between the husband and his wife.

The sound of the screen door opening and banging against the wall pulls me back to the present. I lift my eyes from the page and close the book. Liesbet steps out onto the stoep, her white starched apron taut over the prow of her stomach. She only comes in once a week these days, and without fail she'll moan about her painful knees as she cleans the house.

'Another book?' she says, stacking my plate and teacup onto her tray. 'Everywhere in the house, books, books, books.'

'Yes . . . another book . . .'

She puts down her tray and peers more closely at me. Offering a watery smile to her, I take the book with me into the house.

In the sitting room I walk past my watercolour paintings of old Penang shophouses to the wall of photographs above the Blüthner piano. I lean back and study the photographs, searching for a particular one I have in mind. I have not looked – really looked – at them in years.

Many of the photographs are of Robert and me with our two sons. A few of them show people who had visited us in Penang: stage actors, MPs, members of the aristocracy, writers, opera singers. I can't even recall their names now; and anyway, they are probably all long dead. Claiming pride of place on this wall of imprisoned time is my wedding portrait. Robert and I are standing on the steps of St George's church in Penang. I straighten the slight tilt of the silver frame, wiping the thin layer of dust from it with my forefinger.

People around here had expected me to pack up and return to Penang after I buried Robert. There were days when I asked myself why I didn't do it. But – sail home . . . to what? And to whom? Everyone I had known in Malaya was either dead or had disappeared into distant lands and different lives. And then war had broken out all over the world and the Japanese had invaded Malaya. So I had remained here, a daub of paint worked by time's paintbrush into this vast, eternal landscape.

Below my wedding portrait hangs a photograph of two women, their blouses and frocks and hats quaintly old-fashioned, from another age: Ethel and me, each with a rifle in our hands, the mock-Tudor façade of the Spotted Dog in Kuala Lumpur looming behind us. The photograph had been taken after a shooting competition on the padang. Poor, poor Ethel. My eyes glide to the photograph next to it. I unhook it and study it in the light of the windows. Looking at the four of us – Willie Maugham and Gerald and Robert and myself – lounging in our rattan chairs under the casuarina tree in the garden, my mind loops back to the two weeks in 1921 when the writer and his secretary had stayed with us at Cassowary House.

I put down the photograph. The morning is decanting its light down the slopes of the far mountains. It is the autumn equinox today; here, in the southern bowl of the earth, the portions of day and night are exactly equal. The world is at an equilibrium, but I myself feel unsteady, off-balance.

There is not the slightest stir of wind, and there is no sound, not even the usual petulant bleating of sheep from the valley. The world is so still, so quiescent, that I wonder if it has stopped turning. But then, high above the land, I see a tremor in the air. A pair of raptors, far from their mountain eyrie. For a minute or two I want to believe they are brahminy kites, but of course they cannot be.

My eyes follow the two birds as they drift on the span of their out-stretched wings, writing circles over circles on the empty page of sky.

Chapter One

Willie
Penang, 1921

Somerset Maugham woke up choking for air. Violent coughing rocked his body until, finally, blessedly, it subsided, and he could breathe again.

He lay in his bed inside the cocoon of the mosquito netting, waiting for his breathing to return to normal. There was the faintest aftertaste of mud on his tongue. He swallowed once, licking his lips, and the taste disappeared from his mouth.

His body felt waterlogged as he pushed himself up against the head-board. He had been dreaming: a great wave had swept him overboard into a turbulent river; muddy water poured down his gullet, flooding his lungs and weighting him down into the sunless depths. It was at that point that he had jerked awake in a frenzy of apnoeic snorting.

Parting the mosquito netting, he sat up on the edge of the bed, planting his feet on the floorboards. He felt more fatigued than he had been when he went to sleep. He had kicked the Dutch wife onto the floor, and he was certain he had cried out at the instant he awoke; he hoped no one had heard. He cocked his head to one side, listening; there was only the slurring of the waves on the beach.

His room was sparsely furnished: a rattan armchair by the windows, a low bookcase spilling out with old and yellowing novels, an oakwood chest of drawers against one wall and, in the corner, a washstand with a porcelain basin. Taking up half a wall was a teak almeirah, his bags and trunks stacked on top of it.

He touched the framed photograph of his mother on the bedside table, making a minute adjustment to its position, turning her face more towards the windows. Her brown eyes had always looked mournful, even in his memories; this morning they seemed more melancholy than usual. He picked up the Dutch wife from the floor and set it back on his bed before padding barefoot across the room. He opened the window shutters and leaned out.

The world still lay under a grey ink wash, but at the edges of the sky a pale glow was seeping in. Set in a corner on the first floor of the house, his room had extensive views of the garden below. To his left, about ten yards away, a low wooden fence ran along the bottom of the garden, marking the property from the beach. By the fence grew a tall casuarina tree, a wrought-iron garden bench in its shade. Squinting at the beach, he made out the figure of Lesley Hamlyn. She was standing at the waterline, staring out to sea. A moment later she turned around and started back towards the house. She slipped through the wooden gate and strolled up the lawn, disappearing beneath the verandah roof without looking up at him.

The houseboy had yet to bring Willie his ewer of hot shaving water. He rinsed his face at the basin and picked out a fresh set of clothes from the wardrobe – a long-sleeved white cotton shirt, a pair of khaki slacks, and a cream linen jacket, pressed by the dhobi the previous evening while they were at dinner. He found his shoes lined up outside his bedroom door, polished to an opulent sheen. The Hamlyns' bedrooms were across the wide landing, their doors closed. Halfway down the landing was a living area, jutting out to form the top of the porch, the windows on its three sides over-looking the front lawn and the crescent driveway. Beyond this square space were four more rooms. On his side of the landing were the guest bathroom and, next to it, Gerald's room. Gerald's brogues had also been shined and set down outside his door. Willie proceeded along the landing to the staircase, pausing now and again to study the row of watercolours on the wall. They were paintings of local shophouses, their thin, black lines – architectural in their precision – detailing the elaborate plasterworks of the shopfronts. The meticulousness of the drawings was enlivened by the brushstrokes of vivid colours, artfully capturing the atmosphere of the teeming, cacophonous Asiatic quarters in the towns of the Straits Settlements. Each one of the paintings had a title in the bottom right corner – Moulmein Road; Bangkok Lane; Ah Quee Street; Rope Walk – and all of them, Willie discovered as he squinted at the signature, had been painted by Lesley Hamlyn.

Downstairs, he made his way through the bright, airy house to the verandah at the back, nodding to the houseboys who stood aside for him in the corridors. Robert and Lesley were already at the breakfast table, walled off from each other behind their newspapers. Willie studied them from the doorway. He remembered Robert as a handsome man, tall and bull-shouldered, so he had been dismayed by the stooped figure who had met him under the porch the previous afternoon, leaning on a gold-headed Malacca cane walking stick and breathing in shallow gasps; the thick head of hair Robert once possessed was gone, the dome of his head now a depilated basilica, with just a narrow fringe of sparse grey hair above his ears. He hadn't recognised his old friend's voice either – the resplendent baritone he used to envy had shrivelled to a querulous, fissured tone.

The Doberman lying at Robert's feet lifted his head and barked as Willie approached the table. Husband and wife lowered their newspapers. 'Don't be rude, Claudius,' Robert said, reaching down to rub the dog's ears. 'Morning, Willie. You're bright and early. Sleep well?'

'Like a . . . baby,' Willie stammered.

'Help yourself, Willie,' Robert said, nodding his chin at the sideboard.

Willie opened the lids of the chafing dishes. Kippers and bacon and sausages and eggs and toast, as he had expected. There were also plates of cheeses and bowls of local fruit – bananas and mangoes and starfruit. He filled only half his plate and sat down at the table.

'Don't be shy, Willie,' said Robert.

'I still can't get' – Willie's jaw jutted out, struggling to force his next word out – 'get used to the Falstaffian appetites of you people here,' he said, finally overcoming the blockage in his throat that made people regard him with pity and impatience. 'The heaps of food at . . . every meal . . . in this . . . heat . . .' He turned towards Lesley. 'I saw you . . . on the . . . beach.'

'My morning walk,' she said. 'Your secretary – Gerald – is he up yet?'

The hitch in her words was delicate, but Willie caught it. Holding her gaze, he said, 'He's not an . . . early riser. It won't cause any inconvenience, I trust?'

'Don't be daft, Willie,' Robert replied, and added to Lesley, 'Tell Cookie to set something aside for him every morning, won't you, my dear?'

Robert cut a wedge of Camembert and fed it to the Doberman. The dog wolfed it down, licking its chops. 'Claudius loves his cheese.' Robert grinned as he fed the dog another piece. Lesley's lips, Willie noticed, had disappeared into a thin, taut wire.

'You have a visitor.' He pointed to a monitor lizard emerging from the bottom of the hibiscus hedge. The creature was about three feet long, its thick tail almost the length of its body. It crawled across the lawn with a squat, muscular grace, its tongue flicking in and out. The sparrows pecking on the grass flew off.

'Oh, that's just Monty,' said Robert. 'He showed up here a few years ago. Takes his daily dip in the Warburtons' pool next door. So what's on the cards today, old chap? Lesley'll be delighted to show you the sights.'

Lesley cut in before he could reply. 'I'm meeting the church bazaar ladies today, and I have errands to run in town afterwards.'

'Well, one of these days, then,' said Robert. 'The old girl's quite the expert on our island's history, Willie. Knows everything about the place. Used to give our friends from abroad tours of the town. We showed that German writer around when he was in Penang – what was his name, dear? Hesse, wasn't it? Yes. Hermann Hesse.'

'Quiet, lazy days on . . . the beach, that's all I want,' Willie said. 'I've piles . . . of books to read, and Gerald hasn't fully recovered yet. He needs his rest, lots . . . of it.'

'The poor boy did look rather peaky last night.' Robert peered over his spectacles at Willie. 'And so do you, if you don't mind me saying.'

'The past few weeks have been rather . . . trying. Herman Hesse was in Penang?'

'Eleven or twelve years ago. I've never read any of his stuff. Have you?'

'A couple of them. If you're finished with that paper, Robert . . .'

Robert passed him the *Straits Times* and they ate their breakfast in a comfortable silence. Lesley excused herself and went inside when Robert left for his chambers in town. Willie remained at the table, nursing his cup of tea.

A squeaking noise made him look over the balustrade. A white-haired Tamil in a singlet and khaki shorts had come around the side of the house, pushing a wheelbarrow. He stopped at the edge of the lawn and selected a short-handled scythe from his bundle of tools in the wheelbarrow. Sinking onto his haunches, he began to swing the scythe in a languid rhythm, the sickle blade spitting out tufts of grass as it skimmed over the lawn.

Going up to his bedroom, Willie stopped outside Gerald's room and pressed his ear to the door. He heard nothing. 'Gerald,' he called softly. There was no reply, not even the faintest stirring from within. Hardly surprising, thought Willie, considering the number of drinks he had polished off the previous evening.

He collected his journal and returned downstairs. The houseboys had already cleared the breakfast table. Stepping out onto the lawn, he decided to follow the gravel path and explore the garden. The turning and twisting path gave the impression that the grounds were more extensive than they actually were, an illusion heightened by the tall, impressive trees: a fig tree buttressed in place by the triangular wedges of its roots; nutmeg trees in fruit, remnants of the spice plantations which Robert told him used to cover this side of the island; a pair of pinang trees from which, he recalled reading somewhere, the island took its name. And there it was, the raintree Robert had boasted about last night. 'Three hundred years old, Willie. One of the oldest on the island. Its trunk is so wide it takes three men with their arms fully stretched out to encircle it. Walter – he's the superintendent of the Botanic Garden – he regularly brings people to see it.'

Willie pressed his palm to the hard, crocodilian bark. He pictured the great roots of the tree clawed deep into the earth, keeping the colossus upright. The trunk itself climbed almost sixty feet to the sky, spreading out into an intricate filigree of branches and leaves that reminded Willie of the network of bronchioli and alveoli in a set of lungs.

He resumed his stroll, nodding a greeting to the syce washing the Humber outside the garage. Behind the garage lay a tennis court, the scuffed white lines interrupted here and there by mounds of dead leaves and puddles of rainwater. A crow perched on a rusting net pole, turning its head left and right as though refereeing a game.

Willie returned to the bench under the casuarina tree. The area around the tree was littered with its twigs and small, spiky seeds. He pulled down one of the low-hanging branches and examined it, his thumb rubbing the long, grey-green twigs and the leathery leaves.

The kebun dropped his sickle blade and scuttled towards Willie, grabbed the rag slung over a knobbly shoulder and with a show of vigorous effort wiped the dew off the bench. When he finished Willie offered him a cigarette. The man flashed him a vampiric smile. Willie winced inwardly: even after all these months travelling around the

Federated Malay States, the sight of teeth stained blood-red by betelnut juice still made him queasy.

He settled into the bench and opened his journal to a new page, uncapped his fountain pen and printed the date on the top right corner: 2nd March, 1921. He tapped his pen against his teeth, then added in his neat writing: 'Arrived in Cassowary House yesterday afternoon. Still weak, but feeling much improved today.' He ran his writer's eye over the house. Gerald's windows were open, a breeze pawing at the curtains. He thought for a moment. 'The house is of a comfortable size, square and double-storeyed, similar to many of the Anglo-Indian styled houses I've seen in Malaya. Compared to the houses along Northam Road I saw on the drive from the harbour yesterday – mansions with Corinthian columns and great pediments capping cavernous porticoes – Cassowary House looks unpretentious, it is a house at ease with its own unassuming lines.' He paused, before adding, 'The terracotta roof tiles – they look like a pangolin's hide.'

He paged back to the entry he had written on the evening over a month ago when he and Gerald had returned to Kuching from the interior. He scanned a few paragraphs, then stopped. The events were still too upsetting to read. He scanned the notes on Penang he had made from his copy of *Bradshaw's Through Routes to the Chief Cities*. The island was once part of the territory ruled by the Sultanate of Kedah on the mainland. In the late eighteenth century Captain Francis Light obtained a lease on it for the East India Company from the Sultan and named it Prince of Wales Island. Light had turned it into a free port to divert trade from the Dutch colonies on the other side of the Straits of Malacca. The island was Britain's first outpost in South-East Asia and the capital of the Straits Settlements ('Britain's most important Crown Colony in the Far East', his Bradshaw proclaimed). From Penang they had extended their reach down to Malacca, Singapore and, eventually, into the Federated Malay States and the Unfederated Malay States. In the eighteenth century, tin mining attracted coolies from southern China, while indentured Indian labourers were shipped in to work in the rubber plantations.

He studied the map of Penang he had copied into his journal. The island was about a third of the size of Singapore, its shape reminding him of a wildebeest's hide Syrie had splayed on the floor of his sitting room. He had found it loathsome and had demanded that she get rid of it. This had, inevitably, sparked off another one of their rows.

Willie pushed her out of his mind. From the moment he left England, months ago, he had not thought about her, and he had no desire – or any need, thank God – to think about her now.

The kebun was padding barefoot around the garden, his soles surprisingly pink, his footsteps as light as . . . Willie foraged in his mind for a description, finding it a second later: *as though he was but a brief sojourner in a strange land*. He murmured the sentence to himself a few times, testing out its rhythm. He liked it, and jotted it in his journal. He eyed the page lying open on his lap. He had written just two sentences since he sat down. He closed his journal and pocketed his fountain pen. I'm not going to feel guilty. I came here to recuperate. I'm not going to do a stitch of work. I will rest and swim. I will read the books I want to read and play bridge and explore the island.

The wind frisked the topmost branches of the trees. Golden orioles flitted around the garden. Listening to the waves fizzing on the sand, Willie felt the knots in his body slowly unravelling. He was looking forward to a slothful, restorative stay here with Gerald, free from all cares.

Lesley had appeared on the verandah. She waved something she was holding at him. His eyes followed her as she came down the steps and crossed the lawn, heading straight towards him. She was of medium height, her slender build and rigid posture adding inches to her and giving her an assured bearing. Probably hard on forty, Willie guessed. She was dressed in a cream silk blouse and a matching skirt. She had been solicitous when they arrived yesterday, serving them tea and sticky rice cakes in the sitting room, but there was something wary about her, something tightly closed-up.

'Don't get up, Willie,' she said as he half rose from the bench. 'Your mail from Singapore.' She handed him a bundle of letters and a small parcel wrapped in brown paper. Her long, thin fingers moved with the articulated grace of a spider's legs. 'I'm off to town. Cookie will have tiffin ready at one. Robert will be home by then.'

'Is he . . . well enough to work?'

'He'd be bored stiff if he stayed at home all day. Anyway, he only works until lunchtime. Oh – if you're going out, get one of the houseboys to run out to the road for a rickshaw. It's fifteen cents into town. Don't pay more than that.'

'We're not going anywhere today—'

'Excuse me, Willie.' She beckoned to the kebun weeding by the cannas. 'Bala!'

The man hurried towards her, the cigarette Willie had given him still unlit and tucked behind his ear. Lesley strode around the garden, pointing at the shrubs and beds, the kebun nodding vigorously at her instructions. Willie listened to her giving a list of tasks to the gardener; she spoke not the hodgepodge of English and Malay that the mem-sahibs used when giving orders to the natives, but what sounded to his untutored ears like fluent Malay.

Willie put on his reading spectacles and thumbed through his mail. The letters were graffitied in tangles of crossed-out addresses and arrows of various colours, pursuing him around the world. He recognised a letter from his lawyers in New York and one from his wife. He frowned – most likely Syrie would be asking for more money – she had been going on and on about redecorating their house before he left London. He dropped her letter to the side, unopened, and turned all his attention to the package.

It was from his publisher, and he knew straightaway what lay inside. He unwrapped it slowly, resisting the urge to rip it open, and took out a copy of his latest book, *On a Chinese Screen*. It was the first time he was holding it in his hands – he had left England shortly after delivering the manuscript to his agent.

He examined the cover and was pleased to find no mistakes or imperfections. He brushed his fingers along the spine, turned the book over and then to the front again. Bringing it to his nose, he thumbed through the pages, losing himself in the ascetic fragrance of a new book. He stroked the title and his name on the jacket. Even after so many novels and countless short stories, he still felt a warming surge of pride every time he held his latest book in his hands.

Resting the book on his thigh, he picked up the letter from his lawyer and opened it. It was probably an offer from a publisher or a theatre producer. He read it once, then he read it again. He had invested £40,000 – all of his money – with Trippe & Company, a brokerage firm in New York. He had hoped that he would make enough from the investment so that he would never have to write for money again.

Trippe & Company had collapsed, his lawyers regretted to inform him. He had lost all his money, every penny of it.

A hot, acidulous nausea flooded his stomach, searing his throat. He fought back the urge to vomit. He sat there, the letter pinched between thumb and forefinger, its corners twitching in the breeze.

'Are you all right, Willie? Willie?'

He jerked his head up, squinting against the bright sunshine. Lesley had come back to him. Her face, hovering over him, was blurry. 'My goodness, you're white as a sheet.' Her eyes darted to the letter in his hand. 'Not bad news, I hope?'

He swallowed once, and then swallowed again, forcing down his nausea. 'Just the . . . the . . . colitis, that's all.' He was mortified that he was stammering more than usual. Fighting against it would only make it worse, he knew, but he couldn't help himself. 'It comes and . . . goes. I haven't . . . completely . . . recovered from it. Caught it . . . in . . . Java.'

'You don't look well. I'll send for Dr Joyce.'

He raised his palm. His arm, his whole body, felt leaden. 'I'm . . . all right.' He folded the letter and stuffed it into his shirt pocket. His movements tipped his book off his lap onto the grass. He bent down to retrieve it, using the opportunity to draw in a few long, deep breaths to calm his thoughts.

'Are you sure?' said Lesley.

He wished she would stop talking. 'I'm all right, Lesley,' he said again, peevishly. To divert her attention he showed her the book. 'My latest book.'

'Oh, how marvellous,' she said, 'you must be terribly pleased.' She noticed the title on the cover. '*On a Chinese Screen*. Very evocative. A novel?'

'A collection of . . . sketches . . . of what I saw in China — the places I visited, the people I met.'

A watchful expression stilled her face. 'When were you there?'

'Two years ago.' He patted the space on the bench beside him.

Lesley remained standing. 'Where did you go?'

'We started . . . from Shanghai. We travelled two thousand miles up the Yangtze in a rice barge, into the heart of China. The Yangtze is the longest—'

'The longest river in China, yes, yes, I know all that. How long were you there?'

'Four or five months. We travelled deep inland, walked our feet flat.'

'Did you ever . . .' She stopped, then began again. 'Did you ever come across any mention of Dr Sun Yat Sen?'

'Just about everywhere we went. Intriguing chap, from all that I heard. Speaks English fluently too, apparently. I wish I could have . . . met him and talked to him.'

'He passed through here about ten years ago.'

'Really? What was he doing in Penang?

'Raising money for the Tong Meng Hui, his party. He planned his revolution while he was staying here, you know.'

'Did you meet him?'

'Robert and I did, yes. A few times.'

Willie stared at her. This was getting more interesting. 'I'd like to hear more about him. I've been thinking of writing a novel about China for some time now. Sun Yat . . . Sen would make a most unusual . . . character.'

She took a step forward, into the shade of the casuarina. 'What was it like there?'

His gaze turned inward, down into the long tunnel of his memories. 'I've worked in the worst slums of London, but I'd never witnessed so much misery until I went to China,' he said, relieved that his stammer had left him. 'Warlords fighting one another, the bodies of slaughtered soldiers and civilians piled high in the fields; townsfolk fleeing their homes to hide in the countryside. We saw villages lying in ruins and thousands of peasants dead or dying from hunger and pestilence.'

'Ten years after the revolution, ten years after they got rid of the emperor,' said Lesley, 'and nothing has changed, has it? Nothing.'

The bitterness in her voice made him study her more closely. On his travels around the Federated Malay States and the Straits Settlements he had never met any European – man or woman – who had shown the faintest interest in China or, for that matter, in any other country in the East. Instead, they had wanted to hear only about the happenings in England, the latest West End shows, the newest cafés and shops in Piccadilly. Willie had found himself travelling from London to the opposite end of the earth, only to be interrogated about the world he had left behind.

'When were you there?' he asked.

'China? I've never been there.'

She reached out and took the book from him. She turned the pages unhurriedly, her eyes skimming them from top to bottom. She seemed, Willie thought, to be dredging the text for something buried in it.

Keeping his body completely still, Willie studied her. Lesley's hair was a pale blond, falling down to an inch or two above her shoulders. The sunlight sculpted out her sharp cheekbones. The climate had not sagged her skin or smudged the line of her jaw, but fine lines sprouted from the outer edges of her deep-set eyes, which were the colour of old tea. The corners of her mouth were slightly curled, pulled downwards by another tangle of lines, giving them an anatine look.

Not a great beauty, Willie had decided when he first met her yesterday afternoon, and now confirmed it to himself again; nevertheless, her face had a compelling, doleful quality.

She closed the book before she came to the end. She studied its cover once more, then relinquished it to Willie.

'Would you like . . . to borrow it?' he asked, surprising himself – he never lent anyone the first editions of his own books.

'Oh, I'm sure Robert's ordered a copy already – he has all your books, you know. We have an excellent bookshop in town – Ackroyd's on Bishop Street. It's as good as any in Singapore.'

'You won't find this on the shelves here for a few more months yet.'

'I'll wait.'

Giving him a nod, she turned around and strode across the lawn. He watched her take the three low steps onto the verandah and disappear inside the house.

A voice was hailing him. He looked up and saw Gerald leaning out of his windows. 'Bloody gorgeous morning, eh?'

Even with his hair mussed by sleep, his cheeks gaunt and unshaven, he looked magnificent, Willie thought. The heaviness in his chest lifted momentarily.

'Be down soon!' Gerald said, tucking his head back into his room.

Willie pulled out the letter from his pocket and read it again. Forty thousand pounds. All the money he possessed in the world, gone up in smoke.

Chapter Two

Lesley
Penang, 1921

The traffic heading into town was still heavy when I left home. Motor cars honked at us whenever my rickshaw strayed from the edge of the road. 'Sorry, mem,' my rickshaw-puller called over his shoulder.

'Ignore them, Ah Leck,' I said.

Just a few years ago the only vehicles you'd see were bicycles and horse-drawn gharries and carriages, but the rubber boom had drawn countless motor cars onto the roads. The Chinese towkays, they had to have the largest and most expensive motor cars, naturally, and everyone thought nothing of speeding around at fifteen, twenty miles an hour. Twenty miles! Sheer madness.

Any other day and I would have been lulled by my rickshaw's steady, lilting rhythm, but my thoughts continued to linger on Willie Maugham as I was conveyed into town. The fact that he knew something about Sun Yat Sen had surprised me. The letter he was reading had obviously rattled him – the poor man had looked positively bilious. I just hoped he wasn't going to have a relapse while he stayed with us.

The writer's travels had been documented in detail by the news-papers from the moment he arrived in Singapore. A few weeks ago

Robert announced to me that he had cabled Maugham in Singapore, inviting him to stay with us.

'Is that wise?' I asked. We hadn't had any house guests since Robert came home from the war.

'I haven't seen Willie in twenty years,' Robert said. 'It'd be marvellous if he comes, absolutely marvellous.'

The house *did* feel empty ever since our boys returned to England for their new term. The writer's presence would certainly liven things up.

'Does he know you're here?' I asked.

'I doubt it – we lost touch after I moved to Hong Kong. But he'll be delighted to see us, I'm sure of it.'

Robert's invitation to the author elicited no response, and I thought the matter had all been forgotten, but a few days ago at lunch he had waved a telegram at me. 'He's replied. Willie's replied. I knew he would. He's astounded to hear from me, he says. He couldn't believe it. Anyway – he's coming to stay.'

'He certainly took his time replying.'

'He was in Sarawak, that's why he didn't get my letter. And he's been awfully ill.'

'How long is he staying?' I asked. Cookie had made Robert's favourite: deep-fried chicken chop swimming in a thick brown gravy of Worcestershire sauce and served with peas and a banana fritter.

'Two weeks.'

'That's rather long, isn't it?'

'Stop fretting, my dear. He won't be a difficult guest. We shared rooms for a year, did I ever tell you?'

His eyes were shining, and there was an excited note in his voice. I had not seen him in such high spirits in ages. 'I'll prepare a room for him.'

'He's travelling with his secretary. Chap by the name of—' He checked the telegram again. 'Haxton. Gerald Haxton.'

'Oh. Two rooms, then.'

Robert looked up at me. He blinked slowly. 'What? Oh, yes. Two rooms. Yes. Of course.' He withdrew into his own thoughts, chewing his food. A moment later he lowered his knife and fork. 'Just one thing, my dear.'

'What is it?'

'Watch what you say to Willie. He's my friend, but he's also a writer, and there's nothing he loves more than snuffling out people's scandals and secrets.'

'Oh dear.'

'During the war there was talk that he was working for the Secret Service.'

'You mean . . . he was a *spy*?'

'The word was that he ran a network of agents in Geneva.'

I found the notion of a spy staying with us – snooping through our cupboards and drawers and prying into our lives – not at all pleasant.

'All this constant travelling of his – it's probably a front for gathering information, spying for the government,' Robert went on. 'I wonder if he still stammers. He used to, you know. Quite painfully.'

'Like Clive Featherstone.'

'Clive doesn't stammer. He stutters.'

'Is there a difference?'

'Clive tuh-tuh-tuh-talks luh-luh-luh-like th-th-this. A stammerer doesn't. A stammerer battles . . . to squeeze . . . the next . . . word in his sentence out of his mouth. Verbal constipation, you could say.'

'We should've had the rooms repainted.' I cut off a small piece of chicken and swirled it through the thick gravy. 'They're looking tired and shabby. And we *must* get new furniture for the house, darling. And new cushions and curtains and rugs. Too late to do it now, but we *must* do it after Maugham leaves.'

'I've been thinking,' Robert said, 'about Bernard's offer.'

I swallowed and set down my knife and fork carefully on the edge of my plate. 'I'm not leaving Penang, Robert.'

'Dr Joyce feels strongly that the desert air will work wonders for me.'

Damn that meddling old quack. 'Your doctors are here. Your clients. All our friends. And what about the boys? This is their home.' I drew in a long breath and exhaled heavily. 'It's completely mad to abandon everything here and move to the other side of the world, to a . . . to a sheep farm, for goodness' sake, in the middle of nowhere. At your age?'

'We'll have to sell the house, naturally,' he said.

'Sell the house? You didn't think you should discuss it with me first?' I stared at him; he looked evenly back at me.

For the rest of the week I barely spoke to him. I would not put it past him to have cunningly timed his announcement. He was probably hoping – calculating – that my anger would dissipate during Maugham's stay. After fifteen years of marriage, it wasn't hard to see right through him.

The syce was dispatched to meet Somerset Maugham at the harbour on the afternoon he arrived. I was making a few final adjustments to the lilies in the sitting room when I heard our old Humber rumbling up the driveway.

'They're here!' Robert shouted, limping from his study, Claudius at his heels.

I checked my appearance in the vestibule mirror before joining him under the porch. 'Come along, darling,' he said, tapping his walking stick on the ground. 'Come along.'

A thick, hot breeze was thrusting in from the sea, ripe with the smell of the tidal flats. The Humber stopped beneath the porch. Hassan got out of the car – at close to sixty his movements were stiff but dignified, the black songkok on his head adding to his distinguished appearance – and opened the back door. A man of medium build climbed out, eyes blinking against the afternoon glare. His cream tropical jacket hung slackly on him, and his dark hair, glossed back from his brow with pomade, was beginning to grey. The earliest hint of jowls weighted down his cheeks, heightening his pugnacious jaw and giving his face a turtle-like aspect.

Robert's smile spread open almost as wide as his arms. 'My dear, dear Willie – welcome to Cassowary House.'

I caught the flash of dismay in the writer's eyes before he masked it smoothly. 'Robert, how . . . good to see you,' he said, his nasal voice compressing his words. 'You haven't changed . . . a jot.'

'My wife, Lesley,' said Robert.

Maugham shook my hand and turned to the man who had come around from the other side of the car. 'Gerald Haxton, my secretary.'

He was about twenty years younger than Maugham, a slimmer and more handsome version of the writer, with the same slicked-back hair and small, neat moustache. Their close resemblance to each other was heightened by their sickly pallor.

The houseboys untied the luggage from the Humber's roof and carried it into the vestibule: two metal trunks and a long, bulging canvas and leather bag. The larger trunk had SOMERSET MAUGHAM printed in large letters on its side.

How vulgar, I thought. 'The rest of your luggage will be sent here, Willie,' I said.

We had tea before I showed them to their rooms. I had given Willie the larger and better appointed one; Gerald's room was further down the landing. In the evening they came downstairs and joined us for drinks on the verandah, looking fresh and dapper in their white dinner jackets.

'Well, Willie,' said Robert. 'You must be awfully glad you didn't end up a ship's surgeon after all.'

'A narrow—' Willie's mouth opened and closed a few times, like a fish; the muscles in his neck strained visibly. 'Escape,' he finally managed to expel the word from his lips.

'But why a ship's surgeon?' I asked.

'Years ago,' Robert said, leaning in towards me, 'just before Willie's first book was published, he vowed that if he couldn't make it as a writer, he'd take a job as a ship's surgeon.'

'That was the only way' – the writer's stammer reared up again; it was painful watching him grinding the words out – 'a man with no money is able to . . . see the world. I was desperate to travel to the East – China, Siam, the Malay . . . Archipelago. I wanted to leave my footprints on every island in the South Seas.'

He offered us a cigarette from a silver case, but I shook my head. 'I'm afraid Robert can't have people smoking anywhere near him,' I said. 'His lungs, you see.'

He snapped the case shut. 'Terribly sorry. Of course. Utterly thoughtless . . . of me.'

'I breathed in something I shouldn't have in the Belgian country-side,' said Robert. 'I even had to give up my pipe. You were in the war too, I believe?'

'Red Cross ambulance driver in France. So was Gerald.'

'That's where we met – in a makeshift hospital set up in a chateau,' the younger man said, giving Maugham a sleek smile.

The realisation jolted me. Why had I not seen it sooner? The two of them were lovers. They were homosexuals. We had a pair of bloody homosexuals under our roof. I shot a look at Robert – he knew; of course he knew.

I said, 'Willie, how did you and Robert first meet?'

'It was at a Sunday . . . luncheon in Edmund Gosse's home, wasn't it, Robert?' Willie said.

'I believe so. It was about a month after your first book came out.'

'That must have been around October '97. *Liza* was only . . . modestly successful,' Willie directed this to me, 'but enough people found its subject matter offensive, so I was in great . . . demand by London's . . . fashionable hostesses.'

'Henry James was there too, remember?' said Robert. 'I simply can't understand why people think so highly of him. The man writes like a fussy old spinster.'

'He uttered barely a dozen words all through lunch.' Willie turned towards me again. 'Robert and I were . . . both young bachelors.'

'Hard to believe, isn't it? A quarter of a century ago. Why, I remember that day when you—' A squall of coughing buffeted Robert. I sprang to the teapoy by the sideboard and hurried back with a glass of water. I held it to his lips, rubbing his back in long, hard strokes. He drank half his glass and patted my hand, thanking me with a look.

'We continued to meet up regularly after that luncheon,' Willie said as I arranged myself into my chair, 'usually at White's.'

'I'm still a member,' said Robert.

'We shared a flat for eight months,' Willie went on. 'The arrange-ment was very . . . much to my advantage: during the day he'd be working in his . . . chambers, so I would have the flat all to . . . myself to write. In the evenings we would go out, catch the latest shows, have dinner with our friends.'

'Wonderful times,' said Robert, his eyes hazy with memory. 'Just wonderful.'

'And then both of you got married,' Gerald broke in. 'You, Robert, to a lovely, gracious woman' – a lopsided smile and a piratical wink at me – 'and you, Willie, well, you married Syrie.'

I stole a glance at Willie; his eyes were half-lidded, his face placid. 'A top up, Gerald?' I said, reaching for the bell.

'No need to summon the slaves, Lesley.' Gerald got up and ambled over to the sideboard.

'A great shame our boys're away,' Robert said. 'They'd have loved to meet you.'

'Where are they?' asked Willie. 'KL? Or Singapore?'

'Reading, actually,' Robert said. 'Boarding school. Edward's thir-teen; James is fourteen. They'll be going up to Oxford in a couple of years, we hope. Follow in their old man's footsteps. What about you, Willie? Any sprigs from the old branch?'

'A girl, Elizabeth. Six years old and a delight.'

'Your wife – Syrie? – does she ever travel with you?' I wondered if the poor woman knew her husband slept with men.

'Syrie and I have . . . different interests; we like to go to different places, see different things. I travel . . . luxuriously when I can – it's senseless to rough it just for the sake of it – but I'm also quite willing to put up with the most insalubrious conditions if I have to. Syrie, on the other hand . . . simply can't live without her creature comforts. My wife has many admirable . . . qualities but' – the writer gave a rueful, indulgent smile – 'she's not the . . . most intrepid type. She doesn't even relish going over to the Continent.'

His articulate reply gave me the impression that he had been asked that same question many times.

'Oh, sweet darling Syrie wouldn't have lasted fifteen minutes.' Gerald flopped back into his chair, a replenished drink in his hand. 'We've sailed on rusting tramps, on liners and schooners; we've travelled by train, by car, by sedan chair. We've hiked up narrow mountain passes, slept on straw pallets in cow sheds. We've gone on foot, ridden ourselves sore for days on mules.' He took a big swallow from his crystal tumbler and jerked his chin at the Dyak shield hanging on a wall. 'We saw plenty of those in Sarawak, in their longhouses. We nearly lost our lives there too, you know.'

Willie shot a cautioning frown at his secretary. 'Gerald . . .'

'What happened?' Robert asked.

'We were sailing downriver from the jungle, heading back to Kuching,' Gerald said. 'It was a bright, hot day, cloudless, the river flat as day-old bubbly. And then, suddenly, with no warning at all, this *massive* wave came roaring towards us.' He drained half his glass in one gulp and wiped his mouth with the back of his hand. 'I'd never seen anything like it. It was terrifying. It swept all of us overboard, flipped our boat over like a leaf. And still more waves came rushing in, each one just as huge. The river was like the Atlantic in winter, I tell you.'

'You were caught in a tidal bore,' Robert said. 'Alexander also nearly lost his life to one.'

'Friend of yours?' asked Gerald.

'I may be ancient, my dear boy, but I'm not *that* ancient. Alexander the Great.'

'I don't know that story,' said Willie.

'Quintus Curtius Rufus recorded it in his *Historiae Alexandri Magni*,' Robert said. 'Alexander dreamed of expanding his empire to the ends of the world, but after failing to conquer India, he turned his exhausted, homesick troops around.'

Robert started coughing again, and he had to take a few sips of water before he was able to resume his tale.

'On their journey home Alexander and his army camped by the banks of the Indus River. He took some of his men on boats downstream to find out how far they were from the sea; he nurtured the hope that they could sail home by sea instead of travelling over the high mountains. After a few days on the river they discovered it was running upstream – and what was more promising, the water smelt strongly of salt. Alexander's men rejoiced, believing that they were nearing the sea.

'But a second later their cheers were cut off. They saw towering waves thundering upriver towards them. The waves hit them and smashed Alexander's flotilla to pieces. More than half of his men drowned.' Robert stopped abruptly. 'Do forgive me rather for going on and on – I'm sounding like a tidal bore myself.'

Willie and his secretary laughed. Even I, who had heard that story more than once, couldn't help smiling. Robert and Willie fell back into the remembered rhythms of their old friendship. From the easy manner they chaffed each other, it was obvious that they had once been close friends. Occasionally Gerald stepped into their conversation, but mostly he kept silent and drank, and drank. At one point, as I observed Robert laughing heartily, it struck me that I couldn't remember when he had last done that with me. Or for that matter, I with him.

The garden was receding into twilight, trailing the fragrance of flowering jasmine and frangipani. The houseboys went around switching on the electric lamps, and I winced at the sudden glare. Within a minute or two moths were flaking around the lamps, hurling themselves again and again at the fire sealed inside the glass. Less than a decade ago the only illumination after sundown came from oil lamps and candle-flame. Recalling those days, I was flooded with a powerful yearning to sit in the shadows again, like a Buddha in an abandoned temple at nightfall, remembered only by the flame of a guttering candle lit by a passing pilgrim. Another evening from ten years ago buoyed to the surface of my memory, an evening when another traveller from a distant land had visited us, an exile from China, Dr Sun Yat Sen. Sun Wen, as he had asked us to call him. That particular evening seemed so far away in time, irretrievable.

The monarchy in China was dead, but the revolution had only pushed the antique land into a civil war that seemed to have no end. In the last few years I had stopped reading about the news from there – I found it too upsetting, too painful. China slipped out of my thoughts, out of my dreams, like a cloud pulling away to another sky below the horizon. But ever since Robert had announced his intention to sell our house and move to the other side of the world, the urge to find out what was happening to Sun Wen had begun to tug at me.

A letter. I must write a letter to him. But to where in the whole of China could I send it? With the collapse of the old empire the Chinese Consulate had been abandoned, and even the Tong Meng Hui had dissolved its reading club. But perhaps there was still someone at its headquarters in Armenian Street I could speak to, someone who might be able to dig up Sun Wen's address from their records.

I felt the cold prickle of Willie's gaze on me; I had the unpleasant sensation that he had been observing me for some time. I looked directly into his eyes. He turned his face away.

'Cassowary – that's a bird, isn't it?' Gerald was asking Robert. 'Rather strange name for a house.'

'Nobody has a clue why it's called that,' Robert said, 'but we decided to keep the name when we bought the house.'

'It's named after the casuarina tree — that big tree by the fence.' My throat felt rusty, and I took a sip from my drink. 'The Malays call them "kasuari", because their leaves look like the cassowary's feathers.'

'Where did you hear *that* from?' Robert asked.

A chichak on the ceiling spat its disapproving clicks over us. The dinner gong rippled from inside the house. 'I hope you're all hungry,' I said, rising to my feet. 'Cookie's laid out a feast.'

'Ravenous,' Gerald said.

As I led the men across the verandah into the house, I heard — and felt — the soles of my shoes crushing the bodies of the moths and flying ants that had fallen to earth, their wings scorched when they flew too near to the electric suns.

Ah Leck dropped me off at the gates of St George's church. I waited by the gatepost until the rickshaw had disappeared around a corner. A breeze swelled up, tearing the tiny yellow flowers from the angsana trees lining the road. A blizzard of petals blew past me, scattering themselves on the church grounds and crumbing the dome of Francis Light's memorial.

A tram rattled past, its bell clanging. Opening my parasol, I joined the pedestrians going into town. Outside the Goddess of Mercy Temple I waited for a gap in the traffic. Rickshaw-pullers, their ribcages hollowed by opium, squatted over games of Chinese chess played on grids chalked on the flagstones of the forecourt. The temple's terracotta-tiled roof reared over them like a black wave in the sea. Four stone dragons pranced on the edges of the roof's upturned eaves, a familiar sight on the island. 'The skies of Penang are crowded with dragons,' my youngest son once remarked to me.

Continuing down Pitt Street, I squeezed my way between the fat open gunnysacks of shallots and dried ikan bilis and salted fish that crowded the shaded passageway running along the front of the shops. A yard or two after the Kapitan Keling mosque I turned right into Armenian Street.

I looked around me. It had been years since I was last here, but the shophouses appeared unchanged; even the people in the street seemed cloaked in an air of timelessness. That incense-maker laying out trays of hand-rolled sandalwood incense sticks under the sun – why, I was convinced he was the same man who had given me an incense stick ten years ago. His hair was now completely white, as though it had been dusted by the ash from his own joss sticks.

There is something about the shophouses of Penang I find beautiful and evocative. When Robert had been away at the Front I had spent many a morning with my easel and stool on a street corner in town, sketching and painting watercolours of these shophouses. Built at the turn of the eighteenth century, these buildings blended elements of southern Chinese and Indian architecture. With their exteriors lime-washed in a variety of bright colours and embellished with detailed and eye-catching features, they are an artist's dream. Their first floor formed a narrow porch, creating a connected walkway about five feet wide, what the Hokkiens called 'goh kaki'. This five-foot way is usually laid with brightly patterned terracotta tiles, while the front doors – often a two-leaf comb door opening up to reveal a plain and more sturdy pair of inner timber doors – are flanked by shuttered windows on both sides. Above the windows usually sit a pair of air vents, shaped to symbolise bats and secured by thin vertical iron bars. The façade of the second floor is taken up by timber louvred shutters and, more often than not, a strip of parapet wall perforated with a row of jade-green ceramic air vents.

I squinted at the house numbers stamped in oval metal tags on the lintel as I walked up the street. I stopped at number 120. A blackwood signboard hung above the doorframe, as it had in my memory, but this one was carved with a pair of Chinese ideograms and not the quartet I remembered. The yellow limewash had been replaced by a coat of pale green, and the red altar of the God of Heaven hanging on the wall next to the doors would have infuriated Sun Wen. The comb doors were open; pasted on each side of the half-opened inner doors – doors which in my recollection had always been unadorned – was a strip of vermilion paper brushed with black strokes of Chinese calligraphy, the usual auspicious words to welcome fortune and good luck.

I stepped onto the five-foot way and peered through the doors into the front hall. A middle-aged Chinese woman with a batik sarong wrapped around her bosom was napping in a rattan lounge chair, a newspaper lying on her fat stomach. I knocked and called out a greeting. She jerked awake, the newspaper sliding onto the floor.

'I'm looking for the Tong Meng Hui,' I said in Hokkien.

She sat up, blinking at me in confusion. 'What? Oh, those people-ah? They're not here any more-lah.'

'Do you know where they went?'

Scratching her armpit, she reached down and gathered up her newspaper. 'They long, long time already left.'

'Does Ah Lim still own this house?'

She shook her head. 'He sold it to my daughter.'

I thanked her and walked away. In the shade of a Chinese apothecary's five-foot way I paused to arrange my thoughts. The old apothecary was busy behind his counter, pinching dried herbs from a wall of labelled drawers and weighing them on a hand-held brass sliding scale. He gave me an enquiring look. I smiled and shook my head. The bitter scents of ginseng and cordyceps and a hundred other herbs I couldn't name drifted out from the shop, medicating the air, but they couldn't fumigate the despair from my heart. All this time I had been nursing the weak flicker of hope in my heart that the Tong Meng Hui would still have some link, however tenuous, to that house. But the Tong Meng Hui did not even exist any more.

I shaded my eyes against the glare and studied the street. I should turn left at the junction in front of me into Pitt Street again and make my way back to St George's church. Before my resolve could falter, however, I changed my mind and dashed across to the opposite side of the road. I continued down lower Armenian Street until I came to the last building in the long row.

This particular shophouse stood on a corner and was separated from the next row by a shady side lane. The front doors were locked, the wall above the lintel bare. Flanking both sides of the doors were a pair of windows, protected by thin iron bars and tightly shuttered. Despite appearing regularly maintained, an air of absence brooded within the house.

Walking right up to the doors, I tugged my right glove off and brushed my bare palm slowly over their surface. The wood was unpainted, with a warm, powdery texture. I pulled my hand away and turned it over. My palm was coated in a skin of soot, the lines of my fate etched out in stark relief.

The sun slipped into a hidden seam in the clouds, and the world faded to monochrome. I wiped my palm, put on my glove and stepped out into the street. Before I left I gave one last look at the doors, and then I walked back the way I had come, back to my own world.

Chapter Three

Willie
Penang, 1921

Normally he would have instructed Gerald to do it; instead Willie quietly asked the Number One Houseboy to go to the telegraph office in town and wire a message to his lawyers in New York. Number One Houseboy Ah Keng was in his fifties, and he had appointed himself Willie's personal servant, looking after all his needs. He accepted the task – and the tip Willie slipped into his palm – with a sacerdotal demeanour.

'I have read your book, Mr Willie,' said Ah Keng.

'Oh, which one?'

'The one about the bad woman, the whore.' Ah Keng wagged an arthritic forefinger at him. 'It is not a story for decent people. You must write decent stories, Mr Willie. Nice stories.'

'I shall bear that in mind, my good man,' said Willie drily.

After breakfast with the Hamlyns, he and Gerald headed down to the beach with their books and towels. Lying in the restless shade of the coconut trees, Willie tried to read, but his mind kept wandering off the page.

'For God's sake, Willie, stop fidgeting,' Gerald complained. 'What the hell's the matter?'

Willie laid his book on his stomach. 'I haven't . . . been sleeping well, that's all.'

'It's Syrie – again – isn't it?' Gerald's voice was muffled by the straw hat covering his face. 'What does the bitch want this time? A new sable coat? A new house? Or – dare we even hope – a new husband?'

'It's this . . . bloody illness – it just won't let go of its grip.' He watched the coconut fronds high above them stabbing at each other. 'And don't call my wife a bitch.'

He picked up his book, but it wasn't long before his attention drifted away again. Finally he clapped his book shut and struggled to his feet. 'I'm going inside. Do some work.'

Gerald raised his hat off his face and squinted up at him. 'You're supposed to rest. The doctor said—'

'I'm just going to scribble down some ideas,' said Willie. 'Stay here – don't get up.'

'Not a bloody chance,' Gerald said, dropping the hat back on his face.

Back at the house he found Lesley in the dining room conferring in low, insistent tones with a portly man in a brown suit. They broke off when they saw him.

'Dr Joyce is here to see Robert,' Lesley said.

'Mr Maugham.' The doctor cranked Willie's hand as though he were trying to start a reluctant automobile. 'An honour to meet you. A great honour indeed.'

'Is Robert all right?' Willie asked.

'It's the humidity – plays havoc with his lungs. I've given him a sedative, but there's not much else I can do for him, I'm afraid. Now if we were in London I might be able to rig up an oxygen tent.' He angled a reproving look at Lesley. 'And as I've advised before, a dry climate will certainly ease his suffering.'

She received his words with a tightening of her jaw and turned to Willie. He asked for a writing desk and a chair to be placed in his room. She told him to give her fifteen minutes. He thanked her and, on the way up to his room, decided to look into the library.

The room, located on the eastern side of the house, was spacious and bright. The oil landscapes and the photogravures, the floor-to-ceiling teakwood bookshelves and the pair of studded leather wingback chairs made him think that he was back in the Athenæum's reading room. The illusion was marred only by the Straits Chinese porcelain displayed in corners and niches around the room: lidded pots and plates and vases in gaudy pinks and greens and yellows, decorated with dragons and phoenixes and peonies.

He searched for his books (the first thing he always did whenever he stepped into a bookshop or someone's library) and was gratified to find them – he was even more happy to see them shelved prominently at eye-level. Robert had acquired every single title he had ever published – his ten novels and two collections of short stories. There were also, unsurprisingly, works by Shakespeare and Hazlitt and Dickens and Scott and H. G. Wells; translations of French and Russian and German novels; Robert's Classical passions – Horace and Homer and Virgil and Cicero – and an impressive selection of books on Malaya. But what caught his curiosity was the extensive collection of books on China, the shelves of Chinese history and art, poetry and fiction.

He pulled out a thick volume bound in Morocco calfskin. *The Taiping Rebellion*. Printed on the frontispiece was Lesley's name and a date: 30 May 1910. At random he picked out more books about China – books on the Taiping Rebellion, the Opium Wars, the Boxer Rebellion. Every one of them was inscribed with her name in a neat, elegant hand. All of them were dated from April 1910 or after.

He moved away from the bookshelves to a camphorwood sideboard crowded with silver-framed photographs. They showed the Hamlyns and their two sons, taken over the years, the boys pallid-faced and unremarkable-looking. There were also photographs of

Robert and Lesley with glamorous-looking people on the verandah of Cassowary House and on the lawns of other homes. His eye was drawn to a photograph tucked right up against the wall. He picked it up by a corner of its frame, careful not to send the others toppling. Lesley, looking ten or fifteen years younger, stood in front of a mirrored dressing table staring at the camera, her chin tilted up slightly, her left hand resting on the back of a Chinese rosewood chair. She was dressed in a long-sleeved blouse which draped over the curve of her hips, matched with a long, plain skirt that reached to her ankles. Her hair was styled in a chignon. He had seen the Straits Chinese women attired in the same type of outfit in Singapore, but never a European lady. She had retained her figure over the years, he noted with approval. She looked regal and, in an unconventional way, even beautiful.

Ah Keng appeared at the door and informed him that mem was asking for him in his room. Willie replaced the photograph carefully and hurried upstairs. Lesley was directing a pair of houseboys as they positioned a writing desk at the windows.

'A view of the garden and the sea.' She clasped her hands at her chest and beamed at him. 'That should inspire you when you're writing.'

'Thank you. However . . .' Willie pointed to the opposite corner. 'I would prefer it there.'

'But . . . you'll be facing the wall.'

'It's how I work.'

'If you're sure . . .' Still looking doubtful, she fired off a short burst of instructions in Chinese to the houseboys. They hefted the desk and the Windsor chair over to the spot he had chosen.

'I've been scribbling down some ideas,' said Willie, 'for my book about Sun Yat Sen.'

'Knowing your reputation, I don't suppose it'll be completely flattering to him, will it?' she said. 'But I hope you'll at least be . . . fair . . . to him?'

'My characters are never completely beyond redemption, Lesley.'

She weighed his words for a moment or two. Then, indicating to him to wait, she went across the landing to her own room. She returned with a book and handed it to him.

'It's about Dr Sun's activities when he was in Penang,' said Lesley. 'You might find it useful.'

The book was slim, hardly even eighty pages. *A Man of the Southern Seas*. 'Southern Seas?' he asked.

'That's what the Chinese call this part of the world – Nanyang.'

He studied the photograph of the man on the cover. The revolutionary was dressed in a dark three-piece suit and seated in an antique Chinese chair. He had a sensitive, scholarly face, and his eyes, large and round for a Chinaman, gleamed with intelligence. 'Handsome chap.'

'That was taken in Penang, in his party's headquarters. He was already in his mid-forties.'

'How long did he stay here?'

'Five or six months.'

'I'd still like to hear what he was like from you.'

She looked around the room, her eyes alighting on the framed photograph on his bedside table. She picked it up and studied it. 'Your mother?'

'Yes.'

'You look like her. What was her name?'

'Edith.'

'She has such sad eyes.' She placed it back on the bedside table. 'Do you have a photograph of your wife?'

'I don't carry one with me.'

'Oh. I see.' She continued to stand there. It was obvious to Willie that she wanted to ask something of him. 'Your book, the one you showed me the other morning . . . I'd like to borrow it. Robert would like to read it too.'

He took the book from his bedside table and gave it to her. 'I'm sorry to . . . hear that he's feeling . . . poorly. If it's all right, I'll pop into his room afterwards.'

'He'd like that. Perk him up a bit.'

'Poor Robert. Perhaps we shouldn't have come.'

'Oh, don't say that, Willie. He was terribly keen for you to visit, couldn't stop talking about it.' She smiled. 'Your presence here is the best tonic for him. He'll be right as rain in a day, you'll see.'

'I have not the slightest doubt.'

He sat at his desk after she left and thought about what she had said. Her words, sanguine as they were, could not hide the knowledge in her eyes – Robert would recover after a day's rest, true, but his bad spells would only worsen. And soon the day would come when he would no longer be able to breathe at all. He would drown in the very air that had given him life.

Willie opened his journals and began reading the anecdotes and character sketches he had recorded over the months of travel around the Federated Malay States, panning them for nuggets he hoped could be smelted and hammered into stories.

Two years ago he had journeyed to the Far East for the first time. Departing from London on a dull winter's morning, he had sailed to Chicago, where Gerald was waiting for him. They took the train to San Francisco where they boarded a ship bound for Hong Kong. They lingered a week there before catching another ship for Shanghai. With guides and porters organised by Gerald they had set off into the hinter-lands of the Middle Kingdom, travelling on riverboats and rice barges, tottering on pack ponies up narrow footpaths etched into the sides of vertiginous gorges. Willie had revelled in every minute of it. They spent a few months in China before he sailed home to London, his trunks bulging with presents for Syrie and Elizabeth: porcelain and silks and jade and artworks and books. But they weren't all that he brought home: teeming inside his head were the stories he had been told on his travels.

'You missed Liza's birthday,' Syrie reminded him barely half an hour after he had stepped inside 2 Wyndham Place, his four-storey

Regency house in Marylebone. 'I threw a party for her, with thirty children. I wrote you about it. Didn't you get my letter?'

The familiar irritation pricked at him: he always called their daughter Elizabeth, but Syrie preferred Liza.

Their daughter was looking up at him, her eyes wary. She hasn't seen you in eight months, he told himself. She's probably forgotten who you are. He knelt on one knee and smiled at her. 'Elizabeth, my darling, look what I got . . . for your birthday.' He took out a dark blue coolie suit from his trunk and presented it to his daughter.

She reached out a shy hand for the suit, but Syrie pulled her arm away. 'No, Liza darling, you're not wearing *that*. Really, Willie – do you want her looking like some Chinaman coolie?'

'Oh, I think Elizabeth . . . will look utterly charming in it, utterly charming.' He pressed the clothes gently into his daughter's tiny hands and kissed her cheeks. 'Don't you . . . think so, my darling angel?'

He relished being home again. Settling back into his routine, he began working on a book about his travels in China. Each day from morning till noon he wrote in his study on the top floor of his house. No one was allowed to disturb him. Submerged in his writing, he was oblivious to the bells from St Mary's church up the road rippling the hours over the quiet neighbourhood. But occasionally, when he became aware of them, he would lift his face from the page and pause in his writing, and a deep feeling of peace would spread through him like a warm summer breeze.

The invitations came, and he resumed the rounds of socialising with Syrie, attending opening nights at the theatre and the opera where he caught up with their friends. In the mornings they went riding in Hyde Park. He spent time with Elizabeth, taking her to the little park in Bryanston Square in the evenings; he read to her at bedtime (for some unfathomable reason he never stammered during those occasions). She wore the blue coolie suit day after day, refusing to change out of it, much to Syrie's annoyance.

For a while he was content, even happy. But, as always, it wasn't long before he felt the walls pressing in. He missed Gerald, who had remained in America. As much as Willie enjoyed London, the urge to escape England, to leave everything behind, was always lurking inside him, gnawing into his bones, into his soul. Syrie sensed it too – she had been keeping her eyes peeled for it, ready to pounce on it the moment it stuck its head above ground. She constantly sought assurances from him and made frequent demands for sexual congress. Willie resisted all her attempts, and their old, familiar quarrels boiled over again. He barricaded himself in his study and worked; and when he wasn't writing he found refuge in the Garrick Club, or he wandered the streets, letting the hours seep away in his favourite bookshops and art galleries, anything to postpone the inevitability of going home. He just could not cope with the scenes Syrie made.

He had assumed that they had an unspoken understanding when he married her: she wanted a rich and famous husband and a father for her child; he needed a glamorous wife who could make sparkling conversation at parties and who was at home with the fashionable people of London. In the beginning it had satisfied them both, but their marriage had soured into a marriage of inconvenience. 'Like many unhappily married women I've known,' Willie once remarked to a friend, 'Syrie had made the . . . mistake of falling in love with her husband.'

Their rows grew more frequent and stormy. After another quarrel, he told himself that the situation could not go on. That evening, after he had tucked Elizabeth into bed and read her a story, he asked Syrie to join him in the sitting room.

'Oh, don't look so terribly grim, darling,' she said. 'You're not still angry with me, are you?'

He edged away from her kiss and went to the sideboard to make their drinks.

She sat down on the Regency sofa she had bought the previous week, crossed one leg over the other and lit a cigarette. He gave

Syrie her gin and tonic and, settling into his Chesterfield armchair, sipped his drink as he studied his wife. Her face was growing fleshy. She was forty, five years younger than himself. Her grey silk dress warmed the creamy lustre of the pearls he had given her after her divorce from Henry Wellcome. Her hair was styled into flat, elegant curls. Her dark brown eyes, shrewd and inquisitive, remained her most striking features.

He said, 'My book will . . . be finished in a week's time.'

'Darling, what marvellous news.' She tipped her tumbler at him in a toast. 'Let's celebrate. We'll give a big party, we'll invite everyone.'

'No parties, no celebrations.' He raised his palm as she started to protest. 'After my book is done,' he went on, 'I will be going abroad. To . . . America.'

Syrie frowned. 'You've only just got back.'

'Paramount's asked me to work on . . . the screenplay for Chaplin's film in Hollywood.'

'My goodness, how thrilling! I'd love to meet him. I'm sure he'll be happy to introduce us to the other stars there.'

'I'm going . . . on my own, Syrie.'

A long silence fell between them. Eventually she said, 'I presume that secretary of yours will be there?'

'It's a working trip. That's what I . . . employ him for. And after I've finished the work there,' he forged on, 'I'll be going to the Far . . . East with him.'

'*I* should be going with you. I'm your wife – although you seem to forget that all the time.'

'My dear Syrie, I assure you that I find it . . . extremely difficult to forget that you're my wife.'

Her eyes narrowed, uncertain of what he meant. 'I'm a writer,' Willie continued before she could say anything, 'and to write I . . . need to find fresh material.'

'You leave us on our own for months on end. Liza cries herself to sleep every night when you're away, do you know that?' She mustered her next words and fired them off in a broadside. 'I feel more like your widow than your wife.'

'Listen to me . . . carefully, Syrie . . . don't . . . interrupt.' He willed his stammer into retreat. 'I need to write. And to do so I must have complete freedom to travel anywhere I like, on my own, for as long and as often as I have to. If you can't accept this . . .' He dreaded the inevitable explosion, but he forced himself to go on. 'If you can't accept this, then either we separate, or we get a divorce.' He cupped his hands on his knees. 'It's up to you. But make your decision now.'

For three or four seconds her expression remained frozen. Then slowly, with almost a tragic grandeur to it, her face collapsed. It was like watching a heavy flank of ice calving from an iceberg into the sea, Willie thought.

'You bastard!' She hurled her crystal tumbler at him. He ducked, the tumbler's contents splashing his arm as it flew past. It hit the wall behind him. It didn't shatter, but dropped onto the thick carpet with a dull, lifeless thud.

'Bastard!' she screamed again. 'Bastard!'

He sprang from his armchair and backed away from her. 'Don't make . . . me a scene, Syrie, please don't make me a scene.'

She hunched into herself, buried her face in her palms and started weeping, her body rocking back and forth, back and forth.

He stared past her to the street outside the windows. A hansom cab clopped past. He envied the houses opposite, with their warm, inviting lighted interiors, but he supposed that anyone looking at his glowing windows would receive the same impression too.

To his relief, Syrie finally stopped sobbing. She straightened herself on the sofa and dried her eyes with his handkerchief. 'All right.' She cleared her throat. 'You must travel. I accept that.' She coaxed her hair back into place and adjusted her pearls. 'I can't go gallivanting around the world with you anyway – I have tons of work to do here, thrilling ideas for the house.' She looked around the sitting room, taking in the walls and the ceiling and the furniture. 'It needs more white.'

Willie blew out a silent breath. He was not completely free, but it would have to be sufficient for now.

The next morning he started organising his trip, one that he intended to be longer than any he had ever done before. Once he had finalised his plans he telegraphed his instructions to Gerald and delivered his manuscript of *On a Chinese Screen* to his agent. Syrie was her usual affectionate self as his departure neared, even buying him a new set of leather trunks from Selfridges and offering advice on what he should pack.

He sailed from Southampton on a grey, misty morning. The crossing was pleasant. Gerald was waiting for him in New York, his broad, familiar smile blazing from the crowds in the harbour when he saw Willie. They caught the train to California and stayed in Hollywood for two blissful months before driving up the coast to San Francisco. From there they boarded a ship bound for Honolulu, then sailed to Sydney before continuing north onwards to Singapore.

Bound to no itinerary, they explored the islands of the Malay Archipelago, tracing coastlines thick with mangroves, their roots stitching land to sea; they travelled upcountry to the Federated and Unfederated Malay States. They stayed in hotels and rest houses and, when those were not available, in the bungalows of Residents and District Officers. The Europeans, many of them living thirty, forty miles from the nearest town, were desperate for any form of distraction, and the wives of planters and out-station civil servants squabbled over the chance to host Willie and his secretary.

Now, less than a week after coming to Cassowary House, he was forced to resume his working routine again.

Each morning, as dawn began to thin the darkness around him, he would go down to the beach for a brisk walk. The crescent moon was a Cheshire cat's grin in the sky, fading away into morning. The stretch of the bay in front of Cassowary House was about a quarter of a mile long, lined with four or five mansions spaced far apart and screened from the beach by tall casuarinas. At the end of the bay was a stream, barely two strides across, simmering over the shallow sand bed as it siphoned the rains from the mountains to feed the sea's unquenchable thirst. Pinned to the banks on spindly stilts was a cluster of fishermen's shacks. Beyond the stream lay a tumble of big boulders, blocking the access to the next beach. George Town was no more than a mile or two away, and Willie could see the dome of the Hong Kong and Shanghai Bank poking out above the trees like some strange onion.

At half past seven he would have a quick breakfast with the Hamlyns. After a bath and a shave he changed into a freshly pressed cotton shirt and long trousers. For the next four hours he would remain at his desk, writing. At a quarter to one, even if he were deep in the middle of a scene, he would screw the cap on his fountain pen, keep his exercise book away in the drawer and head downstairs to the verandah for a martini prepared by Number One Houseboy Ah Keng. He had had to show the houseboy how to make it the first time. Following a light lunch with Gerald and the Hamlyns, he would while away the rest of the afternoon on the beach with Gerald. They would read in the shade of the coconut trees and bathe in the sea. Despite his problems, the languorous climate was working its powers on him, and he felt his health improving, like a warm, rich tide replenishing a depleted lagoon.

Gerald's body, he saw, was filling out again too, his skin varnished to a glossy teak by the sun. It wasn't long before he started frequenting the gambling dens and the brothels in the Chinese quarter, returning home only in the early hours of the morning.

'I'm telling you, Willie – you should come with me,' he said one evening. He lay sprawled on Willie's bed, watching him dress. The Hamlyns were taking them to the Penang Club for dinner. 'The boys here are so skilful, so eager to please us Tuans.'

As was usual everywhere they travelled to, he had snuffled out the company of men who shared similar tastes. Willie envied his knack – he himself could never do it: meet someone, a stranger he found attractive, and convey his desires to the man with nothing more than a look exchanged between them.

Gerald grinned. 'I should bring them back here for you.'

'Don't you dare.' Willie shot his cuffs towards Gerald. 'Are you listening?'

From the earliest days he had made it clear to Gerald that he was free to do whatever he liked, as long as he did not bring anyone back to their hotel or the houses they had been invited to stay in, as long as he did not cause any embarrassment to Willie. He was a famous writer and a married man; he had his reputation to preserve.

'Robert and Lesley aren't stupid, you know,' Gerald said, working the cufflinks into Willie's cuffs. 'Maybe I ought to give them all the gory details.'

'God forbid. Even *I* don't want to hear all your gory details.' Willie slipped into his dinner jacket and gave himself a final spruce-up in the mirror. 'Our memsahib's very curious about the devilries you get up to, have you noticed?'

'They don't talk much to each other, those two, do they? He chats more to his dog than to her. Treats it better too – look at all the cheese he's always feeding that bloody beast.'

Gerald was right, thought Willie – there were days when husband and wife barely exchanged more than a handful of words to each other. But that wasn't at all uncommon in many marriages, was it?

'There's something about her,' said Willie, 'something clenched up . . .'

'Just another woman in the colonies stuck in an unhappy marriage,' said Gerald, 'and we've met a fair number of those here, haven't we? Thank Christ at least she's not one of those effusive females – you know, the ones who're always slobbering over you.' Gerald's shoulders made an extravagant shudder. 'One of my poker mates told me she used to be very tight with a bunch of Chinamen rebels. Their leader – that chap called Dr Sun – he stayed here in Penang. Apparently she became close to him.' Gerald leered. 'Very close.'

On their travels around Malaya he and Gerald had encountered many memsahibs; a number of them had been eccentric, and a few had been plain barking mad, but in the main they had been ordinary, middle-class, as Lesley had seemed to him. He was beginning to suspect that she was not as conventional as she made herself out to be.

'When you see your friends again, my dear boy,' Willie said as they went downstairs to join the Hamlyns, 'find out what she got up to with this Dr Sun, will you?'

Chapter Four

Lesley
Penang, 1921

In spite of my reservations, Willie and his secretary turned out to be easy-going house guests. We hardly saw them during the day: the writer spent his mornings holed up in his room working, while Gerald – the employee, mind you – lazed under the coconut trees. At midday the four of us would meet for lunch before dispersing back to our own preoccupations. In the evenings, like animals coming together at the watering hole, we gathered on the verandah for drinks. Robert and I weren't bridge players, and Willie didn't feel inclined to engage in a game with strangers at the Penang Club, so after dinner we would usually adjourn to the sitting room and have a few drinks. Fidgety with boredom, Gerald would drain his whisky and dash off into town. Robert retired to bed early, which left me to entertain Willie. The writer was easy to talk to – too easy – and I often had to remind myself not to let anything slip from my lips. Funnily enough, his stammer no longer set my teeth on edge; in fact I thought it gave his speech an odd rhythm that was distinctively his alone.

I read *On a Chinese Screen* late into the night. The slender volume was a collection of vignettes of places Willie had visited and the characters – corrupt Mandarins and Confucian philosophers, mission-aries and consuls and nuns and Mongol chiefs – who had crossed his path in China. He had recorded their quirks and weaknesses with an unsparing eye, but he did so without any sneer of superiority. In fact he seemed to give the impression that he saw himself in some of those people. Reading those stories, I imagined myself in the towns and villages he had written about, all those places in that country that I knew I would never be able to visit.

Following my fruitless visit to the Tong Meng Hui's old headquar-ters, I had made some enquiries around town, but no one could tell me where its members had scattered to. In the end I had no alter-native but to visit my brother at the *Penang Post*.

Geoff and one of his friends had bought the newspaper two years earlier to save it from going under. They had managed to turn its ailing fortunes around, transforming it into one of the most successful newspapers in Penang (there weren't many, admittedly, but still . . .). Geoff enjoyed telling people he had bought it solely to keep his job. 'Who else would employ a fat, lazy, middle-aged editor who spent far too many hours of the day at the club bar?'

A peon showed me into my brother's office, a hot, noisy space above the printing press. 'How's your famous house guest?' Geoff asked from behind his desk, which was, as always, a chaotic landscape of files and documents and books and crumpled-up balls of paper.

'Willie lent me his new book,' I said. 'It's about his travels in China—'

'Any chance I could take a quick look at it?'

'Oh, I don't think he'd like that – it's not out yet. As I was saying before you so rudely interrupted me, he told me he'd heard quite a bit about Sun Wen when he was travelling in China, and he wants to write a book about him.'

My brother gave me a shrewd look. 'Somerset Maugham wants to write a book about Sun Wen? That'll be a tremendous coup for him. A book by Willie Maugham, a book that's sympathetic to Sun

Wen could persuade more influential and high-ranking people in England to give their support and assistance to him, to his dream of China.'

'I wanted to write to Sun Wen and let him know. I went to the Tong Meng Hui's headquarters to ask for his address.'

'Tong Meng Hui.' My brother leaned back into his chair. 'Haven't heard *that* name in a while.' He looked at me. 'The Tong Meng Hui doesn't exist any more, Les. I'm sure I told you already.'

'What about all those people who went there to fight for his cause? Have any of them come home yet?'

He shook his head. 'Most of them were captured or killed.'

I could still recall some of their faces, if not their names. I remembered how young and determined they were, those men and women of the Tong Meng Hui.

'Makes one wonder if they made any difference at all, doesn't it?' said Geoff. 'Poor old Sun Wen – he couldn't even keep the whole country together.'

I wasn't about to give up so easily. 'What about your friends at the *Kwong Wah*? They'd know how I could get in touch with him, wouldn't they, wherever he is in China?'

Geoff pushed a stack of files from one side of his desk to another, but it only made it look even more cluttered than before. 'How's the old man?'

Sooner or later he would have to be told, I thought to myself. 'He wants to sell our house. He wants us to move to his cousin's farm in the Karoo.'

'Darkest Africa, eh? Well, well . . .' Geoff leaned forward, his stomach pushing against the edge of his desk. He had put on even more weight since I last saw him. That wife of his didn't give a fig about his health at all. 'No doubt his doctors feel it's for the best. I've always wanted to see the place. You'd better have a guest room for me.'

'I'm not going anywhere. My home is here.'

'Shouldn't your husband's health be your priority?'

'I just feel it's a grave mistake to move.' I had no desire to pursue the question of my responsibility where Robert's health was concerned. 'He's much better, you know. Willie's presence has lifted his spirits tremendously. Did you know he's homosexual? Willie, I mean. He and that "secretary" of his, they travel everywhere together.'

'Lots of wealthy and famous men travel with their secretary.'

'For a journalist you're awfully reluctant to believe the worst of people,' I said. 'Oh, I've seen how Willie looks at Gerald – and let me tell you, no man – no *normal* man – looks at his secretary that way.'

'Even so, that's their own private business, isn't it?' He smacked his palms together and rubbed them. 'So, when do I get to meet the famous author? All of Penang is sick with jealousy that he's staying with you, but I'm sure you're not unaware of that. Would he be willing to give me an interview, do you think?'

I stood up to leave. 'You speak to your friends at the *Kwong Wah*, Geoff, and I'll make certain you get your interview.' I sounded more confident than I felt.

'All right, I'll talk to them.' His face became serious, and he was silent for a moment or two. 'Just remember, Les – we're pieces of Sun Wen's past now,' he said. 'I very much doubt he'll ever come back to Penang again.'

The cards had been flocking to Cassowary House ever since Willie arrived – invitations for luncheons and tea, for cocktails and dinner parties. That evening he came out to the verandah and spilled an armful of them onto the coffee table.

'Good Lord,' said Robert, looking at a small mound of cards and envelopes and letters. 'They just keep flooding in, don't they?'

'I had hoped no one knows we're here,' said Willie.

'Well, what did you expect when you announced your itinerary – in exhaustive detail – to the *Straits Times* before you left Singapore?' I said.

He was annoyed by my tart comment. 'So, before I sweep . . . them all into the bin, who are these people?'

We were still sifting through the invitations when Gerald came around the side of the house. He staggered onto the verandah and collapsed into a wicker armchair. The front of his white cotton shirt was blotched with blood, and he was pressing a handkerchief to his nose.

'What happened?' I asked. 'Are you all right?'

'Get me a drink, Willie,' he mumbled through his handkerchief.

'What the hell have you done now?' Willie asked.

'Had a spectacular run of luck at my poker game and the bloody Chinks wouldn't let me leave.' Gerald peeled away his handkerchief, grimacing at it. 'Stole all my money too. Had to teach the bloody buggers a lesson, didn't I?'

'For God's sake, go and clean yourself up,' said Willie.

'A drink, Willie. A strong one – chop–chop.' Gerald crumpled his handkerchief on the table, screwed a cigarette in his mouth and lit it, but Willie stopped him. 'Ah fuck, sorry, Robert.' He dropped the cigarette onto the floor, grinding his heel into it.

While Willie fixed Gerald his whisky I went inside, returning with a box of cotton wool and a bottle of hydrogen peroxide. 'You got cut in your face too,' I said.

'One of the bastards had a knife.' He dabbed a finger gingerly on the wound and winced. 'Well, there go my dashing good looks.'

'I'll take you to the hospital,' I said. 'You need to get that stitched up.'

'Forget it, Lesley. I've had bloodier scratches from a cat.' Gerald smothered the mouth of the hydrogen peroxide bottle with a wad of cotton wool, turned it upside down, then pressed the soaked cotton wool onto the cut.

Willie looked at us, mortification flushing his face. 'I'm terribly . . . sorry about this.'

'Ah, we saw worse in the war, didn't we?' said Robert. 'Much, much worse.'

I returned to the invitations, fanning them out across the table. 'The Resident-Councillor and his wife; the manager of the Chartered Bank; this one, from Judge Harry Yorke. The usual boring—' I stopped. There – right there, lying under my nose – was the means of obtaining Sun Wen's address.

'Send them my regrets, Gerald,' said Willie. 'All of them.'

'*I* want to go,' said Gerald. 'It'll be fun, hobnobbing with the locals. Don't you think so, Lesley?'

I stabbed at the white, gilt-edged card with my forefinger and skimmed it across the table to Willie. 'Say yes to this one, at least.'

Willie picked up the card. 'Noel Hutton. Who's he?'

'Noel owns one of the oldest trading companies in Malaya,' I said. 'Legend has it that Hutton & Sons was founded by one of his ancestors who had been with Francis Light when he landed in Penang. They say it was this Hutton who had given Light the idea of firing silver dollars from the ship's cannon into the interior – a way of spurring the men to clear the jungles.'

'A fairy tale spread around by the Huttons themselves,' Robert said. 'But Noel's a solid chap. Poor bugger lost his wife a few years ago.'

'Istana – that's "palace" in Malay, isn't it?' Willie asked, studying the card.

I nodded. 'That's the name of his house. It's magnificent, utterly magnificent,' I said. 'You'll meet heaps of fascinating characters at his party. Not just the Europeans, but Malay royalty and Straits Chinese.' I knew the words were tumbling out of my mouth, but I couldn't help myself. 'Everyone will be there. Everyone. You'll find lots of ideas for your stories.'

'A quiet verandah, within the circle of . . . light from a paraffin lamp – *that's* where a man feels the strongest inclination to unburden himself to a stranger passing by,' said Willie. 'Not at a . . . party, oh no.'

In my desperation I even looked to my husband for support. 'He's invited us too. We *must* go, darling.'

'Very considerate of him, as usual. But it'll be crowded and noisy, and everyone'll be smoking like blazes.'

'Oh, for heaven's sake, Robert, when was the last time you went to a party? And Noel's one of our oldest friends too. He'll be hurt if we refuse.' I looked at Willie and Robert. 'Fine, if you two don't want to go, I'll go on my own.'

'Well, *I'll* take you, Lesley,' Gerald said. 'It's bloody boring staying home every night.' He winked at me. 'No aspersions cast on your gracious hospitality, of course.'

I flashed him a grateful smile. 'Noel would lose face if you don't accept, Willie. You can't hide yourself away,' I said. 'Your readers in Penang will be bereft if they don't catch a glimpse of you, absolutely bereft,' I pressed on. 'You've come all this way here, you can't disappoint them.'

Willie's fingers drummed a tattoo on the armrest, his eyes never leaving my face. All at once his fingers stopped moving. 'We'll all go, all of us.' He raised his palm as Robert began to object. 'You'll enjoy it, Robert. We'll leave any time . . . you want to. But we'll march in there, you and I, and we'll charm the . . . socks off the ladies. It'll be just . . . like the old days, eh?'

I retrieved the invitation card from Willie and rose to my feet. 'I'll telephone Noel straightaway.'

For dinner I had asked Cookie to prepare a variety of local dishes for our house guests. I gave Willie brief descriptions of every dish brought to the table – its ingredients, the way it was cooked, how it should be eaten: jiu hoo char, tau eu bahk, assam fish, assam laksa, char kway teow, otak-otak. Willie could not get enough of Cookie's famous choon pneah – deep-fried crab meat spring rolls served with a dipping sauce that he had concocted himself, a blend of soy sauce, Worcestershire sauce, some cinnamon and cloves and star anise, and finely chopped red chillies.

'My compliments to your cook,' said Willie when we came to the end of dinner. 'This was the best . . . meal I've ever eaten in the East. This evening I tasted flavours I had never . . . known existed.'

'You won't find anything like it anywhere in the world,' I said. 'Over the centuries Penang has absorbed elements from the Malays and the Indians, the Chinese and the Siamese, the Europeans, and produced something that's uniquely its own. You'll find it in the language, the architecture, the food.' I cast a cool eye towards Robert. 'I can't think of anywhere else in the world I'd want to live.'

Robert pretended he had not heard me. 'You know what the locals' favourite pastime is?' he asked Willie. 'Eating!' He slapped his palm on the table and laughed.

Gerald stretched across the table for the last piece of spring roll. The cut on his cheek had stopped bleeding, but the skin above his left jaw was ripening into a monsoon cloud. 'Thank God we're only here a fortnight,' he said, popping the crunchy piece of spring roll into his mouth and chewing it noisily. 'I'd grow fat as a hog if we stayed longer.'

Perhaps it was just my imagination, but a shadow seemed to fall across Willie's face.

As we left the dining room, Willie's attention fell upon a wooden panel hanging in the passage. The panel measured one and a half feet wide by six feet long. Painted upon it was a hawk drifting over a misty gorge, the bird no larger than a child's palm.

'It's the left leaf of a pair of doors,' I said. The paintwork was faded, leaving blank patches in the mists. Emptiness swirling within emptiness. 'Taken from a clanhouse in Penang. Late eighteenth century.'

'Lesley picked it up in an Armenian Jew's shop in town.' Robert flicked a questioning glance at me. 'Got it for a song too, didn't you, darling?'

Willie pointed to the quatrain of Chinese calligraphy above the hawk, its brushstrokes as delicate as new bamboo shoots. 'What do they say, do you know?'

"'Evanescent path of dreams/in the summer night/O Bird of the mountain/carry my name beyond the clouds".' Brushing my palm lightly over the panel, I recalled the other morning when I had done the same on the doors of another house. 'A Japanese warrior composed it, just before he killed himself.'

We proceeded down the passageway into the sitting room (I watched with mild amusement as Willie, certainly not a man of considerable height, dipped his head slightly as he went through the doors, as though he were a much taller man – it was one of his habits which I had started to notice) and settled into our usual chairs. The lilies I had bought at the Pulau Tikus market on the day of Willie's arrival were already wilting. I made a mental note to replace them.

Looking around me, I felt anchored by the objects in the room, objects that had become so familiar that I scarcely noticed them any more – the William Daniell watercolours of early Penang scenes; my Blüthner piano in the corner which Robert had bought for me; but most of all, my collection of Straits Chinese porcelain – the kamcheng and tiffin-carriers, the teapots and teacups, the plates and bowls – which I had built up over the years. Robert didn't care for them – he thought they were gaudy – but to me they were exquisite.

The imperfections of the room were comforting to me as well: the long, thin crack in the wall above the sideboard which always appeared again no matter how many times we painted over it, the light fitting that had begun to slip out of its bracket, the corner of a window frame that had been chipped off. I lifted my eyes to the white wooden floorboards that formed the room's ceiling. My sons often got a good telling-off from me if they thumped across them when we were entertaining. The sitting room had the faint, medicinal scent of the old teakwood floors mingled with the fragrance of the star jasmine from the garden. All these smells, blended by time into a sillage that could never be replicated in any other house.

From the day I married Robert, this house had been my home. We had watched our sons grow up here; we had taught them to swim in the sea outside, to dig for horseshoe crabs on the beach; their birthday parties had been held in the garden under the trees. I couldn't imagine living anywhere else in the world, especially a place hundreds of miles from the nearest sea, the sea that was eternal yet ceaselessly changing, from wave to wave, swell to swell.

Willie reached for a piece of pulut tai-tai on the Straits Chinese porcelain plate. He had, I discovered, a sweet tooth for these colourful, rhomboid-shaped glutinous rice desserts, cooked in coconut milk and dyed a vivid blue. They were my favourite too. He ate it in two bites, wiped his fingers with his handkerchief and pointed to the painting of a brown-skinned youth clad in a loincloth hanging behind Robert.

'Gauguin, isn't it? Bought it after you . . . won a case?'

'Ah, you still remember my old habits.' Robert's eyes lit up. 'You collect his works too?'

'The odd piece or two.'

'"The odd piece or two",' Gerald said, smirking. 'Tell them about Papeete, Willie.'

The writer gave his secretary a warning shake of his head.

'Oh, go on – tell us,' Robert said.

'We were there three years ago,' Gerald said, when Willie remained mute. 'The village headman's wife – she was massive, built like an elephant – she told us there were some of Gauguin's paintings in another village a few miles away. We drove there immediately. The place was a slum, like all of the villages there. Naked filthy brats running about, mongrels slinking through the lanes. We asked the villagers about Gauguin, and they directed us to a house on a slope. The place was falling to pieces, but right before our eyes was the Gauguin. On the door.'

I leaned forward. 'Painted on the door?'

'Painted on the glass panel.'

'What did you do?' I asked.

'We knocked – carefully, of course. The owner came out. He told us that his parents had looked after Gauguin when he was sick, and

Gauguin had painted the glass panels on three doors for them. "Where are the other two doors?" Willie asked. "Oh, it break," the owner said. Seems his little brats had been chucking stones at them. Willie asked him to sell us the door. "But I must buy new door," the owner said. "Well, how much is a new door?" "One hundred francs." "I'll give you two hundred." The man agreed. I walked – as casually as I could, of course – to our car and got a screwdriver from the toolkit. I had to stop myself from running like the devil back to the house. We got the door off its hinges and somehow managed to cram the whole thing inside our car. I still don't know how we did it. Anyway – back at our hotel we sawed off the top half with the glass panel, packed it in a crate and shipped it back to London.'

'Two hundred francs.' Robert punched his fist into his palm. 'A bargain, an absolute bargain. What was the painting?'

Willie took another pulut tai-tai from the plate. 'A bare-breasted Tahitian . . . Eve holding an apple under a tree.'

'You cheated that man,' I said.

'Cheated?' Gerald said. 'Nonsense. He got what he wanted – a new door – and we saved a priceless piece of art from being lost for ever.' He crooked an eyebrow at me. 'Would you rather we'd left it there? It would've been smashed to pieces sooner rather than later.'

'I'd rather that you had paid him a fair price for it.'

'I'm sure the man found it more than fair,' Robert said.

Before I could deploy a stinging retort Gerald drained his tumbler, plonked it on the table and announced he was off to town. The writer's eyes clung to him as he slouched out of the sitting room. It was obvious what Gerald saw in Willie, but what on earth did Willie find desirable in him? Perhaps Gerald was a fantastic lover. The idea of the two of them writhing about in bed – the very idea of two men in bed – was grotesque. His poor wife – how did she put up with it?

'Some of your stories were related to you by people you met on your travels,' Robert said, reeling Willie's attention back to us. 'Isn't that so?'

'They were *based on* the stories that were told to me,' Willie replied, a tetchy note souring his voice.

'Why on earth would people reveal the shameful things they've done to you, a complete stranger?' I asked.

The writer crossed one leg over his knee. 'I see myself as an anonymous gentleman in the parlour, a traveller sitting in the half-shadows, ready and . . . willing to listen to anyone with a tale to tell. I suppose they see me like that too.' He paused. 'I'm also a traveller who'll be gone by the morning, never to come their way again.'

'But, even so, why would they do it?'

The answer was obvious, the look he gave me said. 'The urge to confess, of course. For some people, getting away with a crime is a heavier . . . burden to bear than the fear of being caught.'

'Poppycock,' Robert said. 'Nobody ever gives a full and complete confession. A chap will only confess to as much as he needs to exonerate himself. I've seen it in court time and again. Witnesses edit their memories about the things they've said and done; they rearrange the facts. All of us do it – we play with truth, mould it into the form that shows our best side to the world.' He laid his chin on the trestle of his interlaced fingers. 'You only hear one aspect of it. You can never get the whole truth, the whole story.'

'No one can, Robert. All we ever get is the incomplete picture,' said Willie. 'A writer's job is to fill in the gaps. And he decides how the story ends.'

It was something that had never occurred to me before: we all had the power to change our pasts, our beginnings – or our perception of them, at least – but none of us could determine how our stories would end.

'Speaking of endings, Willie – my God, those last lines of "Rain"!' Robert leaned towards the writer. 'Sadie Thompson – she leaps off the page. I suppose you must have based her on somebody you knew?'

The writer's reluctance to elaborate was obvious, but perhaps he knew Robert well enough to know that he wouldn't be fobbed off easily. 'We were . . . in Pago Pago for two . . . weeks,' he was stammering again. 'Sadie Thompson was in . . . the room next to mine.'

'So, everything you wrote – the missionary, what he did with her, all of that actually happened?'

'Not all of it. Despite what . . . some critics aver, Robert, I *do* possess a smidgen of imagination.'

'You shouldn't have used her real name,' said Robert.

'Oh, for . . . Christ's sake, Robert, not you as well. I *liked* her name. It suited her character. And I admired her.'

'A prostitute?' I said. 'Surely not.'

'Why not? She wasn't a hypocrite.' His sleepy, brown eyes slid from me to Robert and back to me again. They blinked once, slowly, and I had the feeling that I was a fly being observed by a chichak on the wall. 'Can any of us in this room say that about ourselves? I know I can't.'

A heavy silence weighed down on us. Robert, looking more drawn than usual this evening, yawned and announced that he was turning in. We watched him walk slowly out of the sitting room; a minute later his slow and heavy tread could be heard crossing the floorboards above our heads.

'I'm glad you talked him into going to Noel's party,' I said.

'You seemed so terribly . . . set on going, I couldn't disappoint you, could I?'

Had I been so obvious? 'Oh, Noel gives the best parties, it would've been unforgivable if we had missed it. We used to go out every evening, every evening, would you believe it?' I said. 'But Robert was . . . changed . . . when he returned home from the war . . . he was . . . different. He couldn't cope with crowds or noisy places. He'd lock himself away in his room, refusing to come out, refusing to eat or talk to anyone.'

'It's shell shock, Lesley.'

'I know what it's called,' I said sharply. Softening my tone, I went on, 'Do they ever get over it?'

'Perhaps he just needs a change of scenery, a holiday somewhere in a dry climate.'

'A change of scenery. A dry climate.' A laugh, abrasive and bitter, scraped out from deep within me. A mystified expression came over Willie's face, and I decided to enlighten him. 'Robert has a cousin, a sheep farmer somewhere in the Karoo – I don't even know where the bloody place is – he's offered to build us a house there. The air will work wonders on Robert's lungs, he says.'

'You've decided to go?'

'Robert has. He told me – he *announced* it to me – just before you came. He wants to move there by the end of the year.'

'But . . . why the deuce didn't he tell me? Good Lord, you must have a thousand . . . things to do! It's totally unacceptable – I'll tell Gerald to move us into the E&O tomorrow.'

'You'll do no such thing. You hear me, Willie? You will do no such thing.'

I had expected him to put up a spirited fight, but to my surprise he caved in without even putting up the semblance of a struggle. 'If you're sure,' he said.

'I won't go,' I said. 'I won't leave Penang. I refuse to.'

'The desert climate *will* ease his lungs, you know.'

There was not a trace of condemnation in his voice, nevertheless I felt myself bristling. 'What would you do if your wife – if Syrie – were ill, like Robert?' I asked. 'Would you give up your exciting life in London and move to some place in the middle of nowhere because it would make her remaining days more bearable?'

He slapped at a mosquito on his wrist. 'You're not moving . . . to Ultima Thule. Believe me, modern travel these days, there's nowhere on earth you can't get to. And, anyway,' his mouth softened into a reassuring smile, 'I'm sure . . . you'll be back here again, once Robert's health improves.'

'He's not going to get better, and you know it. He's worsened in the last few months, in fact.'

For a while he was silent, his gaze resting on something far away in time. The garden seethed with the tinnitus of the cicadas. 'After *Liza* was published,' he said, 'I told Robert I wished I could give up . . . medicine and make my living as a writer. He encouraged me to do it. Urged me. Said I'd be wasting my . . . talents if I didn't. He gave me money to . . . tide me over.' He smoothened a crease in his trousers and looked at me. 'Did he ever tell you that?

'He doesn't talk much about his London days.'

Lying in bed that night, I thought about the man sleeping in the room next to mine, the man I had married. Willie's words had polished the lens through which I had always viewed my husband, and yet, at the same time, they shifted him slightly out of focus.

Chapter Five

Willie
Penang, 1921

Number One Houseboy Ah Keng brought the cable to his room around mid-morning. Willie pushed aside his exercise book and contemplated the thin brown envelope lying there on his desk. Now that it had finally arrived, he dreaded what its innards augured.

He picked up his letter opener, disembowelled the envelope and drew out the piece of paper inside.

The message was brief and to the point. There were no legal recourses for him to recover the money from his stockbroker, his lawyers informed him. It was imperative that he return to London immediately to consult his accountants. Arrangements had to be made – he would have to mortgage his house in Wyndham Place, perhaps even sell it, not to mention auctioning off his works of art and antiques.

He slapped the cable on the desk. Mortgage his home and sell off the paintings he had spent his life collecting from around the world. How the bloody hell had the situation descended to this?

The room seemed to list when he stood up. He lurched for the back of his chair, clinging tightly to it. After a minute or two, feeling steadier, he made his way gingerly to the windows.

The sea was emerald and turquoise, chipped with a million white scratches. In the garden below the kebun was resting in the shade of the casuarina tree, puffing on a kretek and scratching his groin through the folds of his shorts with an abstracted, canine pleasure. Looking at him, a longing for the man's simple life gripped Willie.

Envious of a native fiddling with his balls under a tree, he thought. How the mighty have fallen.

He swore softly at himself. The wisest thing to do would be to sail home immediately and confront the disaster, salvage what he could from the wreckage. Returning to his desk, he tore a clean page from his exercise book and began making a list of instructions. The most immediate task for Gerald would be to change their travel arrangements.

Halfway down the page he stopped writing. He could already hear Syrie shrilling at him, blaming him for this catastrophe and the public humiliation she would suffer. The scenes she would make swilled through his mind: the recriminations, the rows and – most horrifying of all – the torrents and torrents of tears. He shuddered.

There was, of course, another thing he had to consider, the only one he truly cared about: this trip with Gerald was probably the last one he would be able to afford for the foreseeable future. He wanted to postpone, for as long as he could, the moment when they would have to part and go their separate ways – he to London, Gerald to Europe or America or wherever his fancy took him. Who knew how long it would be before they could be together again?

A few weeks ago, while he was recovering from his illness, he had made a decision: once he returned to London he would inform Syrie that he would be moving out of their home. She could keep her married name and continue living there; he would provide her with a generous allowance. Naturally Elizabeth had to stay with her. A child needs her mother.

It would be costly, but it would be worth it. It would all be worth it. The veil of their marriage would not be pulled aside; there would be no divorce and no scandal, not even the faintest whiff of it, but he would be free again. Free. The very sound of the word itself seemed to shift a huge weight off him. He would move to the south of Europe, he would buy a villa high up in the hills where the air was saturated with sunshine, and Gerald would come and live with him.

All his plans, all his dreams, swept away. He was penurious now, and he was trapped, with no choices, no escape. Most of all he feared he would lose Gerald: after seven years with Willie, he was accustomed to the very best in life. He would not take kindly to the news that Willie was broke.

A familiar set of rapping at the door pulled him back from his thoughts. He slid his lawyers' cable under his exercise book and spun around in his chair.

'Come in, Gerald.'

His secretary entered, nudging the door shut behind him with his heel. Willie crossed his arms over his chest and scrutinised him. Gerald was dressed in a short-sleeved cotton shirt and blue bathing shorts. In his hands were a rolled-up mat, a towel and a straw hat. A scab, translucent as rice-paper, was beginning to form over the cut on his cheek. A vivid bruise blotched the skin above his left jawline.

'I'm going down to the beach,' said Gerald, 'put some colour in me.'

'Your face looks colourful enough already, wouldn't you say?'

Gerald stroked his jaw tenderly. 'Sorry about yesterday. Abominable behaviour. Won't happen again. Swear to God.'

Both of them knew that oath would be broken again and again, as it had been before. There was no point pursuing the matter.

'I found out a few more things about Lesley last night,' Gerald said. 'Her father was a clerk in the Chartered Bank. Douglas Crosby. A well-known womaniser. Died of a heart attack when Lesley was just twelve. Her mother had to turn their home into a boarding house. The old lady – the talk was she had some Chinese blood in her family – died in her sleep a few years later. Our memsahib had just started teaching at a school in town.'

'She doesn't look Eurasian to me,' said Willie. 'And Sun Yat Sen? Did your friends tell you what she got up to with him?'

Gerald shook his head. 'Nothing interesting, really. She helped publicise his cause, raised a bit of money for him. Speaking of which . . .' Gerald held out his palm.

Willie gaped at him. 'I gave you twenty . . . pounds just two days ago.'

'Those bloody Chinks stole all my winnings.' He pointed to the bruise on his face. 'In case you've forgotten?'

'Can't you just . . .' Willie bit back his words. 'Just be more . . . prudent, will you?'

'Fuck it, Willie, I'll win back whatever I've lost. Fortune favours the bold – I'm one of the boldest men around, and you're one of the richest.'

For days now he had wanted to tell Gerald about the financial disaster he was facing, but then he remembered how close he had come to losing Gerald in Kuching. Life without Gerald was too bleak to even contemplate. Sighing inwardly, he found his money clip, peeled off a handful of notes and handed them to Gerald.

'Sod the work, Willie,' Gerald said, tucking the money in his shorts. 'It's a bloody crime to chain yourself to your desk on such a perfect day.' He peered more closely at him. 'What's really bothering you?'

'Just a knot I'm trying to . . . unravel in my story. Now bugger off. Some of us have to work for a living, you know.'

Gerald dropped his towel and his hat on the floorboards and bent towards Willie. He curved his palm around Willie's nape and kissed him hard on the lips. Willie closed his eyes, all his doubts and frustrations and irritations disintegrating, obliterated in the kiss. He was aware of Gerald's hand sliding up between his thighs. His excitement surged, and then, unbidden, thoughts of his money problems breached his mind, and seconds later – he could actually pinpoint the precise instant – he felt himself wilting rapidly.

He pressed his hand over Gerald's and gently pushed it away. Gerald stopped kissing him. He looked at Willie. 'You've never had this problem before – at least not with me.'

He felt his face flushing. 'I'm just . . . preoccupied . . .'

Gerald continued to study him. Then he pressed a tender kiss on Willie's lips. 'It's only a temporary thing.' He winked at Willie. 'It's like a cat – it'll come back when it wants to come back.'

He collected his towel and mat, jammed his straw hat on his head and left the room, closing the door quietly behind him.

Willie took out his lawyers' cable and read it again. After a while he picked up his fountain pen, moistened the nib with the tip of his tongue and, with the bitterness of ink seeping across his mouth, tried to slip back into the story he had been labouring over.

Half an hour later he put down his pen. He had barely filled two pages after Gerald left. Over the past week he had written only one story. Re-reading it, he found the writing inert, the characters flat. His well of stories had always brimmed over, but now, while the well had not run completely dry, the water was brackish. For the first time in his life, the irresistible inclination to write – his companion, his solace, his sustenance for as long as he could remember – had deserted him.

He screwed the cap on his pen, put away his exercise book and his lawyer's cable in the drawer and plodded downstairs.

The house was silent, the servants resting in their quarters. Wandering through the corridors, he caught himself assessing how much the William Daniell paintings on the walls were worth. He had started doing this recently – unable to fall asleep at night, he would mentally list all his works of art in Wyndham Place, all his jewellery and the expensive trinkets he had acquired over the years, and estimate how much each one of them would fetch at Sotheby's.

On the verandah he fixed himself an ice-cold martini and sipped it in the shade of the casuarina tree. It was just past noon, that time of the day when the wind swelling off the sea seemed to have been transmuted into the hot, searing light itself, but even in the full flood of the midday sun the casuarina's foliage had a brooding, corvine aspect.

His thoughts crept back to the mortifying failure with Gerald. It's just tension, that's all, he told himself, and besides, his health was still on the mend. Gerald's right – the bloody cat will slink home when it feels like it. And to hell with work – I'll write when I get home.

He was just finishing his martini when Lesley joined him under the tree. She was dressed in a pale green chiffon blouse and a yellow skirt. She removed her toque with its plume of white egret feather.

'Had your hair done?' he said. 'Very fetching.'

'What sharp eyes you have, Willie. I've been meaning to ask you – my brother would like to interview you for the *Penang Post*. Geoff owns the paper.'

'Interview?'

'Oh. It's an imposition.' Her face fell. 'I do understand. I'll tell him you're not interested. It's just that – and *please* keep this to yourself – but his paper isn't doing well, you see . . .'

Don't be a fool, he scolded himself. An interview will help sell your books, particularly your latest one. And Christ knows you need to sell as many books as possible. Every little bit helps.

'I'd be . . . delighted to talk to him,' he said. 'Tell him it'll be an exclusive.'

'I say, that's very generous of you. Geoff will be terribly chuffed.' She indicated his glass. 'A top-up?'

'I allow myself only one drink before lunch when I'm working.'

'You're slaving away like a coolie – I thought you came here to recuperate?'

'A writer never . . . stops working.' He did not want to talk about his work. 'How long have you two been married?'

'Fifteen years. It was our anniversary last month, actually.'

'Congratulations.' He made a mental note to get Gerald to buy them a present – nothing exorbitant, of course.

'Robert was forty when I met him. He's changed much, hasn't he? Oh, no need to lie, Willie — that afternoon you arrived, that look on your face . . .'

The high surf of the wind through the trees merged with the sound of the waves; it was hard to tell what was sea and what was merely air.

'We've all changed. Age. Illness. The war. And marriage, of course. Marriage changes a . . . man.'

'Not as much as it changes a woman.' They watched Gerald emerging from the sea, his body glossy with saltwater and sunlight. 'Some men don't change even after they marry,' Lesley went on, her eyes following Gerald as he sauntered up the beach to lie in the shade of the coconut trees. 'Did you?'

He took his time moulding his answer into the shape he wanted. 'In some ways . . . yes.' His stammer was worse than usual. 'And being a . . . a father . . . changed me.'

She looked sidelong at him, the mocking arch of an eyebrow telling him she was fully aware that he had not answered her question. He shifted his feet, shaking out the stiffness from his knees. 'You must miss your sons awfully.'

'I wanted them to go to Victoria Institution in KL, but Robert was set on sending them to his old school.'

'I loathed boarding school.' Willie hawked up a gob of disgust in his throat. 'The . . . beatings and the bullying, the hundreds of imbecilic rules . . .'

'At least your parents didn't have to sail halfway around the world to visit you.'

'My mother died . . . when I was eight. Two years later I lost my father.'

Her lips parted slightly, then closed again; she brushed back a sickle of hair from her forehead. 'Robert never told me. Who looked after you?'

'I was sent to live with my uncle in . . . Whitstable.' He kept his eyes on the coconut trees on the beach as he spoke; they looked like sea anemones waving in the current, he thought. 'He was a vicar. Uncle . . . Henry and Aunt Sophie. She was German. They were childless. They had no clue what to do with me.' He snorted. 'No clue at all.'

'You were an only child?'

He shook his head. 'No, but I felt like one. My two brothers were already at school by the time I . . . popped out into the world. When I went to live with Uncle . . . Henry the boys at my new school . . . mocked my accent.'

'What accent?'

'I was born in Paris. I grew up there. We spoke French at home. I was shy and I had no . . . facility for games. I had no friends. I read all the time.'

He remembered how he used to climb beneath his mother's blankets each morning, and how she had held him in her arms. Never again had he felt such warmth, such a feeling of security.

'She was bed-ridden – my mother, I mean,' he said. 'She had . . . tuberculosis. But one morning she slipped out . . . of our apartment and walked to a photo . . . studio a few streets away.' He paused for a moment, then for a longer moment. 'The effort was too much for her. She died a week later.'

'Oh, Willie . . . How terribly awful for you.'

'The photograph in my room – it's the one my mother had taken that morning. She wanted me to remember what she looked like. She was afraid of being forgotten.'

'All of us will be forgotten eventually. Like a wave on the ocean, leaving no trace that it had once existed.'

He shook his head. 'We will be remembered through our stories. What was that poem? The one written on your door? A bird of the mountain, carrying a name beyond the clouds. Well, a story can carry a name beyond the clouds, beyond even time itself.'

She nodded slowly, as though trying to convince herself of the truth of his words. 'I suppose you're right in a way – all those people you put in your stories – the world might know Sadie Thompson as a whore, but because of you, Willie, she will live for ever. She will never be forgotten.'

He was taken aback by the fervour in her voice. 'You sound as if you envy her.'

The corners of her mouth curled downwards. 'Infuriating, isn't it? For a woman to be remembered, she has to either be a queen or a whore. But for those of us who lead normal, mundane lives, who will remember us?'

'You have your children. They're a form of remembrance too.'

'Children?' She looked unimpressed. 'They have their own lives; and they'll leave their own marks, obliterating ours.'

The wind brushed a low-hanging branch across his face. He grabbed it and pulled it towards him. 'I can see why the . . . Malays liken it to the cassowary.' He rubbed the casuarina's hard scaly leaves between his fingers. 'Ugly, aren't they? Not like oaks or raintrees or banyans.'

'No tree is ever ugly, Willie. But I must say I prefer the name the Malays gave it. Did you know they call it "the whispering tree"?'

'Really? Why?'

'They say that if you stand under a casuarina when the moon is at its fullest, you can hear its leaves whispering to you.'

'And what would they be whispering?'

'Your future, and all the things you desire to know.'

'Is it true?'

A wan smile ghosted across her face, then disappeared, as though it had been filched by the wind.

'I've never heard it say anything to me,' she said.

Chapter Six

Willie
Penang, 1921

The coastal road tracing the northern shoreline of the island was narrow and twisting, stretches of it tunnelling through high, over-hanging tree branches. Thick ferns and shrubs covered the steep slopes on their left; to their right the road was sheared off by a sharp drop into the rocky sea. Lesley drove, Willie sitting beside her; Robert and Gerald were wedged into the seats behind. Willie was comfortable with her driving. Her fingers − long and slender in their red calfskin driving gloves − trimmed the steering wheel with an assured touch. And, unlike women drivers he knew, she never glanced at him or the other two in the rear-view mirror when she was talking or directing their attention to a fishing kampong or a temple by the sea. Traffic was sparse, but she kept her eyes fixed on the road ahead.

Now and again he stole a glance at her from the corner of his eye. Just another unhappily married woman in the tropics. His instincts told him she had had an affair with the Chinaman revo-lutionary, but then he would have heard about it − something like that would never have stayed a secret, and mauvaise langue, he had discovered, afflicted many people in the FMS. No blade is as sharp as a man's tongue.

Two or three miles past the Penang Swimming Club, Lesley slowed down and made a sharp right turn into an imposing entrance. A barrel-chested Sikh guard saluted them through the granite gateposts and onto a long driveway that inclined gently past expansive lawns to the mansion at the top of the rise. Istana was painted entirely white, its façade barricaded by a Doric colonnade with an imposing pediment. To Willie it looked more like the Parthenon than a Malay palace.

They relinquished the motor car to a valet beneath the porte-cochère and a houseboy escorted them into a vestibule. The chequered marble floor made Willie feel they were the remaining pieces of an abandoned chess game. Faint jazz music drifted in from somewhere deep within the house. Willie rotated slowly on his heels, taking in the paintings on the oak-panelled walls rising up the cavernous stairwell to the square gallery – tapestries of medieval hunting scenes and portraits of venerable old men seated in leather armchairs gazing confidently into some distant horizon. He couldn't help but feel let down – Lesley's fervid praise-singing had led him to expect something much more, instead he could have been in any grand country house in England. He was about to say this to Lesley when a tall and well-built man strode into the foyer, his footsteps clipping off the marble floor. He was in his late forties, with blue eyes and short, greying hair. The set of his features seemed oddly familiar to Willie, then he realised they echoed the faces on the walls.

'Welcome, Willie, welcome. I'm Noel.' The man shook Willie's hand. 'Robert, how good of you to come. Marvellous to see you, marvellous. Welcome, Gerald.' He kissed Lesley on her cheeks fondly. 'Looking splendid as ever, my darling.' He stepped back. 'I'll give you a tour of the house later, Willie, and introduce my children to you, but right now everyone's dying to meet you.'

He guided them along a series of teak-panelled corridors and they emerged onto the terrace behind the house. Willie made appreciative murmurs as he took in the unobstructed view of the sea.

The jazz band on the low wooden stage dribbled off into silence; the raucous chatter and laughter subsided. There must have been close to a hundred people milling on the lawn, Willie estimated, Europeans and a fair scattering of Asiatics, the women shimmering in their silk and velvet evening dresses while the men, like himself and Gerald and Robert, were anonymous in black tie. Waiters bearing trays of drinks patrolled the lawn; servants filled plates with food on the long tables. In a corner of the garden a team of perspiring Malay men were squatting over a long brazier, grilling hundreds of sticks of satay over the charcoals, basting the meat frequently with stalks of lemongrass soaked in oil. The sweet fragrant smoke drifted across the lawn, twisting the insides of Willie's belly.

'The whole of Penang's come to kowtow to you, Willie,' Robert murmured into his ear.

'My dearest friends,' Noel proclaimed to the crowd with the gravitas of a Roman senator, 'our guest of honour – Mr Somerset Maugham!'

Cheers and applause gusted across the lawn. Willie smiled, pressed his palm on his stomach and offered a short bow. Noel herded them down the steps onto the lawn where they were immediately surrounded by the guests. Robert beamed each time Willie told people that they were old friends. Men and women swarmed around him, telling him how much they liked his books. Many of them also took pains to inform him how scandalised they were by his story "Rain". At least his latest book was selling, even out here in the East.

At some point in the evening Willie realised that Lesley was no longer with their little group. He scanned the crowd around them, but there was no sign of her anywhere.

The currents of the party eddied him across the garden. When he noticed Robert beginning to flag, he whispered to Gerald, 'Sit him down somewhere and get him a drink.'

The effort of being charming and witty was wearying. His stammer grew more pronounced. He made an excuse to Noel about needing to use the bathroom. Noel clicked his fingers at a passing houseboy and instructed him to show Willie into the house.

Emerging from the bathroom, he wandered through the house, admiring the paintings on the walls. Female laughter pealing down a passageway diverted him into the nearest open doorway. He shut the doors stealthily and, when he turned around, couldn't help letting out a quiet chuckle at the sight of the walls of bookshelves – by some homing instinct he had found refuge in the library.

In the centre of the room stood a large round walnut table, mellowing in a strip of evening sun coming in through the tall windows. His own books were laid out in two orderly piles upon the table. No doubt he would be asked to scratch his name in them before the night was over.

He orbited the table to the windows. Peering through the glass down onto the lawn, he sought out Gerald and Robert in the crowd and found them drinking at the bar, his old friend flinging his head back and roaring with laughter at something Gerald said, no doubt one of his endless store of smutty jokes.

The sounds from the party seemed to float in from far out at sea. Willie's gaze skimmed over the little groups of guests and came to rest upon Lesley. She was standing by the stone balustrade at the far end of the garden. She held her champagne flute to her lips, but she was not sipping from it. Her body was completely still.

Her attention was fixed on an elderly Chinaman making his stiff and tentative way down a flight of granite steps. The moment the man disappeared from view she put her champagne flute down on the balustrade and squeezed her way through the crowd. Reaching the top of the steps, she hesitated, her hand stroking the stone finial. Then, gathering up the hem of her dress by an inch or two at her hips, she descended the steps.

'There you are, Willie!' Noel called from behind him. 'I thought you'd got lost.'

Willie turned away from the windows. 'Those steps at the end of the lawn – do they go down to the . . . beach?'

'There's a path halfway down there that goes around the cliff to another set of steps. Those'll take you all the way down to our little bay. You're most welcome to come and swim there any time, Willie. The water's clear as gin.' He curved out his arm. 'Come on, old chap – don't hide yourself away now – everyone's keen to talk to you.'

Arranging his face into an expression of polite interest, Willie allowed his host to reel him back into the party.

He managed to slip away again when Noel was distracted by one of his friends. He crossed the lawn, nodding to the people who wanted to talk to him but never allowing himself to be detained. He went down the same granite steps he had seen Lesley taking and continued along the narrow path. He soon came to a small wooden deck. Lesley was leaning against the railing. She glanced at him when he went to stand beside her.

'Your legion of admirers released you from their clutches? Where's Robert?'

'Sinking a few down the . . . hatch with his friends. Don't worry – Gerald has strict orders to look after him.'

'Since you're here – will you sign this?' She handed him the book in her hands.

It was, he saw, a copy of *The Trembling of a Leaf*. 'For that venerable Chinaman you followed down here just now?'

She gave him a steady look. 'It's for his son. You're his favourite writer.'

Willie took out his fountain pen and unscrewed its cap. 'What's his name?'

'Make it out to . . .' Her voice tapered off. 'I didn't ask his name. Oh, just write "Welcome home".'

His pen hovered above the page, its nib a golden beak in the sun. 'And from where is he coming home?'

'He's in China.'

'Big place, China.'

'Just sign the bloody book, Willie.'

He looked at her. She gazed coolly back at him.

He scrawled the inscription and signed his name. He blew tenderly on the page before returning the book to her. She checked his signature and closed the book.

'His son left Penang many years ago to fight for Sun Yat Sen,' she said.

Curious, Willie thought, how the Chinaman's name kept bobbing up from her lips.

'You remind me of him, you know,' Lesley went on. 'I thought so the first time I saw you.'

'In what way?'

'Your fastidiousness over your clothes.' She tapped the skin above her lips. 'Your perfectly groomed moustache. The deceptively disinterested air you give off when you observe people from the corner of your eye.' She leaned back at a slight angle, taking the measure of him from head to toe. 'And you're about the same build.' A new thought struck her. 'And you were both doctors too. Fancy that.'

'First time I've ever been likened to a Chinaman.'

They watched the waves scrolling across the sea. He was beginning to understand her refusal to leave the island.

'I've always dreamed of getting a place with a view like this someday,' Willie said. 'A small villa overlooking the sea. Somewhere in the south of France, or one of the . . . Greek islands. With a sparkling swimming pool and gardens fragrant with herbs and . . . lemon trees.'

'A nice holiday home.'

He shook his head. 'I'll move there permanently. I'll write, and grow old and cantankerous in that villa, surrounded by my books and my . . . paintings.' He smiled. 'I'll invite you and Robert to come and stay.'

'What's stopping you from buying it? You're already one of the wealthiest writers in the world, aren't you?'

He was conscious of his smile unstitching itself from his face. He peered over the railings. Far below them creamy white waves were lathering the beach. He pointed to an islet half a mile or so from the shore, deserted but for a cluster of wind-contorted trees clinging to it.

'Looks close enough to swim out to, doesn't it? Anyone staying there?'

'You should ask Noel,' she said. 'He owns it. Perhaps you could build a hut there. It'd be the perfect place to write, wouldn't it? Cut off from the world, with only your own words and thoughts to keep you company.'

It *was* appealing – how he longed to flee from the financial quagmire waiting for him back home! – but Gerald would loathe every second of it.

'It comes with breathtaking views of sunsets too,' Lesley went on. 'You'll have endless inspiration to describe it.'

Brahminy kites wheeled above the islet. 'I'll let you in on something I've never told anyone before – and I'll deny it if you ever . . . spread it around.'

She leaned slightly into him. 'I'm good at keeping secrets.'

He kept his gaze on her face, then nodded slowly. 'This was, oh, eight, nine years ago,' he said. 'I was strolling down a street one autumn evening – I had just lunched with my agent at the Garrick, a very long and boozy lunch during which he informed me that my first three plays had been so successful that I didn't have to worry about money ever again.' He paused, sensing a stammer waiting in ambush. 'I was strolling down the street,' he repeated, 'the sun was setting, and the colours in the sky were just extraordinary. I stopped and stared at the sky. Just stared at it. And all I could think of at that moment—' He broke off, smiling at the memory.

'For God's sake, Willie, don't be such a tease.'

'I thought,' he said, laying out each word carefully in a clear, precise line, '"Thank God I don't have to describe another pretty sunset ever again."'

She stared at him, a shallow groove etched between her eyebrows. And then a luxuriant laugh gushed from her throat. Perhaps it was only the light gilding her face and firing up her eyes, but to Willie she suddenly looked vividly alive. For the first time since he arrived in Penang, he could see why she had caught Robert's eye.

'I vowed to myself at that moment: I would never write another book again,' he went on, 'I would . . . devote myself for the rest of my life to writing plays.'

Her laughter ebbed into a smile. She crooked an eyebrow and held up *The Trembling of a Leaf*.

'Ah yes, well . . . Writing stories still calls to me.'

'No to mention the wealth it showers on you.'

'You know what . . . money really is? Money's the sixth sense. If you don't have it, you can't make . . . the most of the other five.'

He lit a cigarette for himself and gave one to her. She took the silver cigarette case from him and turned it over in her hand, stroking the red precious stones embedded in its lid. She examined them more closely. 'My goodness, these aren't *rubies*, are they?'

'I should bloody . . . well hope so. Sylvia – the Rani Brooke – gave it to me before we left Kuching.' He hefted the case in his palm, wondering how much it would fetch at Sotheby's. It pained him that he might have to part with it. 'It used to . . . belong to James Brooke.'

'Now there's one man you should write about – the Rajah Brooke and his whole mad family,' said Lesley.

'It wouldn't make for an interesting story.'

'Wouldn't make for—' Her eyes widened in disbelief. 'James Brooke founded the only European royal family in the East, and that family's still on the throne today, seventy years later. Why, his life must've been chock-full of adventures and escapades.'

'It *was* an eventful life – but it lacked one essential element.'

'And what's that?'

'Simple, really. There's no love interest in his life. And a story without love . . . well, it just wouldn't work.'

'He never married, did he?' A sly, knowing smile curled her lips. 'And I've never heard any mention of a woman in his life.'

He never married, and the throne, Willie recalled, had passed to Brooke's nephew after he died.

'So all the stories that've been written,' said Lesley, 'they have to be about love?'

'Think of the books you remember, the stories that have lodged . . . themselves in your heart – aren't they all, ultimately, about love?'

She let his words steep in her thoughts for a while. 'So,' she said eventually, 'a life without love is a life not worth writing about? I don't know whether that makes you a cynic or a romantic.'

He flicked his cigarette over the railing. 'I've never been . . . accused of being the latter.'

'Perhaps he *had* loved someone, but he couldn't tell anyone about it,' she said. 'To love, and to be loved, and yet not be able to let anyone know about it. And every trace of that love obliterated when you're gone.' Willie was struck by the pain in her eyes. 'No one would ever know it had ever existed, that it had given you great joy,' she said, 'perhaps the only joy you'd ever experienced in your life.'

Her melancholy mood affected him. Would anyone ever know how much Gerald meant to him? Did it matter?

Her eyes dropped to the book in her hand. 'You say you write about love, Willie, yet so many of your stories are about unhappy marriages and adulterous affairs.'

She had spoken quietly, but her words stung him nevertheless. 'I don't just write about adultery – I write about the human weaknesses that create these unhappy marriages – cowardice, fear, selfishness, pride, hypocrisy . . . All these emotions are . . . found within love too, you know.'

'Well, you must feel godlike, sitting in judgement over the people you put in your books.'

'I'm the last person in the world to judge anyone, Lesley,' he said quietly.

The brahminy kites were still circling above the islet. The sea was creped in a million ever-shifting creases. In silence they watched the sun slip away, two people bearing witness to the last light of the day depleting from the sky, from the world.

Chapter Seven

Lesley
Penang, 1921

Towards the end of the night, after his guests had departed, Noel showed us around his house, finishing the tour in his library where a set of Willie's books – from *Liza of Lambeth* to *The Trembling of a Leaf* – lay waiting on a table. Willie obliged Noel by signing and inscribing every one of them.

Robert had had a jolly time at the party – being Somerset Maugham's old friend had given him a huge amount of face – and he nattered on about the evening as Gerald drove us home. Sitting in the back of the car, I stared out of the window into the darkness, adrift on the currents of my memories.

Gerald dropped us at the front door before speeding off into town. Willie helped an unsteady Robert to his room while I went around the house locking up the doors and windows. For most of the evening at Istana I had stayed by Willie's side, a smile starched onto my face, and it was with a great sense of relief that I finally stepped into my bedroom and shut the door behind me.

One of the houseboys had placed a note on my dressing table. It was from Geoff, informing me that he had not been able to obtain Sun Yat Sen's address for me. I crumpled up the paper and threw it away.

I changed and climbed into bed, propping myself against the pillows. A large, pale moth fluttered around the room and alighted on the rim of the lampshade, imprinting its shadow on the wall. I reached over to flick it away, but my hand was stayed by a voice in my head. *They're the souls of the people we once loved, come to watch over us.*

I picked up Loh's copy of *The Trembling of a Leaf* and opened it to the title page. My fingers mused over the spidery crawl of Willie's inscription. In my mind I replayed my conversation with the old Chinese man earlier that evening.

Noel never failed to invite the pillars of the local communities to his parties, and Willie's presence there would undoubtedly be irresistible. I was certain to see Loh Swee Tiong at the party – even though the old philanthropist's name had disappeared from the pages of newspapers over the years. I kept my eyes peeled for him from the moment we arrived at Istana and as Noel introduced his guests to Willie I let myself lag behind them. At the first opportunity I slipped away into the crowd to find Loh. He has to be here, I said to myself as I searched the faces around me. He *has* to.

I did not see him, and I was resigning myself to the fact that he wasn't there when, through a momentary gap in the crowd, I caught a glimpse of him. I pushed my way through the throng and found him in conversation with an Indian couple. I knew he would be an old man now, but he had aged even more than I had expected; his face was drawn, his cheeks sunken. I took a flute of champagne from a passing servant and waited nearby. The band launched into another jaunty tune, but I paid scant attention to what they were playing. My patience was fast wearing thin when, at long last, the Indian couple moved away. Loh craned his neck and searched the terrace, looking for somebody, probably his wife. I was about to go over to talk to him when, with the timid movements of a man fearful of falling, he made his way down the steps.

The minutes crawled past. Finally I set down my glass and followed him. At the bottom of the steps I continued along the path, going around the promontory. The music from the party faded as the path led me further and further away from the house, until there was only the flapping wind and the waves below. I passed a flight of steep, wooden steps that descended all the way down to the beach, but I was sure the old man would not have attempted them. I kept walking and soon came to a wooden deck. The old man was there, staring at the horizon. Sensing my presence, he half-turned from the view and gave me a polite nod.

'Good evening, Mr Loh,' I said, then went on quickly, 'we've never met. My name's Lesley, Robert Hamlyn's wife.'

'Hamlyn . . . the engineer?'

'Barrister. He's with the George Town Chambers.' I indicated the book he was holding. 'You came to meet Willie Maugham too?'

'I was hoping he would sign this for me' – he showed me the front cover – *The Trembling of a Leaf* – 'but I could not get anywhere near him.'

'You enjoy his books?'

'It is for my son, actually.' A forlorn smile crumpled his face. 'Somerset Maugham is his favourite writer. Every time a new book by him comes out, I buy a copy and keep it for him. For the day when he comes home again.' His smile shrivelled away, leaving a residue of sadness to stain his face.

'Where's he now?' I asked.

'He followed Dr Sun Yat Sen to China a few years ago.'

It was so easy; I didn't even have to tack the conversation towards the direction I wanted. 'How is he? What's the latest news?'

'Dr Sun?' It was undoubtedly the last question he had expected from me. 'He's very sick, I was told.'

I took a hesitant step towards him. 'What's the matter with him?'

'His liver, according to the rumours. They say he has a year – maybe two if he's lucky. You have not heard about this?'

'Our English papers here have little interest in him or what's happening in China, Mr Loh.'

'But you know of him? Not many angmohs here can say that.'

'My husband and I knew him,' I said. 'We became friends when he was in Penang.'

'That was a long time ago. Yet you still remember him.' His ponderous nodding loosened a knowing smile over his face. 'You still think of him.'

I refused to look away from his gaze. 'He's a remarkable man.'

'Many people would agree.'

'But not you.'

'He stole my son, Mrs Hamlyn. He stole our sons and our daughters.' The old man's face hardened, as though it was chiselled from granite. 'I wish that man had never set foot in Penang.'

'But you gave money to his party,' I said, 'you were one of the biggest donors to the Tong Meng Hui.'

'Money? Money is easy to give, Mrs Hamlyn. I would give away every cent I have for my son to return to us, safe and unharmed, for my granddaughter to have her father back again.' His voice fissured. 'I would give everything I own just to know he is still alive.'

'You haven't heard from him?'

All at once he looked frail, as though the scaffolding that had been propping him up all this time was breaking apart at the joints. 'We haven't heard any news from him in two years. Nothing. Not a single letter. Not even a word.'

I wanted to reach out and touch his arm, to comfort him, but I held back. 'Did you ask Dr Sun?'

'My contacts in China have no idea where Dr Sun is. All they can tell me is that he's constantly moving from one place to another – there have been a number of attempts to kill him, apparently.' The old man's body seemed to sag. 'Even so, I hope my son is keeping close by his side – it's probably still the safest place for him to be.' Loh pulled out his pocket watch and brought it to his eyes, squinting at it. 'I must go home. My wife is very ill, but she insisted I had to get Mr Maugham to sign our book. She'll be very upset that I failed.'

'Give it to me.' I held out my hand. 'I'll get him to sign it for you.'

'I can't make you go to all that trouble, Mrs Hamlyn . . .'

'It's no trouble at all. Willie's staying with us.' Loh didn't resist when I tugged the book gently from his fingers. 'I'll deliver it back to your house.'

'You know where we live?'

'Who in Penang doesn't, Mr Loh? Your son will be home before long, I'm sure of it, and he'll have Willie's books to catch up on.'

His eyes sharpened, turned astute. 'The money I gave to the Tong Meng Hui, Mrs Hamlyn, it was never allowed to be made known to the public, it was never reported in the newspapers. That was my condition to Dr Sun. I wonder – how did you know about it?'

He did not wait for my reply, but gave me another nod and walked away. I watched him until he disappeared around a bend, and the path was empty once more.

I shifted in my bed, staring into the shadows above me. Sleep was far away. After a while I got up and went over to the windows. The moon was smothered in cloud, and the sea was fretful, stirred by the restive currents in its depths.

I slipped into my dressing gown and padded downstairs with *The Trembling of a Leaf*. I had intended to go into the library, but a weak spill of light drew me to the sitting room. Willie was slouched in his usual armchair, reading by the glow of a table lamp. He looked up from the page when I sat down across from him.

'Can't sleep either?' He squinted at the book in my hand. 'Well, some of my critics would say you've picked the perfect . . . soporific.' He showed me the book he was reading: *A Man of the Southern Seas*.

'Any good?' I asked.

'Competent prose, if superficial. But it hasn't made me nod off yet.'

'My brother's rather proud of that book, you know.'

He checked the author's name on the cover. 'Geoffrey Crosby's your brother?'

'The very chap who's so eager to interview you.' I smiled. 'Don't worry – I won't tell him what you said.'

'Please don't. The last thing I need right now is a . . . bitchy article from someone eager to . . . bury an axe into my . . . back.'

The despondence in his voice seemed uncharacteristic of him. 'You've been looking strained since you got here,' I said. 'What's troubling you?'

His face closed up. 'Nothing at all.' A moment later he appeared to relent. 'Just a bit of unwelcome news . . . from my lawyers. I made an, ah, unwise . . . investment. It's nothing too serious, but I do need to come out with a new book as soon as . . . possible.'

It was obvious that he was more worried than he let on. 'So *that's* why you've shackled yourself to your desk every day. How many stories have you written?'

'A couple . . .' His eyes sidled to the book on my lap.

'But not one of them comes within a mile of "Rain",' I said. A pained expression flitted across his face. 'Surely you've picked up a great store of tales on your travels?'

'It's not as simple as just going to some place and "picking up" a few stories,' Willie said. 'The story must *demand* to be set down on paper. With my . . . best stories, I always felt that I was merely their . . . conduit.'

I nodded slowly. 'Like a pianist,' I said. 'The music doesn't come from you, but flows through you.'

'Quite so.'

I showed him the title page of *The Trembling of a Leaf*. 'This strange-looking symbol you put in your books,' I said. 'What *is* it?'

'It's called a hamsa. It's a Moorish sign to ward . . . off the evil eye,' Willie said. 'It symbolises a sword breaking open the . . . darkness to let the light shine in.'

Hamsa. I savoured the strange word silently on my tongue, this short intake of breath, followed by its long surrender into the air. 'I always thought it looks like a casuarina tree — that long straight line down the middle is the trunk, and the two curving lines over it the outline of its droopy foliage.'

'I suppose it does, now that you mention it.' Willie shrugged. 'We see what we want to see.'

'How did you come across it?'

'It was my father's . . . he saw it in North Africa. After my mother died, he decided to build a summer house on the . . . banks of the Seine, a few miles west of Paris. Every Sunday he'd take me downriver to check on it. He had this same device engraved onto . . . its windowpanes.' Memory softened his voice. 'Those boat trips with him down the river on those still, misty mornings, they were the only occasions when the two of us spent any time alone together, the grieving widower and his grieving son. But we never stayed in that house, not . . . even for one night.'

'Why ever not?'

'He died shortly . . . after the house was completed. But ever since then I've adopted the hamsa as my own . . . symbol.' His eyes wandered to the Blüthner half-submerged in the shadows. 'Will you play something for us?'

I had not touched the piano in a long while, but I got up and went over to it. The stool creaked discreetly when I sat down. I opened the piano cover and flexed my fingers above the keys. I began pecking out the opening bars of a Chopin nocturne. My playing was wobbly, but grew more assured as I went on. I missed a few notes here, tripped over a cluster there, but Willie clapped softly when I finished — more out of politeness, I knew, than for my insipid performance.

My shoulders rose and dipped with the long, rolling swells of my breathing as I opened myself to the stillness, to the silence of the long, long years, until it filled me completely. And then, barely aware of my own being, I pressed down a key, and another, and another. The tentative notes wove themselves into the ribbon of a simple, plaintive melody. The piano had not been tuned in a long time, and the music seemed to emerge from an old, warped shellac disc, with an unsettling, forlorn quality to it. I played the piece all the way to the end. I never dropped a note, not even once.

This time Willie did not clap. His voice, when it came over my shoulder, was subdued. 'What was that?'

'Reynaldo Hahn,' I said, my eyes fixed on the keys. '*L'heure exquise.*'

'From Verlaine's poem?'

Slowly I swivelled around to look at him. His face was in the light, the rest of his body in the shadows.

'You know it?' I asked.

'When I was a young man – oh, a hundred years ago – I used to . . . traipse around the hills with a book of his poems. That particular one is, if I recall correctly, from *La Bonne Chanson*.' He closed his eyes and in a steady voice that never once stammered, he began to recite:

La lune blanche
luit dans les bois.
De chaque branche
part une voix
sous la ramée.
O bien aimée.

L'étang reflète,
profond miroir,
la silhouette
du saule noir
où le vent pleure.
Rêvons, c'est l'heure.

Un vaste et tendre
apaisement
semble descendre
du firmament
que l'astre irise.
C'est l'heure exquise!

The last word sibilated from his lips, evaporating into the shadows, and slowly his eyes opened again.

The silence around us, the very weave of the night itself, felt denser. Even the waves outside, fraying away the margins of land since the beginning of the world, seemed to have stilled into stone. In the hallway the weighted heart of the grandfather clock went on beating, as indifferent as an aged monk thumbing his prayer beads on their long and infinite loop.

'Where does a story begin, Willie?' I asked.

For a while he did not say anything. Then he shifted in his chair. 'Where does a wave on the ocean begin?' he said. 'Where does it form a welt on the skin of the sea, to swell and expand and rush towards shore?'

'I want to tell you a story, Willie,' I said. Yes, I thought to myself. Tell him your story. Let him write it. Let the whole world know.

The music I had just played seemed to go on unspooling in the air between us, this song that had no beginning and no ending; the song of time itself.

BOOK TWO

Chapter Eight

Lesley
Penang, 1910

I

If I were a novelist, Willie, I would tell you that I woke up on the morning of April 25th with a sense of uneasiness, a feeling that my life would never be the same again after that day. That's what a novelist would do, isn't it? But truth be told (and I intend to be completely truthful here), I felt nothing of the sort, nothing at all, when I got up that morning. I opened my eyes, as I usually did, at half past six. I lay in bed for a while, listening to the drowsy waves as the light outside changed, the ink of night diluting to dawn. On my way downstairs I looked in on my sons in the nursery. They were still fast asleep in their cots, curled up like piglets under the mosquito net, but my old amah Ah Peng was already up and garbing herself in her Sor Hei uniform: black cotton trousers and a starched white blouse buttoned up to her neck. Her hair was pulled back from her brow into a glossy bun. These women of the Sor Hei sisterhood had taken vows to remain unmarried and celibate, to live together and look after one another in their old age. Ah Peng's exact age was a mystery; I guessed her to be in her sixties, but even she herself wasn't certain.

Robert was at the breakfast table on the verandah, dressed for the office in a starched white Turnbull & Asser shirt and a striped tie, his hair combed and pomaded. After four years of marriage I thought he was just as handsome as the first time I had laid eyes on him. He was also regarded as one of the best-dressed men in the Straits Settlements and the FMS. He had grown heavier now – over the years he had acquired a taste for the local food, which was usually sweet and oily – but he was one of those fortunate men for whom a thickening waist only gave him an added gravitas, like a majestic tree with a wide, solid trunk.

He glanced up from his mail, smiling at me. 'Morning, my dear,' he said.

'Good morning, darling,' I said.

I paused at the top of the verandah steps and cast my eyes over the garden. Bulbuls darted around the lawn. The tall hibiscus hedge dividing our property from the Warburtons' was pinned with corsages of red flowers; in the beds below the verandah a sparrow thrashed its wings among the leaves, bathing in the dew. Down at the beach an old man was walking his terrier. I breathed the morning deep into my body. This was my favourite time of the day, when the world was cool and fresh.

'Cantlie's asked me to meet his former pupil when he arrives from America,' Robert said as I took my seat. 'A Dr Sun Yat Sen.'

'A Chinaman?'

'Worse – a revolutionary. The Chinese government has put a bounty on his head, a sizeable one too.'

We had entertained all sorts of characters in our home over the years – MPs and diplomats, writers and actors and singers and artists – but a revolutionary would be a first for us. 'He's not dangerous, is he?'

'Cantlie knows better than to send a madman our way – at least I hope so. But it'll be interesting to hear what this chap has to say about China.'

'When's he arriving?'

He checked the letter again. 'Any day now.'

I spread a thick layer of homemade kaya on my toast, bit off a corner and picked up the *Penang Post* from the pile of newspapers. The news was, as usual, dull and inconsequential: a list of men and women who had fallen ill or who had injured themselves; people who had gone back on Home Leave; the names of shipboard passengers who had disembarked in Penang; the latest books now available on the library's shelves.

I was about to turn the page when a small headline on the bottom left corner caught my eye. 'My goodness!'

'What's the matter?'

'Ethel's been arrested!'

Robert peered at me over his mail. 'What on earth did she do?'

I skimmed over the cramped, small lines of text in the article. 'She killed a man.'

'Mousy Ethel Proudlock?'

'He tried to rape her.'

'Good Lord. There's no accounting for tastes, eh?'

'That's not funny, Robert.'

'Who's the poor chap?'

'His name . . .' My voice stalled, and I had to try again. 'His name is William Steward. She shot him two nights ago.'

A hundred thoughts were jostling about in my mind. I was only half aware of Robert pulling the newspaper gently from my hands. '"Mrs Ethel Proudlock's appearance in the KL magistrate's court yesterday morning lasted less than five minutes",' he read aloud. '"She was released after her father paid sureties amounting to a thousand dollars. An inquest will be held in the Police Courts next week to determine if she is to be charged with murder."'

The clamour in my head was silenced – at least momentarily. 'Murder? But she was only protecting herself.'

'If she's admitted to killing him, then they have to decide if she is to be charged. That's the law.'

'The man tried to rape her!'

'Do calm down, my dear. The inquest is purely a formality, that's all. She'll get off with nothing heavier than a slap on the wrist.'

'I must go to KL,' I said.

'Cable her first. Visitors might be the last thing she wants right now.'

Robert slipped his jacket on and came around to kiss me. A trace of his Floris cologne lingered in the air after he left. I had always loved that scent on him.

Robert and I had been introduced to the Proudlocks at one of Bennett Shaw's dinner parties in Kuala Lumpur three years ago. Bennett was the headmaster of Victoria Institution, one of the oldest schools in KL. He and his wife lived in a spacious bungalow in a secluded corner of the school grounds.

Ethel was born in KL. She was a year younger than me. Her husband William had come out from London to take up a teaching post at VI. They had been married for less than a year when we met them. Robert found the Proudlocks insipid and unsophisticated, but Ethel and I warmed towards each other. After that evening we wrote weekly to each other and met whenever I was in KL. On their infrequent visits to Penang she and William stayed with us. The wives of Robert's friends were quick to enlighten me that Ethel's father, the chief of the fire brigade, was a person of no consequence, but I ignored them.

Earlier this year the Shaws returned to England on Home Leave. They would be away for ten months. In Bennett's absence William Proudlock was appointed acting headmaster, a position which allowed the Proudlocks to move into the Shaws' bungalow. Ethel never said it, but we both knew that her husband's new appointment was a big rung up the social ladder for them.

Sitting at my breakfast table on that April morning, the newspaper still in my hand, my thoughts went back to the last time I had spoken to Ethel. It had been about a month ago, when I had followed Robert down to KL for one of his trials. I recalled what she had told me that morning in Whiteaways' bustling tea room. I had sat there, growing increasingly appalled as she talked. I had warned her that she was acting recklessly, and that there'd be terrible consequences, but this was worse than anything I could have ever imagined. Far, far worse.

Later that morning I was coming out of the George Town Pharmacy on Beach Street when I saw my brother strolling down the pavement, hands shoved into his pockets. He stopped to admire something in a shop window. I waved to him, and he came over to me.

'I'm dying for a cup of tea,' I said. 'Tiffin Room?'

'Sorry, Les, I can't,' he said. 'Deadlines. I've just spent the morning interviewing the president of the Anti-Opium Campaign and I have to write it up.'

Ever since we were children I could always tell when he was lying. 'You didn't look to be in much of a hurry to me,' I said. 'I haven't seen you for weeks, Geoff. Come along now.'

I marched us up Beach Street to the Tiffin Room on the corner. The tea room was the latest place for the mems to meet up after a morning's shopping. The owner, a Hainanese former chef who had never been to England, had decorated the place according to his idea of how a café in London would look. Watercolours of Big Ben and Buckingham Palace and Trafalgar Square and St Paul's hung on the walls. I nodded to one or two people I knew as the waiter showed us to our table by the front windows.

'What have you heard about Ethel Proudlock?' I asked my brother after we had ordered.

'You haven't spoken to her?'

'I sent her a cable this morning.' I leaned in closer. 'What's the story, Geoff? Do you know?'

Throughout the whole morning everyone I had met in town had wanted to talk about nothing else but the killing, but no one had any details of what had actually happened between Ethel and William Steward that night.

'The police and Ethel's lawyer are as tight-lipped as Freemasons,' said Geoff. 'William Steward was buried this morning. There were only a handful of people at the funeral. Poor chap.'

'Was he a planter?'

'Manager of a mine in Salak South till it went *phut*. He got another job with a firm of engineers, driving out to mines and rubber estates to fix their machinery.'

Our tea and scones arrived, and I kept silent while my brother filled our teacups.

'What did he look like?' I asked after I had taken a sip of tea.

'Big, burly man. Balding, although he was only thirty-four years old.' Geoff stirred three spoons of sugar into his tea. 'A formidable rugger player. Quiet and shy, I was told. Not many friends. Not too fond of a—' Geoff made drinking motions with his hand. 'Perhaps that's why.'

There were fewer than eight hundred Europeans living in KL, so I would probably have seen William Steward at the Selangor Club at some time or another, but if I had, then it had left not the faintest impression on me. 'Was he married?'

'Bachelor,' garbled Geoff through a mouthful of scone. 'He was sending money home to his mother and sister in England every month. God knows how they'll cope now.'

For the first time since I had read about his death, William Steward was becoming real to me, coalescing into an actual human being, not merely a name in a newspaper. He had been alive – eating, thinking, chaffing his friends and being chaffed by them – until Ethel had taken all of that from him.

Geoff set down his teacup. 'How's Robert?'

Something in his voice made me wary. 'He's extremely busy. Old Stephen Mayhew died—'

'Heart attack, yes, I know. Two months ago.'

'Well, Robert's the most senior now, so he's had to take over his cases. He's been slogging away late every night.' I stopped buttering my scone and set it down on my plate. 'Oh, what *is* it, Geoff?'

'He's having an affair.'

For a second or two his words made no sense to me. Then the shock hit me. 'For heaven's sake, Geoff.' I shot a furtive glance at the other tables, but nobody else seemed to have overheard my brother. I asked quietly, 'How do you know?'

'I saw him.' He kept his eyes on the world going about its business outside the windows. 'I saw them.'

'Who is she? Who's the bloody bitch?' Before he could answer I gripped his wrist. 'No, don't tell me. It doesn't really matter, does it?' I let go of him. 'Just some bored and unhappy wife, I suppose. No shortage of them here.' I sat back into my chair. 'Is this why you've been avoiding me?'

He looked relieved to be freed from the burden of his secret. 'I didn't know how to tell you,' he said.

'Who else knows?'

'I haven't heard anything. Not a whisper.'

'I suppose I should give him top marks for keeping it so discreet.'

'Even so, you know what Mother always said: "Penang is a kampong—"'

'"—and everybody knows everyone's secrets."'

Gharries and rickshaws and bullock carts and traps clattered up and down in the street outside. From where I sat I could see the dome of the Hong Kong and Shanghai Bank, black on a white stone turret. The dome was visible from almost every part of town; its topmost half could even be glimpsed from the beach outside my home. Robert's chambers were in the building just next door to the bank.

'So what are you going to do?' asked my brother.

I turned away from the street. 'Oh, for God's sake, Geoff – I've only just found out. I don't know.'

'You *have* to do something, Les.'

I cocked an eyebrow at him. 'What would you have me do? Shoot him?'

'I meant confront him.'

'What if he doesn't deny it? What if he says it's true? And it leads to a divorce?' A middle-aged matron at the next table twisted around to stare at us. I lowered my voice. 'There'd be a terrible scandal.'

'It'll blow over.'

'It would *never* be forgotten. Never. No – I can't do that to my boys. I can't.' I had to get out of the place, away from my brother, away from everyone. I rose to my feet. 'I must go. Lots of chores still on my list.'

'And you have to look glamorous for the Pyketts' anniversary party at the E&O tonight.'

'You always know everything, don't you?'

'An essential requirement of my job.' He moved to get up as well. 'I'll take you home.'

'Stay and finish the scones,' I said. 'Don't waste them.'

'Yes, Mother.'

I gave his shoulder a tight squeeze. His hand came up and clung to mine for a moment, and then he let go.

I felt Geoff's eyes on me as I flagged down a rickshaw. Thank God the first one stopped immediately. I gave my brother a smile, threw my shopping bags onto the seat and instructed the puller to take me home. He hefted the shafts of his rickshaw and set off. I lowered the canvas screen, hiding my face beneath it, and then, finally, I allowed my dammed-up tears to spill down my cheeks.

When I reached home I avoided Ah Peng – her dozy eyes seldom missed a thing – and stole down to the beach. I walked barefoot over the burning sand. At the end of the bay I crossed the cool ankle-deep stream and climbed to the top of the highest boulder.

I sat there, staring out to sea. The water was clear, the shoals of rocks on the seabed stark as bruises on skin.

My eyes were sore, but dry: I had done all my weeping in the rickshaw. Despite what I had told my brother, I was now filled with an overpowering urge to confront Robert; I wanted to slap his face, scream at him, but he would only deny my accusations. I knew him only too well. Divorcing him would be supremely satisfying, but then I remembered Mrs Logan – she was a lodger in my mother's boarding house, recently divorced from her husband. In my mind's eye I saw again the despair in her face, the bitterness contorting her mouth as the months passed; I remembered how she continued to wear her wedding ring, clinging on to it for dear life, like a lifebuoy. My mother had had to ask her to leave when she couldn't pay her rent any more. I had seen how divorce diminishes a woman: I would be pitied at first, tolerated, but eventually I would be shunted out of the world I had married into, and the doors would be shut and bolted behind me. Other women would avoid me, fearful that I would steal their husbands. I would be forced to relinquish my position as my sons' mother, and then one day another woman would slip in and replace me. Oh yes, I knew what would happen to me if I divorced Robert.

I had met Robert for the first time at one of Mrs Millicent Skinner's Friday musical evenings. Her regular pianist had been thrown off his horse that morning, and she begged me to accompany a visiting lieder singer from Singapore (normally that woman would barely deign to nod at me when she saw me in the shops – she was a surgeon's wife, and I was, after all, merely an inconsequential junior music teacher at the Light Street Convent School).

The evening's programme was not taxing – Schumann for the lieder singer, some Gilbert & Sullivan and a selection of Chopin's ballades – I could play them all with my eyes closed. We were about a third of the way through our recital when the Skinners' Burmese cat sauntered into the room and jumped onto the piano. The cat made himself comfortable in front of my face and, pointing one hind leg into the air, started licking his nether parts in complete absorption.

Shaking with suppressed laughter – exacerbated by the sight of Millicent Skinner's flushed and mortified face in the front row – I played on valiantly. I became aware of a tall, stocky man in his forties at the back of the drawing room – he was rocking with silent laughter as well. At the end of my recital I picked up the Burmese and the three of us – the lieder singer, myself and the cat – bowed to enthusiastic applause and a good deal of merriment from the audience. I was packing away my music when the man came up to me and introduced himself.

'You played marvellously – the cat thought so too,' he began, but before we could chat further Millicent Skinner swooped in and dragged him away to be introduced to the other mems and their unmarried daughters. Later in the evening Robert approached me again and invited me for tea at the E&O Hotel the next afternoon.

He was waiting for me at his table on the seaside terrace when I arrived. He put down the book he was reading – John Galsworthy's *The Man of Property* – and helped me into my chair. Couples and families were chattering and eating at the tables around us. Tall pinang trees lined the terrace, their long spiky fronds combing the breeze. Ships and tongkangs and steamers chalked thin white lines across the water.

'Reminds me of Hong Kong,' Robert said, drawing my attention to a Chinese junk heaving into the harbour. 'Ever been there?'

'I was born here,' I replied. 'Singapore's the furthest I've ever been.'

Our tea and scones came. As we ate I found out that he had been a barrister in London before moving to Hong Kong, where he had worked for a few years before deciding to move to Penang. He had arrived just over a week ago.

'And no doubt the mems have already staked their claim on you for their daughters,' I said, taking a dainty bite of my scone.

He laughed. 'Penang's not so different from Hong Kong.' He

smoothed his palm over his temple. His black, pomaded hair was greying, adding to his worldly aspect. 'I picked up a fair bit of Cantonese in Hong Kong, but that doesn't help me at all here, as I've found out.'

'The locals here are Hokkien.'

'You speak it?'

'My amah taught me. I speak Malay too.'

'Well, then, you'll have to teach me, won't you?'

My face flushed. I glanced away from him, thrilled that he wanted to ask me out again. 'Why did you leave Hong Kong?'

Everyone had fled Peking for Hong Kong when the Boxers went on their rampage, he explained. They brought with them stories of what the Boxers were doing to the foreign devils. 'The way I see it, there isn't much of a future for us whites in China.'

I had only the faintest notion of what he was talking about, but I nodded sagely anyway. Not having much interest in China, I pressed him to tell me about his old life in England instead. 'Ever since I was a girl,' I said, 'I have wanted to live in London. Oh, to be far, far away from Penang. Where I could become a different person, with no ties to the past, or to anyone.'

There was a silence. Robert, I saw, was gazing at the Chinese junk again, its sinister bat-winged sails flexing in the wind. His eyes, so blue and penetrating, were dusked by some emotion I could not decipher.

'"Caelum non animum mutant qui trans mare currunt" – They change their sky, not their soul, when they speed across the ocean.' He looked back at me. 'A Roman poet wrote that.'

So why did you travel halfway around the world, and what part of your soul were you seeking to change? I wanted to ask him, but I did not. Years later, whenever I recalled our conversation on the E&O's terrace that afternoon, I wondered what answer he would have given me if I had asked my question. Would my own life have turned out differently?

In the weeks that followed, whenever he took me out – for evening strolls on the Esplanade, to a play, to dinner at the E&O – I would teach him phrases in Hokkien and Malay. He was a quick learner, with an absorbent memory.

We were married in St George's church two months after we met. He was forty, and I was twenty-two, but I derived great pleasure from being the young wife of an older man. Under Robert's culti-vated eye I learned to dress and carry myself in a style that played down my shortcomings and accentuated my strengths. Robert was knowledgeable about books and music and theatre, and he knew a lot about politics and history. He introduced me to Flaubert and Tolstoy, de Maupassant and Dante and a long list of writers I had never heard of. He taught me to lose myself in the operas of Donizetti and Bellini (Robert couldn't tolerate Puccini; he particu-larly loathed *Madame Butterfly*, and so did I – such an idiotic and improbable tale, even for an opera). I read widely and kept myself informed of events around the world, but I did not exhibit my knowledge at any social occasion unless the conversation required the sparkle of a mot juste or two. It warmed my heart to see the pride on Robert's face when his friends broke off from their conversations to look at us whenever we entered a room. And I relished the nights when he slipped into my bed. He was a consid-erate lover, and he never outstayed his welcome.

I gave up my job and threw myself into the activities that were expected of the wife of a barrister: dancing and tennis, the Penang Amateur Dramatics Society and the Women's Shooting Club. I volunteered in the church choir and sat on the committees of various charities; I organised 'at home' musical evenings, which were, I must say, always better-attended than Millicent Skinner's.

Our firstborn arrived, and we named him James, after Robert's father. The birth of Edward, our second son, was fraught with complications, and the doctor warned us that I would not be able to have any more children. Robert's nocturnal visits to my bedroom tapered off and eventually ceased completely. I missed him in my bed, but I had a handsome and loving husband and two beautiful sons, and we lived in a house by the sea. What more could I ask for?

The tide was pulling out. I climbed down from the rocks and walked the length of the bay back to the house. That evening when Robert came home he found me lounging on the rattan sofa on the verandah, pretending to be engrossed in a book.

'Darling, you've burnt yourself,' he remarked, unknotting his tie and draping his jacket over a chair.

'Yes, I have.'

He gave me an odd look, but I ignored it. We chatted idly about our day before we went upstairs to bathe and change for the Pyketts' party. It was just another evening in the life we had made together.

The ballroom of the Eastern & Oriental Hotel was packed with the Pyketts' guests. Even with all the French windows opened onto the garden, it was stifling. I nursed my glass of wine and eyed the women around me. I knew almost everyone there, and they knew me too. I groaned inwardly when I saw Mrs Biggs, the wife of the director of the Rickshaw Department, making a beeline for me. In a booming voice that could be heard over on the mainland, she asked me if it was true that Ethel Proudlock had been having an affair with William Steward.

'Absolute bunk,' I told her sharply. 'People should keep their mouths shut when they don't know anything.'

'Well, no need to take it out on *me*, my dear Lesley.' She spread her fingers over her mountainous bosom. 'But you know what they say – "No smoke without fire."'

Watching Mrs Biggs waddle away, Robert said, 'Everyone at the office can't stop talking about it, you know. The poor devil, shot like a rabid dog. Awful way to die.'

'What on earth is wrong with you and Geoff? "Poor devil" my foot! In case you've forgotten, the "poor devil" tried to rape Ethel.'

'We don't know what actually happened, do we?' He peered at me. 'Are you all right, darling?'

I was saved from having to come up with a reply by a Chinaman greeting Robert. He was in his late twenties, slim and bright-eyed, dapper in black tie.

'Darling,' said Robert, 'my new assistant, Peter Ong Chi Seng.'

'I hope you're helping out my husband,' I said. 'He's working far, *far* too hard these days.'

The man's smile squashed his eyes into slits, making him look like a sleeping cat. 'He has very exacting standards, Mrs Hamlyn.' His English was beautiful, each word emerging from his lips with angular precision. 'I am acquiring a great deal of knowledge from Mr Hamlyn.'

The Chinaman had read law at Gray's Inn, he replied to my questions, and in a month's time he would be marrying a Nyonya girl his parents had arranged for him. A few minutes later he made his excuses and wended his way across the ballroom to another group of people.

'He seems competent and industrious,' I said.

'He's still wet behind the ears,' said Robert, 'and he needs to pay more attention to his drafting. I only took him on because I owed his father a favour.'

People were still filing into the ballroom. Noel Hutton and his wife Emma joined us in our corner. We made small talk, but all the while I was aware of Robert's gaze roving casually around the ballroom. I watched his face covertly for a sign — a hesitation, a gleam in his eye, a gaze that lingered a fraction too long on a particular woman — but there was none. In truth I had not the faintest idea what I was looking for.

With no warning at all the faces around me blurred; I felt invisible hands squeezing my throat tighter and tighter. Pressing my wine glass into Robert's hand, I mumbled some excuse to Noel and Emma and shoved my way through the crowd out into the garden. Barely even aware of what I was doing, I took the gravel path that wound between the pinang trees, past the row of cannons mounted on concrete plinths pointing out to sea. I kept walking until I reached the sea wall at the end of the hotel lawn. I pressed my hands on the edge of the sea wall and forced myself to breathe slowly.

Robert caught up with me a few seconds later. 'What's the matter?'

'Nothing. I needed some air, that's all.'

From here I could almost catch a glimpse of our house. At that moment I wanted nothing more than to go home and hold my children tightly in my arms.

The waves slapped weakly at the rocks below the wall, the evening breeze tousling the tops of the pinang trees. I leaned against the wall and gazed at the low buildings of the hotel. On the terrace a waiter was lighting the candles on the tables; and there, beneath the pinang trees, was the very spot where I had first met Robert for afternoon tea, barely five years ago.

Robert fussed with his pipe until he got it going. I noticed him gazing at the terrace as well, a distant look in his eyes. Was the same memory also drifting through his head?

'Those two over there.' I jerked my chin at a couple of Chinamen striding across the lawn, making directly for us. 'I think they want to speak to you.'

Robert exhaled a thin plume of smoke, studying the two men. 'Never clapped eyes on them before.'

The two Chinamen had stopped in front of us. 'Mr Robert Hamlyn?' the younger one said, extending his hand to Robert. 'Dr Arthur Loh. And this gentleman here' – he presented the man beside him – 'is Dr Sun Yat Sen.'

The man touched his palm against his stomach and gave us a brief little bow. He was in his mid to late forties, dapper in a grey suit, with a waistcoat of the same colour buttoned over a white shirt, and a dark blue bowtie. He had refined features, with bright, intelligent eyes and a nose that was narrow and well-shaped for a Chinaman. His moustache was neatly trimmed, his brilliantined hair cut short and meticulously parted on the side. I thought he looked more like a diplomat – and a handsome one at that – than a revolutionary hunted by his government. Our eyes met. I held his gaze for a heart-beat longer, then I looked away.

'When did you arrive?' asked Robert.

'I came in from Singapore this afternoon. Dr Cantlie asked me to look you up. He sends his regards.'

'You're taking a grave risk, aren't you?' Robert waved the stem of his pipe at a huddle of Chinamen staring openly at Dr Sun. 'From your legation. And I'm sure I saw the Chinese Consul somewhere inside too.'

'This is British territory. They would not dare lay a finger on me here.' Dr Sun curled a contemptuous smile at the Chinamen; they continued to watch him, their faces expressionless.

Dr Sun chatted with us until Dr Loh touched his elbow. He broke off and pulled out a gold pocket watch. 'Please excuse us, Mr Hamlyn. I have to give a talk at the Khoo clanhouse.'

'A political talk?' Robert asked with feigned innocence.

'I'm sure you are well aware that I would be deported immediately if I did anything of the sort here. No, no – my talk tonight is on Chinese literature and history, nothing seditious in it at all.'

'With, no doubt, *Romance of the Three Kingdoms* featuring prom-inently,' Robert said.

'Well, it *is* one of the great novels of China, after all.'

'Your audience will certainly lap up its stirring tales of rebellions and plots to overthrow emperors,' said Robert. 'Come for drinks tomorrow. You too, Dr Loh. We're at Cassowary House, Northam Road. Shall we say half past five?'

Dr Sun gave us another quick bow, and the two men left. I noticed the Chinamen from the legation were also watching them as they strode through the grounds out to the road.

'A revolutionary,' Robert said. 'I hope he doesn't stir up any trouble here.' He tapped his pipe against the sea wall and pocketed it. 'We'd better trot back inside, my dear,' he said. 'Charles is sure to give one of his long-winded speeches and I'll need a big glass of wine to survive it.' He shook his head. 'Thirty years of marriage. Which one of them do you think deserves a medal more?'

II

The Chinaman revolutionary showed up at our home at precisely half past five the following evening, and the houseboy brought him out to the back verandah. Robert had just got home and was still in his shirtsleeves, his collar undone, his tie coiled on the coffee table.

That morning, after he had left for his office, I sent the boy around town to cancel my engagements, pleading a cold. I couldn't bear the thought of facing my friends, all the while wondering if they knew about Robert's affair. I stayed home and played with my sons, but their fussing and crying only made me more irritable than usual. I found fault with everything the servants did. I banged out loud, tempestuous chords on the piano, and when that didn't dull my anger I switched to rambling, melancholic pieces. I decided I would confront Robert; a while later I told myself I would not; half an hour after that I changed my mind again. This went on until I felt I was going mad. I escaped to the beach and swam up and down the bay, losing myself in the pounding of the sea. When I eventually stumbled out of the waves, I collapsed onto the sand and lay there. Exhaustion numbed my thoughts, and I welcomed it, but the moment I stepped inside the house they came screaming back at me again. So it was with a warm and grateful smile that I welcomed Dr Sun – his presence would make the long evening easier to endure.

'Dr Loh sends his regrets,' Dr Sun said. 'His daughter is not feeling well.'

'Your English is faultless, Dr Sun,' Robert said. 'Where did you study?'

He asked us to call him Sun Wen. He was born in a small village by the sea in southern China, less than thirty miles north of Macau, he told us that evening. At the age of twelve he was sent to live with his older brother in Honolulu. For five years he stayed there, attending one of the top schools, but his brother, alarmed by his growing interest in Christianity, decided to send him back to their village in China.

'Having seen the world, I was appalled by my own country. I found my village backward, our people shackled by their superstitious beliefs,' Sun Wen said. 'I caused some . . . problems . . . at home, so my parents sent me to Hong Kong to further my studies.'

A tendril of smoke rose from the mosquito coil at our feet. 'What sort of troubles?' I asked.

'I broke into the village temple and desecrated the statues of the deities,' Sun Wen replied. 'And for good measure I smashed the villagers' ancestral tablets as well.'

'Following in the footsteps of that chap Hong, were you? The leader of the Taiping Rebellion?' Robert said. 'He started out just like you too, didn't he? Smashing the idols and tablets in his village temples.'

'My teacher in the village had fought with the Taipings. He used to entertain us with stories about them,' Sun Wen said. 'Unlike Hong Siu Chuan, I assure you that I am not the younger brother of Jesus.'

The two men realised that they had lost me completely. 'Sorry, my dear – Hong Siu Chuan was a scholar in a village in the Kwangtung province,' Robert explained. 'His ambition was to be a court official, but he kept failing the Imperial Examinations. Following his third – or was it fourth? – anyway, following another failed exam, he was struck down by a fever. In his delirium he dreamed that he had been taken up to Heaven to speak to God, who told him He was Hong's father, and that his elder brother was Jesus.'

'When Hong recovered,' Sun Wen said, picking up the story, 'he told everyone in his village that he was now a Christian, and he had been commanded by God, his father, and Jesus, his elder brother, to end the emperor's reign and to found a new Jerusalem.'

'Surely no one took him seriously?' I said.

'Oh, but they did. Hong began to study the Bible intensively, and he travelled around the countryside converting people to Christianity – or rather, his version of it.' Sun Wen gave me a wry smile, and I smiled back at him. 'Within a year he had hundreds of followers, then thousands, then tens of thousands.'

'You're a Christian too?' Robert asked.

'I do not belong to the Christianity of the churches. I belong to the Christianity of Jesus, who was a revolutionary himself.'

I didn't have to look at Robert to know that his eyes were rolling upwards. 'Sun Wen,' I said hurriedly, 'how do you know Dr Cantlie?'

'He taught me at the College of Medicine in Hong Kong. I was his interpreter whenever he went out to the leper villages for his research. But more than that, I wouldn't be sitting here now if it weren't for him. I owe my life to him.'

'He cured you of some rare disease?' Robert asked, smiling.

'If only everything in life were so simple,' replied Sun Wen.

'How did he save your life?' I asked.

It happened a few years after he finished his studies. Sun Wen had gone back to China and organised an uprising in Canton, but it had failed. He fled the country and travelled the world – San Francisco, New York, Hawaii – to raise funds for the Revive China Society. In the autumn of 1896 Dr Cantlie invited him to London, where they found him lodgings in Gray's Inn. It was his first time in the city, and he knew no one except the Cantlies, to whose house he paid daily visits. He was strolling up Portland Place one morning on his way to the Cantlies' on Devonshire Street when a pair of Chinamen accosted him on the pavement. They started talking to him and before he knew what was happening he had been manhandled into an impressive-looking house just off the street.

'The moment I was inside they slammed the door shut and

barred it,' said Sun Wen. 'Fear gripped me when I saw the large number of Chinese inside, all of them in mandarin attire. Too late, I realised I had been trapped inside the Chinese Legation.'

'If I recall correctly, Cantlie lives just around the corner from the legation, doesn't he?' said Robert. 'Surely he'd have warned you to give it the widest possible berth?'

'He did warn me, but I didn't think they'd dare do anything to me in England. They were going to smuggle me back to China, where I would be tried for treason.' Sun Wen paused. 'They would have judged me guilty, and they would have cut my head off.'

'So what happened?' I asked.

They locked him in the basement. The windows had been boarded up so he couldn't shout for help. Days passed, but no one knew what had happened to him. He was starving but, terrified of being poisoned, he didn't touch the food they gave him. Finally he managed to persuade the guard to deliver a note to Dr Cantlie. A week passed, and he had given up hope, when one afternoon the door opened and three men came down into the basement. They dragged him upstairs and threw him out onto the street.

'Dr Cantlie was waiting there with a crowd of photographers,' said Sun Wen. 'I had never been happier to see anyone in my whole life. Back at his home, he told me he had approached Scotland Yard and the Foreign Office with my note, but they were not interested. So he went to *The Times*. After that every newspaper in London printed the story of my kidnapping. The legation had no choice but to let me go.'

'What a terrifying experience,' I said.

Sun Wen pulled out his gold pocket watch and showed it to Robert. 'A present from Dr Cantlie, to mark my narrow escape. I carry it with me everywhere I go.'

Robert examined the pocket watch and passed it to me. The Breguet was slightly warm from his touch. I rested it on my palm for a moment before returning it to Sun Wen.

'That all happened fourteen years ago,' Sun Wen said. 'Since then I have been travelling the world raising money for my party, the Tong Meng Hui.' He slipped his watch back into his waistcoat pocket, patting the slight lump it made. 'In all these years I have never returned home to China. Not even once.'

'What is it you hope to achieve with your revolution?' I asked.

'The revolution is not mine alone,' he said. 'It belongs to all Chinese people, all over the world. We are going to establish a republic, a republic where everyone is equal, where everyone is free – men *and* women.'

'And for that they would sentence you to death?'

'To bring down the emperor is to go against the natural order of Heaven, Lesley. But the emperors have stolen China's wealth. Piece by piece they have sold my country to the West. My people are dying of hunger, they have no future to look forward to. The dynasty is corrupt and decaying.' His hand reached up and grabbed a fistful of air. 'The time has come for us to take back our country.'

'Take back China?' I said. 'But China's ruled by your own people.'

'My dear,' said Robert, 'the Manchus are not Chinese.'

'What do you mean, not Chinese?'

'The Manchus stormed down from the northern plains three hundred years ago, breached the Great Wall and vanquished the Ming emperor,' said Robert. 'They've been the rulers of China ever since.'

'They forced all Chinese men to tie their hair in a queue,' Sun Wen said, 'the symbol of my people's enslavement to the Manchus.'

'But you don't wear it,' I said. Strange, but I had never questioned why some of the Chinamen I saw – even our houseboys – wore pigtails.

'I cut it off when I left China.'

'The Straits Chinese here already did that,' said Robert. '*Ages* ago.'

'These Straits Chinese of yours – they speak only English, they ape your customs, your traditions.' A derisive grunt crawled out from Sun Wen's throat. 'They think England is their motherland.'

Dusk rouged the sky. Inside the house, the servants were going around lighting the lamps. Ah Peng brought James and Edward out to the verandah; my boys were fragrant from their evening bath, their neatly combed hair still damp. James curled his arm around my leg and goggled at our visitor.

'Good evening, young man,' the Chinaman said. 'My name is Sun Wen. What is your name?'

'James.'

'A strong, noble name. How old are you, James?'

'Four.'

'My goodness, you are a big boy already.'

Robert dandled Edward on his knee. 'Tell Dr Sun how old you are.' Edward buried his face in his father's chest. Robert kissed the top of his head and smiled at me. In that brief moment I felt I could forgive him anything. 'This little rascal here's three,' he said to Sun Wen.

I caught a glimpse of pain in the Chinaman's eyes. 'You have children, Sun Wen?'

'I have a son and two daughters. Sun Fo is nineteen. He is studying in Hawaii. Jin Yuan and Jin Wan are sixteen and fourteen. They are with my wife in Hong Kong.'

'It must be hard on your wife, all this travelling around the world.' I kissed my sons and handed them back to Ah Peng, indicating to her to take them inside.

'They accept it.'

'They?' I asked.

'Both of my wives.'

Having more than one wife was an acceptable, even admired custom among the wealthy Chinese, and it was none of my business how many wives Sun Wen had, but all evening I had sat there listening to his talk about equality and freedom and modernising China; I had even begun to sympathise with his cause.

'I'd have thought,' I said, 'that you of all people would be against something so backward.'

'How many wives he has is none of our concern, Lesley,' Robert said. 'Another drink, Sun Wen?'

'One is enough for me,' Sun Wen replied.

'You should apply that rule to wives as well,' I said.

'Darling!' said Robert.

'It's all right, Robert,' said Sun Wen. 'My first marriage was arranged for me when I was a young man, Lesley. The second one was of my own choosing.'

'A prettier – and younger – woman, no doubt,' I said.

'I've yet to meet a man who'd choose differently.' Robert laughed, slapping his knee. 'Have you, Sun Wen?'

'I don't find that funny at all, Robert.' I turned back to Sun Wen. 'All night long you've been talking about equality.' I jabbed my forefinger at him. 'Let me ask you this: after you've established your republic, will you allow us women to take as many husbands as we like? Younger and handsomer, more virile ones? It's only fair, isn't it? It's only *equal*.'

'What you are demanding, Lesley – it goes against the natural order of Heaven,' said Sun Wen.

'So does rebelling against your emperor – or at least that's what I've been told.' The anger I had been holding in check ever since I found out about Robert's affair was threatening to spill out of me. I felt lightheaded, reckless. The life I had built with Robert seemed so fragile; I could so easily smash it all to smithereens with just a few words.

'Your talk of equality means nothing,' I went on. 'You men, you can have all the women you want, but for us women – oh no. *We* have to stand by our husbands. *We* have to tolerate you marrying another woman, tolerate you rutting with anyone you like—'

'You're ranting, Lesley,' Robert broke in. He was crouched forward in his chair, his palms pressed onto the armrests, his feet planted firmly on the floor; he seemed ready to spring at me.

With an effort I took hold of myself; after a moment or two my breathing began to slow down, became normal again.

Sun Wen dug into his pocket and drew out his watch again. 'I must go,' he said. 'I'm expected at the Chinese Chamber of Commerce.'

'Another edifying talk on Chinese literature?' Robert asked.

'Yes, and to convince people to part with their money, to . . . ah . . . help us purchase more books for our reading club. Perhaps you would like to make a donation?'

My joints seemed rusted with fatigue when I stood up. I felt I had been trekking across an endless desert. 'I should warn you, Sun Wen: Penang Hokkiens are great misers. The wealthier they are, the tighter their fists.' I rubbed my thumb and forefinger together. 'They're kiam-siap, and proud of it.'

'I will make them change their minds.'

Robert showed him out of the house. I left the verandah and went into the garden. Twilight was roosting in the trees. I stood beneath the casuarina and stared out to the narrow sea. I can't continue like this, I told myself; I can't keep pretending that everything is fine between me and Robert. I'll crack; I'll shatter. I *must* get away from him.

The light was fading from Mount Jerai, the highest peak in the mountain range on the mainland. Closer by, a fisherman was setting off from the beach. A lantern hung on the sampan's prow, spreading its light on the darkening waters. I watched him rowing, his movements slow and fluid, ploughing his sampan further and further away from the shore. Somewhere out at sea the fisherman would stop rowing and cast his nets into the water. Beneath his boat they would bloom open, and as night thickened, the glow from his lantern would mesmerise the fish from the deep and into his nets. It was all as timeless as the circuits of the tides.

Robert was finishing his drink on the verandah when I walked back to the house.

'I'm going to KL tomorrow to see Ethel,' I said. 'I'd like to attend the inquest.'

'I'll cable the Hubbacks.'

The thought of having to be sociable, to pretend to our friends that everything was going swimmingly in my life, was more than I could bear. 'I prefer to stay at the Empire.'

'By yourself?' He saw the set expression on my face. 'All right, fine. If that's what you want.'

I turned back to look at the sea again. The fisherman had shrunk to a tiny silhouette, and on the far side of the channel the mountains had already dissolved into night.

III

A dusting of stars still clung to the sky when Robert helped me down from the buggy outside the railway station, but the streets around Weld Quay were already busy with trams and bicycles and bullock carts piled high with sheets of smoked rubber and tin ingots.

'Safe journey, my dear,' Robert said, kissing my cheek.

I had to restrain myself from turning my face away. 'Remember to cable Ethel.'

No causeway tethered Penang to the mainland, yet it had always tickled me that we had our own railway station (we couldn't very well lose face to KL or Singapore, could we? After all, we *were* the first British settlement in the East). I bought my ticket and crossed the road to the landing platform to board the railway ferry. I found a spot by the gunwales – ever since I was a schoolgirl I have preferred to stand on the open deck, my spirits always invigorated by the sight of the activities in the noisy, teeming harbour.

Tongkangs and sampans and launches and prahus were moored four, five vessels deep. Seabirds dipped and wheeled above the swamp of riggings and swaying masts. Gangs of shirtless Chinese coolies, bent double beneath huge, bulging gunnysacks, clambered from vessel to vessel to unload them onto the bullock carts queueing on the pier. A crane was lowering pallets of smoked rubber sheets into the hold of a Norddeutscher Lloyd ship; scrawny Indian labourers disembarked from a rusting hulk of a steamer, their worldly belongings in a knotted bundle on their heads; and further down the dock, a line of Mohammedan pilgrims were boarding a vessel bound for Jeddah.

I held on to the gunwales as the ferry churned its way across the busy channel, slipping between tongkangs and Malay schooners and Bugis ships with sinister-looking eyes painted on their prows. At Butterworth the Eurasian stationmaster took my valise and escorted me to the first-class carriage. The train steamed out of the station punctually at a quarter past seven. The godowns and factories soon gave way to kampungs and endless paddy fields, the new shoots of rice fluorescent green in the early morning sun. And then the thick jungle pressed in, so close that I could have reached out my hand and stripped a handful of leaves from a branch flashing past.

The sun had dropped behind the Moorish domes of the railway station when my train drew into KL. It was much busier here than Penang and I had to queue for a rickshaw. At the Empire Hotel the Ceylonese concierge hurried out from behind his desk to welcome me into the high-ceilinged lobby.

'Ah, Mrs Hamlyn.' He looked past my shoulder. 'Mr Hamlyn will be joining you later?'

'Mr Hamlyn will *not* be joining me, but he has reserved a room for me. Has it been prepared?'

A middle-aged planter reading his newspaper beneath the flapping punkahs peered at me as I was signing the register. It struck me that I had never stayed in a hotel on my own before – I felt I had been caught red-handed in an unseemly act.

The clerk handed me my key. There was also a handwritten note from Ethel, informing me that she was expecting my visit.

The headmaster's bungalow stood at the western end of VI's sports field, by the banks of the Klang River. A tall dense hedge of bamboo shielded the bungalow from the eyes of the school. Going around the hedge to the entrance gave one the feeling of being out in the countryside, a feeling heightened by the lush jungle crowding down to the banks on the other side of the river.

The houseboy showed me into the sitting room. A heavy, late afternoon stupor lay over the house. Looking around the room, I tried to recall the last time Robert and I had been here: it must have been three months ago – at the Shaws' farewell party before they departed for London. By now the news of William Steward's death would have been reported in the London dailies. How would they feel when they found out that a man – someone they would have known, given how small the European community in KL was – had not only been killed in their home, but had been killed by the acting headmaster's wife?

The sitting room opened onto the verandah. I went out to take a look. Built on four-foot-high concrete piles, the house had an unimpeded view of the river crawling past. The bamboo chicks beneath the eaves had been lowered partway down, cutting out the glare from the water. I recognised the Shaws' rattan chairs and sofa and their prized teapoy from Japan on the verandah; their teakwood bookshelf was now filled with the Proudlocks' yellowing issues of *London Illustrated News* and *Punch*. Peering around the corner of the verandah, I spied my rickshaw coolie squatting under a tembusu tree, smoking a kretek. The sickly-sweet clove scent of his cigarette wafted over on the hot breeze.

Below the verandah the well-tended lawn sloped gently down to the river. It was difficult to imagine the low and sluggish river bursting its banks during the monsoon. Bennett had once regaled us with the story of how during the rains he and his wife had had to paddle in a sampan from the bungalow across the flooded school field to High Street, with him at the oars while his wife stood on the prow with a rifle, scanning the turbid waters for crocodiles.

Footsteps from the corridor inside sent me scurrying back into the sitting room. Ethel entered a moment later. We stood facing each other, and then I took her hands and pulled her in, kissing her cheeks.

'Oh, Ethel. What an awful, awful thing for you.' We sat down across from each other. 'Where's Will?'

A vague, distracted air hovered about her, as though she had just awakened from a drugged slumber. 'Still in his office, I suppose,' she replied, finally. 'Strange, isn't it? The man who . . . who attacked me . . . has the same name as my husband.'

What an odd thing to remark upon, I thought, sweeping my eyes over her. She had lost weight but not her sense of style. Her peach-coloured skirt and cream long-sleeved blouse were tastefully matched, and her dark brown hair was knotted into a chignon.

'Are you coping?' I asked.

'Will's been an absolute pillar – but, oh! I just wish the whole deuced thing were over and done with.'

'It'll all blow over in no time. Your lawyer's Wagner, isn't he? You're in capable hands. Robert thinks very highly of him.'

'How is he? And the boys?'

'They're growing up so quickly. And Robert . . .' My fingers dug into my palms, then uncurled open again. 'He's . . .'

'What is it?'

I felt an overpowering urge to tell her about Robert's infidelity. My mouth opened, but I clamped it shut again. It would be utterly selfish of me to burden her with my problems; she had more serious troubles to worry about. And there was another thing which had silenced me, which I had not expected: for some reason I couldn't explain, I did not feel comfortable confiding in her.

'He's working too hard as usual,' I said crisply.

She leaned forward, squinting closely at me; she always did have a sensitive nose for truffling out gossip. 'Is everything all right, Lesley?'

I flicked open my fan and began flapping it vigorously. 'KL's always so humid, isn't it? I don't know how you can stand it.'

The houseboy came in with a tray of tea. His black, glossy queue dangling down the back of his starched white tunic made me think of a long stroke of Chinese calligraphy brushed onto a sheet of paper.

'We met someone terribly fascinating a few days ago.' I continued to fan myself. 'He's a revolutionary, a Chinaman. Born in China, but speaks perfect English.'

I started telling Ethel about Sun Wen, but very quickly I realised that she wasn't listening to a word I was saying. My gaze strayed to the verandah doorway.

Ethel pounced on my lapse in attention. 'You're wondering what happened that night, aren't you?'

'I was thinking—' I cleared my throat. 'I was thinking of the first time we met. Bennett had asked us over for dinner, do you remember? We all sat out there that evening . . .' My eyes slid to the verandah again.

'They're saying that I was sleeping with Steward,' Ethel said, her voice dull, emotionless.

'Was William Steward the man . . .' I faltered. 'Was he . . .?'

The last time we had seen each other, in the tea room of Whiteaways, Ethel had been uncharacteristically fidgety. She kept turning her silver bracelet round and round on her wrist. 'You look as if you're bursting with news,' I said, wondering if she was expecting again – there was a self-satisfied glow about her. After some prodding, and after swearing me to secrecy, she told me that she was having a mild flirtation with a man. Those were the very words she used: 'a mild flirtation'. It had started in December the previous year, when her husband was away in Hong Kong. In his absence she had gone for drives outside KL with the man, and had occasionally even spent nights in his house. She did not tell me his name, and I did not ask. I was appalled, and I didn't care to know too much about it.

'Who else do you think it was?' Ethel snapped at me now, her eyes narrowing. 'You think I sleep with every man I meet? Is that what you think of me?'

'Oh, don't be silly, Ethel.' She seemed touchier than usual, and I chided myself for not being more sensitive to her plight.

'"People will find out," you said. "People will talk."' She dropped her head and buried her face in her hands.

'Oh, Ethel . . . what a mess. What an awful mess.'

She looked up, her eyes spearing mine. 'You didn't blab to anyone, did you? You didn't tell Robert?'

'I promised you I wouldn't, didn't I?' I reached across the coffee table and took her hand, giving it a gentle squeeze. 'Why did William Steward visit you that night? Did you invite him?'

'Of course not. I had told him that it was over between us, I told him a month ago. But he couldn't accept it. He just couldn't. The miserable wretch was utterly besotted with me, you know, utterly besotted. He kept writing me letters; he sent me flowers and presents. I told him to stop. He tried to see me, many times, but I avoided him.'

'So what *was* he doing here that night?'

'What was he doing here? He came to beg me to change my mind, of course. Oh, how he begged and pleaded. But when I still refused, he . . . he flew into a rage and attacked me. He was like a . . . a monster. Oh, Lesley, I had never been so terrified in my life.'

Pity for her, for what she had endured, wrenched my heart. 'What will you tell the inquest tomorrow?'

She looked evenly at me. 'I don't have to tell them *anything*, Lesley.'

For a second or two I did not know what to say, but then I realised that she was right, of course. The inquest was purely a formality to determine if there was a need to hold a full trial for murder; Ethel would not be required to present her side of the story in tomorrow's proceedings.

'I'm awfully tired, Lesley.' Ethel's gaze wandered around the sitting room. 'I must give Dorothy her bath. Will should be home soon – and Mr Wagner wants to go over some matters with us for tomorrow.'

I folded my fan, returned it into my handbag and stood up. 'Of course. I must go. I haven't even unpacked yet. I'll see you at the inquest tomorrow.'

Ethel rang the brass bell by her side. I wanted to offer her some words of comfort as the houseboy showed me out, but whatever words I wanted to say stalled on my lips when I looked at her. When I left she was still sitting there in her chair, staring out to the verandah, a void behind her eyes.

IV

The next morning I left the hotel just after eight. My solitary presence in the hotel's dining room at breakfast had drawn disapproving looks from the other guests. I ignored them, taking my own sweet time over my meal. I had slept fitfully; sometime during the night I had jerked awake, convinced that I had been firing my revolver at someone, a man whose face was hidden from me.

It was a short and easy stroll into town. At the Selangor Club I stopped to watch a group of elderly Chinamen practising tai chi on the padang. They seemed to be dancing to the music of the spheres audible only to themselves, and their rooted yet fluid movements reminded me of the fisherman I had watched rowing his sampan out to sea the other evening.

To the left of the padang stood St Mary's cathedral, its English Gothic architecture half hidden by its colonnade of fan palms. Ethel had told me that she and William had been married in that church. What she did *not* tell me was that they had rushed off for their honeymoon in England just a few hours after the ceremony. People had whispered that it was because she was already pregnant; naturally I paid no heed to the gossip, although I couldn't help but wonder when I heard she had given birth to their daughter in England during their honeymoon.

Facing the black-and-white Tudor frontage of the Selangor Club directly across the main road were the Government Buildings. The sight of their salmon-pink stonework and domes and pointed arches never failed to make me think of *A Thousand and One Nights*, a book my father had often read to me when I was a child. As I waited to cross the road, I looked at the clock tower, wondering if, just this one time, I might catch a glimpse of Prince Hussain on his magic carpet, whizzing around the clock tower's gigantic onion-shaped dome.

The air inside the Government Buildings had a damp, subterranean chill that seemed to have seeped in from the river behind the buildings. Signs on the walls directed me through the labyrinth of passageways to the Police Court. Every courtroom is the same, the one indistinguishable from the other, I thought as I looked around me. They even have the same stale, dusty smell. The public gallery was empty but for a handful of Europeans, including a young man who I guessed was a junior reporter from the *Malay Mail* or the *Straits Times*, and four or five Asiatics chatting quietly among themselves in the Natives section.

In the early days of my marriage I had often attended court whenever Robert was arguing a case. How my heart had swelled with pride to witness him in his black robes and wig; how it had thrilled me to hear him wielding his authoritative voice with an actor's art as he methodically and ruthlessly demolished his opponents' arguments into rubble.

That morning, as I sat there in the public gallery, it occurred to me that it had been years since I had watched my husband in a courtroom. When did I stop doing it?

At a quarter to nine Ethel, flanked by her husband William and her lawyer E. A. S. Wagner, entered the courtroom. The murmurings in the public gallery ceased. She looked stylish in a pale blue dress with a narrow collar and fitted sleeves that came down to her slender wrists. Her face was lightly powdered, her lips rosy, and I marvelled that she had found the time to have her hair done. Her artfully assembled façade of self-possession made her appear older than her twenty-three years. She received my smile with the slightest of nods as William pulled out a chair for her. He kissed her cheek, murmured something to her, and then sat down in the front row of the gallery.

The older man next to William leaned over and whispered something to him. He was slight and dour and dressed in a badly tailored brown suit. He looked vaguely familiar, but it was only after a moment or two that I recognised him as Ethel's father. Ethel never told me much about him, nor her mother; she had once mentioned how wretched she had been growing up in their house, but when I pressed her for details she had changed the subject.

The clock in the tower began tolling. The sound chiming in through the thick walls seemed to have travelled from some distant hilltop. The Sikh bailiff motioned us to our feet as the magistrate entered the courtroom. The magistrate, Daly, looked to be in his mid forties, thin and balding.

The punkahs above the bench and the lawyers' tables began flapping languidly. Ethel was asked to step into the dock. Magistrate Daly looked at her, then murmured a few words to the bailiff. A chair was carried in by a guard and Ethel was invited to step out of the dock and sit below the bench, facing the magistrate.

It boded well, I thought. She would be cleared of any wrongdoing by the day's end; she wouldn't be charged with any crime. Just a slap on the wrist, as Robert had assured me.

Wagner commenced proceedings by requesting the magistrate to exclude members of the public from the inquest. 'There will be delicate and sensitive matters raised in the hearing,' he said, 'matters that carry a certain amount of . . . indecency . . . that would certainly cause great embarrassment to Mrs Proudlock.' He half swivelled his tall, angular body to cast a meaningful look at the Natives gallery. 'There are a great number of persons in court who have no business here, and this would adversely affect Mrs Proudlock.'

Disgruntled murmurings came from the Natives gallery, only to be muted by a scowl from the bailiff. I had a clear view of Ethel's profile from where I was sitting. She held herself erect, and she did not look around her.

Paul Hereford, the Deputy Public Prosecutor, raised himself to his full height; the DPP was a narrow-shouldered man with thinning grey hair and a lean, handsome face.

'Your Worship,' his voice rang across the courtroom, 'rightly or wrongly, English law stipulates that persons having no interest at all in a trial or an inquest are entitled to attend. This is a fundamental principle of our legal system.'

The magistrate rejected Wagner's application and ordered DPP Hereford to present his case for the police. An expectant hush fell over the courtroom – this would be the first time we heard what had actually taken place the night Ethel shot William Steward.

'On the night of 23rd April, Sunday,' began Hereford, 'William Crozier Steward was dining with two friends at the Empire Hotel. Halfway through the meal, and announcing that he had another appointment, he excused himself and left for the Proudlocks' bungalow.'

Only the accused and the cook were at home that night, Hereford went on. Ethel's husband William was dining with his friend, and the amah and the houseboy had been given the evening off. When William Steward arrived at the Proudlocks' bungalow he told his rickshaw coolie to wait a short distance away. Steward then walked the rest of the way to the bungalow. The coolie made himself comfortable in his rickshaw, his back turned to the verandah. About ten minutes later he heard two or three gunshots. Startled, he left his rickshaw and crept warily up to the bungalow. The light on the verandah, which had been shining when he arrived, had been extinguished and the house was in darkness. Moments later he saw the Tuan who had hired him staggering down from the verandah, pursued closely by a European mem. He saw that she had a gun in her hands. Frightened, he ran back to his rickshaw and sped away with it. Pausing at the High Street gates to catch his breath, he heard three more shots being fired.

'The rickshaw coolie, Tan Ng Tee, identified Ethel Proudlock as the woman he had seen pursuing the deceased,' said Hereford.

The cook, Hereford continued, was smoking opium in his room behind the bungalow when he heard a man shouting. Seconds later he heard gunshots. He did nothing, but went on smoking his pipe until he heard Ethel Proudlock calling him from the side of the bungalow. There were no windows in his room. Ethel asked him to fetch William Proudlock from his friend's house. The cook went out by the side entrance. He did not see Ethel Proudlock, but she sounded upset.

'When William Proudlock arrived home,' said Hereford, 'she told him that she had shot a man.' He pursed his lips. 'Mrs Proudlock, the accused, does not dispute that she killed the deceased. However, she claims that she had killed him in self-defence.' He paused, then repeated, 'Self-defence.' In a clear, steady voice he said, 'Ethel Proudlock shot William Steward six times – one shot went into his chest, another shot went into the back of his neck, and four shots into his head.'

Gasps and shocked whispers filled the gallery. I was stunned. Six times. She shot the man six times.

'Your Worship,' said Hereford, 'we are here today to determine if Mrs Ethel Proudlock is to be charged with murder. And to that objective, we begin by stating that we doubt that she was telling the truth when she said that she was not expecting William Steward's visit on the night of the 23rd of April.'

I looked hard at Ethel; she was gazing with unruffled calm at Hereford. Not once did she look to her husband or her father. She gave the impression that, for her, there were no other people in the courtroom except Hereford.

'As stated earlier, the deceased, Mr William Steward, was dining at the Empire Hotel that evening,' said Hereford. 'Halfway through dinner, and announcing to his companions that he had an appoint-ment with a lady, he left. He must have known that Mrs Proudlock would be alone at home. But how could he have known this, unless she had told him? There *must* have been some communication between them before that fateful night; they must have made some arrangement to see each other.'

There was also the question of the timings, the DPP went on. William Steward left the Empire Hotel at approximately 8.50 p.m. It was drizzling and he was in a hurry, so he took a rickshaw; nevertheless he would only have arrived at the accused's bungalow by about 9.10 p.m. at the earliest. After the shooting Ethel Proudlock's cook had rushed to summon William Proudlock from his friend's home. The cook got there at 9.25 p.m. At the most, William Steward could not have been with Mrs Proudlock on the verandah for longer than ten minutes.

'It is highly improbable that the deceased would have gone straight into Ethel Proudlock's house and proceeded immediately to assault her on the verandah,' said Hereford. 'The fact that he was there for such a brief period of time also makes her story hard to swallow. Inspector Wyatt discovered the deceased's body lying on the grass, and on examination found his clothing to be entirely intact. He was still wearing his mackintosh, and his trousers were buttoned up.

'Mrs Proudlock claims that she was dining alone at home that evening,' Hereford continued, chiselling away at the rock face of Ethel's story, 'yet she was attired in a tea gown, a tea gown that was cut very low.' He cleared his throat ostentatiously. 'Why was she dressed to entertain, unless she was expecting a caller? We have to ask ourselves whether it does not indicate that she was expecting a visit from Mr William Steward.'

I had to restrain myself from leaping up from my chair to correct Hereford – it was *entirely* probable, I wanted to shout at him. Ethel adored wearing beautiful clothes; she would often dress up for the most trivial of occasions at home. I made a mental note to raise this with her lawyer.

'. . . and what is more, the signs of struggle on the verandah were minimal,' Hereford was telling the court. 'A Japanese teapoy had been overturned, scattering a pile of books onto the floor; the rug was only slightly ruffled up. There were no bloodstains on the verandah.'

In her statement to the police Ethel Proudlock had said that she shot Steward once, when he was attempting to rape her on the verandah, Hereford told the magistrate. Then her mind had gone blank, she averred. She could not remember what had happened subsequently until she found herself standing over William Steward's body on the lawn a few yards away from the house.

'If it were the fact that the revolver had only been fired on the verandah,' said Hereford, 'the case would carry a very different aspect, but the evidence will clearly prove that this is not so.'

Ethel's face had grown more and more taut during Hereford's presentation. When the proceedings were adjourned for lunch, William Proudlock spirited her home before I could have a few quick words with her. Disinclined to eat at the Selangor Club – I was bound to bump into Robert's lawyer friends there – I walked down the tree-shaded Embankment behind the Government Buildings and crossed the bridge over the river into Old Market Square. In Whiteaways' tea room I found myself a table and had a bowl of mulligatawny soup.

The inquest reconvened at two o'clock and went on until Magistrate Daly adjourned proceedings for the day at a quarter to four. He ordered Ethel to stand.

'The accused,' he announced, 'is hereby ordered to be taken to Pudoh Gaol.'

I felt sick; I could not believe what I was hearing. Ethel swayed slightly on her feet. She gripped the edge of the box, steeling herself with a visible effort of will.

Wagner shot to his feet. 'We wish to apply for bail, Your Worship.'
'Denied, Mr Wagner.'

Detective Inspector Wyatt, the man in charge of the investigation, offered to drive Ethel to Pudoh Gaol in his own car. I was glad for her sake – at least she was spared the humiliation of being transported there in a police van. I offered her words of encouragement as she was led out of the courtroom, but she did not look at me, did not even seem to have heard me. Her face was blank, a mask.

The next morning I was again one of the earliest to arrive at the courtroom. Having told no one I was in KL, I had spent the previous evening alone in my room, writing the details of the inquest in my journal.

People were taking their seats in the public gallery. I nodded to a few I recognised from the previous day, but there were also more new faces this morning. The low chatter around me broke off when a pair of policemen brought Ethel into the courtroom.

Her hair was still done up in a chignon, although it was not as immaculate as it had been the day before. Faint half-moons hung under her eyes, and her clothes, the same ones she had worn yesterday, had lost their crispness. She glanced at her husband in the front row; if she saw me, she gave no sign of it.

Wagner nodded at me. I had dropped by his office yesterday afternoon. 'This will be helpful,' he had remarked after I had explained to him about Ethel's habit of dressing up at home. 'Will you testify to this if there's to be a trial?'

'Surely it won't go as far as that? The inquest's just a formality, after all.'

'Well . . .' He spread his palms over his paunch and regarded me across his desk. At that moment I realised that Ethel was in grave trouble.

No chair was provided for Ethel below the bench this morning; instead she was ordered into the dock. For his first witness DPP Hereford called William Proudlock to the stand.

The DPP established a few preliminary facts about William Proudlock, then asked, 'Can you tell us what happened on the evening of the 23rd of April?'

'I had been invited to dine with my friend Goodman Ambler at his house. I went alone. Ethel stayed at home. Shortly after dinner Cookie turned up at Ambler's house. He was visibly agitated, but he refused to tell me what was wrong. He would only say to me, "Mem panggil lekas-lekas balik." Fearing that something had happened to Ethel, I rushed home immediately. What time was it?' He stared at the punkahs, turning the DPP's question over in his mind. 'Oh, about half past nine. Ambler went along with me.'

'What happened when you arrived home?'

'It was dark, and it was raining softly. I saw Ethel walking down the road, coming towards me. She was swaying on her feet and she looked . . . at first I thought she had had one drink too many, but then I noticed that her dress had been torn below her waist.'

'What happened next?'

'We – Goodman and I – helped her back to the house. She was incoherent; we couldn't make head nor tail of what she was saying. I gave her a sherry to calm her nerves. I waited a few minutes and then I asked her to tell me what happened.' William stopped and glanced towards Ethel. His wife's face was impassive.

'Please continue,' said Hereford.

As William described it, Ethel told him that she had been writing letters on the verandah when she heard a rickshaw pulling up the driveway. She was surprised to see William Steward coming up into the verandah moments later. Thinking that he wanted to speak to her husband, she told him that he was dining at Goodman Ambler's. William Steward said it wasn't important. They sat on the settee and chatted for a while. When she got up to the bookshelf to get a book she wanted to show him, he went and switched off the light. Suddenly he lunged towards her and started assaulting her.

'She screamed for Cookie,' said William Proudlock. 'She fought Steward and tried to put on the light. That was when her fingers came upon the gun.'

'Where was it?' asked the magistrate.

'The light switch is set into the bookshelf,' William explained. 'Just under the switch is a small recess. We sometimes keep the gun there.' He waited for the magistrate to write down his words. 'She grabbed the gun and shot Steward. That's all she remembered. At this point she started shaking and gibbering away again. I gave her another glass of sherry and made her drink it all down.'

William paused, running his tongue over his lips.

'Once she had calmed down again,' he resumed, 'I asked her where Steward was. "I don't know, I don't know," she said. "He ran. He ran." I went out into the garden to look. I stumbled upon the body about thirty or forty paces from the bungalow. The man was lying face down on the ground. I did not touch him, but it was obvious that he was dead.' William paused, arranging his thoughts. 'I left Ethel with Goodman and hurried to the High Street police station.'

Proceedings were adjourned for lunch. When we resumed an hour later Hereford called Dr Thomas Cooper, who had conducted the post-mortem on William Steward. Under Hereford's questioning he stated that he had found four bullets embedded in Steward's skull and another one in his neck, but the fatal wound, he declared, was a bullet that had penetrated Steward's heart and gone into his spine.

For the first time since hearing about Steward's death, I thought: the poor man. Robert was right – cut down like a rabid dog.

At the close of the inquest Ethel was ordered to her feet. She gripped the brass railing of the dock, pulled herself up stiffly and raised her face to the bench.

A slap on the wrist, I repeated to myself. Nothing more than a slap on the wrist. She'll go home today, back to her husband and her daughter, back to her life.

Magistrate Daly peered down at her over his pince-nez. 'After listening to the facts of the case,' he said, 'I have decided to refer the matter to trial.

'Ethel Proudlock, you are charged that on or about the 23rd of

April, 1910, in Kuala Lumpur in Selangor, you, Ethel Proudlock did commit murder by causing the death by shooting of one William Crozier Steward and thereby committed an offence punishable under section 302 of the Penal Code.'

Shouts and cries erupted from the gallery. I sat there, trembling with shock. My best friend had just been charged with murder. Murder.

The trial was set down for the 7th of June in the KL Supreme Court. Once again the magistrate refused Wagner's request for bail and ordered Ethel to be taken immediately to Pudoh Gaol.

Ethel was weeping as William helped her from the dock. She clung to her husband's arm, but still he had to hold her up. Her father pushed his way through the throng to her as a pair of policemen led her out of the courtroom. I wanted to say a few words to her, words that I hoped would give her strength, but I was shoved aside by the journalists shouting their questions at her.

Sitting by myself in the hotel's dining room the next morning, I looked around me as I added a few drops of soy sauce and some white pepper into my bowl of soft-boiled eggs. William Steward had dined here on the night of his death – I wondered which table he had been sitting at, drinking and eating and laughing with his friends before he made his excuses and hurried off to Ethel's house in the rain.

Outside the hotel the rickshaw–pullers squatting by the road all shook their heads when I told them where I wanted to go. Pudoh Gaol was only a mile away, but it was built on a former Chinese cemetery and none of them wanted to risk a horde of angry ghosts trailing him home. Finally one rickshaw coolie agreed to take me there, but demanded three times the normal fare.

The ride to Pudoh Gaol took me past the cemetery where William Steward had been buried. I looked at the graves, wondering which one of them was his, and what words were carved onto its headstone. Would they tell the world that he had been killed by another person? Or would they merely bracket the brief span of his life with a pair of dates?

The rickshaw stopped in the shadow of the gaol's high, crenellated walls. Telling the coolie that I'd only pay him when he took me back to my hotel, I brushed aside his protests and entered the gaol through the normal-sized entrance cut into the massive wooden doors. A Malay guard escorted me across a sun-baked quadrangle into the gaol. The warden came out of his office to meet me. Warden Clarke knew Robert, and we had occasionally had drinks with him and his wife at the Spotted Dog. I was too early for visiting hours and I was not a family member, Warden Clarke said, but of course he would make an exception for me.

The room I waited in was furnished with only two wooden chairs facing each other across a narrow table. The windows were open but barred. A calendar with a watercolour print of a Malay kampung hung on a wall; someone had already crossed out the 1st of May. I counted the squares until the 7th of June. Ethel would be locked up here for more than a month.

A bored-looking guard brought Ethel into the room, then sat on a bench in the corridor and watched us. Ethel was dressed in prison garb: a plain beige blouse over a brown skirt that came past her knees. Her eyes and nose were raw from weeping.

'Oh, my dear . . .' I said. 'Is there anything you need?'

'I was defending myself – he was going to rape me! Why is this happening to me? Why?'

Glancing at the guard, I lowered my voice to a whisper. 'Ethel, you have to tell them about your affair with William Steward. You *have* to. It's the only way you can explain why he came to the house, why he attacked you – he was furious at you for breaking up the affair. *Tell* them, Ethel.'

'I can't,' she said, shaking her head. 'I can't have everyone know that I'm an . . . an adulteress.' She reached across the table and grabbed my hands, squeezing them so hard that I winced. 'You won't tell?'

I looked at her in despair. Her eyes hardened; she let go of my hands and pushed away from me. 'If you tell anyone about it,' she said, 'I'll deny it. I'll deny everything, you hear me, Lesley? I'll tell them you're a damned liar.'

'What does it matter now? Everyone's saying that you were sleeping with him. For God's sake, Ethel – just tell them the truth.'

'It's nothing more than gossip. Gossip dies, people forget after a short while – they'll always find something new to tattle about. But if *I* were to tell them I had been having an affair with William, if *I* confirmed the stories . . .'

I saw her dilemma, and I felt a rush of pity for her, but I couldn't accept that her decision to remain silent was the right one. I just couldn't. 'Does Will know?'

'He doesn't believe the rumours.'

Recalling how her husband had looked at her when he was being questioned by Hereford, I wasn't so sure, but I refrained from saying anything. I was glad when the guard announced that it was time for her to return to her cell.

'Don't come again, Lesley,' she said to me as she was led out of the room. 'I don't want you to see me inside here. Do you understand me?'

Outside the gaol, I looked up and down the road for my rickshaw-puller, but there was no sign of him. The man had abandoned me.

V

My stay in Kuala Lumpur had given me the space to view the troubled waters of my marriage with more equanimity. There were times when I even forgot about Robert's affair, but as I stood on the ferry's deck and watched the green hills of Penang rising over the town, the feeling of oppression returned, pressing down hard on me.

The moment I arrived home I went straight upstairs to the nursery.

I swept my sons into my arms and embraced them tightly. 'Mummy missed you so much. Did you miss Mummy?'

'This one-ah,' Ah Peng rubbed Edward's head, 'cry all the time.'

'I didn't cry,' Edward said.

'Cry-baby, cry-baby,' James said.

'I'm not a cry-baby!' Edward's face trembled with incipient tears.

'Oh, my darling, it's all right. James, don't be mean.' I took out a pair of brightly painted toy sailing boats from a shopping bag. 'Look, Edward, look what Mummy got for you.'

I took them down to the beach. At this hour of the evening there were just a few people there – an elderly man walking his terrier; a pair of young and shirtless European males lying side by side on their bamboo mats. The Malay woman digging for horseshoe crabs at the tideline greeted me as we walked past. A sampan, moored to a pole, lay on the exposed seabed, scuttled by the retreating tide.

At a shallow tidal pool I knelt and helped my sons set their boats on the water, showing them how to keep their hands on the sterns.

'Ready?' I waved my handkerchief above my head. 'One, two, three!'

The boys launched their boats even before I had dropped my hand. Edward's boat surged ahead, but James's wobbled, listed, then righted itself. We screamed and cheered as the boats glided across the smooth, reflective pool, dragging their overlapping wakes after them.

I sat on the beach, watching my sons splashing in the water as dusk poured its ink into the sea. I couldn't leave all this behind, I couldn't walk out of my marriage. I had no choice but to suffer Robert's betrayal in silence.

At dinner Robert wanted to hear all that had transpired at the inquest. Everybody, he said, was talking about the murder charge.

I observed Robert as I related the events of the inquest to him, a part of me wondering if he had visited his lover while I had been away. On the train coming home from KL I had wrestled with the idea of talking to him about Ethel's affair, but his unfaithfulness made me reluctant to discuss Ethel's infidelity — *anyone's* infidelity, for that matter — with him.

'The facts just don't add up,' he said when I finished. 'If I were Daly I would have charged Ethel with murder too.'

'But Steward tried to rape her. She was in a . . . a disturbed mental state . . . she didn't know what she was doing. She wouldn't simply accuse Steward unless it's true — and rape is not easy to prove, is it? You said that to me once.'

'Rape is very difficult to prove,' said Robert, 'but it's even more difficult to *dis*prove.' His eyes took on the familiar sleepy look he had whenever he was trying to drill his way into the bedrock of a complex legal problem. 'If she *was* sleeping with him, what would drive her to kill him?' he said, as though he were talking to himself. 'A lovers' quarrel? Did he want to end the affair? Or perhaps he was throwing her over for another woman, and she killed him in a fit of jealous rage.'

He was skirting very close along the edge of the truth. But what *was* the truth? Perhaps Ethel had lied to me, and the events of that fateful night had played out in the manner Robert was speculating.

'By the way, the Macalisters have electric lights now,' said Robert, as our new houseboy Ah Keng came and took our empty plates away. 'They're giving a party to brag. We've been invited.'

'But . . . *we* should've got them first. We moved in a month before they did. It's because Mary's cousin is in the Public Works Department, that's why.'

I forgot my annoyance with the Macalisters when Ah Keng returned with, to my delight, two bowls of shaved ice and a brass pot of chilled coconut milk. Floating in the milk were little worms of lentil noodles, dyed green with the juice of pandanus leaves. Chendol, my favourite pudding. I lifted my eyebrows at Robert. He grinned as he ladled the coconut milk into our bowls of shaved ice.

'I got it from your favourite stall — the fat old Teochew in Swatow Lane. You wouldn't believe the queue.'

I looked down at my bowl, hiding the sudden heat of tears in my eyes. I blinked them away and poured a lavish serving of gula Malacca syrup over my chendol. The coconut milk was cold and creamy, and the green noodles, fragrant with pandanus, lifted the sticky, smoky sweetness of the gula Malacca.

'It was worth the queue,' I said, giving him a smile.

For a while we ate our chendol in silence, and then Robert said, 'Maybe Ethel was the one who had wanted to end the whole thing. He couldn't take the insult; he threatened to expose their affair. So she lured him to her house one night while she knew her husband would not be at home, intending to silence him. Half a dozen bullets into his back would certainly do the trick, oh yes.'

A cold-blooded murder. No, it was impossible. I refused to believe that Ethel was capable of it. I refused to believe it, but still I couldn't help asking, 'What will happen to her if she's found guilty?'

The candles had burned down, and the dining room seemed to be shrinking in upon us. The sea sounded far away.

Robert helped himself to another serving of chendol. 'Then she'll hang.'

Chapter Nine

Willie
Penang, 1921

The last piece of music Lesley had played unfurled in his head when he opened his eyes. The song seemed to have wraithed through his dreams.

Propping himself up against the headboard, he thought back to the previous evening. Watching her close the piano and return to her chair, he had waited, saying nothing, keeping absolutely still — as a young medical intern on duty in the slums of Lambeth he had learned that any sudden movement tended to shatter the spell and mute the person on the brink of revealing something. And for the entire time as Lesley undammed the flood from within her he had not said a single word. She had only stopped talking when they heard the car rattling up the driveway. For the first time ever Willie wished fervently that Gerald had stayed out at his debaucheries until dawn.

He wasn't at all surprised by Robert's affair. But he suspected that Robert's infidelity was not the sole cause of the sorrow buried inside Lesley. Something else, something much more painful, had happened to her.

After breakfast he wrote down in his journal everything she had told him, occasionally referring to the notes he had made before he went to sleep. She and Sun Yat Sen had been lovers, he felt it in his bones. He had struck his first seam of gold; a thin seam, but it was promising, and he intended to quarry the rest of it from the depths of her memories.

Locking away his journal, he changed into his swimming trunks and a cotton shirt, jammed his Panama hat on his head and strolled down to the beach. The earth had tilted the sea away from the shore, exposing a vast mirror that reflected the white clouds foaming across the sky. Gerald was lying at his usual spot beneath the coconut trees, shirtless and flipping through a magazine.

'This is an unexpected visit,' he said, wriggling to one side to make room for Willie on his mat.

Willie rested on his elbows, stretched out his legs and breathed deeply. The wind, hot and salty, crackled the coconut fronds. He felt Gerald's hand stroking the inside of his thigh.

'Just checking if the cat's returned,' Gerald said.

He took Gerald's hand in his, brought it to his lips and kissed each knuckle. He opened his senses to every detail of the moment – the coconut fronds casting fish-skeleton shadows on the soft, fine sand, the smooth, warm touch of Gerald's skin, the whiteness of his smile against his brown, glowing face. He wanted to remember all of it, absorb every element into his being, because he knew that when he opened his mouth and spoke, everything would be taken away from him.

Stammering more than usual, he began to tell Gerald about the money he had lost.

Gerald sat up and gaped at Willie. 'You're fucking joking.'

It wasn't quite the reaction he had been hoping for. 'I never joke about money.'

'You've lost everything? You're completely broke?'

'I'll need to speak to my . . . manager when I get back to London, find out how brutal the . . . damage is, but yes.'

'Christ.'

'No more first–class cabins for us; no more luxury . . . hotels. In fact, no travelling at all for a while.'

'How long is "a while"?'

'I haven't a damned . . . clue, Gerald. Three, four years, maybe longer,' replied Willie. 'No one must know about this, you . . . understand? No one.'

'We're not cutting short our stay here, are we?'

'Of course not.' He took Gerald's hand again, gripping it tightly. 'I want us to be together for as long as we can.'

'We can't hide out here for ever.'

Wouldn't that be wonderful? Willie thought.

White egrets spiralled down from the sky onto the exposed seabed, their wings flagging the temporary truce between land and sea.

'What about my salary?'

'You'll have to survive on your army pension for a while, my boy.'

'But it's a pittance.'

He lost his temper; he couldn't help it. 'Damn it all, Gerald. I'm aware of that. But I – we – have to tighten our belts. And one more thing – I can't afford to keep paying off your debts. So please, stop being so bloody . . . reckless.'

'Reckless? That's fucking rich, coming from a man who's lost all his money in some idiotic investment. What a fucking disaster.' Gerald gave a sidelong squint at Willie. 'How did your darling wife take it?'

'You're the only one I've told.'

'Perhaps she'll divorce you now that you're a pauper.'

The possibility of Syrie leaving him had not occurred to Willie; he didn't know whether to be overjoyed or dismayed by the prospect.

'So all your talk of us living together in a villa by the sea – I suppose that's off the table now?'

'I can't afford it now, my dear boy.'

Without another word Gerald got to his feet, hitched up his swimming trunks, knotted the drawstrings and strode down to the dried-up sea. Willie watched him, shading his eyes against the sun's glare. Gerald walked between the pools of marooned water turned to mercury by the sun. The egrets flew off at his approach and settled down a short distance away. Gerald kept walking, heading towards the thin white strip of surf in the distance, until he was nothing more than a small, wavering mirage.

Late one evening in the autumn of 1913, Willie had been looking forward to some quiet reading in his flat when he received a last-minute invitation from the Carstairs next door. They were hoping he could replace a guest at their dinner party, and then attend a play in the West End with them afterwards.

He was introduced to Syrie Wellcome when he stepped into the Carstairs' sitting room. She told him that she was recently separated from her husband Henry Wellcome, the pharmaceutical tycoon. She was already in her late thirties, and she was not pretty, but Willie found her charming and gay, and he was flattered by her interest in him. When they were putting on their coats to leave for the theatre, she whispered to him, 'I wish we didn't have to see this play. I'd much rather spend the evening listening to you.'

A few days later he invited her to the opening night of his new play. After the curtain came down he rushed off to the party she had organised for him in her house. The audience had been rapturous about his play, and he was in high spirits. That evening he and Syrie became lovers. She was a famous hostess among London's fashionable set; she was fun and stylish. They attended parties and opening nights at the opera and the theatre together. Willie felt flattered to be seen as her lover, and she relished basking in the glow of his fame. Although she was separated from her husband, she was still involved with Gordon Selfridge, but Willie didn't mind. He viewed his own affair with her as nothing more than a fling that both enjoyed, with no long-term prospects in it for either of them.

Her husband had insisted on sending their son to boarding school.

Syrie pined constantly for him. Willie was horrified when one day she told him she wanted to have his child. He talked her out of it and considered the matter closed. Two months passed, and then one morning in late summer she telephoned him. She sounded in great distress, demanding that he see her immediately. Rushing to her house in Regent's Park, he found her sitting up in bed, her eyes swollen from crying, her hair unkempt.

'What's wrong, Syrie? What happened?'

'Oh Willie, I lost the baby. I lost our baby.'

He felt as if he had been punched in the face. 'But . . . damn . . . it all, Syrie, we had . . . agreed.'

'I was going to tell you . . .' she choked her words out through her tears, 'when . . . when I was sure . . .'

He wanted to walk out of her oppressive bedroom, out of her house, he wanted to have nothing to do with her ever again. But instead he sat by her bedside, consoling her. He felt sorry for her, but secretly he was glad that she had lost the baby.

After she had recovered, he told her unequivocally that he would not have a child with her while she was still married to Henry Wellcome. They resumed their rounds of socialising, but he grew bored with her and her possessiveness. He longed to be free, but when he thought of the tearful scenes she would make, he couldn't bring himself to end the affair. He was almost glad when war broke out in Europe. He applied to the Red Cross ambulance corps; with his medical qualifications and his French he was accepted immediately. After a day spent learning to drive an ambulance at an army depot he was given his uniform and assigned to Boulogne.

On the afternoon before his departure, Syrie informed him that she was with child again. His child. Willie sat in her expensively decorated sitting room tight-lipped with rage. Bitch. Deceitful bloody bitch. But most of all he was furious at his own stupidity.

The next morning he left England on the first boat and, with an immense feeling of freedom and relief, rushed headlong towards war.

His ambulance unit was assigned to a makeshift hospital set up in a chateau fifteen miles outside Boulogne. The drivers were called out at all hours of the day to drive into the battlefields to collect the wounded, often coming under heavy enemy shelling themselves. When he was not on ambulance duty, he worked in the overcrowded wards, resurrecting the medical training he had not used in years to treat the maimed soldiers. He cleaned the men's wounds and changed their dressings; he calmed their fears and did his best to ease their torment. Never a squeamish man, he was horrified by the injuries, injuries he had never seen on anyone before, and hoped he never would again – the shattered bones, the gaping wounds seething with pus and rot, men with half their faces blown off.

One night, trudging up the grand marble staircase to his quarters, hours after his shift had ended, he was overcome by a powerful longing to gaze at the stars, to look at something pristine, something unpolluted by the war.

The drawing room on the first-floor landing had been closed up. He slipped into it, shutting the door behind him. There was just enough light from the gaps in the heavy velvet drapes to guide him between the strange shapeless forms shrouded beneath dark sheets to the French windows. He opened one of them, stepped out onto the broad balcony and drew in a long, deep breath. The bracing purity of the cold night air felt wonderful.

He had wanted to be alone, so he was peeved to discover someone else already there, leaning against the balustrade and staring out into the night. The man peered at him over his shoulder. Even in the milky starlight Willie had no difficulty recognising him – one of the volunteers in the Red Cross who had helped him restrain a ranting, badly injured patient earlier that day.

'Gerald Haxton,' the man said. 'And I know who you are.' His teeth flashed in the darkness. 'Knew the second I clapped eyes on you.'

'I forgot to thank you – for this morning.'

'It was bloody chaos, wasn't it? That poor bastard . . .'

They stood shoulder to shoulder at the balustrade, their breaths flouring the hard, frosty air. There was no moon, and the privet hedges and flowerbeds of the formal gardens below were buried in darkness. It was one of those rare nights when the constant shelling had ceased and the sky over the horizon was not haemorrhaging its usual infernal crimson. The world was at rest, at least for the moment.

Lifting his face, Willie offered up an incantation to the stars: '"Tempora cum causis, lapsaque sub terras ortaque signa canam."'

'What does that mean?'

'"Of Times and their reasons, and constellations sunk beneath the earth and risen, I shall sing."'

'That's beautiful. You wrote that?'

'If only I had.' Willie smiled. 'Ovid. A poet from . . . ancient days.'

They started talking, stumpy, tentative sentences at first, testing the ground between them. Gradually they drifted away from the war and began telling each other about what they would do once the madness was over and life returned to normal again.

'I want to travel, see more of the world – Polynesia, the Far East, the Malay Archipelago,' said Willie. 'And you? What do you . . . want?'

He would always remember the natural ease of the young man's reply. 'From you, or from life?'

He felt his face flushing, and he was grateful for the darkness. 'Why not . . . both? They might turn out to be . . . the same in the . . . end.'

The silence seemed to seep out from deep inside the earth and rise all the way to the stars above. And then, in the darkness, he heard Gerald Haxton saying, 'I've got a bottle of gin in my room.'

And it was as simple as that.

Lesley had arranged for her brother to interview Willie after lunch. While waiting for him, Willie went through his latest correspondence on the verandah. There were no further letters from his lawyers, thank Christ – at least they had given up trying to get him to go home. He stacked the invitations to one side of the coffee table for Gerald to deal with. The party at Istana had tired him, and he didn't feel inclined to go to any more of them.

Gerald had been uncharacteristically subdued during lunch. He would leave him, Willie was certain, now that he knew Willie was broke. He was young and handsome, he would have no trouble attracting another wealthy patron to provide him with the lotus-eating life he had become accustomed to.

He was still fretting over the problem of keeping Gerald by his side when Lesley brought a tall, fat man to the verandah. She introduced them to one another and left.

'I appreciate you giving me an exclusive interview, Willie,' said Geoff Crosby.

Lesley's brother shared her faded colouring and her deep-set eyes. He would have been an attractive man once, thought Willie as he noted the vestiges of his looks. 'Lesley's older than you?'

'Younger by two years, actually, but she always behaves like Big Sister.' Geoff opened his notebook. 'Shall we begin?'

His questions were the sort Willie had been asked countless times in every foreign port he had ever set foot in: What did he think of Penang and the people? Was he going to write a book about it? What was his favourite food in Penang? Where did he find his inspiration? How many hours a day did he write? Did he write with a pen or a typewriter? Who were his influences? Willie gave his oft-repeated answers, refused to entertain any questions about his wife or his daughter, and he steered their conversation to his latest book, *The Trembling of a Leaf*.

'It's a splendid collection of tales,' Geoff said. '"Rain" was particularly . . . disturbing. Do you think you'll write another story like it?'

The very same question had been troubling him for some time now, although he was not going to admit it to anyone. 'For any writer to come up with a story like that, even once in his life, is already a gift. I'd be greedy to hope for another one.'

'Lesley says you have a new book coming out soon.'

'*On a Chinese Screen*. It's a . . . record of my recent travels in China.'

'What's it like there? Is it as hopeless as I've been told?'

Willie took a few moments to craft his reply. 'I did my practical midwifery . . . training in St Thomas's—' he began.

'Somerset Maugham, midwife. Now *that's* hard to imagine.'

'Yes. Quite. As I was saying, in one month I went into Lambeth's slums over sixty . . . times,' said Willie. 'I delivered babies in the most appalling . . . surroundings. Ten, fifteen men and women crammed into a tiny room, with no running water, no fire. I'd never been so weary in all my life. There's nothing noble about poverty, despite what people — and it's always the rich — tell you.' Willie sipped his tea and dabbed his lips with the corner of his napkin. 'TB and . . . diphtheria and poverty; the booze-soaked husbands . . . thrashing their wives and children. Criminal gangs terrifying people in the streets. Hopelessness and violence hung like a thick fog in the air. That's what the . . . villages in China reminded me of — the slums of Lambeth.'

'Must have been terribly frightening.' Geoff was scribbling away furiously. 'Were you ever robbed? Assaulted?'

'I could stroll into the most dangerous slums with more impunity than the . . . police. My doctor's black leather bag was my talisman. Of course, in the beginning the women — and their husbands — distrusted me. They kept absolutely tight-lipped about their ailments and symptoms; I had great problems trying to . . . diagnose them.'

Geoff stopped writing. 'How did you get them to trust you?'

With the air of someone about to divulge a secret of the ages, Willie leaned forward, drawing Geoff closer to him.

'A man is more willing to open up to you once you've revealed something . . . personal, something shameful, about yourself,' he said. 'If you want someone to confide in you, you must first offer him some private . . . morsel of your own.'

Willie sat back, giving Geoff time to finish jotting down his words.

The wind had come up, planing long white curls off the surface of the sea. 'Speaking of China,' Willie said, 'I've just finished your book on Dr Sun Yat Sen.'

'Ah – *A Man of the Southern Seas*. Did you enjoy it?'

'It's an . . . alluring title.'

'I wish I could say I came up with it, but it was Lesley's idea.' He paused. 'She said you're thinking of writing a book about him.'

'She's been telling me about him,' said Willie. 'I didn't expect to find such a . . . *personal* link to China here.'

'I was the only one from the English newspapers he spoke to,' Geoff jabbed his forefinger at his own fleshy chest, 'the only one he trusted. He was *here*, Willie, he sat where you're sitting now, the first time I met him. Probably even in the very same chair.'

'What was he like?'

Geoff stared off into the distance, paging through his memory. 'To be honest, Willie, the first time I met him I didn't think much of him.'

'What did you not like about him?'

'He reeked of failure – all his attempts at starting a revolution – and there'd been five or six of them already – had gone *phut*. I found it perplexing that he had so many supporters. It was only after I got to know him better that I realised he was a masterful manipulator of people. He could have them eating out of his hand, and they'd still beg for more.'

'And popular with the ladies too, no doubt.'

'Oh, he collected more than his share of female supporters – he *was* a very good-looking chap, you know.'

'Lesley became close to him, didn't she?'

A careful expression draped itself over Geoff's face. 'She supported his cause,' he said.

'Not many white women here did, I'm sure.'

'My sister's always been a bit of a contrarian. Anyway,' Geoff slapped his knees and pushed himself to his feet, 'I've taken up too much of your time, Willie. Oh, I almost forgot.' He pulled out a copy of *The Trembling of a Leaf* from his satchel. 'Would you mind inscribing something for me and the missus?'

In his room, Willie picked up *A Man of the Southern Seas* from his writing desk and studied the photographic plates of Sun. The majority of them had been taken in Penang. One photograph showed Sun seated with the Hamlyns on the verandah of Cassowary House. The last photograph, dated October 1918, was of an older Sun sitting alone in a Ming blackwood chair, his face hewn with a noble, almost saintly, suffering; it made him look even more attractive. Willie recalled seeing this particular photograph in a newspaper when he was in Shanghai.

On a map inside the book he traced the elliptic lines of Sun's travels around the globe. They were as extensive as his own. He and Sun had been in London at about the same time, he realised, and now here he was on the same island where Sun had once spent half a year of his life. And what was even more curious, he was staying in the very house where the Chinaman had been a frequent visitor.

He recalled reading about the kidnapping in the London papers, but his memory of it was blurry – at the time he had taken no more than a fleeting interest in the story. He had been busy with his practical midwifery training. And furthermore, he and his friends – and countless others in the stratum of London society in which they moved – were reeling from the death knell rung across England by poor Oscar Wilde's fate. They were all frantically consigning caches of letters and notes to the flames, letters and notes that should never have been written and sent; and how many more men were fleeing across the Channel to the civilised havens of the Continent. What did he – or anyone else – care about the abduction of some Chinaman by his own government?

Chapter Ten

Lesley
Penang, 1921

Just like the night before, I found Willie already in the sitting room when I came downstairs. The rain, which had started after dinner, had weakened, but frog-song continued to bloat out into the cool, dripping night. Geoff's book lay open on his lap, but the writer's eyes were closed, his head tilted at a slight angle. He seemed to be listening intently to something in the air.

'The songs of Anura,' Willie said, opening his eyes when I joined him within the small circle of lamplight. 'Even in London, it never fails to remind me of the . . . tropics whenever I . . . hear it.'

All day long I had been troubled by doubts. By telling my tale to Willie I was betraying not only Robert, but Ethel as well. And yet I must confess that it had felt liberating to tell my story to this man sitting in the half-shadows, this gentleman in my parlour.

Making myself comfortable in the armchair, I picked up my tale from where I had left off the previous night.

Chapter Eleven

Lesley
Penang, 1910

I

One of Sun Wen's supporters had lent him a bungalow not far from our house. He became a regular visitor, dropping in on us once or twice a week in the evenings. We enjoyed his company, and he provided Robert the opportunity to keep his Cantonese honed. He relished his robust debates with Sun Wen about the political situation in China. I tried to keep up with them, but their discussions – which often turned into heated verbal jousting – were usually lost on me.

He always stayed long enough for just one drink. When his tumbler of whisky was empty he would click open his pocket watch, squint at it, and take his leave. He had work to do, he would announce, people to address at the local business associations and clanhouses and guilds; or he was needed at the Philomatic Union on Armenian Street, the reading club set up by a group of Chinamen to provide books and magazines for its members.

'They named it wrongly,' Robert remarked one evening after Sun Wen had just left. 'A philomatic society is for people interested in the sciences. And reading club, my foot – it's nothing more than a front for his party.'

As I had expected, it didn't take long for my brother to catch wind of our friendship with Sun Wen: nothing seemed to happen in Penang – or for that matter in the rest of the Straits Settlement, not to mention the FMS – without Geoff knowing about it. At his request I arranged for him to meet Sun Wen at our house one rainy evening.

'Things all right?' my brother asked when he stepped into the vestibule.

'Oh, I'm quite fine.' I had not spoken to him since that morning in the Tiffin Room. In those three weeks my old, comfortable life had been turned upside down. 'Robert's working late this evening,' I said, and I couldn't refrain from adding acidly, 'He sent his peon to tell me at the last minute.'

'You haven't talked to him about—'

'Good Lord, no.'

'Maybe it's better you don't,' Geoff said. 'You were right – it's none of my business. I shouldn't even have told you.'

Not for the first time I wondered if he had been mistaken about Robert. For weeks now I had been waiting for some well-meaning mem to draw me aside and with barely concealed glee whisper into my ear the gossip about my husband's infidelity. I had been hardening myself for that moment, but nobody had said anything to me. Not a single person. Surely I would have heard something by now; there were no secrets on this little island of ours.

'Any news about Ethel?' I asked. The newspapers had been muted about her since she was sent to Pudoh Gaol.

'Still refusing to speak to us lowly reporters. She refuses to see anyone except her husband.'

'How awful for her, locked up in that horrible place.'

'She's in the European women's wing, Les. Granted, it's not *quite* the E&O, but it's clean and, under the circumstances, comfortable enough. They're allowed to cook their own meals, and they're encouraged to spend their time sewing and knitting and reading.'

'All the things Ethel finds tedious,' I said. 'I just wish there was something I could do for her.'

'You write to her, don't you?'

'She hardly ever replies, and when she does write back, she doesn't tell me much.'

In one of my first letters I had pleaded with her to inform her lawyer Wagner of what she had told me (without explicitly mentioning what it was, as I suspected the warden was probably reading her mail), but she never once alluded to it.

'Her story sounds plausible,' my brother said, 'but a number of things about it just don't ring true . . .'

'Come along, Sun Wen's waiting,' I said.

Sun Wen sat drooped in his chair on the verandah, nursing a whisky. His eyes, when he looked up at us, seemed lifeless. I had never seen him looking so defeated.

The fundraising had not been going well, he admitted under Geoff's questioning. 'They're — what's that word in Hokkien — kiam-siap, as your sister had warned me.' He rubbed his thumb and forefinger together. 'Even the rich ones. Especially the rich ones.'

'Or maybe they don't think much of your chances of success,' Geoff pointed out. 'These people didn't make their fortunes backing the wrong horses.'

'Don't be cruel, Geoff,' I said, although I felt a twinge of vindication — I was still bitter at Sun Wen for what he had said about a man having multiple wives.

Geoff held up his palms at me, then turned to Sun Wen again. 'Your own people in Singapore didn't think you'd succeed either. They wanted you out of your party, that's why you washed up here, isn't it? Fact is, you've been deported from every place you've set foot in — Hong Kong, Japan, Siam, Singapore. Penang's the last haven that's still open to you.'

Moths flew around the lamps, flirting with the light. Sun Wen shifted in his chair to face Geoff directly. 'Do you know how many times I have tried to bring down the Manchu government?' The light in his eyes, which a few minutes ago had been low and dull, had intensified. 'Seven. And every one of those uprisings failed, every single one. Thousands of people died for our cause.' His hands, resting on his knees, curled into fists. 'But I won't give up. I cannot.'

The anguish in his voice seemed to silence the usual sounds of the evening. Gradually I became aware again of the cicadas' tintinnabulation in the trees, the waves hissing on the shore. From within the house drifted the faint clinking of silverware and china. The servants were setting the dinner table.

'You've been throwing all your efforts into winning over the Chinese-educated locals,' Geoff said. 'What about the Straits Chinese? Why haven't you enlisted their help?'

'Those people? They have no loyalty to the motherland. They cannot even speak their own tongue. They side with the English; they think England is home. And your English newspapers here – they have no interest at all in my country unless it's to pour scorn on it.'

'Ah yes, what was it the *Straits Echo* said today?' Geoff foraged in his pockets and pulled out a page from a newspaper. He unfolded it. '"With Dr Sun Yat Sen it is money, money, money all the time, and never anything to show for the stream of gold that has flowed his way. As a revolutionary he doesn't revolute."' He handed the piece of newspaper to me. 'I never knew that "revolute" was a word.'

'We do not have a newspaper, we cannot fight a polemical war,' said Sun Wen. 'I am a foreigner here, it is easy for them to say whatever they want about me. It has always been so, everywhere I go.'

I felt sorry for him. 'Geoff, why don't you interview him?'

'Nipped the idea right out of my head, sis,' said Geoff. 'How about it, Sun Wen?'

The revolutionary looked sceptical. 'The Straits Chinese read the *Post*,' I said. 'You can explain your cause to them, tell them what you want to achieve.'

'This is no time to be shy, Sun Wen,' said Geoff.

Sun Wen left his chair and walked over to the balustrade. He stood there looking at the shadows in the dripping garden. After a minute or two he turned around again.

'I want full approval of what you publish,' he said.

'Forget it. That's not how we do things, old chap,' Geoff said.

'Then there will be no interview.'

'He'll be fair to you, Sun Wen,' I said. 'Fair and objective. I'll make sure of that. I promise you.' I turned to my brother. 'You will show him what you've written before you publish it. If there's anything he disagrees with, you will include his counter-arguments in the final article. You will let him clarify things from his point of view.'

'Fair enough,' Geoff said. He raised his tumbler of whisky. 'To the revolution?'

Sun Wen looked at him, and at me. He picked up his glass from the coffee table and held it in the air. 'The revolution.'

For the next hour Geoff asked Sun Wen questions and recorded his replies in his notebook. At length Sun Wen stopped talking and looked at his watch. 'I must go.'

'Where're you off to?' asked Geoff. I could almost see his nose twitching.

'I'm speaking at the reading club.'

'The Philomatic Society in Armenian Street?' Geoff got to his feet as well. He stood a head taller than Sun Wen. 'I'd like to tag along.'

'You won't understand a word.'

'Doesn't matter. I want to see *how* you say it.'

'All right.'

'I'm coming too,' I said.

'Robert won't like it,' Geoff said.

'Robert's not here to like or dislike anything.'

'What about the boys?'

'Ah Peng will feed them and put them to bed.'

'It's raining.'

'I won't melt.'

Geoff appealed to Sun Wen. 'It's not proper, not proper at all.'

'We have women members too in the Tong Meng Hui,' Sun Wen said.

Trundling through the rainy streets of George Town in our rickshaw, Geoff and I couldn't help grinning at each other. I knew the same memory was bobbing around in our heads.

'Did Ah Peng ever win the lottery?' my brother asked as our rickshaw turned down into another street.

When we were children Ah Peng would sometimes take us to the Chinese quarter. In a smoke-filled temple she would get down stiffly onto her knees before the blackwood altar in the main hall, clasp her hands together and beseech the resident deity to grant her some lucky numbers. We had to promise not to tell our mother, a promise bought with a glass of cold sugarcane juice from the hawker outside the temple. All morning she would go from one temple after another, repeating the same prayer to different gods.

'She always vowed she'd go home to China if she won, don't you remember?' I said.

We followed Sun Wen's rickshaw down dark, quiet streets hemmed in by two-storeyed shophouses. Blackwood signboards perched above door lintels, their carved, gold-leafed Chinese calligraphy glowing in the shadows like candle flame glimpsed through clouds of smoke. Through doors and windows thrown open to catch the cool evening air I glimpsed families seated around tables eating their dinner. At a crossroad junction my ears caught the lines of a Chinese ballad from a gramophone.

We stopped outside a shophouse at the upper end of Armenian Street. Geoff helped me down from the rickshaw and we joined Sun Wen on the goh kaki. A signboard carved with four Chinese ideograms hung above the doors, and nailed to the centre of the lintel was a small oval brass plate embossed with '120'. Sun Wen knocked and tilted his face to the porch ceiling.

'What's he looking at?' I whispered to Geoff.

'A spyhole.'

I peered at the ceiling, but I saw only tattered cobwebs in the shadows.

The lock turned, a bolt was pulled back and then one side of the double doors opened, just wide enough for a person to enter. Sun Wen went in, followed by Geoff. I hesitated, then, gathering my skirt above my ankles, I stepped over the threshold.

The front hall was lit only by the frail glow of an oil lamp. I could just about make out the shapes of armchairs and a few low bookcases huddled in the murky corners.

We followed Sun Wen behind a folding screen into the dining hall. The hall was open to an air-well paved in granite and overlooked by the shuttered windows of the rooms upstairs. A dark flag – black? Blue? It was impossible to tell in the sallow light – with a yellowing sun in the centre hung on one wall. Milling around the hall were thirty or forty people, women as well as men. They were in their twenties and thirties, many of them in Western clothing. Seated at a long, rectangular rosewood dining table were more people. Everyone fell silent as they became aware of us.

Sun Wen introduced us, then added to me, 'Ah, here comes Arthur – he will interpret for you.'

I recognised the man from the evening on the E&O's terrace. He smiled at me and led us to the back of the room. The people standing there shifted aside, making space for us.

Sun Wen stood at the head of the table. The room was silent as he cast his gaze over the members. Then he began to speak. Arthur whispered to us, but his voice soon fell away as he struggled to keep up with Sun Wen's torrent of words. But Sun Wen's fury needed no interpreter. I was swept up by his passion, by his towering, implacable conviction. And so was Geoff, I thought, glancing at him.

My brother was watching Sun Wen with total absorption, his pen and notebook forgotten.

Everyone in the hall clapped and shouted Sun Wen's name the instant he finished speaking. He stood there in the storm, his eyes seeking out each and every person around him. For just a second or two he and I looked at each other, and in that eye-blink of time I felt that he was binding all of us to a covenant, a covenant for a future he would sacrifice everything for, even his life, to bring into existence.

Robert had not come home yet when I got back to Cassowary House. I tried not to think where he was, or who he was with. I went around the rooms downstairs putting out the lamps, leaving one burning in the vestibule for him. I wound the grandfather clock outside the sitting room and corrected its hands. I looked in on my sons in the nursery, checking that there were no gaps in the mosquito netting over their cots. Ah Peng was snoring away thunderously in her bed, her head resting on her porcelain brick. Long ago I had given up trying to convince her to sleep on pillows — she complained they gave her a sore neck.

Before going to sleep I wrote in my journal all that I had seen and heard at the reading club. What a tempest Sun Wen's words had roused in the hearts of his audience. He was going to transform the world, I was sure of it. I was witnessing a turning point in history, and this evening I had even been a part of it. It was all very thrilling.

Sun Wen. How strange his name looked on the page: Sun, the brightest star in our firmament, emitting waves of life-giving heat and light, with all the other planets circling it for eternity in their invisible grooves.

The excitement of the evening was still fizzing in my blood. I tried to read the new Somerset Maugham novel but put it down after a page or two. Why were his stories so frequently about adultery and unhappy marriages? I was about to switch off my bedside lamp when I heard Robert's trap coming up the driveway. I caught his 'Selamat malam' to the syce, and then I heard him coming into the house. My ears tracked his footsteps creaking up the stairs. A long silence followed – he would be checking on James and Edward; he never missed doing it, however late he got home. Moments later I heard his quiet rapping at my door.

'I'm still awake,' I said.

He opened the door and stood there, his body a black void against the light from the landing.

'Have you eaten?' I asked.

'Ate at the club. I took Peter Ong there. Mutton curry tonight. Tough and gristly. Might've been dog, for all I know. We had a swim too. How did Geoff and Sun Wen get along?'

'Geoff's going to write about him.' I was reluctant to tell him anything more, but he would find out about it eventually. Nothing was secret on this island. 'We went to hear him give a speech at his reading club.'

'That was bloody reckless – and stupid. Geoff should know better than to take you there.'

'I never felt unsafe, Robert, not for a second. You ought to go and listen to him sometime. He spoke with such power, such fury, he was like a typhoon.'

'Typhoons often leave destruction in their wake.'

'Goodnight, Robert,' I said.

'Goodnight, my dear,' he said, and shut the door.

The susurrations of the sea filled the night. A nightjar called out, like a stranger knocking at the door. A long time passed before the waters of sleep closed over me.

II

Over the years of living in Hong Kong Robert had built up an extensive collection of books on Chinese history and philosophy and literature. I had never been interested in them, but the next morning after he left for work I raided our library for them, pulling out volume after volume from the shelves.

More than two thousand years ago, I discovered from my reading, the ruler of Ch'in unified several warring states into a single powerful empire, with him as its first emperor. To keep out his enemies, he started construction of a wall that would stretch for hundreds of miles. I followed the glories and defeats of the Ch'in empire's subsequent dynasties; I learned about its emperors, its cities and states, its poets and philosophers, its artists and writers, and its gods and demons. The Middle Kingdom's present decay could be traced to 1644, when the Manchus vanquished the Ming emperors. And in 1839, more than forty years before I was born, England went to war with China to enforce its right to sell opium to the Chinese.

How utterly outrageous, I thought, using arms against another nation to force it to buy opium. No wonder the Chinese called us barbarians.

Defended by an outmoded army and incompetent military leaders, and undermined by a corrupt civil service, it was hardly surprising to anyone that China lost. The defeat saw its territories carved out by the victors – England and Germany and France – and it was made to pay millions of silver dollars in indemnities. Instead of modernising itself, however, the Ching monarchy retreated further into its dream world behind the walls of the Forbidden City, while the country outside descended into turmoil and chaos. But even as China was struggling to recover from the crippling wounds of the Opium Wars, a rebellion erupted in the south and rapidly spread north, inching its way to the capital.

The Taiping Rebellion. I wondered why it sounded familiar, and then I remembered Robert's remarks during Sun Wen's first visit to our home. Hong Siu Chuan, the leader of the Taipings, a scholar who had failed his Imperial Examinations, not only believed he was the brother of Jesus, but that he had been commanded by their Heavenly Father to overthrow the emperor and found a new Jerusalem. I had thought he was mad, and in all probability he was stark raving, but as I read more about him I discovered that in just two years Hong and his half a million converts conquered Nanking and made it the capital city of the Kingdom of Heavenly Peace. Hong proclaimed himself the Heavenly King, and for fourteen years they had controlled Nanking. Missionaries and bible-printers from the West had visited the city, hoping to form alliances with them and spread the gospel to the whole of China. Some of them stayed in Nanking for years, but in the end they were repelled by Hong's warped ideas of Christianity. The Kingdom of Heavenly Peace fell to the imperial army in 1864. Hong died of food poisoning, and his son and thousands of his supporters were executed by the emperor.

The Taipings, I was happy to find out, viewed women as the equal of men. From the earliest days of the rebellion their women had been fighting shoulder to shoulder with the men against the emperor's troops. I couldn't think of the last time in history, and in any other place in the world, when a similar thing had taken place.

My burgeoning interest in China delighted Robert, and we spent many an evening discussing its convoluted history, although he thought I was becoming too obsessed with the Taipings. But it had been a long while since we shared something that engaged us; it gave us something safe to argue about, something to hold back the tide of silence that had, unknown to us, crept into our marriage.

'We must help Sun Wen,' I announced to him one evening.

'That unrepentant, incorrigible polygamist?'

I ignored his chaffing. 'Just imagine if he succeeds – a society where everyone is equal – the rich and the poor, the educated and the illiterate. Why, once he's achieved that, the women would no longer be powerless.'

'There will always be inequality, Lesley. That's the way of the world.'

'So we should just do nothing?'

'I strongly advise it,' Robert said. 'The authorities will be keeping an even more attentive eye on him after that piece your brother wrote, mark my words.'

Geoff's interview with Sun Wen had been published the day before. With its details of his turbulent, rootless childhood, his family and three children (Sun Wen had allowed mention of just his one wife), the interview had painted a sympathetic portrait of the revolutionary. Pleased by the interview, Sun Wen had invited my brother to follow him around and write a series of articles about his cause.

During his next visit to our home Sun Wen mentioned that he was translating the Tong Meng Hui's pamphlets and articles into English so they could be disseminated among the Straits Chinese.

'Your translations had better be up to scratch,' I warned him, 'or the Straits Chinese will laugh at you.'

'Arthur – you've met him, you remember? – Arthur does as much as he can to check the translations, but he can't really spare us the time.'

'I can look them over for you,' I said.

'You're not going there, Lesley,' Robert said.

'There are other women there too, Robert,' Sun Wen said, 'even some young ladies from Penang's finest families. And I will be there, of course.'

'That may be the case, but I forbid it.'

Sun Wen's smile withered away. 'Ah, yes. Of course. Your wife should not be seen in the company of us Chinamen.'

'You know quite well that the rest of Penang isn't as . . . accepting . . . as we are.'

Sun Wen put down his half-finished tumbler of whisky. I felt awful for him. How often did he have to choke back his rage and swallow his pride, all for the sake of his cause?

I said to Robert, 'I can collect the papers tomorrow morning. I'll do the work at home.'

'It's very kind of you, Lesley, but . . .' Sun Wen shook his head. 'You must obey your husband.'

'Tomorrow morning,' I repeated firmly.

Sun Wen got to his feet and gave us a clipped bow. 'Thank you, Robert, and Lesley, for welcoming me into your home.'

I rounded on Robert after he left. 'Write him a note and apologise.'

'I'll do nothing of the sort.'

'What he's trying to achieve will end the suffering of millions of people, Robert, *millions*. I – we – *have* to do whatever we can to help him.'

'You find him attractive, don't you?'

It was the last thing I had expected him to ask me. I fumbled for an answer. 'He has attractive qualities, yes,' I said finally. 'But I'm not attracted to him.'

A sour smile distorted Robert's lips. 'A perfect lawyerly answer.'

I stared at him. Robert – *Robert* of all people – accusing me of having feelings for another man. All at once I was fed up with the pretence. I was tired of it, tired of not knowing. For weeks now I had been standing on the edge of a precipice, wondering what lay waiting beneath the bank of mists.

Enough. No more. I stepped off the ledge and into the void.

'Are you having an affair, Robert?' I knew, even as those words left my lips, that my marriage would be irrevocably changed by them.

In the middle of lighting his pipe, he froze, his hands rigid in the air. 'Am I *what*?'

Time stopped; a roaring noise flooded my head; my voice sounded muffled in my ears, hollow. '*Are* you sleeping with another woman?'

He struck his match in one sharp stroke and cupped the flame to his pipe-bowl. He sucked in his cheeks a few times, puffing out smoke.

'Is this why you've been acting oddly – because you think I'm having an affair – with another woman? Where the hell did you get this, this *lunatic* idea from? Those dried-up hags at the club? Pykett's barren wife and her mahjong coven? Or Mrs Biggs? That bloody woman's mouth is as big as her arse.'

'Somebody saw you with . . .' I wished I hadn't confronted him, but it was too late now. 'With another woman.'

He stared at me; and then he started to laugh. The sound of it was horrible – harsh and frightening. I had never heard him laughing like that. 'And who's this woman, this seductive siren?'

'They didn't say.'

'Of course they didn't. Typical, isn't it? Bloody cows. You remember how their malicious – and need I remind you, ultimately baseless – tittle-tattle scuppered the Fitzpatricks' marriage?' He took a couple of long, lazy draws on his pipe and looked directly into my eyes. 'I am not sleeping with another woman, Lesley.'

III

Standing outside the house on Armenian Street, I studied the black signboard above the doors. My eyes followed the thick, fluid strokes of the Chinese characters carved into it. These signboards were common all over town, but on this morning the ideograms with their tarnished gold leaf felt oppressive to me, alien.

Robert had been aloof towards me during breakfast, barricading himself behind his newspapers. When he left for his office he didn't come around the table to kiss my cheek.

I knocked on the doors and checked the ceiling boards. If there was a spyhole, it was well-camouflaged. A minute later the bolt was pulled back and a man peered out from a partly opened door.

'Dr Loh,' I said, relieved to see a face I recognised. 'Lesley Hamlyn. I'm here to collect—'

'Yes, yes. Come in, come in.'

He bolted the door behind us. He was in a crisp white shirt, grey trousers and a blue-and-red striped tie. He had a narrow, almost rectangular face, with a thin, well-shaped nose, and his eyes were alert with humour and intelligence.

'Come along,' he said. 'And call me Arthur. We're all on first-name terms here.'

The dining hall looked more salubrious in the morning sun flooding into the air-well. Half a dozen people were seated around the long rosewood table, books and sheets of papers spread out before them. One or two glanced up from their work, giving me a nod. Telling me to wait, Arthur hurried to a pile of boxes taking up a corner of the dining hall. I looked around me. The walls were blistered with damp; documents were stacked high on tables or jammed into overflowing shelves. An empty bamboo birdcage hung by the air-well. From the dining hall a short passageway led to a pair of rooms at the back. To the right of the passageway was the kitchen where a blackened kettle was brooding on a charcoal stove, steam whispering from its spout.

Arthur came back and handed me a bundle of papers. 'The printers need them by noon tomorrow.'

'I'll bring them back before then.'

'You're already here. Why not just stay and finish it here?'

I looked at the documents and then back at him. 'I'll need a pen and writing paper.'

The work was not as easy as I had expected. The documents – articles and pamphlets and editorials describing in histrionic tones the corruption of the Chinese government, the abuses of power, the sufferings of the common folk – were riddled with errors and mangled grammar. I frequently had to ask Arthur to clarify phrases or names as I tightened the meandering sentences, sheared the paragraphs and did the best I could to make them coherent. Arthur also asked me to remove anything that could be construed as seditious or critical of our own government, however vague it was.

We chatted during a short break for tea. He was thirty years old, and he was a GP sharing a clinic in Campbell Road. Through a series of questions – who his parents were; to whom he was related – I charted his coordinates on the map of our social world (it was a habit everyone here – especially the Chinese – indulged in when meeting someone for the first time), and I was fully aware that he was doing the same with me. I had heard of his father – a tin merchant and the president of the Chinese Anti-Opium Association; his mother was from an old and prominent Straits Chinese family.

'Is that the party's flag?' I nudged my chin at the flag displayed on the wall behind him; in the full daylight it was dark blue, the sun blazing from its centre an empty white circle.

'Yes. And one day it will fly over the whole of China.' He looked at me. 'Have you ever been there?'

'No.'

'I thought as much.'

The disdain in his voice stung me. I suddenly realised how I appeared to him: just another bored memsahib slumming with the locals, looking for a bit of excitement in her humdrum, unsatisfying life.

'Why do *you* care about China?' I flung the question at him. 'You Straits Chinese, you all went to English-speaking schools, you all speak English at home, dress like Europeans. You kowtow only to England.'

I had expected him to be provoked into anger, but he merely smiled. 'The Chinese-educated ones here say we chiak angmoh sai,' he said. '"We eat the white man's shit."'

'I know what it means.'

He became serious. 'I'm here because of my grandmother. She was eighteen when she joined the rebels fighting the Manchu emperor.'

'Your grandmother was a Taiping rebel?'

'You know about them?' Surprise tussled with doubt on his face. I gave him a quick summary of what I knew of the rise and fall of the Taiping Rebellion. He seemed quite impressed with me when I concluded.

'What happened to your grandmother?' I asked.

'She grew disillusioned with the Taipings after they took Nanking, after they founded their Kingdom of Heavenly Peace. She had been assigned to work for a Scottish bible-printer there. He helped her escape. He had contacts in Penang, and he gave her money to come here. She worked for a small printer in Bishop Street – she bought the business from him after a few years. It's still operating, my second uncle runs it.'

'Is she still alive?' I wanted to meet her.

He shook his head. 'She died when I was fifteen. She used to fill my head with tales of her life in China when I was a child. When I was old enough I decided to go there, see it for myself.' He seemed to be addressing the flag on the wall. 'I was shocked by how bad it was there – the poverty and the misery, the corruption. China must be saved, and every one of us Chinese in the world must play his part.'

'Until I met Sun Wen, I had hardly any interest in his country,' I said. 'But that night when we came here, when I heard him speak . . .'

He looked at me, and I felt he understood what I was trying to articulate. 'Every one of us would have willingly marched off to war for him,' he said.

I finished editing the last article and handed the whole bundle back to him. He checked a few of them, then put them aside.

'Can you come again next week?' he asked.

IV

Every Tuesday morning, after Robert had left for work, I would take the rickshaw to the house on Armenian Street. Arthur was usually there already, helping out for an hour before he departed for his clinic. In the beginning I felt out of place, sensitive to the curious glances from the other members, but they soon lost interest in me after a few visits.

Robert's late nights became less frequent. He would often find me lying on the verandah sofa when he got home, lost in a book. We would chat over stengahs before we went in for dinner, but he never asked me what I was doing at the reading club, and I never mentioned anything about it. My eyes raked him covertly for signs – a long curlicue of hair on his clothes, or a trace of perfume – as to where he had been, and whom he had been with, but I never found anything incriminating.

★   ★   ★

By now Ethel had been locked up in Pudoh Gaol for a month. I couldn't imagine the awfulness of her predicament. I wrote to her regularly, hoping to lift her spirits; I sent her novels and the latest issues of the *Illustrated London News*, even though she wasn't much of a reader. The warden and the other prisoners were decent to her, she told me in one of her infrequent letters, and William visited her without fail every day, but she missed her daughter terribly. People seemed to have forgotten about her, but as the first day of her trial loomed her name surfaced on their lips again. Like everyone I knew, Arthur was intrigued by her case, often airing outrageously slanderous speculations about her and William Steward when we were working at the long table.

'Your prurient interest is unbecoming,' I scolded him on one occasion. We had fallen into the habit of speaking in a rojak of English and Hokkien. 'You're worse than anyone.'

'It's not prurient.'

'Oh, of course not.'

'No European woman in Malaya has ever been on trial for murder, do you know that? Ethel Proudlock's the very first one. And she didn't just kill any man, Lesley – she killed someone of her own exalted race. You angmohs have always taken pride in telling us natives that "everyone is equal before the law, white or brown, black or yellow". Well, now with one of your own on trial – with her very life at stake – how will you angmohs mete out justice? That is what I find compelling.'

'She'll be judged fairly, like you and me, like every one of us.'

'Oh, of *course* she will.' He mimicked my sarcastic tone perfectly. 'The judge will put on a show of impartiality and fairness, but in the end the verdict will be "Not guilty".'

'That's because she's *not*.'

Realisation pulled up his eyebrows. 'You know her.'

'She's my closest friend.'

'So was she sleeping with him?'

'Arthur . . .' I warned him.

He raised a pair of mollifying palms to me. 'Well, even if they find her guilty,' he said, 'they'll fashion some loophole for her to slip out of the noose. They'll say . . . oh, she had amnesia, or that she blacked out temporarily; or they'll say that she was hysterical, she didn't know what she was doing. They'd never hang a white woman. Never.'

He was wrong, I thought. I held my tongue and returned to the work at hand, but I couldn't help remembering what Robert had said – that Ethel had shot William Steward with the intention of killing him.

I glanced at the clock on the wall when Arthur began packing his pens and writing pads into his doctor's bag.

'Patient's appointment?' I asked. He was leaving earlier than he normally did.

'My doors are being delivered.' He hefted the leather bag in his hand. 'Would you like to see them?'

'I know what doors look like.'

He grinned. 'Come on – it's not far, just down the road.'

He seemed so terribly keen for me to go with him that I could not refuse. I made one last amendment to the essay I'd been working on and handed it to one of the women down the table.

'All, right, Arthur,' I said. 'Let's go and look at your doors.'

It was not yet mid morning, but the sun was already ferocious, and I was grateful for my parasol as we followed the gentle curve of Armenian Street towards the harbour. A boy no older than nine or ten sped past us on a bicycle too big for him, one tiny paw on the handlebars, the other hand balancing a tray with a bowl of steaming wonton noodles; a rickshaw weighed down with a pair of stout Nyonyas chased us out of its path. Nobody looked twice at me – the people here had become used to the sight of this angmoh woman.

This was his favourite section of town, Arthur said. The neighbourhood had seen fierce fighting between the Ghee Hin and the Hai San in the riots, he told me. They had been outlawed afterwards, but they were still here, the secret societies, thriving in the shadows.

I could see why: the lanes and alleys provided convenient escape routes to the harbour, and I wondered if Sun Wen had this in mind too when he chose this neighbourhood for his base.

A man sitting on his haunches outside his shop and kneading a lump of almond-brown dough in a basin called out to Arthur. 'Loh loke-kun, chiak-pah buey?'

'I've eaten already, Ah Tong,' Arthur replied in Hokkien. 'Eh, your wife's stomach better or not?'

'No pain any more, no pain any more. Your medicine very best-lah.' Ah Tong throttled off a fist-sized lump, worked the dough into a long thin roll and skewered it on a thin wooden stick. He stuck it in a tray with the dozen or more he had already made; they looked like rows of sausages. 'This morning she even told me she wanted to eat roast pork. I said to her, "Roast pork? Siau-ah? Ah Lan, you think you married a rich man's son like Dr Loh-ah?"'

'Tell her I'll buy her a plate of sio-bahk, but she must keep taking her pills.'

Ah Tong laughed. He chose a stick from the tray and presented it to me. The dough was still moist and soft. I brought it to my nose. The smell of sandalwood pulled me back to the smoky temples my amah used to take me to when I was a girl. I handed it back to the incense-maker, but he motioned me to keep it.

'Tell her a few hours in the sun and they'll be as dry as biscuits,' the incense-maker told Arthur.

'Kamsiah,' I said. I smelled it again. 'Very fragrant,' I said in Hokkien, grinning at him as his eyes widened.

'You should see the incense he makes for the Hungry Ghost Festival,' Arthur said as we continued on our way down the street. 'Six feet long and thick as a telegraph pole, each one of them, with dragons and phoenixes twisting up and down the whole length. They burn for a whole week.'

He stopped walking when we came to the last shophouse in the row. It stood on a corner next to an alley, as unremarkable as every other shophouse we had just gone past. The front doors were plain, with no glass insets or fretwork, and the windows were shuttered. A wooden bench and a flowering purple bougainvillea in a terracotta pot stood on the five-foot way, which was tiled in a green-and-white geometric pattern.

From a ring Arthur selected a key, spindly as a twig, and unlocked the doors. He didn't invite me inside, but nodded at something behind me. Peering over my shoulder, I saw a coolie coming down the street pushing a handcart stacked with a pair of doors wrapped in grubby jute sacking. He grunted a greeting at Arthur and hefted the doors into the house. He emerged again, accepted his payment and disappeared with his cart back to wherever he had come from.

Arthur held out his hand to me. I took it and stepped over the shin-high threshold.

It was cool inside, the leaded windows casting a milky light into the guest hall. Except for a Coromandel screen at the opposite end, the hall was bare of any furniture. The walls, however, were hung with wooden doors painted with birds and flowers, or mist-covered mountains. The upper halves of some of the doors were decorated with intricate fretwork of dragons and phoenixes.

'I got them from shophouses and temples that were about to be torn down,' Arthur said. 'It always made me so sihm-tnhia' – he used the Hokkien word for 'heart-pain' – 'knowing that they were going to be chopped up into firewood. One day I thought: why don't I buy them? My grandmother had left me this house, and it was standing empty. It's a place to store them.'

I went over to the pair closest to me. They were carved with vertical, sinuous strokes of Chinese calligraphy papered in gold leaf. Carefully I lifted the lower corner of one of the doors half an inch away from the wall. I knew I wouldn't see anything of course, but I was disappointed when I found only the limewashed wall behind it, and not a doorway leading into another room, perhaps into another world.

'Let me show you my latest acquisitions,' said Arthur.

He was waiting for me by the Coromandel screen. I hesitated – it suddenly occurred to me what people might say: I was a white woman alone in another man's house, and not just any man, but a Chinaman.

He looked across the length of the hall at me, and then, without uttering a word, he walked back to the front doors and flung them wide open, exposing the interior of the house to the street. The thought struck me that perhaps he was more worried about what people might say about *him* being alone in a house with an angmoh woman.

I followed him behind the screen and down a short corridor. Emerging into the dining hall, I pulled up abruptly.

'Goodness . . .' I said, my voice hushed.

The walls here were also covered with doors. And hanging from the ceiling beams were more doors, carefully spaced apart and suspended on wires so thin they seemed to be floating in the air.

We walked between the rows of painted doors, our shoulders and elbows setting them spinning slowly. Each door pirouetted open to reveal another set of doors, and I had the dizzying sensation that I was walking down the corridors of a constantly shifting maze, each pair of doors opening into another passageway, and another, giving me no inkling of where I would eventually emerge.

We came to the back of the dining hall. A wrought-iron spiral staircase twisted upstairs, like the remains of a giant nautilus shell. By the foot of the staircase was a Chinese zither resting on its stand.

'You play this . . . what is it called?' I asked. The zither was about five feet long and a foot wide.

'A guzheng.' He strummed the strings, stirring up a liquid arpeggio. For some inexplicable reason the sound made me think of a cold, clear stream flowing down a bare and rocky mountainside.

I looked at the doors; they were still turning languidly from the ceiling beams. 'How many of them do you have?'

'Oh, thirty or forty pairs.' His laugh sounded embarrassed, but it was also tinged with the pride of the true collector. 'I've lost count. These two here' – he showed me a pair of doors hanging on a wall – 'they're the oldest set in my collection. I bought them from a temple on the day before it was demolished. Eighteenth-century. Painted by an artist from a village in the Hokkien province.'

Each of the doors was painted with a crimson-faced, fierce-eyed man in military garb. The figure on the left door brandished a great, lethal-looking axe while the one on the right wielded an intimidating halberd. The paintwork was weathered, and in some places the colours had completely faded.

'Who are they? Warriors? Or deities?'

'In the T'ang dynasty, an emperor was harassed by demons and evil spirits outside his sleeping chambers,' said Arthur. 'This went on for night after night. The emperor couldn't sleep, and his health deteriorated. His advisors despaired of finding a solution. Then General Qin and General Yu, two of the emperor's most loyal men, stepped forward. They declared to the emperor, "In our whole lives, your two humble servants have killed men as they would slice open a melon. We have stacked up bodies as high as mountains. We fear neither ghosts nor demons. We shall stand guard outside your royal chambers; we shall keep watch all through the hours of the night." The emperor agreed to their suggestion, and that night no ghosts or demons disturbed his sleep. But the next morning he summoned the two generals. "You have kept watch over me all night," he told them, "but you have had no sleep. This cannot continue." The emperor thought for a while, then he found a solution: he ordered his court artist to paint the likenesses of the two generals on his doors, one on the left, the other on the right. And from then on he was never disturbed by evil spirits again.

'Over time, this practice spread across the land. General Qin and General Yu became known as the Gods of the Doors.'

He went over to another pair of doors propped against a sideboard. 'These you saw carried in just now. They're two hundred years old.' He pulled away the jute covering and adjusted the position of the doors. A small brown hawk was painted on the left door, floating over a high, misty gorge.

My fingers hovered above the four vertical lines of Chinese characters brushed over the mists. 'What do they say?'

'"Evanescent path of dreams/in the summer night/O Bird of the mountain/carry my name beyond the clouds." A poem by Shibata Katsuie, a sixteenth-century Japanese samurai, a warrior. He was betrayed in a battle. He composed it moments before using his sword on himself.'

Something stirred inside me, something mournful. How strange that the words of a Japanese warrior from more than three hundred years ago – his last few breaths, given shape – should still exist, inscribed on a weathered door thousands of miles from his home. I murmured the poem a few times, lodging the words in my memory.

'You collect these painted doors.' I stroked the powdery wood, thinking of the uncountable number of people who had passed through these doors over the centuries. 'Yet your own front doors are bare.'

For the first time since I met him, he seemed parched for words. 'You know,' he said, 'it's never occurred to me.'

'I like the idea of your plain, unremarkable doors concealing these' – my hand swept over the painted doors around us – 'from the world outside.'

He reflected on what I had said. 'I like it too.'

The doors spun slowly in the air, like leaves spiralling in a gentle wind, forever falling, never to touch the earth.

V

Geoff's articles about Sun Wen had made him more widely known among the Europeans and the Straits Chinese, but the flood of funds he had been hoping for was still not even trickling in. Arthur decided to hold a fundraiser tea party for all his friends at his house. Sun Wen would give a talk and enlighten them on what he was trying to achieve.

'It's this Saturday, three o'clock. You must come,' Arthur said. 'Bring Robert too.'

'He's going to KL this weekend,' I said. 'He has a trial on Monday.'

'But you'll come?'

I shook my head. 'My darling husband's already none too happy about my being here.'

'Everything all right between you two?' He had the perfect bedside manner of a trustworthy GP: sympathetic yet unobtrusive. I had to fight the temptation to confide in him.

'Couldn't be better,' I replied.

The reading club was having one of its rare quiet mornings, with only a handful of people working at the long table. I was getting irritated with a shoddily translated pamphlet when Sun Wen turned up with a woman. I had never seen her before. We put down our pens and gathered around the couple. Sun Wen beckoned me to his side.

'I have long wanted you to meet Chui Fen, and now she is finally here in Penang,' he said. 'Chui Fen is one of our most loyal supporters.'

The woman looked only a few years older than me, but she already had a strong presence about her. Her hair was pulled back into a low bun, revealing a smooth brow and an oval-shaped face. Her eyes were large and intelligent, her nose long and well-proportioned. She had plump, perfectly shaped lips. She took my hands in hers and, with Sun Wen interpreting, thanked me for helping their cause.

'She's one of his wives, isn't she?' I whispered to Arthur the moment they left. 'The second wife. She's young and pretty enough.'

He didn't lift his head from the document he was checking. 'They're not married, actually.'

'Oh? So she's his concubine?'

'You'd better not let her hear you. She's handy with a gun, and she knows martial arts – she's roughed up a few men in her time.

Chui Fen's been by his side for twenty years. As far as he's concerned – as far as *we* are concerned – she's his wife.'

Twenty years together. I had been married to Robert for only a quarter of that. 'Well, I feel sorry for his first wife.'

He scribbled a few words on the margin. 'You can convey your sympathies to her yourself – she'll be joining them in a few days.'

'You mean . . . they'll be living together? All three of them under the same roof?'

'Every marriage has its own rules, Lesley.'

The softness of his voice, the absence of condemnation in it, made me look sharply at him. 'Was your marriage arranged?'

'It was, as a matter of fact.' He raised his eyes from the sheet of paper he was reading. 'Ah, memsahib thinks it's a barbaric native custom.'

Were my feelings so transparent? 'It's . . . antiquated.'

'After I finished my studies and came home, my father told me over breakfast one morning I was to marry his business partner's daughter. Everything had been arranged.'

'Did you know her?'

'Since I was ten years old.'

'You didn't object?'

'Even Sun Wen had to obey his parents.'

'But do you love her? And does she love you?'

'Marriage is not only about love. It is the duty of every son to ensure that the family name does not die out. The tree must produce branches. Anna is a dutiful daughter-in-law, a devoted mother, and a good wife.'

'It's so . . . sterile. What about romantic love?'

'Why did you marry Robert? He's nearly twice your age. Was it romantic love?'

From the way he was looking at me, I wondered if he had heard something about Robert's infidelity. 'You'll be telling me next that Sun Wen's got another wife hidden away somewhere,' I said, 'a third one, waiting to spring out into the open.'

'He has. She's the one he loves the most.'

'Who is she?'

'You already know her.'

I dredged my memory for the faces of the women I had met since I started coming here. 'Who is she? Tell me.'

Arthur laid his pen on the table. His eyes, I saw, were stained with sorrow.

'China,' he said. 'He is married to China. He loves her the most, and he's loved her the longest. And of all his wives, however many he will have in his life, she will allow no competition from anyone else. She will demand everything from him. And in the end, after he has given her all that he has, she will crush his heart.'

VI

The monsoon edged closer to the island, bringing heavy afternoon storms that flooded the streets around the harbour when the tide was high. I welcomed the respite from the heat – I have always loved Penang when it rains, when the harsh tropical light softens, and the world feels hushed and cosy.

Returning home from the beach with my sons one evening, I found Ah Peng waiting anxiously on the verandah, her palms bracketing her ample hips. 'Come inside quick-quick!' she cried. 'Sky black-black, want to rain already.'

She dropped a fistful of papers and coins into my palm. 'Dhobi-wallah find in Mr Robert's pocket,' she added as she took James and Edward to their baths.

It was Friday, which meant Cookie's roti babi for dinner. I was looking forward to it. Robert had taken his assistant Peter Ong with him to KL that morning. They would spend the weekend there preparing for a trial that would run for a whole week. He would have already arrived at the Empire Hotel by now. I pictured him in my head, welcoming his lover into his room, a woman whose face

I could not see. I forced that image away; it was becoming much easier to do, I was surprised to discover.

I smoothed out the crumpled pieces of receipts and bills Ah Peng had given me. Among them was a neatly folded piece of paper. I unfolded it. The words were written in a wine-red ink, the hand-writing loose but elegantly formed: 'My darling Robert, I love the book. Thank you. Peter.'

Cheeky bugger. Someone should knock him back into his place. *My darling Robert.* Impudent, addressing his superior like that, I thought as I read the note again. The realisation coalesced slowly, and then, like a coffin slotting into a grave, everything fell into place. *My darling Robert.*

I sank onto the sofa, feeling sick. All these years, all the effort to make myself attractive to him, and all the blame I had laid upon myself because he no longer showed any interest in me, wondering what was wrong with me. What a fool I had been. What an utter, utter fool.

The wind had stiffened, rattling the bamboo chicks rolled up beneath the eaves. I ought to have dropped them before the storm came, but I couldn't move. My body, my heart, felt heavy, so heavy. I slumped on the sofa, barely aware of Ah Peng when she came to call me. 'Eat rice already.' She clapped loudly. 'Oi, Lesley-ah, you got hear me or not?'

I lifted my face to her. She looked at me. Her gaze flicked to the piece of paper in my hand, then back to my eyes again. An age of silence seemed to pass between us.

'Aiya, so he has another woman,' said Ah Peng.

'How long have you known?'

She nodded to herself. 'Ah, I knew it! All men stray-lah. He'll tire of her soon.'

'It's not . . .' I began, but I was too mortified to reveal the complete truth to her. It still felt as if it was my fault, some deficiency, some grave flaw in me that had driven Robert into the arms of another man. At that moment I said to myself: No one must ever know.

'Ah Peng,' I said, 'do you regret taking your vows? Do you ever wish you had married?'

Her sigh, when she sat down beside me, seemed to emerge from somewhere deep inside her entire being. I caught a whiff of the camphor ointment she rubbed into her arthritic fingers, a scent I had known since my childhood. Smelling it now left a hollow of loss inside me.

'You see this face-lah. Got what man want?' Ah Peng smiled, but swimming in the depths of her eyes was an old, old pain, refracted through the years of resignation. 'I join Sor Hei long time already. Regret got what use?' Beneath her white tunic her mountainous bosom rose with a seismic heave, before settling down again. 'That morning, I light joss sticks and take vow before Kuan Yin's altar, my Sor Hei sister, Ah Suan, she say to me, "Ah Peng, from this day on, no man can bring you sorrow, only yourself."'

The joints of her fingers were knotted with arthritis. Her jade bangle hung loosely on her wrist; it was the only jewellery I had ever seen her wear. Her face was heavily lined, and her hair, gathered into a bun, was completely grey. When had she grown so old?

When I was a little girl she would sometimes take me with her when she visited the letter-writer in town. Outside the entrance of the Prangin Road market we'd sit on low bamboo stools while she dictated the news she wanted to tell her family back in their village in China to the letter-writer, a thin old man with a tidy grey beard down to his chest. And weeks later, when she received a reply, she would take it to the same letter-writer. He would squint at it and give voice to the lines and lines of brush-stroke runes that had been inscribed by her village's own letter-writer, runes that neither she nor anyone else in her family had been taught to decipher. She would perch on the edge of the stool, her hands tucked between her broad thighs, her face, depending on what the runes reported, ripening into smiles or withering into worry and sadness. Occasionally she would chuckle or even laugh aloud, but such moments were rare; more often than not she would sigh or shake her head in sorrow. She seemed so intent, so focused, as she listened to the letter-writer's voice, scolding me sharply if I fidgeted or whined, and it was only when I was older that I realised she was trying to memorise the words recited by him, so that she could summon them up again in her mind, until the next letter arrived from beyond the mountains, from across the seas.

Remembering those moments, I said, 'Ah Peng, do you want to go back to your village? See your family again?'

'All die already-lah. Mother, father, aunty. My sisters, I don't know where.' She patted my hand and stood up, her knees popping. 'My family now here.' She walked her stiff, bow-legged gait back into the house.

The wind banged an unlatched window shutter somewhere again and again. I tore up the note and went over to the balustrade to drop the bamboo chicks. Lightning stabbed the clouds on the horizon. The mountains, the sea and then the beach disappeared behind the thicket of rain as the storm came charging in. Like watercolour on paper, the sky, the trees, the shrubs, the garden itself, were all washed away.

For a long time I continued to stand there, staring into the emptiness, only dimly aware of the wind driving the rain onto my arms, onto my face.

Chapter Twelve

Willie
Penang, 1921

A window shutter kept knocking against the wall. The sound seemed to have been travelling to him from far back in time. He sat up on the edge of his bed, knuckling the sleep from his eyes. Geoff's book had fallen onto the floorboards. He picked it up and placed it next to his mother's photograph, then went to secure the loose shutter.

Clouds were pulling across the sea, trailing long tassels of rain. No walking on the beach this morning.

After breakfast he returned to his room to write down what Lesley had told him, making a list of questions he wanted to ask her. He tried out some ideas of how he could structure the story, but he was frustrated and restless. If only it were night already so she could resume her tale. He was not unhappy for his work to be interrupted when Gerald came in and flopped onto the bed.

'Sodding rain,' said Gerald. 'It's bucketing down, isn't it? Reminds me of that time we were stuck in Pago Pago. You need anything typed?'

'Not yet.'

Gerald crossed his hands behind his head and disgorged a luxuriant yawn. He seemed to have made peace with Willie's new-found poverty. Willie was grateful for that.

'Lesley has been telling me about her story,' he said.

Gerald laughed coarsely. 'So who was she fucking? That Chink Sun? I'd wager a packet on it.'

For a while Willie said nothing. He felt, in a strange way, that he would be betraying her if he revealed her secret to anyone else. Yet she *must* know that there was a great probability that he might write about it – what other reason could she have for confiding in him? She could not be unaware that her reputation would be torn to tatters and her marriage ruined if he were to publish the story she was telling him.

'Robert had an affair a few years ago,' said Willie. 'With a Chinaman.'

'Oh, Robert's been eyeing me from the day we got here,' said Gerald. 'Very, very discreetly, mind you, but he's been eyeing me all right.'

'Robert? Are you sure?'

'Our memsahib finds people like us repulsive, you know. She hides it well, but she doesn't fool me. To think she married one of our kind.' Gerald laughed. 'Oh, the sweet irony of it.'

Willie still had grave doubts about it. He thought back to the old days he had spent with Robert: their regular evenings at the theatre and the opera, their weekly dining at Robert's club.

'If Robert's homosexual, then he's camouflaged it better than anybody I know.'

'Oh, darling Willie . . . and to think the critics say you're cynical.'

'You've been wrong-footed before. Need I remind you about Father Bailey and the deuced mess you kicked up? And that widowed planter in Johor? He was going to shoot you.'

'Oh, those damned old pederasts just couldn't admit to themselves they were lusting after me,' Gerald said.

'According to you every man is homosexual, and every one of them wants to sleep with you. Especially those you fancy.'

'I wasn't far off the mark with you, was I?'

Willie swivelled a lazy circle in his chair. 'Robert intends to sell Cassowary House and move to the Karoo.'

'He's crazy.'

'He's not. The desert air might give him half a dozen extra years, perhaps more. Lesley's none too pleased about it, though.'

'Well, I don't blame her,' said Gerald. 'I know what it feels like – forced to leave your home and never allowed to go back again.'

Willie sighed. Here it came again, the old tiresome problem. 'I did everything possible to help you. I spoke to every person I could think of who had any influence.'

'Well, obviously you didn't try hard enough. Or you're not taking it seriously. I can't go back to England, Willie. Do you understand that?'

'You know . . . bloody well it was your reckless behaviour that got you banished,' said Willie. 'Picking up men in a . . . public lavatory – sooner or later you were going to . . . get arrested.'

'Yes, yes, it's all because Gerald couldn't keep his cock in his trousers again.' He sat up against the headboard, curled his knees and wrapped his arms around them. 'I don't carry my mother's photograph with me everywhere I go, Willie, but that doesn't mean I don't think of her. I want to see her again. I miss her terribly. If she falls ill, I won't be able to visit her or look after her. You realise I'm not even allowed to go back for her funeral when she dies?'

Gerald seldom talked about his mother, and Willie had never heard him speak about her with such intensity of feeling before.

'We've roamed the world together, my dear boy,' he said, 'and I've always been grateful for your presence by my side. You know that it would give me only the greatest of joy if you could be in London with me.'

'It's Syrie. It's her doing. Your bloody wife's made sure I can't return to England. The cunt's not going to share you with me, oh no.'

Willie frowned; really, Gerald could be appallingly crude at times. 'I'll make enquiries again when I'm back in London. I'll speak to someone at the highest level.'

'When we get back – when you get back to London, I mean – I'll be going to America.'

'Don't be hasty, Gerald. I'll find you something closer – Paris, or Amsterdam. We can still see each other once a month.'

'I've done some thinking in the last few days. I know people in New York. I'll get a job easily there. Oh, don't look so put out, Willie – it'll only be until you're back on your feet again.'

So it had already begun, Willie thought, contemplating his young companion. The thing he had feared the most.

By evening the rainclouds had crept inland, leaving the skies clear again. Cooped up in the house all day, Willie agreed without a second's hesitation when Robert suggested a visit to the Protestant cemetery.

They parked the Humber in the forecourt of the E&O Hotel and crossed the busy road to the cemetery. The Tamil jaga was about to lock up, but Lesley spoke a few words to him in Malay, slipping a handful of coins into his palm. The watchman opened the gates and let them in.

The noise of the world outside dropped away, kept out by the cemetery's high walls. In the dripping banyans a koel fluted out its three-note question at regular intervals, deepening the silence. To Willie's eyes the graves were laid out in no particular order. Further inside the cemetery were baroque-looking tombs and imposing monuments decorated with neo-Classical urns on their roofs. The light seemed aged by the grey, weather-beaten headstones.

Robert jabbed his walking stick at a grassy aisle between the graves. 'Follow me, chaps,' he cried, and stalked off.

'Be careful, Robert,' Lesley called after him, 'the grass is slippery.'

'Look after him,' Willie murmured to Gerald.

There were about four hundred graves in the cemetery, although no one seemed to know the actual numbers, Lesley informed him as they followed Robert a few paces behind. Frangipani trees, their branches clotted with creamy white flowers, leaned into the path.

'Perhaps new ones spring up by . . . themselves in the night,' said Willie.

'What a horrible thought, Willie. Now I'll be awake all night.'

The earliest graves dated from the eighteenth century, the final resting places for missionaries and the men of the East India Company. Many of the weathered slabs were inscribed in English, but Willie also noticed French and German and Dutch carved into a number of them.

A memory of his Aunt Sophie buoyed to his mind's surface. He used to accompany her to the graveyard behind the Whitstable church. She was an austere, reticent woman, and he was hobbled by his stammer, so the boy and the woman seldom spoke. In the beginning he had walked self-consciously by her side through the cemetery; then one day he had reached up and taken her hand. She had glanced down at him, a slightly startled expression on her face, and then she had given him a quick, almost shy smile. From that moment on he would hold her hand wherever they walked – in the cemetery, along the high street, or when they went down to the sea to watch the fishing boats returning on the tide.

Now, decades later and a world from his boyhood, he curled his fingers over his palm. He had a sudden longing to feel, for just the briefest moment, her bony, gloved hand in his again, but his fingers closed over only emptiness.

'Not a place for happy memories, is it?' Lesley had turned around and was looking back at him. He was not even aware that he had stopped walking. 'We haven't come here since Robert returned from the war. We used to bring his friends from abroad here – especially if they were writers.'

'Are there writers buried here?'

'You'll see in a moment; I don't want to spoil his fun.'

Willie helped her over a tangle of angsana roots thrusting out from the earth. His feet crushed the frangipani blossoms strewn over the ground, and he imagined them sighing one last fragrant breath into the air. He bent down and picked up a flower. It was perfectly formed, but its white, silky petals were already browning at the edges.

Seared by the unforgiving air, he thought. While we are living, the air sustains us, but the very instant we stop breathing, that same air immediately sinks its teeth into us. What keeps us alive will also, in the end, consume us.

He dipped his nose into the frangipani and inhaled deeply from its yellow-daubed heart. He offered it to Lesley, but she made a face and leaned away from him.

'My amah used to warn me that if you smell a whiff of its perfume in the evening, it means there are ghosts close by.'

'Well,' said Willie, 'we *are* in a cemetery, after all.'

They had stopped at a tomb guarded by a marble angel, his opened mouth singing a voiceless, eternal lament. Lesley's eyes searched the granite crosses and petrified cherubs. She seemed to locate what she was looking for. Beckoning him to follow, she struck off along a half-hidden track between the graves. Once or twice the track disappeared completely and they had to climb over a grave or two. They came to an ancient banyan tree, its broad spreading branches supported by thick columns of roots. Willie would not have been surprised to see a fakir with legs contorted into the lotus position meditating beneath the tree, roaming through space and time in the universe of his mind for the secrets of eternity. Resting in the shade of the banyan were half a dozen graves. They were small and modest, the vertical lines of Chinese ideograms etched on their headstones precise as a surgeon's stitches.

'I told you the other night how Sun Wen and Robert were talking about the Taiping Rebellion,' said Lesley.

'Their leader was the madman who believed he was Jesus's younger brother, wasn't he?'

She nodded. 'When the rebels were defeated, many of them had to flee for their lives. Some of them found their way to the Southern Seas, to Penang. They planted new roots on the island; they made new lives here.' She stopped before one of the headstones. 'This one here is Madam Cheah. She was a soldier in the Taiping army.'

'A woman?'

'Why not? The Taipings believed a woman was just as good a soldier as a man.' She glanced behind them – Robert and Gerald were some distance away, studying the inscriptions on a chest tomb – before adding quietly, 'She was Dr Arthur Loh's grandmother. When Sun Wen heard about her, he asked Arthur to bring him here – he wanted to pay his respects to the rebels. Geoff and I came with them.'

Twilight was foxing the margins of the sky as they retraced their path and caught up with Robert and Gerald waiting by a rectangular tomb.

'Come along, you two. Stop dawdling,' Robert cried. He laid his hand on the top of the tomb. 'Here he is, old Francis Light himself.'

'Who's he?' asked Willie. The block of granite was about five feet by two and a half feet and came up almost to his shoulders. Withered leaves and twigs and frangipani flowers littered its coping, and a snail was oozing down its side.

'One of a pair of men who made Penang what it is today.' Robert made a half-hearted attempt to sweep the leaves off the tomb with his stick. 'Francis Light was the clever chap who leased the island from the Sultan of Kedah to build a victualling station for the East India Company's clippers.'

'"Who first established this island as a British Settlement",' Willie said, reciting the inscription chiselled into the side of the tomb. 'Who's the other fellow, then?'

Instead of replying, Robert set off further into the cemetery, pointing his stick to the gravestones on either side as they skirted past them. 'Settlers, nutmeg-planters, missionaries, sailors, soldiers, traders, scoundrels,' he said. 'You can trace the history of the island here. This one here is a chap called Thomas Leonowens. Low-level clerk of some sort, I think. His widow took a job as governess to the King of Siam's brood. People said she was a half-caste – mother was Anglo-Indian, apparently. We have a copy of her memoir, if you'd like to read it, Willie. Rather dreary and insipid, I must confess. But this is what I want to show you, in answer to your question.'

He tapped his walking stick on the side of a tomb. It was only a little smaller than a hansom cab. On its top, perched in the middle like a knob on the cover of a butter dish, was a stone urn.

'James Scott, Francis Light's business partner.' Robert's eyes glided appreciatively over the tomb. 'Together they founded Penang. He's the cousin of Sir Walter Scott. And one of my great-great-great-uncles. I told you about him in London, Willie, you remember? I grew up hearing about his exploits. Made me long to go out to the East. You could say he's the reason I ended up here.' He smiled sadly. 'I remember what *Waverley* meant to you, Willie.'

Willie circled the tomb. The last thing he had expected to stumble upon in a graveyard in Penang was a link, however tenuous, to the Scottish writer. He recalled his unhappy childhood with his uncle and aunt in Whitstable. As a boy, as an orphan, he had found solace in books, reading at every opportunity he could steal, even secretly on Sundays, which Uncle Henry had forbidden. *Waverley* was the first novel he had ever read; by the age of twelve he had devoured all of Scott's novels.

'It's twice the size of Light's tomb,' said Willie as he completed his perambulation.

'Well, Scott *was* the largest landowner in Penang,' Robert remarked.

'Tell them *how* he became the largest landowner,' said Lesley, but then continued on before Robert could speak. 'Light sired a family with a woman he never married, Martina Rozells. She was Eurasian – Portuguese-Siamese, it was said. Scott cheated her of the properties Light left her in his will, Willie. She fought him in the courts, but of course they ruled against her.'

'It was a different world in those days,' said Robert.

'I don't think it's changed much,' said Lesley. 'Do you?' She went over to a small, plain grave beneath a raintree. 'See if you can make out what this says, Willie,' she called over her shoulder.

The roots of the raintree had prised the headstone halfway out of the earth. Blotched with florets of lichen, it had a simplicity that appealed to Willie. Many of the letters and numerals were already drowned beneath the stone, and what remained lay faint on the surface.

A NA HAMM ND 1 97 – 18 1
H R SU I GO E DO N WH E IT WA YE D Y

He traced the shallow indentations with the tip of his forefinger, stroking the blank spaces between the letters. 'The name's easy enough,' he said. 'Anna Hammond.'

'And the second line? I haven't been able to solve it.'

He studied the headstone again. The answer came to him after a minute, the ghosts of the runes materialising once more in the blank spaces.

'"Her sun is gone down while it was yet day",' he said. 'Jeremiah 15:9.'

'"Her sun is gone down while it was yet day",' Lesley said. 'You *do* know your way around words.'

'I told you – my uncle was a vicar. I wasn't allowed to read anything on Sunday except the Bible.' Willie gripped the corners of the headstone and pulled himself stiffly to his feet.

'All that remains of a woman's life, a woman's story – a few fading lines of missing words,' said Lesley, running her palm over the edge of the headstone. 'A cemetery isn't where the dead are remembered, but a place where they are to be forgotten.'

Robert cocked his head in the direction of the cemetery gates. 'The jaga's calling. We'd better leave before he locks us all in here for the night.'

Watched over by the cataracted eyes of the stone cherubim, they filed back to the entrance. Willie turned to take one last look. The jaga bolted the iron gates, locked them and hung the rusted key around his neck. It lay on his chest like an amulet. Then the old man turned away and walked to his shack under the banyan trees.

Chapter Thirteen

Lesley
Penang, 1910

I

I would never know how I survived the rest of that evening, how I didn't turn into a raving lunatic just thinking about Robert's affair with Peter Ong. And yet I must have slept soundly that night, because the next morning I woke up filled with a sense of clarity I had not felt in many years. I knew what I had to do.

After I had fed my sons and handed them over to Ah Peng, I asked the houseboys to bring out my camphorwood chest from the storeroom. Lifting out the layers of old clothes and sheets, I found what I was looking for at the bottom. I unfolded it and took it to the window, holding it up to the light. The kebaya was creased, but I was relieved to see that its colours had not faded. I sniffed it – the smell of camphor was pungent, but an hour or two in the sun should get rid of it.

Ever since I was a girl I had envied the Nyonyas their kebaya, but Mother had never allowed me to wear one. I used to draw them in my sketchbooks and create my own designs for them.

The Nyonya kebaya, like the Straits Chinese themselves, had absorbed influences from the Malays, the Siamese, the Javanese, the

Chinese, even the Europeans. The long-sleeved blouse narrows at the waist and reaches down to the hips, giving a curvaceous shape to a woman, yet at the same time also ensuring that she looks elegant, refined. The voile blouse is worn over a camisole and matched with a sarong. After I married Robert I had one made by a widow in Kimberley Street who sewed for the old Straits Chinese families. It was based on one of my own designs. 'You look like a bloody native,' Robert had said when he saw me in it. In the end, after having worn it only a handful of times, I had put it away.

My kebaya was the shade of young bamboo. Embroidered flowers of darker green and yellow bloomed at the lapels; ferns sprouted from the ends of the sleeves and curled up from the hem. I matched it with a pale cream camisole and a dark green sarong I found in the chest.

I held the clothes against my body, smiling to myself when I saw that they still fitted me. From inside the chest I dug out the cotton bag containing a pair of cloth shoes hand-stitched with hundreds of tiny colourful glass beads – manek-manek, the Malay name came back to me.

I called Ah Peng to my room and asked her to air the kebaya and the matching garments in the sun before she pressed them. 'I'm going to a tea party for Sun Wen this afternoon,' I said. 'We're helping him raise money.'

'Wearing this?' She held up the garments. 'Lu siau-ah?'

'Yes, yes, I've gone mad, my head is full of wind,' I answered in Hokkien, shooing her out of my room.

After lunch I put on the outfit. I pinned the front of the kebaya together with the kerongsang, a trio of silver orchid brooches linked by a slender chain. The sarong was cool and smooth against my thighs, but it also narrowed my stride, and the manek-manek shoes were so dainty that I was almost afraid of pressing my full weight onto their soles. Once fully attired, the clothes compelled me to move with a languid grace, as befitted a Nyonya with nothing to fill her days but pua' chiki card games and gossip and scolding her daughter-in-law.

It was too complicated to do my hair in the Nyonya style – pinned up with a circle of long jewelled hairpins – so I gathered it into a simple chignon instead. When I finished I studied myself in the full-length mirror. I liked what I saw.

On my way out of the house I stopped by the nursery to give my sons a kiss. James gawked at me. 'You look pretty, Mummy,' he said, but Edward hugged his stuffed rabbit and started wailing when he saw me. Ah Peng picked him up and, rocking him gently in her arms, handed an envelope to me. I gave her a questioning look.

'Me and Ah Keng and houseboys, we collect money give Dr Sun,' she said.

I thanked her and kept the envelope in my purse. As I was leaving, she added, 'No man can cause you sorrow. Only yourself.'

The road outside Arthur's townhouse on Leith Street was lined with gharries and traps. Their syces squatted in the shade of the trees, smoking kretek or reading newspapers. I felt their eyes on me as I walked up the short straight path to the front entrance, and a crude comment or two in Hokkien from them singed my cheeks. Arthur was at the doors welcoming his guests. His eyes widened ever so slightly when he saw me before him.

'I changed my mind,' I said.

He smiled, performed an elaborate salaam and led me into his home. There were twenty to thirty people already gathered in the guest hall, talking and laughing among themselves. Sweeping my eyes around the room, I realised that I was the only angmoh there. A woman with the soft hands and the hard face of the wealthy eyed me from head to toe. I clutched my purse against my stomach and smiled at her; she gave me a cool nod and turned back to her friends' conversation. Ah Peng was right, I was mad to wear the kebaya. I was mad to come here.

I turned to leave, but Arthur stopped me. 'Sun Wen will be here soon,' said Arthur, 'and your brother's coming too.'

'Where's your wife? I'd like to meet her.'

'She took our daughter to my parents' house. I didn't want her disturbing us.' His attention was distracted by another arrival at the front doors.

'Go on.' I gave him a reassuring nod.

Looking around the hall again, I recognised a young woman from the Tong Meng Hui seated at a table in a corner. She gave me a shy wave, as heartened to see a familiar face as I was. Pamphlets and booklets were arrayed in neat rows on the table, and a ledger lay invitingly open for the guests to record their pledges.

'How much have you collected, Ah Ying?' I asked her.

She swept her hand in disgust over the blank pages of the ledger. I handed her the envelope of money Ah Peng had given me. I watched her print the names of the donors and the amount in her careful script, and then I asked for her pen. I wrote Robert's name and mine on the page and put down a figure that made her mouth gape.

'That should kindle the fire,' I said.

I retreated to a corner of the hall with a glass of wine. The windows were open, the late-afternoon breezes swelling the curtains. Arthur's home was similar to the houses of Robert's Straits Chinese clients, reflecting the Eastern and Western worlds they lived in. Bentwood chairs and half-moon tables inlaid with mother-of-pearl were lined against the walls, which were decorated with dados of ceramic tiles. Dominating the hall was a large, round, marble-topped table, a glass epergne in the shape of a swan in its centre. The Stoke-on-Trent floor tiles were laid out in a repeating floral design. Set close to the timbered ceilings were ventilation holes – shaped to symbolise bats because their name in Hokkien sounded similar to 'wealth', one of Robert's clients had once explained to me – allowing the air to circulate and cool the house. The guest hall opened off to a sitting room on either side; one would be furnished in the Eastern style for their family and their Asiatic friends; the other sitting room would be European, used when they entertained their angmoh friends.

A pair of framed photographs on a half-moon table caught my eye. One was of Arthur in a dark waistcoat and tails, standing behind his wife; she was sitting in a blackwood armchair, dressed in her wedding gown, her oval face heavily powdered, a circle of silver pins moulding her hair into an elaborate chignon. The other photograph showed them holding their infant daughter. She had had her fifth birthday a few weeks ago, I remembered him telling me.

From the fragments of conversations I caught around me, everyone here seemed to move in the same circles, travelling regularly to Singapore and London and Europe. Like Arthur, they spoke without the local accent, and it made me think of how my mother had frequently scolded us so that Geoff and I would grow up speaking with the proper accent and not sound like Asiatics. If I closed my eyes I could have been in a room full of Tuan Besars and mems exchanging the latest news about what they had done during their Home Leave.

I was glad to see Geoff. I waved to him and he wended his way between the guests towards me. My brother towered over everyone in the room, and he was not oblivious to the admiring looks from the women; it had always been like this ever since we were young.

He gave me a peck on the cheek, leaned back and cocked an eyebrow at me. 'What's this? Dressing like a native now? I almost didn't recognise you. It does look ravishing on you, I must say.'

'A gentleman would have said, "You look ravishing in it."'

'Well, you look . . . different. And I don't mean the dress. You seem . . . clearer, somehow. More defined. Sharper. How odd.' Geoff lit our cigarettes and cast his eyes around the hall. 'Robert here?'

'KL. Left yesterday.' Cigarette smoke veiled my face. I added quietly, 'He took his lover with him.' I sucked on my cigarette and released another cloud of smoke. 'His Chinaman lover.'

My brother eyed me warily, as though he was only just beginning to realise that he was in the presence of a feral animal. I liked it — it made me feel potent, someone not to be trifled with.

'How did you find out?'

'His catamite left him a note. A rather sweet one, actually.'

Geoff winced. 'I wish you wouldn't use that word.'

'What's so objectionable about "note"?'

Despite himself, he burst out laughing. 'Sometimes I think Mother was right — a woman shouldn't be given too much education or have a large vocabulary.'

'Idiot.' I punched him lightly on his arm.

'I'm shocked, utterly shocked, that you even know a word like "catamite". What unsuitable books have you been reading, young lady?'

'I followed the Wilde trials, you know, just like everyone else.' Robert had been engrossed by the trials, reading the newspapers avidly every morning, and now I understood why. 'The thought of Robert in bed with another man . . .' I shuddered. 'And a Chinaman too.'

'Now that you know, your grounds for divorce have just become much stronger. Unassailable, I'd say.'

'Are you mad? I don't want my sons to grow up knowing that their father is a . . .' I couldn't utter the word aloud, not even to my own brother.

'I'm sure he wouldn't want them to know either, so it's highly unlikely he'll contest the divorce.'

'Word will get out, Geoff. It always does. The mud will stick to us. It'll never wash off. Never.'

'So what are you going to do, then? Stay locked up in a dead marriage for the rest of your life?'

I blew gently on the glowing tip of my cigarette; the ring of fire brightened, eating up the paper. 'Locked up? Not at all. Quite the opposite, in fact. I feel that I've been released from a prison I'd never realised I had been placed in. Strange, isn't it? Do you know how liberating it is, to finally understand that it's not my fault my marriage is a failure?'

'I wouldn't go so far as to call it a failure.'

'The enviable Mr and Mrs Hamlyn, with their perfect marriage.'

'No marriage is perfect, Les.'

'I suppose you know lots of husbands who cheat on their wives.'

'I know wives who betray their husbands too.'

'But not many instances where the husband is sleeping with another man, I'm sure.'

'It's not common, I grant you that, but it's not unheard of either.'

I gave him a penetrating look. 'You're not unfaithful to Penelope, I hope?'

'Me? God forbid. The memsahib would geld me with a parang if I ever cheated on her with a woman – or a man, or a coconut tree.' His voice hardened. 'I detest – absolutely detest – people who are unfaithful. Look how our dear father used to hurt Mother.'

'Yet I don't hear you objecting to Sun Wen's infidelity.'

'He's not hiding Chui Fen from his wife, is he? And anyway, he's a Chinaman, it's their way, having many wives. It's polygamy, not adultery.'

'Splitting hairs.'

He sighed. 'Look, Les, I don't approve of it – but there are much bigger issues at stake, important issues.'

'He's here,' I said.

There was a stirring in the hall as the guests parted for Arthur and Sun Wen. The two men stopped beneath the chandelier in the centre of the hall and took in the faces around them.

'My dearest friends,' Arthur announced. 'The man we've all come to meet – Dr Sun Yat Sen.'

Arthur retreated to the sidelines, leaving Sun Wen alone in the circle. The revolutionary acknowledged the genteel applause with a brief smile to a woman here, a nod to a man there. He was in his customary dark grey suit and matching waistcoat, his hair pomaded and parted precisely at the side, his moustache meticulous. His face, however, looked gaunter than I recalled; the flesh of his cheeks seemed to have been scooped out by a spoon.

An expectant silence settled over the hall, but still he waited, stretching out the anticipation. And then he began to speak. It was the first time that I was hearing him give a speech in English. He had a natural assurance and conviction, his words carrying us on a voyage through China's troubled history; he described how his country had fallen to its present state; and he ended his speech by setting out the vital role the Overseas Chinese had to play in restoring the glory of China, the motherland of every single Chinese man and woman all over the world.

'For the sake of our beloved China, for the sake of our motherland's very life, I appeal to all of you – no, I *beg* you: give as much as you can. Our comrades overseas, people like you here today' – Sun Wen's eyes seemed to blaze at the faces before him – 'they sacrifice their money. But our comrades in China, they sacrifice their lives.'

A round of respectful applause broke out again, but I wondered, as I discreetly wiped the tears from the corners of my eyes and looked around me, how much sympathy he had succeeded in rousing in the hearts of these people.

The servants were bringing out more wine and food, and the atmosphere livened up. They could easily pass as brothers, I thought as I observed Arthur introducing his friends to Sun Wen.

'How graceful you look, Lesley,' Sun Wen remarked when they eventually joined us. 'Everyone can't stop staring at you. Doesn't she look beautiful, Arthur?'

'You haven't visited us for a while,' I said, conscious of the warmth flushing my cheeks. 'I must apologise for what Robert said. I hope you don't bear us any ill will.'

'Of course not. You are both constantly in my thoughts, but there are hundreds of urgent matters that require my attention. Did I tell you that we are going to publish our own newspaper? No? It will be called *Kwong Wah Yit Poh* – the *Glorious China Daily*. And what is more' – a huge smile transformed his face – 'for the first time in twenty years, my family are together again.'

'I'm over the moon for you, Sun Wen,' I said.

His wife and two daughters had arrived in Penang a few days ago. The whole family, including Chui Fen, were living in the bungalow on Dato Kramat Road. Only his son, still in Honolulu, had been unable to complete the family reunion.

'A part of me wishes things would move faster, but another part wants to slow down time, even stop it completely, so we can stay together for longer.' He sighed. 'My daughters, they grow up so quickly.'

A thin, stylish woman elbowed her way into our little group. 'Stirring speech, Dr Sun,' she said, waving an ivory cigarette holder pinched between her fingers. 'Diana Chua, David Chua's wife. Tell me – what are your views on the Suffragettes? Will women in your new China be allowed to vote?'

'I have always believed that men and women are equal.' Sun Wen flicked a sardonic look at me, as if daring me to contradict him. 'And in our new China, our new republic, they *will* be.'

'You're certainly more enlightened than our dear Queen Victoria. Do you know what she said? Women's rights are a "wicked folly". Can you believe that?'

'Well, then, Diana,' said Arthur, 'you'd better make sure David gives generously to us.'

'My poor David would be horrified if the day comes when his wife is considered his equal. And so would I – we all know *I'm* the superior one, don't we, Arthur?'

'That's what you always tell us, Diana,' said Arthur.

An approaching thunderstorm provided Arthur's friends the excuse to take their leave. Most of them walked past the pledge table without even giving it a glance. Geoff had promised to meet his wife at the Penang Club. 'And the memsahib doesn't like to be kept waiting,' he said apologetically. Within a few minutes Sun Wen and I were the only ones left. The servants began clearing up, so we moved into the sitting room – the European one, I gathered from the style in which it was decorated. I could hear Arthur chaffing his guests as he saw them out.

'A waste of time, coming here,' said Sun Wen.

'Oh, don't say that. You convinced many people today.'

'The situation in China is worsening every day, and I'm stuck here, begging for crumbs from these rich, spoilt people.' He paced restlessly around the sitting room. 'These people – they feel nothing for China, for her pain. All they care about is England, bloody England.'

'At least your family's with you again,' I said, trying to lighten his black mood.

He picked up a book from a side table, then set it down again. 'I have a favour to ask, Lesley.'

One thing I had learned about Sun Wen: he was never shy when he wanted something. 'You know I'm more than happy to help in any way I can.'

'I wish to enrol my daughters in a school here, the best one.'

'Well, you really can't do any better than Convent Light Street,' I said. 'I'm an old girl, and I used to teach there.'

'Will you put in a word with someone?'

'I'll speak to the headmistress – Sister Mathilda will want to know for how long they'll be enrolled.'

'I want them to complete their schooling here.'

'But what happens when you return to China? You're leaving your daughters here?'

'The government is on its last legs. One powerful, concerted push, and it'll come crashing down,' he said. 'But a dying animal will use every ounce of its remaining strength to fight, to fend off the killing blow. It will be at its most desperate. My life is in greater danger than ever, but I know my daughters will be safe in Penang. We have friends here – dear friends, like you and Robert.'

Arthur came into the sitting room. 'That's the last of them. Anyone for another drink?'

'Did you speak to your father?' Sun Wen asked.

'He's still perched firmly on the fence, I'm afraid.'

'Tell him we will grant him exclusive rubber import rights for three years if he gives us sixty thousand dollars.'

Over the past few weeks I had begun to realise that Sun Wen viewed the Overseas Chinese largely as a source of money to be milked. I tried not to judge him, but his mercenary attitude made me uncomfortable.

'I must go,' Sun Wen said. 'No need to see me out, Arthur.' He gave a short bow to me and left.

I went over to the bookshelves. I had always enjoyed the mild voyeuristic thrill of seeing what other people read.

'Quite an impressive collection of Somerset Maughams you've got here.' I pointed to a row of books on one of the shelves. 'As good as Robert's.'

'Everything he's written. When I was studying in London I would go to all his plays. I remember one season he had four plays running in the West End at the same time. Four different plays. No one had ever achieved that before.'

'He's an old friend of Robert's.'

'You've met him?'

'He wasn't in London when we were there.'

Arthur ran his fingers across the spines of the books. 'Which one's your favourite? *Mrs Craddock*? Or *The Merry-Go-Round*?'

'I've gone off him, actually.'

'Sun Wen was right, you know.' His voice was soft, but I could hear it clearly. 'Everyone here couldn't keep their eyes off you.'

My body felt very light, almost weightless, as I turned towards him. In the silence we looked at each other, each waiting for the other to speak, to move.

'The House of Doors,' I said softly.

★ ★ ★

We took separate rickshaws. The streets were deserted, the wind roiling up the fallen leaves, driving grit into my eyes. In the low, black clouds thunder prowled like a ravenous god. Many of the shophouses across town were already shuttered against the storm.

Having left first, I arrived before him. I inserted the key he had given me into the lock – I had to jiggle it a few times before it turned – and slipped inside, shutting the doors behind me. Faint spores of dust drifted around in the pallid light. In the dining hall the doors creaked discreetly as they turned in the air. The guzheng was still resting on its stand. I plucked at a string, flexing a solitary note – an E – into the stillness. I plucked it again and again; the notes sounded harsh. I stopped abruptly, clenching my hands. This is wrong. I should not have come here. I must leave this place, now, immediately.

But I did not move; I stayed there, watching the doors spinning above the tiles. The sky ripped open and the storm roared down into the air-well, the deluge so heavy, so mighty that I could have been standing at the foot of a cataract, its spray misting my arms and face.

I saw Arthur come into the dining hall. He slipped his way between the floating doors to me, appearing and disappearing as they opened and closed. And then he was before me, his hair dripping, rain plastering his shirt to his body. We did not speak, did not murmur even a word – we would not have heard each other above the storm anyway. I watched his hand rise from his side and reach past my face. I felt the heat of his palm as it curved over the nape of my neck. He drew me towards him and kissed me on my lips.

Time stopped. Eventually I opened my eyes and pulled away from him. I was conscious only of my heart's stuttering rhythm, and the hard, rapid pounding of my breath. I ran my tongue over my lips; they had a flavour there I had never tasted before, a flavour so different from Robert's. Then I realised that I could not remember what Robert's mouth tasted like any more; I had forgotten it years ago.

I followed him up the spiral staircase, into a room lit only by thin slits of light cutting through the window shutters. In the centre of the room stood a double bed, the brass bedframe stark as the bones of a shipwreck that had come to rest on the ocean floor. In the watery half-light we undressed and reached for each other.

I opened my eyes, disoriented by the absence of sound. The rain had stopped a while ago, and the shadows in the corners of the room had thickened. My eyes were closing again when a sudden panic jolted me – I had been away from home all afternoon.

I got out of bed and hurriedly began to dress. My fingers fumbled with the kerongsang, dropping them. I cried out in frustration. Arthur placed his hands on mine, picked up the brooches from the floorboards and with a few deft movements pinned them on my kebaya lapels.

At the front doors I held out the key to him, the long thin key I had used to enter the house. He glanced at it, then looked at me. I opened my purse and dropped the key into it.

People were already emerging from their houses, families taking their evening stroll in the street, enjoying the cool, crisp air. I hesitated on the goh kaki, weighed down by a reluctance to leave. The world still looked the same, yet the pattern of its weave seemed different now. A lifetime had slipped past since I stepped into the house. Everything had changed, and it could never be undone.

I set off down Armenian Street. Passing a photographer's studio on the corner of Victoria Road, I stopped to study the wedding portraits of the Straits Chinese couples in the window – the Nyonya ladies regal in their kebayas and the Baba men solemn in their Western suits. I pushed open the door and went inside. The Chinese man behind the counter looked up from his newspaper, his bored expression not changing the slightest as he took in my appearance.

He posed me in front of a dressing table with three adjustable mirrored panels to show off the jewelled hairpins worn by the Nyonya women. He motioned to me to sit in the bentwood armchair in front of the dressing table, but I chose to stand beside it. I waited while he developed the plate. When it was ready he put the print and the film into an envelope and gave it to me.

The lights of the shophouses had already come on when I left. Hawkers were firing up their charcoal stoves and setting out tables and stools on the pavements. A night market was springing to life, men and women chaffing one another with coarse jokes and insults as they set up their stalls. I flagged down a rickshaw and told the puller to take me home.

In spite of my newfound knowledge about my husband, I surprised myself by greeting him calmly when he returned from KL, even pressing my customary kiss on his cheek when he stepped into the house.

'Did you win?' I motioned to the houseboy to take his bag upstairs.

'Of course. Trounced Harrison soundly. He was livid, absolutely livid. His client didn't look pleased with him either.' He glanced around him. 'Where are the little rascals? Let's take them for a swim, shall we?'

We played in the shallows until dusk fell. Robert grinned at me whenever he made our sons squeal with delighted terror, and I couldn't help but think back to the earliest days of our marriage. They felt like another lifetime ago.

If Robert detected any change in me, he made no mention of it, not even obliquely. I felt . . . irradiated . . . by my afternoon with Arthur, as though I had fallen asleep in the sun too long, and I was certain it was visible to everyone around me. I was an adulteress now.

II

Two mornings a week I would go to the reading club. It was purgatory, sitting at the long table in the dining hall with the others and feigning interest in my work, when I was burning to be in bed with Arthur. Around mid morning I would leave the reading club and stroll down the street to the House of Doors, trying not to give anyone watching the impression that I was in a mad rush to get there. Arthur and I never arrived together and, except for our mornings at the reading club, I was inflexible that we were never to be seen together in public.

'No letters or written messages, no little notes that might fall into the wrong hands,' I warned him. 'No one must ever find out about us.'

'You're being unduly cautious, aren't you? What if something happened and I couldn't meet you?'

'I will wait here for you. If you can't come, I'll know something's keeping you. I won't be upset.' I remembered the note I had found in Robert's pocket. 'No letters, Arthur.'

At the birthday dinner of one of our friends I glimpsed a face in the crowd I did not expect to see. I nudged Robert. 'Isn't that Wagner over there?'

It was less than a week before Ethel's trial; I would have expected her lawyer to be busy preparing for it in KL instead of attending parties at the Penang Club.

Wagner waved and squeezed his way over to us. 'Hullo, Robert, looking well,' he boomed. 'Wonderful party, what?'

'What are you doing here?' I asked.

'I got here yesterday,' he explained. 'I had a full day of meetings today. I'm heading back to KL first thing in the morning. Just the person I wanted to see, Lesley. You'll be attending Ethel's trial, I presume?'

The canny gleam in his eye made me tread warily. 'She needs the support of all her friends,' I said.

He slapped his palms together. 'Excellent. In which case you'd have no objection if I were to call you as a witness?'

'You want me to testify?' My mouth went dry. 'What . . . what about?'

'Well, what she was wearing that night, for one thing. You know – the fact that it's not at all out of the ordinary that she should be in her fancy tea gown when Steward showed up. I really must thank you again for bringing it to my attention.' Glancing quickly around the room, he dropped his voice. 'The thing is, well, you being her closest friend, I'd like you to testify as to her character too. You could help us scotch the rumours flying around – you know, about her and Steward . . .'

My immediate instinct was to refuse. 'You've discussed this with Ethel?'

'She's very stubborn. She's adamant that we mustn't bother you. Quite adamant.' He shook his head in wonder. 'With all the problems she's facing, she feels it'd be highly inconsiderate to trouble you. I told her you'd be coming for the trial anyway.' He looked hard at me 'It won't harm her prospects at all to have a woman on the stand testifying in her defence. In fact, I am of the opinion that it would strengthen her case considerably. Pooley thinks so too.'

'You've got James Pooley helping you defend Ethel?' asked Robert.

'William and Ethel wanted him.'

'Well, the odds of her getting off scot-free have improved tremendously' – Robert patted Wagner's shoulder – 'not that I ever doubted your abilities, old chap.'

'I haven't really made up my mind if I want to attend her trial.' I was conscious of Robert's eyes on me. 'Have you asked her other friends? Kathleen Simpson? Or Frances Reed?'

'Every one of them told me they won't do it. Look – we're all aware that Ethel's never really endeared herself to the other ladies in KL,' Wagner said. 'You're not just her closest friend, Lesley, you're her only friend now.'

The House of Doors was the first property Arthur's grandmother had bought in Penang. Born to a family of printers in a village in southern China, she had been conscripted into the Taiping rebels' army when they conquered her province. She was twelve years old. A year later, in the spring of 1853, the rebels took Nanking and established it as the capital of the Taiping Heavenly Kingdom, and she was assigned to work with a Scottish missionary in the city, helping him typeset and print the bibles that carried the Heavenly King's warped teachings of Christianity. She learned the technique of letterpress printing from the missionary, who also taught her to read and write English. When the Heavenly Kingdom fell to the emperor's forces in 1864, she fled China with the help of the missionary, who told her she would find a haven in Penang in the Southern Seas. Within a few years of arriving on the island she had saved up enough money to start her own business printing calendars and – something which I found ironic – bibles for the local missionaries – the King James Version, of course, and not the version of the Heavenly King. Over the years she acquired a string of shophouses and larger houses in more salubrious addresses, but she always kept that first shophouse in Armenian Street where she had started her printing business. When she died she had left it to her favourite grandson, with the stipulation that he was never to sell it.

The house was long and deep, its interior cool even on the most scorching of days. I liked its dark chengal-timber floorboards and the bright floral patterns of its encaustic floor tiles. A feeling of timelessness hovered within its four walls, as if the sun had slipped behind the moon and remained there, fixed in a permanent eclipse.

The House of Doors became my sanctuary. I went there even when I wasn't meeting Arthur, just to be by myself and, for a few hours at least, to forget everything outside its walls, forget that I had a husband, and yes, forget even that I was a mother with two young sons. Inside I could become a different woman, living a different life.

I brought little items to the house every time I went there – flowers and pot plants and books. We didn't always spend our time in bed; sometimes we would sit in the dining hall and drink tea and talk. We spoke about many things: our childhoods, the books we were reading, China, Ethel's trial, and always, Penang. From him I discovered so many stories about our home. He had a deep, intense love for the island, a love which I soon learned to share.

Sometimes he would play the guzheng for me. I enjoyed watching the way his hands skated over the strings, his fingers plucking and pressing down on them, summoning up mournful songs from dynasties long crumbled to dust. The notes shimmering from the strings sounded like condensed drops of tears; they echoed in the air, distilling into the silence.

On one of our visits to the house he played a song I had never heard before, singing the lyrics – in French, to my surprise – in his clean, if unremarkable, tenor.

'What was that?' I asked when he finished.

'Reynaldo Hahn, *L'heure exquise*,' he replied. 'The words are from Verlaine's poem. He wrote it for his wife.' He translated the poem into English for me. The words had the chill glaze of moonlight on the surface of a frozen pond.

'He must have loved her very much,' I said.

'Perhaps he did – at least in the beginning.'

'What happened to them?'

'Just before she gave birth to their first child, he invited a young poet to stay with them. When the child was born, a son, Verlaine left her – and their new-born son – and travelled around Europe with the young poet. Rimbaud was his name. Arthur Rimbaud.'

It cut too close to home, this tale. Nevertheless, there was a stark beauty flowing through the song, an icicle purity, and I often asked him to play it for me.

In addition to collecting doors, Arthur was also a tea connoisseur. On one of my visits to the House of Doors he came out of the kitchen with a tray of tea. He said nothing, but from his bearing and expression I knew that it was something special. He filled two tiny Straits Chinese porcelain teacups with the thin, almost translucent liquid, picked up one cup with both hands and set it down on the table before me.

I brought the cup to my nose. 'It smells' – I tried to put my impressions into words – 'it smells of the first drops of rain falling on the lawn on a scorching day.' I took a sip and closed my eyes, letting the tea pool on my tongue for a moment, as he had taught me. 'It has a melancholic taste.' I looked at him, taken aback. 'How strange – that a tea can taste of loss.'

'"The Fragrance of the Lonely Tree",' he said. 'I bought it from a tea merchant in Tokyo a few years ago.'

It was raining, thin sparkling cords of water running off the eaves, flooding the air-well.

'All you need is a few carp swimming in it and it could be a pond,' I said. 'You should have the drains looked at, they're probably blocked.'

He gave me an indulgent smile. 'They're not blocked. The air-well is designed to swirl the water in a clockwise flow before it runs out of the house.'

'Whatever for?'

'To retain wealth and good fortune inside the house, of course.'

Whenever he uttered something like that, or whenever I watched him in a heated discussion with the others at the reading club, a sudden realisation would strike me: But . . . he's Chinese. And then a second later the shock would fade away, and he would be just Arthur again, just a man I knew.

Later, lazing in bed after we had finished making love, I asked him to tell me his Chinese name. He told me, and added, 'It means "To Engrave a Record of Aspiration".'

I repeated his name a few times, trying to get the tones right. Knowing the meaning of his name made me see him in a slightly altered way, as though I had been given a glimpse of him that was only visible to those who were literate in Chinese.

A moth flaked down from the rafters and settled on the sheets. I reached out to brush it away, but Arthur stayed my hand.

'Don't harm it,' he said. 'They're the souls of the people we once loved, come to visit us, to watch over us.'

That disconcerting lurch again, even after I thought I had become used to him. 'Who told you that?'

'My grandmother. The one who left me this house.'

'So it could even be Grandma watching us now?' I gave a cheeky little wave to the moth. 'Ah Mah,' I said in Hokkien, 'I hope you averted your eyes earlier.'

He laughed nervously. 'Don't be disrespectful to my Ah Mah.'

The question that had been lurking in the depths of my mind broke the surface. 'Am I the first angmoh woman you've ever slept with?'

He stared into the rafters, stroking my hand in a slow, distracted way. 'There was a girl in London . . . when I was doing my internship.'

'Were you two in love?'

'We liked each other very much, but no, we weren't in love. She married an Anglican minister in Colchester.' He kissed my hand. 'I went past Cassowary House yesterday afternoon. I stood outside your gates, looking at it.'

I pulled my hand away. I felt I was swimming in the warm sea and had entered a patch of icy current. If I had parted the curtains in the sitting room and looked out at just the right moment, I would have seen him standing at the end of my driveway, and the two worlds I had been determinedly keeping apart would have intruded into each other.

'You shouldn't have done that.'

'I just wanted to see where you live.' He was taken aback by my anger. 'I want to picture you going about your days.'

'I don't ever think of you in your home, Arthur; I don't think of you with your wife and your daughter,' I said. 'I think of you here, only here. If you want to picture me, then picture me here, in this house, our house.'

He sat up against the headboard and looked at me. 'Why are you here, Lesley?'

What could I tell him? Eventually I settled on the truth – a partial version of it, at least. 'Robert stopped sleeping with me years ago.'

'It happens in a lot of marriages.'

'Yours too?'

'My wife doesn't enjoy it. She's never said so, but, well . . .'

'Perhaps she just doesn't enjoy it with you,' I said. 'Perhaps she has a lover too.'

'Don't be ridiculous.'

'Ridiculous? If you can seek gratification elsewhere, why can't she? You and Sun Wen,' I said, 'forever pontificating about fairness and equality, but when it comes to your own wives . . .'

'It's not the same.'

Arguing about it with him – or with any man, for that matter – would be as fruitful as trying to push back the wind. 'I accepted Robert's lack of interest.' My mind groped for the right words. 'I . . . *accustomed* myself to it.' I had never spoken to anyone about the rot in my marriage before, and the words I wanted to use were rusted from lack of use. 'I told myself that he's much older than me, he probably doesn't need . . . intimacy . . . any more. But I like it, I enjoy it.'

'All these years you've never considered sleeping with someone else? Never thought about having an affair?'

'Now you're the one who's being ridiculous.'

'What changed your mind? I know I'm charming and devastatingly handsome, but still . . .'

'Do you remember that evening at the E&O when you brought Sun Wen to meet Robert?'

'The very first time I met you. How could I forget?'

'Well, just that very morning I found out that my husband had been unfaithful.'

The smile was blotted from his face. 'So this' – he swept his hand over our bodies, over the bed – 'all this is just to get back at him?'

If only I could tell him it was much more than that. Once I had discovered that Robert preferred men in his bed, I understood that nothing I did would bring him back to me, to the intimacy I craved.

'Who's he sleeping with?' Arthur went on when I didn't reply. 'One of your best friends? Some pretty young lady from a committee you're on?'

I weighed up what I could say, how much I was willing to reveal. 'It doesn't matter who she is,' I said in the end. By sleeping with Arthur I had betrayed my husband, but I would not betray his secret; I would not shame him.

'You still love him,' said Arthur.

Wings clapping soundlessly, the moth floated back into the shadows of the rafters.

'Every marriage has its own rules,' I said.

Voices drifted up from the street below, only to lose themselves in the canyons of silence between us. Attempting to lighten the mood, I said, 'I've always wondered why it's called Cassowary House.'

He brushed his foot slowly down the side of my leg. He had narrow, well-formed feet. 'It's because of your casuarina tree,' he said. 'The Malay name for them is "kasuari".'

'Why?'

'Because they say their leaves resemble the cassowary bird's feathers.'

'It's an ugly tree, isn't it?'

'No tree is ugly, Lesley. Each and every tree has its own charms, its own kind of beauty.' He remembered something. 'The Malays also call them "whispering trees".'

'I've never heard that before.'

'They say that if you stand under a casuarina during a full moon, you can hear its leaves whispering to you, whispering all the things you want to know about your future.'

'The whispering tree,' I murmured. How strange, that with just a few words something which I had always found unattractive was now transformed into a thing of beauty.

'I've just finished a missionary's account of his experiences in the Taiping Rebellion,' he said. 'It's horrific, but utterly engrossing. I'll bring it next time.'

'I can't see you next week,' I said. 'I'm going to KL for Ethel's trial.'

'I'll come with you.'

'You'll stick out like a sore thumb at the Empire.'

'There *are* other hotels in KL, you know.'

'Oh, for God's sake, Arthur.'

Couldn't he understand that it was too risky for us to be seen together? Sooner or later someone *would* find out about us. I lived in fear of it. I took care to dress plainly and conceal my face beneath a bonnet or a wide-brimmed hat whenever I was in Armenian Street, but I was a European woman, and even though the people here were used to the sight of me by now, I still stood out. The most sensible thing to do was to end my affair with Arthur, but I didn't want to do it. I couldn't.

'Ethel's lawyer has summoned me to be a witness,' I said. 'The prosecutor will probably cross-examine me as well, and there are certain things concerning Ethel I don't want to be interrogated about.'

'She was sleeping with him, wasn't she?'

'Since December last year.'

'Now it all starts to make sense.'

'She had ended it last month, but he couldn't get it into his head that it was over. That evening she shot him – he had gone to see her, to change her mind.'

'But she wouldn't budge.' He assembled the pieces in his head. 'He got angry and tried to rape her. So she shot him.'

'That's what she told me.' I recalled the various scenarios Robert had laid out a few weeks ago. Would the truth, the real truth, ever emerge? 'I begged her to tell her lawyer, but she wouldn't even consider it.'

'It would certainly make her defence more believable. The judge would be more sympathetic to her plight.' Realisation turned its wick up in his eyes. 'Ah, of course. Her affair with Steward is just gossip now, but if she told her lawyer, and if he used that in court . . .'

'She'd be tarred and feathered as an adulteress, whatever the verdict.'

'Well, don't go to KL,' said Arthur. 'It won't matter in the end, you know. I told you: even if they find her guilty, they'd never hang her.'

If only things were so simple. 'Robert would find it suspicious if I didn't go. I've been so supportive of Ethel right from the start. That bloody tea gown – I wish I'd kept my mouth shut about it.'

'There's more to the episode than meets the eye,' said Arthur. 'It'll make for a gripping story.'

'Nobody will give two hoots about the trial – or Ethel – once it's over,' I said. 'By the end of the year they would have forgotten about her. She could return to her old, normal life. And that's how it should be.'

Chapter Fourteen

Willie
Penang, 1921

Robert felt poorly after dinner, but he refused to let Lesley summon Dr Joyce. Willie helped him upstairs to his room and made him comfortable in his bed, propping him up against his pillows. He gave Robert his sleeping tablet and a glass of water.

'I'll be fine after a good night's sleep,' said Robert, his breathing laboured. 'I'm organising a trip for us to go up Penang Hill one of these mornings. We used to take a bungalow up there during the hot months. Lesley and our boys loved it.'

'She's been telling . . . me about Ethel Proudlock,' Willie said from the armchair at the foot of the bed.

Robert looked blankly at him for two or three seconds. 'Oh, not *that* tawdry business. Nobody wants all that muck raked up again.' His breathing had eased. 'Ethel Proudlock,' he murmured. 'Haven't heard that name in years . . . The way they treated her . . . her husband and her own father, what they did to her . . . they should've been hanged . . . and we should have said something . . .'

Willie was suddenly alert, paying close attention. 'What are you talking about, Robert?' He got up and went over to the bedside. 'Robert? What did they do to Ethel?'

But Robert had closed his eyes and was snoring contentedly away. Willie watched him for a few moments, then gently removed his spectacles from his face and placed them on the nightstand. He backed out of the room quietly and closed the door. He left the light on for his friend.

Going downstairs to join Lesley on the verandah, his mind continued to puzzle over Robert's words. What the devil did he mean? He fixed himself a whisky and sat across from Lesley.

'He's nodded off,' said Willie. He told her what Robert had said about Ethel Proudlock. 'Do you know what he meant?'

'I haven't a clue.' She contemplated the ceiling. 'Ethel didn't get on with her father, but I never heard her say anything bad about him. And William, well, he adored Ethel. He would never have done anything to hurt her.'

The night was hot and humid, shrill with cicadas. Somewhere a dog howled once, then fell silent.

'Gerald's gone into town,' said Lesley.

'I'd be more surprised if he had not.'

'It doesn't upset you?'

He heard the real question beneath the one she was asking. 'He's young and full of beans.' He shrugged. 'Whoever he meets out there, whatever he does, he'll always . . . come home to me in the morning. Usually the worse for wear, but he'll . . . come home.'

'And what if, one day, he decides not to come home?'

He peered into his glass as though he was staring into a deep, bottomless well. He said nothing.

'Did you know Robert's homosexual?' asked Lesley.

Slowly he looked up from his glass. 'He never gave me any . . . indication.'

'Oh, come on, Willie, you two shared rooms for, what, eight, nine months? And he must've known about *you*, surely.'

'It was never . . . mentioned between us,' he said. 'Not even . . . obliquely.'

'How does your wife feel about you and Gerald?

It was really none of her business, and he had no intention of discussing it with her. The affronted expression on his face did not deter her, however. 'Does she have affairs?'

'I've never cared to ask.'

'But the thought occasionally crawls into your mind, doesn't it? Oh, don't look so sanctimonious.' Anger flared up in her. 'You know what? I hope she *does* sleep with other men, men who can give her *some* pleasure, make her feel she's desirable and desired. Make her feel like a *normal* woman. It's the least she deserves, don't you think?'

Willie rose to his feet with a rigid dignity. 'Goodnight, Lesley,' he said coldly, and went inside the house.

She came upon him in the library when she was going through the house locking the doors and putting out the lights. He was on his favourite leather sofa, a book open on his lap. They looked at each other, and then she walked across the silence between them to stand before him.

Willie closed his book, shifted to one side and indicated the space next to him. She sat down, adjusting her skirt over her knees. He caught a faint trace of her perfume, mingled with the smell of her. It was a familiar smell to him by now, and it was not unpleasant.

'You're the only one I've ever spoken to about this . . . this matter, Willie.' Her voice sounded strained; there was no trace left of her earlier anger. 'You're the only one to whom I *can* speak about it. For ten years now I've said nothing to anyone about Robert's . . . preference. It hasn't been easy keeping it to myself. It hasn't been easy at all.'

'Syrie has never met Gerald,' said Willie. 'But she has made sure he's not allowed to step foot into England again, ever.'

'What did she do?'

'Gerald was deported from England two years ago. "Undesirable alien." My darling wife,' he said acidly, 'does not lack friends in lofty perches – her father's Thomas . . . Barnardo, and she used to be married to Henry Wellcome. I have not the slightest doubt she called in some favours, dripped her poison into a . . . few powerful ears.'

'Why do you homosexuals do it?' She seemed resigned, shrunken. 'Why do you marry us when you'd sooner hop into bed with a man?'

Willie's reply, when it came, was silted with the sorrow of the world. 'What other choice do we have?'

'No one would think it the tiniest bit out of the ordinary at all if men like you remained bachelors all your life.'

'After what happened to poor . . . Oscar Wilde?' He shook his head. 'The world has turned against us, Lesley. You don't know what it's like to live in fear all . . . the time, knowing that at any moment you could be exposed, your entire . . . life destroyed. By marrying Robert, you have given him a haven. You have kept him safe from speculation and gossip. But most of all, safe from . . . being locked up in gaol.'

'We're wives, Willie,' said Lesley. 'Not martyrs.'

He had no reply to that, and so he said, 'Tell me what happened to Ethel.'

Chapter Fifteen

Lesley
Penang, 1910

I

Every seat in the courtroom was taken on the opening day of Ethel's trial, but Wagner had instructed the clerk of the court to reserve one for me in the front row, next to William Proudlock. He gave me a careworn smile before turning to speak to Ethel's father on his other side. Wagner had given me an outline of what he intended to ask me, but I was still tight with nerves. I wished the whole deuced trial was all already over and done with.

To refresh my memory of the inquest, I had studied my journal again on the train going down to KL. Almost two months had passed since Ethel was locked up in Pudoh Gaol, but it felt much longer. In those weeks my own life had changed so drastically.

A few minutes before nine o'clock Ethel was brought up from a holding cell somewhere in the building. I was appalled by how much weight she had lost, how small she seemed, seated inside the dock. She caught sight of me and her face hardened.

The counsels sitting at their tables — for the Prosecution and for the Defence — were bewigged, collared and bibbed, and robed in black. I studied James Pooley. Robert and I had met him before on a few occasions. A tall, handsome man in his fifties, he was one of the most senior lawyers in Malaya, and I was glad for Ethel's sake that he was defending her.

On the stroke of half past nine the door behind the judge's dais was opened. The clerk of the court appeared and summoned us to our feet. 'God save the King!' he called out.

Mr Justice Sercombe Smith entered, his round, florid face oddly feminine beneath his white wig, his crimson robe endowing him with an episcopal plumpness. He was followed by a pair of European assessors. The two men were in their mid fifties. I recognised one of them – Kindersley – but not the other one. Jury trials had been abolished some years ago, and the task of these two men was to assist the judge in weighing the evidence.

The counsels bowed three times to the judge, who returned their bows, and then there was the sound of rustlings as we all took our seats.

The prosecutor, Hastings Rhodes, opened the trial by calling William Proudlock to the witness stand. He placed his palm on the bible held up by the clerk and took the oath.

'When was the last time you saw the deceased before he was shot dead by your wife?'

His choice of words was, I knew, deliberately provocative, but William Proudlock remained unruffled; only a slight narrowing of the eyes betrayed his anger.

'It was on the day before he went to our house and attacked Ethel. Saturday evening.' From the way William spoke, one could see that he was a firm but reasonable schoolmaster, one that was undoubtedly much liked by his pupils. 'We saw him at the Spotted Dog – the Selangor Club, I mean. He was in the library reading a newspaper.'

'Did the accused speak to him?'

My eyes darted from William to Ethel; she was completely still, her entire attention focused on her husband.

'He called out to us,' William Proudlock replied, taking his time, 'and we chatted with him for a bit. Ethel mentioned that we had not seen him in a while, and that we had moved into Bennett's bungalow.'

'That was all you spoke about?'

'Yes . . . I think so. It wasn't a long conversation.'

'Had the deceased ever been to your house?'

'Not our new house, but he'd popped by our old house in Brickfields Road on one or two occasions.'

'I would like to draw your mind back to the 23rd of April, a Sunday,' said Rhodes. 'What did you and the accused do that afternoon?'

'We had our tea around four o'clock,' William said, 'then we spent some time in our compound practising our shooting. It was about twenty past five when I looked at my watch and realised we had to get ready for church. I gave the revolver to Ethel and told her to put it away while I went to wash up and change. We then walked to St Mary's.'

'You normally keep the gun on the verandah?'

'Of course not.' A note of irritation sharpened William's voice. 'I always lock it away in the pigeonhole of my desk in my bedroom.'

'But it was left on the verandah that evening. Why?'

'I don't know. You'll have to ask my wife. We were rushing to church, I suppose she didn't have time to lock it in my desk.'

'Did you unload the revolver before you gave it to the accused?' asked Rhodes.

William Proudlock shook his head. 'I already told you – I didn't want to be late for Evensong – it was my duty to put out the hymn books, you see. As it was, we got to St Mary's at a quarter to six, which gave me just enough time.'

'The Webley which the accused used to shoot Mr William Steward,' said the prosecutor, 'to whom did it belong?'

The slightest narrowing of the eyes again. 'It's mine. Ethel bought it for my birthday this year.'

'When was this?'

'My birthday's the 18th of April.'

'Five days before the shooting . . .' Rhodes scribbled on his writing pad. 'Where did she buy it?'

'At the Federal Dispensary in High Street.'

'Isn't it rather out of the ordinary – a wife giving her husband a gun for his birthday present?'

'I told her to get it, actually. She asked me what I wanted for my birthday. We were burgled in our home last year – our previous home, I mean, the one in Brickfields Road. When we moved into Bennett's bungalow I felt we'd be safer if we had a gun.'

'When did you move into your present home?'

'Sometime in early February this year. I can't give you the exact date.'

'February. Four months ago, yet you only felt you needed to have a gun in your house in the last few weeks before the accused shot the deceased?'

'Well . . . We had been so busy after moving in that we didn't think of getting a gun.'

'Where did you go after the service was over?'

'We walked home,' William said. 'We changed and I went out to dinner at my friend Goodman Ambler's house. Ethel dined alone at home.'

'The accused also changed her clothes?'

'Yes.'

'Is this the tea gown the accused wore that evening? The tea gown marked as Exhibit B?' Rhodes asked, indicating to the clerk to hold up the gown.

'Yes, it is.'

The clerk presented the gown to the judge and the assessors. We all leaned forward to get a better view of it. The tea gown was chiffon, light green and decorated with a narrow band of paler green floral pattern down its front. It was sleeveless, with a low, round neckline. Even though it had been torn in a few places and its hem was crusted with dried mud, it was still obvious to the eye that it was once an elegant and alluring dress.

'Your dinner with Mr Goodman Ambler,' Rhodes said, 'when was that arrangement made?'

'Saturday – the previous evening,' replied William. 'After we spoke to William Steward at the Spotted Dog's library, we took a walk to Goodman's house – he's staying at our old home in Brickfields Road. He invited me to dine with him the following night.'

'Only you?' Rhodes glanced at Ethel, then back to William. 'Was the accused not invited also?'

William rubbed his palm over the nape his neck. 'Well . . . I don't know why.' For the first time since stepping into the witness box he looked flustered, uncertain. 'Ethel was waiting outside the house when I went inside to speak to Goodman. I . . . I suppose . . . the subject had all been forgotten when she came in.'

A sceptical grunt escaped from the back of Rhodes's throat. 'Do you often dine with friends on your own?'

William Proudlock scratched his cheek ruminatively. 'I've only done it three times this year.'

'You went to dine at Mr Goodman Ambler's house, leaving the accused alone at home,' said Rhodes. 'What happened afterwards?'

Dinner had gone on until about ten past nine, William Proudlock replied. He was playing the piano in the sitting room when his cook arrived at Ambler's house with an urgent message from Ethel, asking him to hurry home. William and Ambler caught a rickshaw in the rain, entering the school grounds by the High Street entrance.

'I saw her as we were coming to the bungalow. She was staggering down the road, heading towards us,' said William Proudlock. 'I ran to her. "Blood . . . blood . . ." They were the first words she said to me, and she repeated them a few times. Then she said, "Oh, Will, I have shot a man." "Who?" I asked her, and she said, "I have shot Mr Steward."'

William caught her as she collapsed. He and Ambler carried her up onto the verandah and laid her down on the settee.

'She was babbling and sobbing,' said William Proudlock. 'I tried to get her to tell me what had happened. "I have shot a man," she said again. "I have shot a man."'

William brushed back a lock of hair from his forehead. 'I asked her, "Where is the man?"' and she said, "I don't know. He ran. He ran." She pointed vaguely beyond the verandah railing. I couldn't see anything – it was dark, and it was still drizzling. I went down into the garden and looked around. I came upon the body lying on the grass just beyond the bamboo hedge.'

'How was he lying on the grass?'

'On his chest, his feet pointing towards the house, the left side of his face turned to the sky. I recognised him the moment I saw him. It was William Steward. He was dead.'

Leaving his wife under Ambler's watchful eye, William had gone to look for Inspector Wyatt at his home. Dr Edward McIntyre, the Senior Assistant Surgeon at the KL General Hospital, was also summoned to the Proudlock bungalow. The three of them went together to look at the body on the lawn. Returning to the verandah, Dr McIntyre asked Ethel to stand up so he could examine her arms and hands and face for wounds or marks.

'Can you describe what she looked like at that stage?' Rhodes asked William.

'Her dress was torn at the knee.' William asked the clerk to hold up the tea gown again and pointed to the position of the tear. 'Her hair was in a mess, dishevelled. After everyone had finally left, I gave her another glass of sherry to calm her nerves. And then I asked her to tell me again what had happened.'

He placed his hands on the railing of the witness stand, corralling his thoughts. The courtroom waited, completely still.

'Please go on, Mr Proudlock,' said Mr Justice Smith.

'She told me that after dinner she had been writing letters on the verandah when William Steward turned up. He said he was looking for me. She told him I was at Goodman's house and that he ought to go there, but Steward didn't leave. Ethel was keen to get back to her correspondence, but felt it rude not to invite him in. They sat on the verandah and talked. She mentioned a book she was reading and got up to show it to him. Steward stood up and grabbed her as she went past him. He embraced her and started kissing her. He said he loved her. "Let me have you," he told her, and . . . and he shoved his hand up under her gown and he . . . he fondled her . . . and started kissing her again.'

Ethel, I noticed, was staring at a point somewhere distant inside her thoughts.

William Proudlock breathed out heavily. 'Steward put out the light,' he said. 'Ethel broke away from him and reached behind her into the nook to switch on the light again. She shouted for the cook, she was in great terror. That's when her fingers curled over the revolver. She grabbed it and pointed it at Steward. She remembered firing once, perhaps twice, and nothing more after that.' William paused again, pressing his knuckles onto his lips. 'She must have blacked out. When she came to, she found herself on the verandah. She went around to the side of the house to call for the cook to fetch me. She said she remembered pacing back and forth anxiously, waiting for me to come home. Suddenly she noticed that she was holding the gun, that her hands were smeared with blood. She dropped the revolver onto the ground.'

'On that particular night, the 23rd of April, when you left the accused alone at home,' said Rhodes, 'was she expecting any visitors?'

'No. She told me she was going to answer some letters after dinner.'

'Yet she was dressed in the tea gown marked as Exhibit B. She was dressed as though she was expecting to receive a caller. In a tea gown with a rather . . . revealing . . . décolletage.'

'You're painting the completely wrong picture,' William Proudlock said, his face flushing. 'It's not uncommon for Ethel to change into a tea gown in the evening, even if we're not expecting anyone. She says it makes her feel cooler. My wife loves dressing up. All her friends know that.' He glanced at me. 'Why, she'd wear a tea gown even if she's dining alone at home. It's a very common thing, very common,' he emphasised.

Mr Justice Smith interrupted them, coins of light winking off his spectacles as he looked at William. 'When you and the accused came back from church, how did you enter your house?'

'We went in by the verandah, as we normally do.'

'Did you notice the revolver lying in the nook?'

William shook his head. 'I did not.'

The judge indicated to Rhodes that he should continue his questioning.

'Mr Proudlock,' said Rhodes, 'are you and your wife on good terms?'

Surprise flashed across William's face, replaced almost instantly by indignation. 'Of course we're on good terms. She's the most wonderful wife, attentive and affectionate.'

'Have you ever had any reason to be unhappy with your wife's moral conduct?'

William Proudlock turned towards Ethel. Husband and wife looked at each other across the courtroom.

'Never,' he said, his eyes still on his wife.

Ethel was straight-backed, her expression placid as she gazed at her husband.

Rhodes indicated to the judge that he had finished his examination-in-chief.

'Mr Pooley, you may cross-examine the witness,' said the judge.

Ethel's counsel asked a few questions to establish the Proudlocks' marital history. 'How is your wife's health?'

'It isn't the best, unfortunately,' replied William Proudlock. 'She suffers from leucorrhoea, you see.'

'Would you explain to the court what that is?'

'Well, at certain times of the month she would experience . . . discharge from her . . . womanly parts.' William's face flushed; he dropped his fidgeting hands out of sight. 'It always caused her great agony. She would take to bed all day. Her nerves would be frayed, she'd cry at the slightest thing. She'd get angry with me for no reason at all.'

I was mortified for Ethel that her most intimate details were being exposed in public, but she appeared oblivious to her husband's words. It was as though he was talking about someone she had not even the slightest interest in.

'How well did you know the deceased?' enquired Pooley.

'Reasonably, I suppose. We'd known him for about two years. We saw him sometimes at the Selangor Club, and he'd been to our musical at-homes at our old house in Brickfields Road a few times.'

'When was the last time you and your wife spoke to him?'

'We saw him on Saturday evening, the evening before he was . . . before he turned up at our house. We had gone to the club to listen to the band. We spoke to Steward in the library. Ethel told him that he had not been to see us since we moved to our new house. He said he would drop in one evening.' William paused, replaying the conversation in his mind. 'She told him not to come after nine, because we usually retire early. And then we had gone home because the band wasn't playing that night.'

'You told the court earlier that you've only dined out three times this year.'

'That's correct. I rarely dine out. My wife is a very nervous woman, she's easily frightened. She doesn't like being on her own at night.'

Pooley finished with William, but he was asked to remain in the witness box for re-examination by Rhodes.

'You were in Hong Kong in December last year, am I correct?' Rhodes asked.

William hesitated for just a second. 'That's correct. Before Christmas.'

'How long were you there for?'

'A month.'

'Did you leave the accused on her own for the whole period of time you were in Hong Kong?'

'No. I asked my friend Hugh Markes to call at the house every night to make sure that she was fine,' William said. 'Ethel adores Hugh – he was the best man at our wedding.'

Ethel angled her face slightly, watching me from the corner of her eye. I knew we were both thinking of that morning when she told me that she had gone out for drives with Steward when her husband was away in Hong Kong, and how she had spent nights at Steward's house in Salak South.

Rhodes next called Goodman Ambler to the stand. His version of the evening's events did not diverge significantly from William Proudlock's, although his recollection added more details to the picture William Proudlock had painted. There were spots of blood on Ethel's face, arms and chest, Ambler informed Rhodes. Her dress was ripped in three or four places, and the strap had slipped off her right shoulder.

'We set her down on the settee. I stayed with her on the verandah while Will rushed off to Inspector Wyatt's,' Ambler said. 'She grew agitated, extremely so. She said, "He lifted my dress" and "He tried to spoil me." I couldn't understand anything else she said. She was lying down, but every so often she'd sit up with a violent jerk and start babbling away randomly.'

'What did she talk about?'

'Really, I couldn't make head nor tail of it. It was all very disconcerting. She'd ramble on about one thing, then abruptly jump to something completely different. And she kept muttering, "He made me do it, he made me do it. Oh, God, oh God, I wish I had never met him!" I tried to calm her; I talked to her, hoping to keep her attention on one thing, but she got furious with me. "Shut up!" she snapped at me. "Just shut up, you stupid man! You don't understand at all! Stop talking!"'

Ambler dabbed at his perspiring face with a handkerchief. Even with the punkahs flapping away, the courtroom was stuffy. The judge, after conferring briefly with his assessors, adjourned the hearing to the following morning.

That night in my hotel room I wrote down everything I had seen and heard in court. I was drained by the effort of concentrating on the witnesses all day long. I longed for Arthur's body next to me, for the touch of his smooth, warm skin on mine. I thought of sending him a telegram, just to tell him how much I missed him, but I resisted the temptation. No letters, no notes.

The following morning the prosecution called Detective Inspector Charles Wyatt as their first witness. The Inspector was a short, thin man in his forties, with cool, watchful eyes and a wispy brown moustache. He spoke in crisp, succinct sentences, anticipating and answering Rhodes's questions even before they were asked.

'On the night of the 23rd of April, Mr William Proudlock knocked on my door at about a quarter past ten,' Inspector Wyatt said. 'He informed me that his wife had shot a man. I quickly changed into my uniform and, after sending a message to Dr McIntyre to meet me there, followed him back to the headmaster's bungalow.'

Dr McIntyre arrived shortly after, DI Wyatt said, and they all went to examine the body. It was lying approximately forty paces from the front of the bungalow. DI Wyatt struck a match and saw that it was the body of William Steward. He was lying on his chest, his right cheek on the grass.

'There was a great bloody wound on the back of his head,' DI Wyatt said. 'He was fully clothed. We turned the body over. His white tunic was buttoned, as were his trousers. We found prints of a lady's shoes in the muddy ground by the body.'

He also came upon a revolver lying on the sodden grass not far from the body. There was blood on the barrel and the cylinder as well as the grip. He sniffed the barrel; it smelled foul. Later, when he examined it, he discovered it held six empty cartridges.

'We left the body there and went to see Mrs Proudlock,' DI Wyatt continued. 'She was wearing the dress marked as Exhibit B. There were flecks of blood on her face, as well as on her neck and dress.

There was also blood in her hair, and her hands were smeared with blood. Her dress was torn, in the manner as shown in Exhibit B. I checked her hands,' he added. 'Her right forefinger was blackened with powder.'

The next witness was Dr Edward McIntyre. Under Rhodes's examination-in-chief, he testified that, after checking Steward's body on the lawn, he went back to the verandah and examined Ethel. He asked her to stand under the electric light hanging over the big table where she had been writing her letters. In addition to the bloodstains on her hands, arms and chest, he also found bloodstains on her back.

'Detective Inspector Wyatt had informed me that there may have been improper advances made on her, so I examined her for bruises and other forms of injury on her body.'

'Did you find any?'

'I found no bruises or scratches on Mrs Proudlock. I asked her if she had any. She replied, clearly and calmly, that she had none. I asked her to wash her hands and the rest of the exposed parts of her body, and then I examined her again. I found no bruises nor scratches.'

'Surely bruises wouldn't show up so soon?' Rhodes asked with the patently feigned ignorance of a man who already knows the answer.

'That's correct. A deep bruise will only show up after twenty-four hours; on the other hand, a superficial bruise will appear within a few minutes. In the case of a deep bruise, there will be pain. There might be abrasion or the skin might be red. I found nothing of that sort.'

'What was her state of mind?'

'She was agitated, and she was shaking. But . . .' For the first time since the questioning started Dr McIntyre appeared hesitant.

'Yes?' Rhodes prodded.

'Well, Mrs Proudlock answered all my questions sensibly. She understood them clearly, I had no doubt about it. Her eyes . . . they weren't clouded or dazed; they had a sharp, intelligent look. She didn't seem to me as if she had just experienced a terrible shock.

After what had happened to her, and after what she had done, well . . . to be quite honest, I had expected her to be in a more traumatised state.'

Excited whispers raced through the courtroom; Mr Justice Smith was too absorbed by Dr McIntyre's testimony to silence them. Ethel was still gazing with cool composure at Dr McIntyre. Was there just the faintest crease of a smile at the corners of her lips? You're imagining it, I told myself.

Pooley, Ethel's counsel, proceeded to cross-examine Dr McIntyre. 'You said you found no bruises on Mrs Proudlock when you examined her on the night of the 23rd of April?'

'That's quite correct.'

'But the next evening, the 24th of April, you saw her again at the home of Mrs Wilhelmina Brown, with whom she was staying, is that right?'

'Quite so.'

'Will you describe her condition to us?'

'She looked different from the previous evening. She seemed terrified, as if some awful event was still happening to her, and she was unable to control it. At times she was incoherent. Her eyes would be aware and sharp, but then a second later she would look away furtively. She was twitching all over. At one point she pressed her head tightly between her palms and moaned that she was going mad.'

'Did you examine her again?'

'I asked Mrs Brown to accompany me into the bedroom with Mrs Proudlock. She came with a powerful electric lamp and shone it on her.'

'When you examined Mrs Proudlock on this occasion, what did you find on her body?'

'Five bruises on her body. She had bruises on her left arm between her elbow and shoulder.' He pointed to the places on his own arm. 'There was some swelling there too, and in the corresponding position on her right arm as well. But no bruising on her right arm. I found extensive bruising over the trochanter of the femur on her right thigh, and another bruise four inches below her left kneecap.'

'In your opinion, how old were the bruises?'

'A day old, I'd say.'

'A day old. I see. So they could have been caused by the assault on the previous evening.'

'It's possible.'

Pooley changed tack. 'How long have you known Mrs Proudlock?'

'I've been attending to her for just over two years. She suffers from leucorrhoea. I've advised her more than once to have an operation, but she's always refused to even consider it. In my opinion she is a nervous and hysterical woman. She is highly emotional.'

'A nervous and highly emotional woman,' repeated Pooley slowly and distinctly so that none of us could miss his words. 'In your opinion, Dr McIntyre, could Mrs Proudlock – being a highly emotional woman – could she have suffered a temporary loss of reason and memory caused by the shock of being attacked by the deceased?'

'It's possible, yes.'

'Thank you, doctor.' Pooley looked to the bench. 'That will be all, My Lord.'

The trial reconvened after lunch. Inspector Frederick Ferrant was called to the stand. He had been sent to search William Steward's house at Salak South the day after he was killed. Not expecting to hear anything out of the ordinary, my thoughts started to drift. I snapped back to attention when I heard Inspector Ferrant saying, 'There was a chest of drawers in Mr Steward's bedroom. When I opened them, I found them full of women's clothes. They were for a European woman. There were also a few items of clothing for a European girl, aged three or four. I didn't find any native female clothing.'

Ethel's lips were slightly parted. I could see her chest rising and falling steadily, but her eyes remained as lifeless as a stagnant pond.

Steward was a bachelor, and the clothes had, in all probability, belonged to his lover. But who was the woman? Had Ethel taken her daughter along with her when she was sleeping over at Steward's house? The very thought of it was repugnant to me.

'There were four Chinese women in the house when I got there,' Inspector Ferrant said in reply to another question from Rhodes. 'They were all sitting on their haunches on the front verandah. No, I don't know who they were. Servants, I reckon. They didn't speak English. I told them that Tuan Steward sudah mati, and one of them started wailing loudly. She wouldn't let up, just went on and on, wailing and beating her chest.'

The prosecution said nothing more, but let the inference hang like a foetid smell in the warm, still air: William Steward had been sleeping with that Chinese woman.

The next witness was one of William Steward's friends. George Spence told the court that he had been dining with Steward at the Empire Hotel on the evening he was shot. At about half past eight Steward had made his excuses and left, saying that he had an appointment at nine, although he did not say whom he was meeting. Spence affirmed that Steward had been having relations with a Chinese woman; the woman had lived with him for the last three months before he was killed.

A clear and distinct pattern was emerging: the prosecution intended to show that Ethel had been having an affair with Steward; when she had found out about his relations with the Chinese woman, she had murdered him in a fit of jealous rage.

II

The newspapers reported on the trial's proceedings each day. I cut out the articles and pasted them in my journal. Ethel's spirits improved visibly, and so did her appearance; she chatted with Pooley and Wagner, and once or twice she even lit a brief smile on me.

'Mr Pooley is very certain that Ethel will be acquitted,' William Proudlock remarked to me as we waited for court to begin.

'That's wonderful, William,' I said.

I was tight with nerves. It was the fourth day of the trial, and the moment I had been dreading had arrived. Pooley summoned me to testify, and with a heavy heart I stepped into the witness box. I avoided Ethel's eyes, keeping my entire focus solely on Pooley.

Under his questioning I informed the court that yes, I was a friend of Ethel's, that I had known her for three years. She was a warm and kind person, vivacious and witty and funny. Did she like to dress up in beautiful dresses? Oh, all the time.

'Ethel's mad about clothes,' I said. 'She'd spend hours leafing through the latest fashions in the illustrated magazines. Whenever I came down to KL we'd always go shopping.'

'In your opinion, was there anything out of the ordinary in the fact that she was wearing a tea gown on the night William Steward was shot?' asked Pooley.

'There was nothing out of the ordinary at all,' I said. 'Ethel is always well turned-out, even if she isn't expecting anyone. Like I said, Ethel loves clothes.'

'Are you aware, Mrs Hamlyn,' said Pooley, 'of the malicious gossip about her and the deceased? Malicious gossip that has been swilling around KL?'

'I'm aware of it, yes.' I knew what was coming, and I forced myself to remain composed.

'Did Mrs Proudlock ever confide in you that she was having an affair with the deceased?'

For the first time since I stepped into the witness box, I looked directly at Ethel. She gazed back at me, her expression unreadable. I could feel a line of perspiration crawling down the hollow of my back. I thought back to that morning when she told me about her affair with Steward. What would happen if I revealed the truth? Would I save her, or damn her?

Still keeping my eyes on her, I said, 'She did not confide in me that she was having an affair with William Steward.' I then looked at Pooley and at the faces in the courtroom. I let my words sink into everyone's minds before I said, with the brisk, unassailable authority of a memsahib putting an intractable servant in his place, 'And there is no truth to the rumours that she was having an affair with William Steward,' I said. 'No truth at all.'

'Thank you, Mrs Hamlyn,' Pooley said. 'We have no further questions for Mrs Hamlyn, My Lord.'

Mr Justice Smith put down his pen and asked the prosecutor if he wanted to cross-examine me. I sat there in the box, drawing on every ounce of willpower to appear imperturbable as I waited for Rhodes to rip my testimony to shreds, to expose my lie to the world.

'We have no questions for Mrs Hamlyn, My Lord,' said Rhodes.

The listless flapping of the punkah was the only sound in the court-room as Pooley summoned Ethel to the witness stand.

'How long have you known Mr William Steward?' asked Pooley.

'My husband and I have known him for about two years.'

'When was the last time you saw him, before he showed up at your house on the 23rd of April?' asked Pooley.

'We saw him on the previous evening, at the Selangor Club. We spoke only for a few minutes.'

'What did you talk about?'

'I mentioned that I had not seen him for a long time, and that he had not been to see us since we moved. He said he didn't know where we lived, so I told him, and I asked him to come and see us. He promised he would drop in one night, but I asked him not to come after nine o'clock, as we retire early.'

'Was your husband with you?'

'He was talking to someone, I can't recall who it was, but yes, he was close by.'

'You did not invite Mr Steward to visit you on Sunday night?'

'I most certainly did not,' she said firmly.

'Please tell the court what you did on Sunday.'

She had not felt well that morning, she said, so she had stayed at home all day. At a quarter past four in the afternoon she and her husband had taken tea on the verandah. He then asked her to fetch the revolver, as he wanted to do some practice shooting in the garden.

'Did you practise too?'

'I fired twice,' Ethel replied.

'Did your husband reload the gun?'

'I did not see if he reloaded it.'

Her husband handed the revolver to her before they went inside to prepare for church, Ethel explained. She was going up onto the verandah when she was distracted by noises coming from the nursery.

'What kind of noises?'

'It sounded like something falling. I was worried that some stray cats had gotten into the nursery,' Ethel said. 'Those cats have been a real nuisance since we moved in. I didn't want them disturbing Dorothy. I placed the revolver on the right side of the bookshelf and hurried into the nursery. It was just as I had feared – a pair of cats had sneaked in there. I chased them out through the window.'

She then went to her room to get ready for church. Her husband was waiting for her when she returned to the verandah, and together they walked to church. Returning home after the service, William Proudlock quickly changed and hurried off to dinner at Goodman Ambler's house. She changed out of her church dress and into her tea gown and ate her dinner, alone. She was catching up on her correspondence on the verandah after dinner when, to her surprise, William Steward turned up.

'What time was that?'

'I'm not sure, but I think it was about half past eight, maybe just before nine.'

It was raining, but not heavily, she said. He asked her if her husband was at home. Before she could reply he had instructed his rick-shaw-puller to wait under a tree.

'I told him William would be back at about ten o'clock,' Ethel said. 'He said it wasn't anything important. I was hoping he would leave as I wanted to answer my letters, but I did not want to appear rude, so I invited him to sit. I asked him to tell his rickshaw-puller to wait in the porch, as it was raining, but he said, "It's not very pleasant having him nearby, spitting all the time."'

They chatted about the weather and the rising level of the river. She was worried that the lawn would be flooded if the rain kept up. They talked about the books they were reading. She went to the bookshelf to get a book she wanted to show him, but he stood up and blocked her way.

'He grabbed me and placed his arm around my waist and he said to me, "Never mind the book. You do look bonny! I love you." He pulled me in roughly and kissed me on my lips. "Let me have you!" he said. "I will have you!"'

'What did you do?' asked Pooley.

'I pushed him away. I told him, "Are you mad? What are you doing?" But he said nothing. There was a strange fire in his eyes. He put out the light and grabbed my arms, very tightly. It was very painful, it hurt me. Then he pulled up my gown and he . . . he began to grope me. Oh, it was horrible, horrible! I struggled against him, but he was so strong, he was so strong. I reached out my hand for the light switch, I thought if I put on the light, that would stop him, make him come to his senses. I was reaching for the switch when my fingers touched the barrel of the revolver. In desperation my hand closed around it, gripped it tightly. He was still pulling me towards him. I was terrified that he was going to drag me into the house and . . . and . . .'

A sob cracked her voice. She pressed her face into her hands, her shoulders shuddering uncontrollably. None of us made a sound, not even the judge and the assessors. Gradually her shaking stopped and she lifted her face from her hands. Her breathing sounded loud and heavy. She accepted a handkerchief from Pooley and dried her eyes.

'I pointed the gun at him,' she said. 'I fired the gun. I think I fired twice.' She dabbed the handkerchief at her eyes again. 'That's all I remember. Everything became a blank.'

'What happened next?' asked Pooley.

When she came to herself again, she realised that she was still standing on the verandah. She had no idea how much time had passed. She went to the servants' quarters to look for the boy, but he wasn't there. The cook answered from his room, and she ordered him to go and fetch her husband.

'I only wanted to frighten Steward by firing a shot over his head,' she said. 'That's all I wanted to do. I didn't intend to kill him.'

Her façade of self-control collapsed and she started sobbing again. Mr Justice Smith paused the proceedings to give Ethel time to compose herself. After a short while she indicated that she was ready to be cross-examined by the Public Prosecutor.

'Did the deceased not see that you had a revolver in your hand?' asked Rhodes.

'I don't know. It was very dark. The light on the verandah was off – he had put it off himself.'

'Did you warn him that you had a revolver?'

'I don't . . . I don't remember. I . . . I don't think . . . I don't remember warning him before I fired. I just wanted to get away from him. Somehow I knew that if he didn't let go of me, he would . . . he would rape me.'

'The deceased was found lying face down in the garden, about forty paces from the verandah.' The Public Prosecutor did not refer to his notes. 'He had six bullets in his body. Four in his chest, one in the back of his head, and another in the nape of his neck. Can you explain how this happened?'

'I can't,' Ethel replied simply. 'I remember firing the first shot. I remember hearing the second shot. It seemed to come from far away. I don't remember anything after that.'

'What happened after you had spoken to the cook?'

Ethel drew in a long breath and exhaled. 'My memory of what happened after my husband returned is cloudy. I was aware of Goodman being there, yes, but I simply cannot recall what I said to them.'

'Had the deceased ever visited you at home, before the evening you shot him?'

'Only once, when William was in Hong Kong. He came to our old house in Brickfields. It was a musical evening – there were other guests there too,' she added quickly to the three men on the bench.

'Did you ever go to the deceased's house in Salak South?' Rhodes asked.

'No.'

'You never spent a night in the deceased's house?' Rhodes pressed on.

'No.'

'Did you ever have an affair with the deceased?'

'Certainly not!' Ethel's eyes swept around the courtroom before coming to rest on Mr Justice Smith and the two assessors. 'I am not a harlot,' she addressed them directly. 'I have never had an affair with William Steward, nor with anybody else.'

I thought she had said all that she wanted to say, but she gripped the railing of the witness box and with a fierce dignity pulled back her shoulders, at the same time jutting her chin forward. In a clear, ringing voice she declared, 'I would rather be convicted of murder than live out the rest of my life under the cloud of being an unfaithful wife.'

It was a powerful and affecting performance, I thought – but would it convince the three men sitting up there deciding her fate?

III

On the final day of the trial James Pooley summed up the case for the defence.

'Mrs Ethel Proudlock is a fine, virtuous woman who suffered a temporary deprivation of reason when William Steward attempted to rape her,' he concluded at the end of his lengthy speech. 'She should not be found guilty of murder.'

Hastings Rhodes made his summation for the prosecution, and then for the next hour and a half Mr Justice Sercombe Smith reviewed the evidence presented by both sides. It was almost five o'clock when he finished summing up the case.

'Mr Wise,' he addressed the assessor on his left, 'what is your verdict on the charge of murder?'

'My verdict says she is guilty.'

Mr Justice Smith looked to his right. 'And you, Mr Kindersley? What is your verdict on the charge of murder?'

'My verdict says she is guilty.'

The judge removed his spectacles and gazed down from the bench at Ethel.

'I concur,' he said.

The courtroom erupted. Screams of disbelief competed with shouts of approval. 'Murderess!' a man behind me cried out. 'Murderess!' Ethel was staring at Mr Justice Smith, her face bloodless. Again and again the bailiffs called for silence until finally the commotion petered out.

'Does the accused have anything to say to the court?' asked Mr Justice Smith.

We waited, straining to hear her speak. For God's sake, say something, Ethel, I urged her in my mind. Tell them what really happened between you and Steward. Speak, Ethel. Fight for your life.

But Ethel just stood there in the dock, silent. The judge gave her a moment longer, but still she did not utter a single word.

'I hereby sentence the accused, Ethel Proudlock,' said Mr Justice Smith, 'to hang by the neck until she be dead.'

The court was adjourned, and the three men on the bench filed out of the courtroom.

Ethel stared at her husband, a stricken expression on her face. A choking noise burst from her throat, and then she broke down. Her awful keening filled the courtroom. William Proudlock rushed to the dock and took his wife into his arms. He stroked her head and whispered into her ear, but she went on wailing.

William Proudlock had to hold her up as the policemen escorted Ethel out of the courtroom. I followed them down the corridors, keeping close to her two lawyers. We emerged into the cobbled courtyard by the Klang River. It was late evening, the raintrees along the river aflame with crows squabbling for their roosts.

A police van was waiting in the courtyard, its back doors wide open. Still sobbing piteously, Ethel hung on tightly to William, refusing to climb inside. The policemen had to pull her from her husband's arms and manhandle her into the back of the van. William demanded to ride with her, but the policemen slammed the doors shut, turned the lock and climbed into the front of the van.

We stood there – William and I and the lawyers – and watched the van pull away, taking Ethel back to Pudoh Gaol.

Chapter Sixteen

Willie
Penang, 1921

The trees were still gauzed in mists when the syce drove Robert and Willie to the Botanic Gardens. The outing was too early for Gerald's liking, and Lesley had elected not to join them. 'You two old friends should have some time together,' she said when she saw them off from the porch.

The bearers were sitting on their haunches at the bottom of a jungle track that climbed to the summit of Penang Hill two thousand feet above. Willie felt a twinge of doubt when he saw the dhoolies that would convey them to the top: two spindly bamboo poles approximately ten feet long threaded through a wicker armchair in the centre.

They settled into their dhoolies, and with whoops and cries the bearers — four Tamils assigned to each dhoolie — hoisted their load onto their shoulders and embarked on the long, steep slog up the hill. Willie held on tightly to the armrests, fearful of being tipped out of his seat, but soon he began to relax and enjoy the bouncing, swaying ride.

'The funicular will be completed in a year's time,' Robert said, twisting around in his dhoolie to look back at him. 'If you come to Penang again you can go up the hill in that.'

'We'll do that with you and Lesley, but I doubt it'll be . . . as thrilling as this.'

They were carried ever upwards, through patches of sunlight and tunnels of dappled green shadows thick with ferns and orchids and bromeliads. Broad-girthed trees pressed in on them, their wrinkled trunks soaring hundreds of feet skywards to spread their branches into the canopy far above. Willie thought there was something crotch-like about the lush and unruly clumps of epiphytes spilling from the forks of the trees. At various points the bearers were forced to squeeze past huge overhanging boulders. The jungle flared with birdsong, and the air was occasionally gashed by the manic screeching of monkeys.

The clammy heat of the lowlands had given way to chilly air by the time they reached the summit just over an hour later. The bearers carried them along quiet leafy lanes lined with brownstone cottages. Willie felt he could have been back in a village somewhere in England.

At the Crag Hotel they climbed out of their dhoolies. Willie shook the stiffness from his limbs as he looked around him. The main bungalow of the hotel was built on the crest of a high rocky ridge surrounded by tall trees, and was connected to a cluster of smaller guest bungalows on the lower slopes by narrow steps and walkways.

It was the quiet season, the manager apologised as he led the way through the airy, empty lobby to the viewing platform at the end of the terrace lawn. A massive angsana tree, its trunk bristling with ferns, thrust out from the centre of the platform, ringed by a circle of benches. A table had been laid out for them by the wooden railings, a waiter standing attentively by. George Town lay sprawled in the morning light far below. Squinting his eyes, Willie made out the godowns lining the harbour. Ships and countless minuscule vessels criss-crossed the channel, like water skimmers skating over a pond's surface. Over on the mainland he recognised the mountains that greeted him every morning from the beach at Cassowary House, and behind them, more mountains, stretching away into the haze.

The journey and the crisp fresh air had sharpened their appetite, and they ate a hearty breakfast.

'I'm enjoying *Chinese Screen*,' Robert said when they were drinking their tea. 'I feel quite privileged, getting my paws on it before it's even on the shelves.'

'I'll send you an inscribed copy.' Willie pushed aside his cup and leaned forward, pressing his palms on the table. 'The other night, just before you fell asleep, you said something . . . about Ethel Proudlock, about what her husband and . . . her father did to her. Something terrible. What was it, Robert? What did . . . they do?'

Robert scratched his cheek, frowning. 'I can't remember saying anything of the sort.'

'You did.'

'Well, I have no idea what I said or meant, old chap.'

If he was lying, Willie thought, it was very convincing.

Robert pointed to the houses on the nearby ridge. 'That's the governor's residence. And that one there – that's Noel Hutton's. We've stayed there a few times. Most of the houses up here are holiday homes or government rest houses.' He pointed to a temple at the foot of the mountains. 'That's the Temple of Supreme Joy. You see that structure on the slope just above it? They're building a pagoda.'

The octagonal stump of the unfinished pagoda was still only three or four storeys high, its sides perforated by rows of tall, narrow windows. Surrounded by the hills and the lush jungle, it looked like a ruin of a forgotten civilisation.

'I won't see it completed, Willie, just like I won't be riding the funicular up here with you.' Robert glanced at him over the rim of his teacup. 'Lesley's told you, I'm sure.'

'She mentioned that you're planning to move to the Karoo.'

'I suppose you think I'm barmy too?'

On the temple's roof a vermilion and yellow banner flapped from a pole, like a flickering flame on a candle. 'When we were being

. . . carried up here,' Willie said, looking at the banner, 'I was reminded of a tale I had heard in Hong Kong.'

'Oh? Do tell.'

'This took place about eight or nine years ago. A middle-aged doctor, English and newly married, found out that his young . . . wife had taken a lover. So he decided to accept a posting as a District . . . Medical Officer in a cholera-stricken village high in the mountains of China.'

'A rather puerile way to numb his pain, wouldn't you say?'

'Actually, he wanted to punish his . . . wife. He ordered her to accompany him, but she refused, so he gave her an ultimatum: either she went with him, or he would divorce her and send her . . . back to her parents in England.'

'What did she do?'

'She went with him, of course. What other choice did she have? It took them . . . five weeks to reach the village. The journey was arduous and perilous. For the last stretch up to the mountains they had to be carried in sedan chairs – that's what made me think of the story when we were riding in our . . . dhoolies up here.' Willie cradled his teacup in his palm. 'Three months after they arrived at the village, this doctor was struck down by cholera. She buried . . . him there.'

'What happened to her – the doctor's wife?'

Willie had to think for a moment or two. The woman had left the village and gone back to Hong Kong, he recalled. She had married her lover, and by all accounts they were still happily together.

'She's still there, in that village in the mountains,' he said. 'She never went home.'

A cool breeze passed by, moulting the leaves from the trees. Robert pointed to the slabs of grey clouds lying above the mountains on the mainland. 'Won't be long till the monsoon,' he said. 'Day after day it rains, for weeks on end. I feel as if I'm drowning. You have no idea what that's like. Of course it's a drastic step, moving to the

Karoo,' he continued. 'You think I don't know that?' His voice, when he spoke again, was jagged at the edges. 'But it's the only alternative left for me.'

Looking at his friend, Willie felt a deep sadness for him. 'I'm glad you invited me to stay, Robert.'

'You'll come and visit me in the Karoo?'

'I'll even bring a big . . . box of the latest . . . books for you.'

'Don't you ever get tired of travelling?'

'Never. I enjoy the . . . freedom it gives me. I feel that when I travel I can change . . . myself a little, and I return from a journey not quite the same . . . self I was.'

'"Caelum non animum mutant qui trans mare currunt",' said Robert. He smiled when he saw Willie's blank look. 'Horace.'

'Ah, yes. Of course.'

Dragonflies with stained-glass wings stitched invisible threads in the air. The two friends gazed down at the land below, watching the cloud shadows bruise the earth.

Chapter Seventeen

Lesley
Penang, 1910

I

After the trial, whenever I went to the reading club the people there would dart warning looks at one another and drop their voices. The atmosphere was taut with tension and paranoia. I suspected Sun Wen was cobbling the final plans together for another attempt to overthrow the emperor, but I never asked Arthur what they were up to.

Sun Wen had formed a committee to publish the Tong Meng Hui's first newspaper in Penang. They had set up a printing press in one of the rooms near the kitchen. I joined the others already gathered in the dining hall to witness the first issue rolling off the press.

'The *Kwong Wah Yit Poh*,' Sun Wen declared, the newspaper held high over his head like a victory banner. 'From today our voices will be heard, loud and clear.'

The *Glorious China Daily* was sold in shops sympathetic to the Tong Meng Hui, but most newsagents in George Town would have no truck with it. Paging through it with Arthur when we were alone, I came upon a photograph of Ethel Proudlock accompanying a long article. It was disorienting to see her face hemmed in by the vertical bars of Chinese writing.

'I wrote it,' said Arthur.

He read the article aloud to me, translating it into English. I thought he had been fair and objective to Ethel, sticking to the facts and never divulging what I had told him about her affair with William Steward.

It was hard to believe that three weeks had passed by since Ethel was sentenced to hang. There were many who felt that she had got what she deserved, but there were letters in the newspapers every day criticising the court's decision — Ethel had been defending her honour, they wrote, and to sentence her to death for this was a gross travesty of justice. It shouldn't be allowed to happen to a European woman.

Ethel's lawyers had filed an appeal the day after her fate was laid down. William Proudlock wrote to the Secretary of State for the Colonies requesting a royal pardon, and the European Women's Club in KL and Penang sent a cable to the Queen, imploring her to persuade the King to grant it. When the Secretary of State rejected William's request and informed him that the appeal for leniency should be sent to the Sultan of Selangor, hundreds of us in Penang, KL and Singapore signed petitions to the Sultan. We were informed that he would only consider our petitions when the result of Ethel's appeal was made known. All we — and Ethel — could do now was wait for the date of her appeal to be set down.

I went to see her. I had to. A guard led me deep into the gaol, down long, chilly corridors hollowed by the echoes of our footsteps. I had lost my bearings by the time we stopped outside her cell. She was lying on her bunk, staring at the ceiling. The Sikh guard nodded to me and went to stand at the end of the narrow corridor.

'Ethel.' The thick, damp walls dulled my voice. She didn't move, and I called to her again, louder.

Slowly, like a heavy stone being lifted, she turned her head towards me. She stared at me for a long time. Eventually she pushed herself up, brushed the strands of hair from her brow and trudged barefoot across the grey cement floor, stopping a few inches from the bars of the cell. I had been warned against any physical contact with the prisoner, so I kept my hands at my side. Ethel's cheekbones were sharper, her hair greasy and tangled. Pouches hung beneath her eyes. She was dressed in prison uniform: a loose grey cotton blouse and long skirt. She seemed to have aged twenty years.

'Oh, Ethel . . .'

'They've put me here. This place, this is where they keep the condemned,' she said. 'I'm not allowed to mix with the other women; I'm locked up day and night. The guards watch me all the time.' Her laugh sounded like a death rattle. 'They think I'll kill myself.'

'Be strong, Ethel. It'll soon be over. The appeal will overturn the judgement. You'll be acquitted. Robert says so. Everyone says so.'

'I've asked Pooley to withdraw my appeal.'

I stared at her, my hands gripping the bars. 'Are you mad? Why on earth would you do that?'

She began to pace up and down her cell: four steps to one wall, then four steps back to the opposite wall. 'I can't stand it here, Lesley. I hate it. I hate it! It'll be another month before they hear my appeal. I have to get out, immediately. Today. Now. I can't bear to stand in court again and have everyone staring at me, judging me again. I can't. I just can't.' She stopped. 'I've asked the Sultan to pardon me.' She started her mindless pacing again.

'But, Ethel . . .' My mind fumbled through the ramifications of her decision. 'You know what that means, don't you? If you with-draw your appeal? Yes, the Sultan might pardon you, but you won't be exonerated of your crime – you'll remain a convicted murderer. You'll carry that stain with you for the rest of your life. It's not fair to Dorothy – or William. Oh, for heaven's sake, Ethel, will you please just sit down! You're making me dizzy.'

She stopped abruptly, flinging me a sullen look. 'I've already told Mr Pooley, and I've written a letter to the *Mail*.'

She fell back onto her bunk bed and turned her face to the wall. I called out to her, but she ignored me.

Robert went down to KL for an urgent meeting with his client. He took Peter Ong with him. I was glad of his absence as it allowed me to spend my days with Arthur. How ironic that Robert and I each had our own Chinese lovers. We had this unusual thing in common, but we could never discuss it. Between us lay this great, heavy silence, accreting over the years, layer upon layer, hardening like a coral reef, except a coral reef was a living thing, wasn't it?

'All everyone could talk about was your friend withdrawing her appeal and asking the Sultan to pardon her,' Robert remarked when he came home a few evenings later. We had just sat down to dinner. 'People are furious that she's putting her fate in the hands of the Sultan. You should hear how they're tearing her to pieces. It's absolutely vicious.'

'I warned her that she'd still be a convicted murderer even if the Sultan pardoned her.'

'The implications are much more calamitous than that.'

'What are you talking about, Robert?'

'Ethel Proudlock has damaged our prestige among the natives. "How can we allow an Asiatic potentate to exercise the power of life and death over a European, an Englishwoman?"'

'They wouldn't care two pins about any of that if it were their own necks in the noose.'

Robert wiped his lips carefully with his napkin. 'Sun Wen gave a speech at a Chinese Club in Macalister Road last week,' he said. 'He attacked British rule in Malaya. Openly. Someone reported it to Sir John.'

'What's he going to do?' I was worried, but I tried not to let it show. The governor of the Straits Settlements was the god who ruled over our lives.

'He's signed the orders expelling Sun Wen from Penang. He's to be put on the first ship out tomorrow.'

Images of bedlam at the Tong Meng Hui headquarters flooded my mind. I forced down the urge to warn Arthur. No letters, no notes; no messages. There must be nothing tangible to link us, no crumbs dropped along the trail.

'What will happen to his family?' I could hear the faint tremor in my own voice. 'His daughters have just started school.'

'The deportation order applies only to him, but they'll pack up and follow him later, I suppose. Oh, don't look so distraught, my dear. It was only a matter of time before he was asked to leave, you know that.' Robert turned his whisky tumbler around in his hand, volleying shards of light onto the walls. 'You'll want to see him off tomorrow. Do convey my farewell to him. I don't think we'll ever see him here again.'

He still suspected that I had been having an affair with Sun Wen. My dearest husband might have his lover, and we might not have shared the same bed in years, but I was still his wife.

We sat there in the silence, our true thoughts camouflaged from each other. What sustained a marriage, kept it going year upon year, I realised, were the things we left unmentioned, the truths that we longed to speak forced back down our throats, back into the deepest, darkest chambers of our hearts.

II

Over a hundred men and women were gathered around Sun Wen and his family when I arrived at Swettenham Pier at dawn. A group of pigtailed officials from the Chinese Legation stood at the sidelines, observing. I pushed my way through the sombre, restless crowd to Sun Wen. Chui Fen's arm was curled around the drooping shoulders of a much older woman. It was the first time I had seen Sun Wen's wife. The short, stocky woman was weeping, her two daughters comforting her.

For a moment or two Sun Wen and I just looked at each other. I thought of the first time I had met him. I thought of how I had been changed by that meeting. He bowed to me and pressed his palm on his heart. 'For all that you've done for our revolution, Lesley, I thank you. My family thanks you. China thanks you.'

'Where will you go?'

'England, and then onwards to America, always onwards.' He glanced at his wife, his daughters and Chui Fen. 'My family will remain here. I shall send for them when the future has been determined.'

'If they need anything, Sun Wen, anything at all, they must tell me.'

'Come to China when we have created our republic, Lesley.' Beneath his calm demeanour I sensed he was putting up a heroic front for his family and his followers; and, perhaps, most of all, for himself. 'Come and see for yourself the dawn of the new country you helped bring into existence.'

He gripped my hands, then let them go. I went to stand beside Arthur. He leaned slightly into me, his arm brushing against mine. I kept my arm there, feeling the warmth radiating off him.

A pair of Sikh policemen escorted Sun Wen to the end of the pier, where the SS *Edinburgh* was waiting to cast off. At the foot of the gangplank Sun Wen stopped and thanked the policemen. He straightened his shoulders, and then he ascended the gangplank, moving at a stately pace. At the top he removed his hat and turned around to look back at the crowd below, his eyes searching for his wife and daughters. He raised his hand in a farewell to them and to every one of us, holding it aloft for a long moment.

The ship sounded its whistle, and the tugboats rumbled into life, pulling the vessel out into the shipping lanes. We lined the pier, Arthur and I and Sun Wen's family and the people of the Tong Meng Hui, and we watched the ship carry Sun Wen away from Penang.

★ ★ ★

Sun Wen's deportation lit a fire under his supporters. The men and women of the Tong Meng Hui travelled around Penang and Malaya making speeches and spreading Sun Wen's calls to rise up against the Ching monarchy; they raised funds by organising Cantonese and Teochew opera troupes to perform in villages and tin mines. I continued to visit the reading club twice a week, working at the long table for an hour or two before slipping off to the House of Doors.

This morning as I stepped onto its five-foot way, something made me look twice at the doors. They were plain and bare, no different from how they had always looked, yet there was something different about them, something I couldn't put my finger on. I took a step back, but found nothing out of the ordinary. I took another half-step back, at an oblique angle. I tilted my head slightly to one side, and I saw it.

Faint lines on the face of the wood, forming an arcane design. The pattern looked familiar, but for the of life of me I couldn't remember where I had come upon it before. I took half a step forward. The lines disappeared, like dust wiped away by a piece of cloth.

'What *is* that odd-looking symbol on your front doors?' I asked Arthur later when we were lying in bed. 'It was never there before, was it?'

'I asked Pak Musa across the street to carve it last week,' he replied. 'Somerset Maugham put it on every one of his books. He said in an interview that it's a sign to keep away bad luck.'

Of course. Now I remembered where I had seen it before.

'I've always liked it,' said Arthur. 'I thought: Why not put it on my front doors? I want it to protect this house.' He shaped his palm to my cheek. 'Our house.'

III

In the dying days of August an insurrection broke out in Canton. We held our breath, wondering if this was the spark that would ignite the powder keg. But two weeks later the rebellion was savagely put down by the imperial army. More than seventy revolutionaries were executed – one of them a schoolteacher from Penang. The mood in the reading club was bleak; quarrels broke out among the members, some criticising Sun Wen's weak leadership, others voicing their unwavering support for him. Listening to the arguments raging around me, I remembered that evening on our verandah, Sun Wen listing his many failures on his fingers. I feared that he would never succeed.

A month later another uprising erupted, this one in Wuchang. It would collapse like all the others before it, I remarked to Arthur. But week after week the neighbouring provinces rose up against the government. The rebellion caught fire and flared across China. Sun Wen, in America raising money, was caught unawares by events and rushed back to Canton on the fastest ship. He had not organised the latest insurrections himself, but naturally he had to be seen to be taking the lead.

IV

One afternoon Arthur and I were sitting by the air-well in the House of Doors, sipping tea and listening to the patter of the falling rain.

'We had a meeting last night,' Arthur began. 'Thirty members from the KL Tong Meng Hui volunteered to go to China. Twenty from Penang.' The water in the air-well had already risen to our ankles. 'I was one of them.'

I put down my cup and stared at him. 'But . . . how long will you be away? When will you come back?'

'Until I'm not needed there.'

'That could take years.' I could not believe what I was hearing. 'You can't do that to your parents, Arthur. What about your wife? And your daughter? You can't do that to them.' And most all, I thought, but did not say aloud: You can't do that to me.

'If all of us felt like that, there would be no revolution, no change for the better, would there? Now is the time for us to act, Lesley, to give all that we can give.'

'You're just bloody selfish,' I said. 'Just like every man I've ever known: Robert, Sun Wen, my father. Even Geoff. Always thinking about your own needs, your own pleasures.'

'We're this close to succeeding.' He pinched a sliver of empty air in front of our faces. 'This close, Lesley. Sacrifices *have* to be made. Sun Wen accepted it long ago. So must I.'

'Why is it that when you men make sacrifices it's always we women who must suffer the most?'

I got up and walked to the end of the hall, my wet footprints following me across the tiles. I touched one of the doors hanging from the ceiling, set it spinning slowly. 'She will break your heart.' I turned around and looked back at him. My footprints were already evaporating from the tiles, as though I had never existed, had never stepped foot inside this house.

He did not understand my words. 'China,' I said. 'China will break your heart.'

We saw each other only one more time before he sailed to Canton. In the dining hall, witnessed only by the spiralling doors, I gave him a maroon velvet pouch.

'Open it,' I said. 'Go on. I won't think you rude.'

He loosened the drawstring and pulled out a silver chain from inside the pouch. Hanging from the end of the chain was a silver amulet in the shape of the lines he had had carved on his doors. I had traced the symbol from one of Maugham's novels on a sheet of paper and given it to a silversmith in Kimberley Street.

I took the chain from Arthur's fingers and looped it over his neck, adjusting the amulet's position until it hung exactly at the centre of his chest. With my palm I pressed it firmly against his shirt, pressed it into his skin.

'To protect you,' I said. 'To keep you safe.'

He took my hand and gripped it. 'I'll write to you,' he said. 'You'll always know where I am, what I'm doing.'

I shook my head. 'I told you from the first day, Arthur – no letters.'

'Everything's different now.'

'No letters,' I repeated firmly. 'I will wait for you here, in Penang. I won't leave. I won't go anywhere.' I nodded at the guzheng in the corner. 'Will you play a song for me?'

He sat down at the guzheng, resting his hands on the strings. Then he started to play *L'heure exquise*, more slowly than I had heard him play it before, as though he didn't want the song to end. The music seeped through the air, into the house, seeped into me, and my heart, beating in its ark of bones, expanded and collapsed with every breath I took, each one heavier than the last. All the exquisite hours we had shared between us – where had they disappeared to? And would we ever hold them in our hands again?

The song came to its end. The final note dissolved into the silence. We embraced and kissed, and I turned to leave. But then I remembered there was still one more thing left to do. I took out the key from my purse and gave it to him.

He placed it back on my palm, folded my fingers over the key, and then pressed his lips on them.

V

A week after Arthur sailed to Canton, an item was delivered to the house. The servants had propped it up in the vestibule when I returned from town. I stood there, looking at the leaf of a pair of doors, at the hawk drifting over a misty crag and the four lines of a poem by a Japanese warrior from long ago.

When Robert came home from work that evening he told me that the Sultan of Selangor had announced that he would be pardoning Ethel, but only on one condition – she had to leave Malaya, and never return.

'That's harsh,' I said.

'Harsher than a rope around her neck? No, my dear. The Sultan is right – it's better this way, better for her that she leave and never come back again.'

'Better for her, or for everyone else?'

'The Sultan may have pardoned her, but her own people – us whites – will never forgive her,' said Robert. 'All everybody wants now is to forget that she ever lived here, forget that she ever existed.'

One of the first things Ethel Proudlock did when she was released from gaol was to give interviews for the newspapers. I found it hard to understand after her steadfast refusal to have anything to do with the press during her trial. She continued to maintain that she was innocent, but her words found no room in the hearts of the people who had once given her all their support, who had written letters to the newspapers and signed petitions demanding that she be freed.

She was given a week to pack her things and leave Malaya with her daughter. I asked her to stay with us on her way to England. She took pains over her appearance and made every effort to be gay and talkative, but she never left our house to go into town, not even once; instead she spent her two days with us in the garden or on the beach with Dorothy.

'I'll miss KL, and I'll miss you,' said Ethel, 'but oh, I can't tell you how terribly glad I am to leave.'

It was her last afternoon in Penang, and we were having tea in the garden. The trees luxuriated in the wind, their leaves seeming almost to be purring.

'You *will* write?' I said.

'Of course. We *must* keep in touch.' She reached over and squeezed my hand. 'You're a dear, dear friend, Lesley. What you did for me in the trial . . . I'll never forget it.'

It was the first time she had ever raised the subject. 'It didn't help much at all, in the end, did it?'

'You didn't betray me – that's what matters most to me.'

'What's William going to do? He'll join you in England?'

The light emptied from her eyes; they took on an absence, a void, as if there was no longer anyone behind them. 'I never want to see him again.'

'You can't mean that,' I said. 'He's your husband. He stood by your side all through your terrible ordeal. He adores you.'

'He made me do it, Lesley.' Her voice sounded dead, as dead as her eyes. Despite the cloudless sky I felt cold all of a sudden. 'I had no choice. He made me do it. He made me kill William.'

'Whatever do you mean? Ethel? What are you talking about?'

She turned her bracelet on her wrist a few times. Then, with a visible lurch, like a motor car jerking into life, she seemed to come back to herself.

'I'm glad we're leaving,' she said, smiling at me.

The next morning I took mother and daughter to the harbour. I was the only one there to wave them farewell as the ship sailed away from Penang, but journalists in every port of call charted her progress across the oceans; I read about her arrival in Colombo and Port Said and, finally, Tilbury. And after that I heard no more of her.

VI

One morning in January 1912 I came down to breakfast to find Robert looking oddly at me over the top of his newspaper. He waited for me to sit down before he handed it to me.

'It's *President* Sun Yat Sen now,' he said.

I read the article. The Ching dynasty was dead. No longer did a Son of Heaven rule over China. The Republic of China had come into being.

I put down the paper and stared out to the sea. He had done it; Sun Wen had achieved his dream. I wanted to cry, but I forced myself to hold back my tears. Not in front of Robert. I prayed Arthur was safe; I prayed the amulet I gave him was casting its protective shield over him.

The moment Robert left for work I quickly changed and rushed off to the reading club. The celebrations were already in full swing when I arrived. People were making extemporaneous speeches and belting out patriotic songs that were regularly interrupted by someone shouting slogans and Sun Wen's name.

I cheered and clapped along with them. But as I looked at the men and women around me – so young, so fired up with purpose – I knew that I did not belong there any more. Perhaps I never did. A small fragment of the larger world, which for a brief moment had extended its hand to me, had moved on, leaving me behind. I chatted and laughed with everyone around me, but not one of them noticed or cared when, after a while, I left the place, closing the doors behind me.

Out in the bustling street, I paused and looked back at the house. I thought of the first time I had gone there, and I thought of the countless times since that evening. And then, silently, I bade my farewell to it.

The winds of old longings blew my sails down the street to the House of Doors. Its window shutters were closed up, the front doors locked and stamped with an invisible seal.

As I emerged onto Victoria Street, my eyes fell upon a line of Chinese coolies at an open-air Indian barber in a back alley. Curious, I stopped to watch them. One after another of the men perched themselves on the barber's high stool. The barber pegged a sheet of newspaper around their shoulders, then proceeded to snip their braid off. Without fail every one of the coolies rubbed the back of their head with their palm when they got off the stool. Some of them picked up their severed plait from the ground, coiling it around their wrist or stuffing it into their pocket; but there were also a great number of them who left their cords of hair lying on the ground where they had fallen. Many of the coolies had tears running down their cheeks, but whether from joy or sorrow I could not tell.

On that morning, as I stood in the back lane and watched the coolies cutting off their queues, I was filled with a great sense of envy for them, for the opportunity they had been given to discard their old self, and to start a new life.

Chapter Eighteen

Lesley
Penang, 1921

For some time after I stopped talking Willie remained silent. I got up and went over to the windows. There was no moon, and the air was sticky and warm; there was not even the slightest breeze to twitch the black fabric of the night.

All these nights, telling Willie about my life and my marriage. What had I accomplished? I had expected to feel liberated, unburdened. But in the end I felt only a deep sadness for myself, and, something which I had not expected, for Robert too.

Something in the dark scrim of the sea flashed in the corner of my eye. I thought I was mistaken, but a second or two later it appeared again.

I turned away from the window. 'Fancy a stroll on the beach, Willie?'

The sea was quiet, the waves listless. The mansions behind the trees were dark. The sand was still warm from the day's sun. I set a brisk pace, guided by a faint glow from a fisherman's hut. The seed of light was as faithful as a mariner's star. We had gone about fifty paces when I pulled up abruptly.

'Look — out there in the sea,' I said.

There was nothing, just dense blackness. Then a patch of blue light flared up in the water. Another patch lit up, followed closely by another, like lightning trapped inside a wall of storm clouds.

'Goodness,' Willie said softly.

He was mesmerised, I could tell. 'You know what's the best thing for a sticky night like this?'

He caught my meaning instantly. 'Oh, no. Absolutely not.'

But I was already unbuttoning my blouse and my skirt. They whispered down the length of my body onto the sand, to be joined a moment later by my undergarments. I stood there in the warm, starchy air, completely naked. I didn't give a flying fig about Willie. Well, he was homosexual, wasn't he? And anyway, he couldn't see me clearly in the darkness; even so, I sensed him averting his face and taking half a step away from me.

'It's pitch-black out there—' he began.

'Oh, stop bleating like an old woman, Willie.'

He took off his clothes, his reluctance palpable even in the darkness. He placed them at his feet and then, naked except for his trepidation, he followed me into the sea.

The water was blood-warm, and I seemed to dissolve into it. It had been a long time since I last swam at night, and I couldn't help picturing shoals of creatures in the water, circling us in a silent tornado of razor-sharp teeth. *Idiot.* I pushed those fears away. We breasted far out to sea, the earth sloping away beneath us into valleys and chasms and broad silent plains untouched by the sun since the beginning of the world. I couldn't make out the coast of the mainland in front of me, couldn't tell where the sea joined the sky. I turned to look back, but the house and the beach had been folded into a crease of the night. Only the distant, faintest hiss of surf effervescing on sand told me that the land was still there behind us, still existed.

All at once we were swimming in cobalt fire, every kick and stroke igniting the tempests of plankton swirling around us. I laughed, the sound rupturing the quiet, windless night, and then Willie joined me as well. We dunked our heads under the blazing sea and came up again, spluttering fire from our lips. Rivulets of blue flames streamed down Willie's hair, his face. I touched my own cheek, felt it glowing; I scooped up handfuls of the sea, marvelling at the fire-snakes writhing down my arms. We grinned at each other with stupid, childlike glee. Our naked bodies were visible in the water, but what was there to be embarrassed about? We were nothing more than two insects preserved in amber, after all.

Whenever the fire dimmed, we would scissor our legs and swing our arms, stoking the watery furnace. 'If we flapped our limbs hard and fast and long enough,' I said to Willie, 'do you think we could light up the entire ocean?'

Like an anchor sliding from a ship, I sank beneath the surface of the sea and cleaved my way down, descending in a cocoon of light. Shadowy fishes darted around me. The water grew colder, but still I kept falling, intoxicated by the sensation that I was travelling back in time. Was it because the sea was so unmeasurably old, existing even before the firmaments had been formed to divide the waters from the waters? I was gripped by an atavistic urge to keep sinking, down and ever down into the impenetrable darkness, boring a narrow tunnel of light into the fathomless sea, nebulae burning from my fingertips, comet-fire trailing in my wake. What would happen if I kept falling, all the way to the beginning of time?

A hand gripped my shoulder, jerking me from my spell. Half-turning around, I saw Willie. I was suddenly conscious of the painful band tightening around my chest. I panicked, realising all at once that I was rapidly running out of air.

As though he could see into my thoughts, Willie grabbed my wrist and kicked us upwards, pulling me along. The surface seemed too far away for me to reach in time. My lungs were screaming when, finally, my face burst through the skin of the sea.

I sucked in gluttonous, choking gulps of the warm night air. We treaded water, Willie watching me. His face was illuminated by the glow in the water, but his eyes were hidden inside caverns of shadow.

'We should head back,' he said quietly.

'I'm all right, Willie.'

I lay on my back and floated in the flat, glowing sea. After a moment Willie followed me. That night, side by side, we drifted among the galaxies of sea-stars, while far, far above us the asterisks of light marked out the footnotes on the page of eternity.

BOOK THREE

Chapter Nineteen

Willie
Penang, 1921

The tide had lured the sea away when Willie went down to the beach. Under the morning sun the mudflats, corrugated by the currents, seemed to stretch all the way to the shores of the mainland.

He had completed only three stories. He would need to write three or four more of them when he was back in London – a satisfying collection, to his mind, required half a dozen stories at the very least. He had written down Lesley's tale of her affair with a Chinaman as she had told it to him, but he had not worked out how he would craft the shape of the story. It would make him a goodly sum of money, of that he was certain – not enough to pay off his debts, but hopefully sufficient to keep the ravening wolves beyond the walls for a few months. Her marriage, however, would be ruined if he published the story. He would change a few details here and there to camouflage her identity, of course, but people in the Straits would know whom he was really writing about.

He looked around the beach and saw Lesley with a Malay woman at the tideline. The Malay woman was digging in the sand with a stick, a bucket by her side. He went over to them and peered into the bucket. He jerked his head back, then looked again. Clambering over one another were the oddest-looking creatures he had ever seen. Their smooth, olive-coloured carapaces reminded him of the helmets worn by soldiers in the trenches; and their tails, long and stiff and tapering to a sabre's point, looked more than capable of inflicting a mortal wound. One of the crabs had flipped onto its back, exposing its gaping mouth, soft, pulsing gills and five pairs of little legs scrabbling desperately at the air.

'Horseshoe crabs,' said Lesley, grinning at his repugnance. 'Their eggs are a delicacy. My old amah couldn't get enough of them.'

The Malay woman had dug up another crab burrowed in the sand; she yanked it out by its tail and dropped it into her bucket.

'I told her to give six of them to Cookie,' she said. 'Oh, don't look so alarmed, Willie – they're for the servants, but you're most welcome to try them.'

Side by side they walked along the beach, sitting down on the sand when they came to the end of the bay. A fish eagle skimmed low over the gleaming mudflats.

'Last night . . .' he began, then stopped, trying to find the words.

Never before in his life had he ever stepped into the ocean after dark, and certainly not with a naked woman, but it had turned out to be one of the most transcendent experiences of his life. Floating in the sea of light, he had felt untethered from the bonds of time, eternal. And after they had emerged from the water and walked home, he was convinced a faint blue glow was fluorescing off his body.

In the end he just said to her, 'I'll carry it in my memory to my dying day.'

'It's rare these days,' she said, 'but when Robert and I were first married we'd see it almost every month. We couldn't run fast enough into the sea whenever we saw it all lit up.'

He wondered what had mesmerised her down there in the deep last night. Fearing the worst when she did not resurface, he had dived in after her and had found her far below, enclosed in a bulb of dimming, wavering light, a lantern adrift in the currents of the sea.

'I was glad when Robert signed up in the war. That sounds terribly heartless of me, doesn't it? But those few years he was away, I didn't have to pretend to be fine. I didn't have to pretend to be happy.'

'Why did you lie for . . . Ethel at her trial?'

'How could I not, when I was in the same situation myself?'

The mountains on the mainland were emerging from the night, hardening once again into their eternal forms.

'They seem so near, don't they?' said Lesley. 'So near, but at the same time as distant as myth, or a memory.' She paused for a moment, then went on. 'They always remind me of a poem I had learned at school: "'What are those blue remembered hills . . .'"

"'That is the land of lost content/I see it shining plain/The happy highways where I went", Willie said, "'And cannot come again.'"

A P&O liner was steaming past, heading out into the Andaman Sea. It was probably making for India and down the coast of Africa, to round the Cape of Good Hope and sail towards Southampton. The sight of it filled Willie with despair – in three days' time he and Gerald would also be on a ship, for their long voyage home.

'The last time you spoke to Ethel,' Willie said, as they strolled back to the house, 'what did she mean when she told you "He made me do it, I had no choice. He made me kill William"?'

'I haven't a clue, Willie. For a long time I kept thinking about it, trying to understand what she meant, but . . .' She shrugged.

'We've travelled around Malaya for months, but no one's told me anything about Ethel Proudlock. I've never heard her name . . . mentioned.'

'It happened so long ago. And people here are ashamed of her. She had let the side down, you see. They wanted to forget about her, erase every trace of her.' She brushed away a leaf from his shoulder. 'And they did.'

'You never heard from her again?'

She shook her head. 'William left KL less than a year later. I don't know if he ever joined her.'

'I'd like to see the house where Sun . . . plotted his revolution.' Willie paused, then added, 'And the House of Doors.'

The rickshaw dropped them outside the squat, grey-stone building of the Chartered Bank and they strolled down Beach Street with its European shops: watchmakers and wine merchants, cafés and tearooms, gentlemen's outfitters and shoemakers. Willie was starting to feel as if he was in Cheltenham on the equator when Lesley led them into the Asiatic quarter. The labyrinthine streets held a trove of Chinese and Hindu temples and mosques; he even saw a forlorn-looking synagogue. The shops sold a bewildering variety of goods – brassware and cloth and biscuits and sesame seed oil and nutmeg and silks and sacks of spices and dried fish hanging on hooks – but there were also mysterious stores where he saw nothing being sold, just one or two old people sitting in the dim and empty interior, gazing out into the street.

Never before had he seen so many races of Asiatics in one place: Malays and Chinamen and Javanese and Bengalis, Siamese and Tamils and many others he couldn't identify. Itinerant vendors shouted out their wares, piling onto the din of motors and buses and rickshaws.

He removed his linen jacket, draping it over his arm. Perspiration fused his shirt to his back. They squeezed their way between rattan baskets heaped with mounds of salted fish and dried shrimp and shallots on the five-foot ways, Lesley giving him the histories of the clanhouses they passed. Strolling down Love Lane she filled his head with lurid tales of the wealthy Chinamen who kept their concubines in the upper floors of the drab little shophouses. They stopped for a few minutes to admire the Kapitan Keling mosque before turning right at a small crossroad junction into Armenian Street.

He had been hearing so much about the street from Lesley, but to him it appeared indistinguishable from the other streets and lanes.

As in the other sections of town the shophouses were gaudily painted, the lower half of their front walls cladded in porcelain tiles, their window frames and shutters picked out in blue or yellow, green or red. Bicycles and pots of flowering plants and bamboo stood on some of the houses' five-foot ways. The smell of frying spices from a kitchen somewhere watered his eyes and set him coughing.

'Belachan,' Lesley said, enjoying his discomfort. 'Fermented dried shrimp.'

'Thank god the Huns . . . didn't use it against us in . . . the war.'

Old men and women sitting on low wooden stools chatted on the five-foot ways; small children giggled and cupped their hands over their mouths when Willie waved at them. From within a shophouse gusted out the hailstorm of a mahjong game in progress.

'Just like every town in China,' said Willie. 'Always at their . . . mahjong tables, the Chinese.'

Lesley walked ahead, then halted at a shophouse, waiting for Willie to catch up with her.

'The Tong Meng Hui's base,' she said.

Willie crossed his hands behind his back and took in the whole house. Above the lintel hung a rectangular blackwood signboard carved with a pair of Chinese ideograms covered in gold leaf. Over each of the barred windows flanking the doors was an oddly shaped ventilation hole that made him think of bats. Through the open doors he glimpsed a pot-bellied Chinaman in tatty white shorts and a singlet sitting in a rattan chair, picking his nose as he read his newspaper.

'The house doesn't . . . draw attention to itself.' Willie looked up and down the street. A few yards to their left was a small playground. Beyond it ran another street, lined with more shophouses. 'It's a stone's throw to the docks, with convenient escape routes if they were raided by the authorities. I can't fault Sun's choice of Penang for his HQ – British banks here to move their funds around the world, a telegraph service, and an . . . extensive transport network.'

'You sound like quite the spy,' said Lesley, giving him a sidelong glance.

'So this is where you used to come?'

'Twice a week. Mondays and Thursdays.'

'You played a role in his revolution too. You're part of the history of China.'

'A tiny, insignificant role, long forgotten already.'

They walked back to the junction and crossed to the opposite side. 'We're still in Armenian Street,' Lesley said. 'It goes all the way down to the harbour.'

They strolled in the middle of the street, stepping aside for the odd rickshaw or a pushcart hawker. They followed the street to the last shophouse in the row. The expectant look on her face told him that they were standing outside the House of Doors.

He studied its façade, imprinting its every detail into his memory so he could describe it accurately later. The windows on the ground and upper floors were shuttered. The space above the lintel was bare, and the main doors themselves were plain, their wood weathered and smooth.

'Have you been inside . . . since Arthur left?'

'No.'

'But you have the key.'

'I will only enter the house again when he comes home.'

She beckoned him onto the five-foot way. He touched the doors, examining them, but he saw nothing out of the ordinary. He tilted his head to the left, and then to the right, feeling slightly foolish. And then he saw it.

Embossed on the doors' surface was a network of lines, each one about an inch wide and spanning the breadth and height of the doors. He reached out his hand and touched the wood, his fingertips following the curve of the lines – they were no deeper than the thickness of a leaf. It was, he thought, like a watermark concealed in a sheet of paper, its shape coalescing before your eyes only when you caught it at a certain angle in the light.

He backed away from the doors. Now that he knew the lines were there, he could clearly see the pattern stamped into them; opening either one of the doors would cleave it precisely in half.

How strange to come upon his own symbol here; he felt off-kilter, as if the humidity had affected him.

'Does it work for you?' Lesley traced the lines of the hamsa with her fingers. 'Has it protected you from danger?'

He detected no hint of scepticism or mockery in her voice; on the contrary she sounded genuinely interested in his answer, hopeful even.

'I've escaped death many times.' They sat down on the dusty bench by the doors. 'When I caught TB the doctors said I . . . wouldn't recover, but I did. Before the war I did something . . . unofficial . . . for the government. I was often in danger; I nearly got killed a few times. And once, during the war, I . . . drove out to a field in my ambulance to look at a building. I was standing right next to it, having a smoke. As I was walking away from it a shell . . . flew across the sky and exploded against the wall, bringing the whole thing down on the very spot where I had been standing just seconds earlier.'

'The tidal bore in Sarawak,' said Lesley. 'What happened there?'

He cupped his hands on his knees. A woman came out onto the five-foot way in the shophouse across the street, three joss sticks in her hands. She closed her eyes, her lips moving in a long soundless prayer. When she finished she inserted the joss sticks into the ash-filled brass bowl of a small red altar hanging on the wall. Smoke unthreaded from the joss sticks, plaiting and dividing as it climbed into the bright sunlight.

'Shortly after we arrived in Singapore,' Willie began, 'I received an invitation from the Rajah Brooke to visit . . . Kuching. I was keen to go – I'd heard so much about the Kingdom of the White Rajah. I liked Kuching – it was small and peaceful after the hurly . . . burly of Singapore. We stayed in the Rajah's palace, on a hill overlooking the town. We wanted to travel up one of the big rivers into the interior, so Gerald hired us a boat. It was crewed by four strapping . . . Dyaks.

'We set out at dawn. The river was brown and smooth and wide. Our boat was a long and narrow sampan, sitting low in the water. During the day we'd recline on cushions under a . . . canvas canopy, watching the riverbank gliding past, or the egrets rising off the banks in white, silent drifts. Monkeys shrieked from the thick trees. Gerald asked the boatmen about . . . crocodiles, but he was immediately shushed – it was bad luck to even mention them when we're on the river.

'At sunset each day we'd moor our boat on the banks of a Dyak village. We were guests of Rajah . . . Brooke, and we were invited to stay with the villagers. Thirty or forty families lived in those long-houses built high on stilts, while underneath them chickens pecked and pigs rooted. We feasted with them. There was usually wild boar on a spit, and muddy-tasting fish steamed with ferns in . . . bamboo tubes. Gerald would get legless on toddy with the village men. I retched my guts out at my first taste of it and I never touched it again.' He smiled. 'They were gentle and friendly, the Dyaks, and sometimes I even forgot that they're headhunters.'

He recalled the clumps of black, round objects hanging from the low roof beams of the longhouses. At first he had thought they were some strange bulbs of dried garlic, but then with a jolt of shock he realised that they were human heads. Throughout the long night, as the Dyaks entertained them with their music and their birdlike dancing, he would glance up at those shrunken heads. Media vita in morte sumus. He could feel their gaze on him even when he looked away, and long after he and Gerald had left the longhouse they continued to leer at him in his dreams.

'How many days did you travel upriver?' Lesley asked.

'A week,' Willie said. 'On our last night, before we turned back . . . downriver to Kuching, I couldn't sleep. I went out to the riverbank and gazed at the night sky. The moon was full, the largest I had ever seen, tinted the colour of rust. Like dried blood, I remembered thinking to myself then.

'We left the next morning. The journey was pleasant, the day bright and hot, windless. I was reading under the canopy when I sensed a change in the movement of our boat. The boatman, standing on the . . . prow with his oars, shouted and pointed downriver. The water was . . . suddenly choppy, rocking the sampan. Gerald and I squinted into the distance ahead, but I couldn't make out anything unusual. And then I saw faint white . . . lines on the water.

'A second later I realised they were waves, heading rapidly upriver. The wind had stiffened, and that was when I heard the sound – a low roar, like a distant waterfall. The waves surged towards us, and the roaring grew louder. The . . . sampan was rocking wildly now. The waves reared up, almost ten feet high. I shouted to Gerald as the first wave folded over us and swept us all overboard. I was spun round and round in the water, dragged . . . down into the muddy depths. I couldn't see anything at all. I felt my shoulder slamming against something . . . hard and jagged. Pain ripped through me. I knew I was running out of air. I kept my mouth clamped tightly shut, but the crazed urge to open it, to breathe, was impossible to fight.

'It was at that moment that I felt my feet sinking into something soft and . . . slimy. I didn't know what it was, but some rapidly dying part of my . . . conscious mind told me I had touched the riverbed. With a last flicker of willpower I kicked myself upwards, up to the surface. I felt I would never get there. But finally, after what seemed like . . . eternity, I broke through the surface. I sucked in the air hungrily, I didn't care that I was swallowing . . . water from the waves.'

Willie pulled out his handkerchief and wiped his neck and face. The air felt as if it had been painted on his skin with a hot, dripping brush.

'Where was Gerald?' asked Lesley.

Willie folded his handkerchief but kept it in his hand. 'I trod water and looked frantically around. There was no sign of him or any of the crew. The . . . waves were still coming, one after another, pushing me under, but each time I clawed my way to the surface again. I caught sight of the sampan; it was overturned, but still afloat. I ducked under another wave and swam towards it. I grabbed its . . . keel but it was too slippery. I tried again and again until finally I managed to cling on to it. I saw Gerald's head breaking the surface, but then I lost sight of him. I shouted at him, but all that emerged from my throat was a rasping . . . noise.

'A moment later Gerald's head breached the surface again, closer this time. He flailed about in the currents, saw the sampan and started swimming towards me. I reached out and . . . hauled him to the sampan. We clung to it. We were in the middle of the river; the banks were far away. My strength was fading, and my shoulder was in agony. The sampan's keel was slippery; I kept losing my . . . grip and sliding beneath the water.

'"I can't hold on," I said. "We *have* to swim for the bank."

'"We won't make it", Gerald said, buoying me up with one arm. "It's too far. Just hold on, Willie."

'We heard shouting. One of our Dyak boatmen was drifting past us, clinging to a plank and . . . kicking himself towards the riverbank. He waved, shouting at us to join him.

'"Come on," Gerald said. He held me tightly to him and we swam to the boatman. We hung on to the plank. The waves were still coming. I didn't know how much time had passed before the river started to settle again. Still clinging to the plank, we kicked our way to the . . . riverbank. I was about to give up when I felt our feet touching the bottom. We crawled out of the river. We grabbed at the tree roots, and Gerald helped me up the muddy, slippery bank. At the top we collapsed on the ground and lay there, gasping for air. We were covered in mud – our legs, arms, bodies, our faces and hair – but we were . . . alive and safe. Or so I thought. Gerald tried to stand up, but then he fell back onto the ground. He was shaking, his fingers rigid, his face . . . contorted with pain.'

Willie stopped talking. The joss sticks on the altar had burned halfway down, powdering the air with the fragrance of sandalwood.

'What was wrong with him?' Lesley asked.

'He was having a heart attack. I recognised the signs. I shouted to the . . . boatman to get help, that my friend was dying. The Dyak looked at me, panic all over his face. And then he turned and . . . ran off into the jungle, disappearing behind the tall grass.

'I was too exhausted to do anything. I cradled Gerald's head in my lap. "You'll be all right," I told him. "Help's coming. You'll be all right."

'I didn't know how long I sat there, stroking Gerald's head, murmuring to . . . him. Finally I heard shouting from the river. A sampan rounded a bend and came into sight. Standing at the prow was our Dyak boatman; he pointed to us on the bank, urging on the rowers. They . . . loaded Gerald onto the sampan. I held tightly to his hand, refusing to let go. We were rowed downriver to a . . . longhouse.'

Lesley nodded slowly. 'No wonder you two looked so sickly when you got here.'

'Gerald's one of the toughest . . . men I know, but I was sure I was going to lose him. If you had seen him then, Lesley . . . But thank God after a few days he recovered. As did I. The headman said the full . . . moon had made the river angry. Except for one boatman, all our crew drowned. It was a . . . miracle we survived.'

'The idea of drowning . . .' Lesley shuddered.

'You know what's the best thing to do if you're . . . drowning? Don't fight it. That was what one of my professors told me. Just open your mouth wide and swallow the water, let it fill your lungs, and you'll lose consciousness in less than a minute.' He gave a mirth-less bark. 'Easier . . . said than done, of course.'

'The hamsa protected you.' She nodded, almost to herself. 'It kept you safe all your life.'

She seemed desperate to believe it, Willie thought. Perhaps she was right. Perhaps his father's symbol, the same colophon he put on every one of his books, *had* kept him out of harm's way.

But if the hamsa did shield him from harm, what was the price for its protection? Was he cursed to live a long, long life, only to watch all his friends and loved ones fall by the wayside? To outlive everyone, even his enemies; to witness his popularity wane, his books forgotten. Perhaps at the end he would beg to be released from life; he would open his mouth as wide as he could and let the water roar down his throat; he would swallow it all in.

Before stepping back into the street Willie looked at the hamsa again. As they walked away from the House of Doors he and Lesley, by some silent agreement, both turned back at the same time to take one last look.

The hamsa had disappeared back beneath the wood, and the cyphered doors were blank and impassive once more.

Chapter Twenty

Lesley
Penang, 1921

Willie was adamant that he did not want an elaborate farewell party, so I invited only Geoff and his wife Penelope. After some thought I dispatched the houseboy with an invitation to the Chinese lawyer Peter Ong and his wife too.

Robert was in his study writing a letter when I went to inform him. He put down his pen and looked at me. 'Why did you ask him?'

'You haven't seen him for years,' I said. 'You used to be very fond of him, didn't you?'

My husband continued to regard me, but I could not read anything in his eyes. 'Is there anyone else you'd like to invite?' he asked.

'There is no one else, Robert.'

It took me much longer to dress and to do my hair than I had anticipated. Before leaving my bedroom I gave myself a final look in the full-length mirror. I almost succumbed to the doubting voices in my head and changed my clothes, but I was already running late.

Robert and the guests were chatting away in the sitting room when I came downstairs. His words broke off in mid flow when he caught sight of me. The others followed his gaze as I, with tiny, languid steps, walked across the room to join them

'My God, Lesley,' Gerald said, putting down his drink, 'how utterly exotic and alluring.'

I was in the full Straits Chinese ensemble: the kebaya, the manik-manik shoes, and I'd done up my hair in the Nyonya style, pinning the bun with a row of jewelled hairpins.

'It's the same one you wore in the . . . photograph, isn't it?' said Willie. 'What's it called now' – he snapped his fingers in the air – 'a "kebaya".'

'The very same one,' I said, accepting a pahit from the houseboy.

Geoff took my hand and spun me around in a slow, small circle. 'It looks beautiful on you, Les.'

'Oh, Geoff. A gentleman would have said . . .' Our smiles were stained with the sadness of shared memories.

The Chinese man standing next to Robert stepped forward. 'My wife sends her regrets, Mrs Hamlyn,' he said. 'She's visiting her sister in Singapore.'

'Peter Ong! My goodness, I nearly didn't recognise you,' I said. 'You've become rather . . . ah . . . prosperous-looking, haven't you?'

The lawyer chuckled, smacking his large paunch affectionately. 'Growing old, Mrs Hamlyn. And too much work.'

He had aged, but he still spoke beautifully. He was four or five years younger than myself, if memory served. He had married well, I had heard. One of the daughters of Towkay Yap. I thought of the first time I had met him, all those years ago.

'Robert was extremely peeved with you when you left him to start your own firm.' I wagged a finger at him. 'And after all that he's taught you, the long hours he spent training you.'

'The memsahib's right,' said Robert. 'But you've made me very proud.'

The dinner gong summoned us into the dining room. In the corridor Geoff drew me to one side, letting the others pass us by. 'Interesting guests tonight, Les,' he murmured, nudging his head at Peter Ong's back.

'It was so long ago. What does it matter any more?'

My brother shook his head. 'Sometimes I have this feeling that I don't know who you are at all.'

The windows in the dining room were open to the evening breeze. Robert and I sat facing each other at opposite ends of the long damask-covered table, with our guests on either side of us. I had placed Peter Ong on Robert's left and Gerald on his right. Willie sat next to me, with Geoff on my left and his wife between him and Gerald.

Sometime during the evening I noticed Robert murmuring into Peter Ong's ear; a smile bloomed over his florid face and he touched Robert's wrist lightly. I looked away from them and gazed around the table. Geoff had put on a great deal of weight in the last few years; he was looking more and more the spitting image of our father. These days he spent most of his evenings at the bar in the Penang Club, avoiding his wife. I watched him pass a bread roll to Penelope, a woman I had never warmed towards, and who felt the same way about me. Robert and Gerald were laughing at something Peter Ong said. And Willie, well, Willie's eyes were, as always, on Gerald.

For the first time in many years I felt a sharp, painful longing for Arthur. Eleven years of silence lay between us. He had kept his word, as I had asked him to – no messages, no letters.

'Are you all right, Lesley?' Willie asked quietly.

Blinking my eyes a few times, I dredged up a smile from deep inside me. 'Some more belachan brinjal, Willie?'

The house had fallen silent. I lay in my bed, listening to the sea.

I had been devastated with grief when Arthur went to China to join the revolution, but, if I were to be honest, a large part of me was also relieved. It was better that way, I had said to myself, much better. It was only a matter of time before we were found out and exposed. We had achieved the impossible – we had kept our affair a secret. Nobody knew about us, nobody suspected a thing. Over the years my memories of all that I had shared with him did not fade, but their sharp outlines gradually softened and blurred, so that there were often moments when I felt as though our affair had never taken place, that it had all been just a story I had read once too often until I could not tell where fiction became memory, and memory, fiction.

And yet sometimes it grieved me that no one would ever know the joy he had given me, and the sorrow I had had to conceal from the eyes of those around me when I lost him. He had given me the strength to remain in my marriage, to endure it. I wanted to tell someone about us, to fill the void of his name, but I couldn't. So I talked about Sun Wen instead. To utter Sun Wen's name was, for me, a way of keeping Arthur alive and vivid in my memory.

I had even tried to write all of it down – how we had met and became lovers, the many hours we had spent together in the House of Doors. But when I read the words on the pages it had felt even more invented to me, even more like a story from a book. In the end I had torn up the pages and scattered them in the sea.

I put on my dressing gown and went downstairs to the verandah. The night was still, lying at anchor. A full, white moon rested on the top of the casuarina tree, bleeding its cold, metallic light over the garden. I was not alone: Willie was leaning against the balustrade, smoking a cigarette.

'Shouldn't you be in bed?' I said.

'I can never sleep the night before a . . . journey.' He blew out a feathery quill of smoke. 'Wonderful party tonight.' He paused. 'It was interesting to see Robert and Peter Ong together.'

'Whatever happened to Verlaine and his lover?' I asked.

'Rimbaud?' He rummaged through his memory, found the pieces he was searching for. 'Verlaine shot him during a drunken quarrel, shot him in the left wrist. Rimbaud filed . . . charges against him.

Attempted murder. He withdrew the charges later, but Verlaine was sent to prison for two years anyway. Their . . . relationship . . . never recovered from it.'

'Poor Verlaine.'

I thought about Robert and me, and about Robert and Peter Ong. I thought about Arthur and myself; and I thought about Willie and Gerald.

'We fell in love with the wrong person,' I said. 'You and Gerald. Robert and Peter Ong. Arthur and myself.'

'I did not fall . . . in love with the wrong person, my dear Lesley. I only made the mistake of . . . marrying the wrong one.'

'How cynical, Willie,' I said.

'What you've told me – your affair with Arthur – it will ruin your marriage if I were to write about it.' Willie took one last drag on his cigarette and flicked it into the garden. 'It will ruin you.'

'That's never stayed your pen before, has it?' I said.

'Is that what you want? To blow your . . . marriage to smithereens?'

I pressed my palms lightly on the balustrade. At dawn the stranger in my parlour would depart from my home; but the day would soon come when I too would no longer be living here.

'I'm tired of the silence between us, Willie. I'm so very, very tired.'

'What about Robert's affair?'

'You must have heard stories like that over the years. Yet you have never written about a homosexual affair in any of your books. You've never even alluded to it in all your stories, not even once.' I looked at him. 'And I think you never will. Why risk drawing the beam of *that* particular light onto yourself?'

His fingers tapped on the balustrade, reminding me of the flicking of an annoyed cat's tail. All at once his fingers stopped moving. 'And Arthur's marriage? Do you have the right to destroy that?'

I unfurled a silky smile at him. 'My dear Mr Maugham, surely you didn't actually think I would have used his real name?'

His face remained tight, then abruptly it slackened. He shook his head, half ruefully but also, I liked to think, half in admiration. 'You've thought everything through, haven't you?'

'I made a decision this evening. I made it at the end of dinner, when we were eating our chendol. When Robert moves to the Karoo,' I said, 'I will be going with him.'

He nodded, but said nothing. In his eyes I saw understanding, and pity.

'Our boys are going to have such a shock when they hear Africa's to be their new home.'

'They'll think it's a . . . thrilling adventure. All boys want to go to Africa.'

I cocked my head at him. 'Did you?'

'I wasn't like the other boys, Lesley.'

'No.' I said. 'You were not.'

I reached over and gave him the lightest kiss on his cheek, and then I went upstairs to bed.

We were having our breakfast on the verandah when Robert lowered his newspaper and told me that, while he had not changed his mind about moving to his cousin's farm in the Karoo, he would be going there on his own. He wanted me to remain in Penang. 'Someone has to look after the house,' he said.

I stared at him. 'You're not selling it?'

'Sell the house? And have my wife and my sons living on the streets?'

There were so many things I wanted to say, but in the end I only managed a tentative remark. 'Money will be tight.'

'We'll just have to manage. You can teach again, can't you? And if we have to, we'll sell our paintings – the Gauguin'll fetch a good price. Should've asked Willie to buy it.' His gaze roamed beyond the verandah to the garden, to the sea. 'I want to come back here, when I'm better again. I want live out the rest of my life here, to smell the wind from the sea.'

He retreated behind his newspaper. I listened to his strained breathing; I studied his hands, his thin, arthritic fingers and his wedding ring, its small diamond winking in the light. What was a diamond after all, but a fallen star that had been buried deep in the earth aeons ago?

'No, Robert,' I said.

My husband put down his newspaper again. 'What's that, my dear?'

'I'm coming with you.' I held up my palm as he opened his mouth. 'No more arguments, Robert. Please. No more.'

We sold Cassowary House and packed our things into crates: the artworks and the furniture; our books, my watercolours, my piano and my collection of Straits Chinese porcelain. I took down the door with the painted hawk from the wall. I would find a place for it in our new house.

We were invited to a few parties before we left Penang. The last one was held in the mansion of a Chinese tycoon in Leith Street. The man's father had been the Chinese Consul appointed by the Ching dynasty, and he had built the mansion for his seventh wife. Arthur had once confided to me that the consul was one of Sun Wen's clandestine supporters. 'The man might be the representative of the emperor of China,' he said, 'but he's also a pragmatic businessman hedging his bets.'

When the string quartet struck up a waltz, Robert turned to me. 'Don't let me stop you, my dear.'

'I think we'll leave the dancing to the young people this evening. Oh look – there's Noel.'

'The poor chap, he's just standing there, all alone. Shall I ask him to dance with you?'

'I don't think he'd be interested,' I said. 'Look again.'

Noel Hutton's complete focus was pinned to a Chinese woman waltzing with a Chinese man. The woman was in her early twenties, with a strong, narrow face and high cheekbones. The instant the music ended Noel pushed his way through the crowd to the young lady. He said something to her; she arched an eyebrow and looked at him. And then, without a word, she dismissed her partner and took Noel's hand.

'My God, I've never seen him so brazen,' said Robert.

Noel took the Chinese woman into his arms as the music started again. They moved awkwardly at first, but quickly adjusted themselves to the other's quirks. Halfway through the dance she stumbled. Still clinging to his arm, she pointed to her shoe.

'She's broken her heel,' I said. 'No more dancing.'

But I was wrong. I watched, wide-eyed with admiration as the young lady slipped out of her shoes and flung them over the heads of the other waltzing couples into a corner of the room. Barefoot, she resumed dancing with Noel, both of them oblivious to the censorious looks directed at them.

We left the party shortly afterwards, but the next day we heard that Noel and the young lady had danced with only each other for the rest of the night. Noel invited us to their wedding, but we had already left Penang by then.

Epilogue

Lesley
Doornfontein, South Africa, 1947

The sun is retreating behind the mountains when I go out onto the stoep. I sit in my wicker armchair – the same pair from our verandah in Cassowary House – and pour myself a full glass of red wine. And then, as I have done every evening since Robert died, I fill his glass as well and set it on the table between us. This is the time of the day when I feel his absence most keenly, when I remember how we would sit here side by side and drink and talk about the books we were reading. More than our conversations, I miss our shared silences as the wick of another day is lowered behind the mountains.

They look different this evening, the mountains – they seem further away, their outlines blurring into the sky. I think of the mountains across the sea from my old home.

Over the course of the day I had drilled down deep into the layers of strata, all the way into the bedrock of my memories, recollecting my life in Penang, the people I had known there – Arthur and my brother and Sun Wen. But most of all I had been reliving the two weeks when Willie Maugham and his lover had stayed with us.

'I received a book today, Robert,' I say to the empty chair next to mine. 'One of Willie's old books. *The Casuarina Tree*. You remember it?' I sip my wine, feeling it warm my insides. 'Forgive me — it was a stupid question. Of course you'd remember it. It wasn't one of your favourites, was it?'

The vastness, the emptiness of the Karoo countryside made me want to weep when we first moved here. Everything was so bleak — the land, the light, the faces of the people. I was a child of the equator, born under monsoon skies; I pined for the cloying humidity of Penang, for the stately old angsana trees shading the roads, for the greens and turquoise and greys of the chameleon sea. I missed my garden in Cassowary House — the trees I had planted, the flowers and shrubs I had tended. I pictured the bright, high-ceilinged rooms in the house, their curtains lifting in the breeze. On the farm, whenever I heard the rumour of thunder, I would stop what I was doing and go out onto the verandah. Seeing the hulls of the heavy clouds rising from the edge of the world, I would silently beseech them to sail towards us and give us rain to revive the earth's scents and quench my soul. But more often than not those cloud caravels would sail further away from me, trailing echoes of fading thunder in their wake.

With time I adjusted to my new life in Doornfontein. People here didn't give two straws about who I was related to, which committees I sat on, or which wives of important men I had had tea with. After a while I realised that I too no longer cared about those things.

The skies were not crowded with dragons, but here I discovered the stars. They were so bright and clear, so different from the constellations above Penang. Every night, after Robert had retired to his bedroom, I would lie on the patch of kweek grass in the garden, searching the night sky with my field glasses, a thrill bolting through me whenever I saw a dislodged star streaking across the heavens. I learned their names and their shapes: the Southern Cross; Auriga; Coma Berenices; Horologium; Orion; Circinus; Apus; Andromeda. I soon knew them all, these constellations in the night sky, constellations that had, since the beginning of the world, been sinking into the earth each morning, to rise again the next night.

Despite my scepticism, as the months passed Robert's lungs unclogged and loosened up; his breathing grew less tortured. His appetite flourished, and with time he grew strong enough again to ride a horse. Following a few lessons from one of Bernard's stable hands, I started going on rambles with Robert around the farm on horseback; it was something we had never done together before in all the years we were married. He cut a dashing figure on his horse and I was reminded of why I had fallen in love with him twenty years ago.

In the waning breaths of autumn we decided to ride out to the farm's northern fences. We set out early one morning, when the air smelled of the rested earth and the day was still just a glowing filament stretched taut across the horizon.

We were high up on an escarpment when there came, from the edge of the world, a soundless explosion of light as the sun rose. We halted our horses and watched the light spreading across the veld: it crisped the peaks of the mountains, then lit up the lower hills and ridges; it blew across the kopjes and the valleys, the kloofs and the stony plains. The world had never seemed so immense to me as during those fleeting moments when the earth was turning its face towards the sun.

We resumed riding, heading down the escarpment onto the plains. The landscape was always the same unchanging dun, dusty emptiness. I was four or five paces behind Robert when I saw him raising his hand carefully, at the same time reining-in his horse. The land was flat and scrubby, broken by narrow reefs of rocks. Mindful of jackals, I reached down for my rifle strapped to the saddle, but I stopped when I saw what had arrested his gaze.

A pair of ostriches was pecking at the ground about ten feet away. The larger bird's plumage was black with patches of white on the lower half of its body; the smaller ostrich was drab and dusty brown all over. They curled up their necks and stared at us, their eyes big, glassy orbs fringed by thick, long lashes. Deciding we were harmless, they lowered their heads and returned to their pecking.

I couldn't help grinning with childlike wonder: I had never seen these birds in the flesh before. They looked like creatures from myth, neither fowl of the air nor beast of the land.

The ostrich with the black feathers fanned its wings. 'That's the male,' said Robert. 'He's on heat – his legs are pink, do you see?'

'They're much bigger than I imagined.'

'They look quite like cassowaries, don't you think?' said Robert.

I studied him from the corner of my eye. He sat upright and motionless, his attention fixed on the birds, the top half of his face shadowed by the wide brim of his felt hat.

'A little bit, I suppose,' I said.

Robert spurred his horse onwards, and I followed him. We had been trotting for about ten or fifteen minutes when the ostriches sprinted past us, soundlessly, weightlessly, their thick, luxuriant tail feathers shaking like trees in the wind. Their clawed feet seemed never to touch the parched, rocky ground, not even to lightly graze it. Looking at them, I understood why ostriches couldn't fly – they had no need to.

We watched the two birds run on and on, into the horizon, into eternity.

Geoff wrote and told me that Willie had visited Malaya again three years after he had first travelled there. *The Casuarina Tree*, the book he had published after his stay with us, had made him more famous than ever. But the people he had met in the Straits Settlements were furious with the stories he had written about them; he had betrayed their trust, and he had not even taken the trouble to disguise the names.

But what had they expected, after all, I said to myself as I read Geoff's letter, when they had revealed to him the secrets interred in the darkness of their hearts?

They stayed three months on their second visit, the writer and his secretary. Willie had asked my brother for our address, but if he did write to us, we never received his letter.

Robert bought a copy of *The Casuarina Tree*. He read it and passed it to me, not saying a word. I opened it with more than a little trepidation. After I turned the last page of the final story, 'The Letter', I remained in my armchair by the windows, watching the sun move over the mountains. I marvelled at Willie's ingenuity and the leaps of imagination he had taken with Ethel's tale. He had woven it into something that was familiar to me, yet also uncanny; factual, but at the same time completely fictional. After a while I opened the book and read the story again.

Later that evening, when I carried our gin pahits out to Robert on the patio, he said, 'Rather impertinent of Willie to put us in his stories, don't you think?'

'Well, he's *your* friend, Robert.'

Willie had crafted a compelling story about Ethel Proudlock, but he had not written about Sun Wen, and there was nothing in any of his stories about my affair with Arthur; in the end he had not betrayed his friendship with Robert. I was disappointed, but in truth I was also glad.

'I just wish he had described me accurately.' Robert looked down at his seated form. 'I'm not "baldish" and "stoutish", am I?'

I laughed. 'He didn't think much of my looks either.'

'We got off lightly, I suppose – even if he *did* cast you as a murderess. The bloody cheek of the man.'

Reading 'The Letter' had brought back to me Ethel's strange remark in the garden of Cassowary House on that balmy afternoon before she left Malaya for ever, and I mentioned it to Robert.

My husband turned his head slowly towards me. 'She said that to you? "He made me do it"?'

'What do you think happened between them? I always thought they had a contented marriage, if not a happy one.'

Robert stretched his bare foot and rubbed Claudius's belly. The dog thumped his tail on the floor; he was getting on in years, but Robert had refused to leave him behind in Penang. It suddenly struck me that since we moved here I had not seen Robert feeding him any cheese, not even once.

Robert took a sip of his pahit and shifted in his chair. 'What I'm about to tell you, Lesley, must remain strictly between us,' he said, looking directly into my eyes. 'You can never reveal it to anybody.'

'I'm your wife, Robert.'

He continued to look at me, and I could see that he was uncertain of what I really meant. He put his drink down on the table and began to tell me a story.

'After Ethel was found guilty and while she was in gaol awaiting the Sultan's pardon, Pooley, the more senior of her lawyers, went to see Sir Arthur Young, the High Commissioner for the Federated Malay States. Certain facts had come to his knowledge during the trial, Pooley informed the High Commissioner, facts which indicated that William Steward's death was premeditated.

'Pooley told Sir Arthur that he had no evidence,' said Robert, 'and that his conclusion was based on facts that he couldn't divulge due to his professional duty.'

According to Pooley, when William Proudlock was away in Hong Kong, Ethel had gone for drives with Steward, and she had made frequent visits to his bungalow. William Proudlock found out about it when he came home. He began to blackmail Steward. Steward, afraid that he would be publicly shamed for being involved with a married woman, gave him the money at first, but then William Proudlock started demanding more, and finally Steward put his foot down. He was supporting his mother and sister in England, he couldn't give Proudlock more money. He asked Proudlock to return the money he had given him or he would go to the police. William

Proudlock refused to return the money, so Steward started pressuring him. If Proudlock did not give him back his money, everyone in the FMS would know his wife had slept with him.

'Rather ironic, isn't it – the victim turning the tables on the blackmailer,' said Robert.

Who would ever have suspected William Proudlock of being a blackmailer, and what was more, blackmailing another man about his own wife's affair? After all these years, I finally understood the reason for Ethel's loathing of her husband.

'What did William do?' I asked.

'He consulted a lawyer in KL. He wanted to know what the legal consequences were, if . . .' Robert paused. 'If a woman were to shoot a man who was trying to rape her.'

'If she were to kill him,' I said.

'If she were to kill him.' Robert nodded. 'William told Ethel what he wanted her to do. He also warned her that he would divorce her if she refused. He hatched a plan for her to invite Steward over one night, and he arranged for himself to be out of the house.'

'But . . . why didn't she refuse? She could have left him. She could have gone back to her father.'

'She couldn't ask her father for help,' Robert continued, 'because William Proudlock had approached her father with his plan, and he agreed to it. If she didn't go along with it, they warned her, William would divorce her, and her father would refuse to take her in. So you see, Lesley, she had nowhere to go and no one to turn to.'

I felt sickened. 'How do you know all this?'

'Sir Arthur asked for my advice – unofficially, of course. You remember that time I had to rush down to KL? He asked to see me urgently. He had written a confidential report of what Pooley told him and wanted my advice before sending it to the Colonial Office in London.'

'Was anything done about it?'

'I told him that, in my opinion, nothing could be done unless

Ethel confessed to what she had been forced to do. Nothing at all.'

'Poor Ethel . . .' I said. 'Poor, poor Ethel.' No wonder she couldn't wait to leave. They forced her to kill Steward. They forced her – her husband and her own father. Bastards.

'Pooley also mentioned that, based on what he was told, Ethel is illegitimate. Her mother – her real mother – was her aunt, the sister of her father's wife. There was also talk that her mother was Eurasian.'

Ethel had once confided in me that she had had an unhappy childhood, and that she had never felt she belonged in her father's house. I thought that she was just being overly dramatic. Now I wished that I had been more sympathetic to her.

'Willie sailed very close to the truth,' Robert said. 'If he only knew just how close.'

One day in the June of 1925 I received a letter from Geoff. He had included the obituary for Sun Wen that had been published in a Hong Kong newspaper a few months earlier. Sun Wen had died of liver cancer. He looked distinguished in the photo that accompanied the obituary. He had divorced his wife and married the daughter of one of the richest men in China. There was not a single reference to Chui Fen in the article; I wondered what had happened to her. I wondered too if Arthur had returned to Penang, to his wife and his daughter.

Over the years Geoff continued to send me newspaper cuttings about Willie. He had lost a great deal of money in an unwise investment, but with the success of *The Casuarina Tree* – a success propelled, I'm not at all too modest to say, by what I had told him over the course of those many nights – he had managed to recoup his losses. In another newspaper article I read about his divorce from Syrie. He was photographed standing by a plain, stuccoed wall painted with 'Villa Mauresque', the name of his new home on the Cap Ferrat; set above its name was his Moorish symbol, as large as the top half of his body. He was as elegantly dressed as always, a cigarette in a long-stemmed ivory holder clamped between his fingers. He had found his house by the sea. I was happy for him.

In the winter of 1938, sixteen years after we had moved to Doornfontein, Robert suffered a heart attack while at his desk. He lived for another five days. Before he died, he told me, his voice weak but insistent, to go home to Penang after his death. I took his hand and kissed it, but I said nothing. To my surprise I found my face wet with tears.

I buried him in the family cemetery on the east of the farm. He had asked that his headstone be engraved with his favourite line from Horace: 'Caelum non animum mutant qui trans mare currunt'. Once, long ago, he had told me what it meant.

I continued to live in Doornfontein, far from the world beyond the mountains. My sons grew up, became men. Edward read law at Oxford and became a King's Counsel, as his father had wanted for him. James found minor success as a novelist in London. Another war came; James enlisted in the army and was posted to Malaya. He died there, his body ploughed into the earth of an unmarked grave, in the land where he was born.

Geoff didn't survive the war, although his wife did. Her last letter to me informed me that she had remarried and moved to Australia. After that we stopped writing to each other.

Night has fallen, and the chill is stealing into my bones. There is no moon tonight. My glass of wine was empty long ago, and I have been sipping from Robert's. I go inside the house to cook my dinner, but I pause before the wooden door hanging in the corridor. The paint has faded even more over the years, but the bird of the mountain is still there, still drifting above the misty gorge, carrying the warrior's name beyond the clouds.

Willie Maugham must be in his seventies now, if he is still alive. I suppose if he had died I would have heard about it, even out here in the middle of nowhere. Does he still write? Does he still think of us — of me — sometimes?

It has been many years since I last read *The Casuarina Tree*. After dinner I open the copy I received that morning and begin to read it again. When I come to the last story, 'The Letter', I don't rush through it. I take my time, opening myself to the echoes Willie's words summon up. And as I read, I have the strange sensation that I am looking down from a great height at Cassowary House. I see the garden and the trees — the pinang, the casuarina, the angsana, and that venerable raintree with its great girth. I see the white arc of the crescent driveway on the front lawn. In a rushing silence I descend, down and down, passing through the terracotta roof tiles and the plastered walls like wind through silk. Unseen and unheard, I glide through the corridors and the rooms of my old home. I see Robert coming out of his study, laughing at something he had read and calling for me to share it with him. I stop to watch myself reading a story to my sons in the nursery. I chuckle at the sight of Ah Peng chaffing our syce Hassan in the kitchen. I follow the salty breeze billowing through the house out to the verandah and onto the sunlit lawn. I am on the beach, empty except for the sky and the mountains on the mainland. And then I am swimming with Willie in the darkness of night in a sea of blue fire.

'The Letter' had been made into a film, and Robert and I had gone to watch it at the bioscope. If it had felt unsettling to read the story, it had been disconcerting to sit in the darkened theatre and watch Bette Davis play Ethel; to watch, my hand pressed to my lips, as she shot her lover on the verandah. Six bullets fired into his body as he was fleeing from her into the tropical night.

I wonder where in the world Ethel is. Is she still alive? Is she happy? If she has read the story, or more probably — she was not one for reading books, I recall — if she has seen the film, there would be not the tiniest shred of doubt in her mind that I had been the one who had revealed the private details of her affair to Willie.

True, I had betrayed my friend, but in doing so I had prevented her from being erased from history. I refuse to feel guilty. Because of Willie's story, Ethel Proudlock will never be forgotten and, in a smaller way, neither will I. What he had worked into his tale was merely a shard he had broken off from the larger story I had given him. It is a small shard, but it is enough for me.

My eyes return to Willie's symbol on the page. With my forefinger I trace the additional lines that had been inked-in by a later hand. They frame the symbol in a rectangle, the line in the middle cleaving it in half, dividing it into the twin panels of the front doors guarding a house, a house with many more doors within it, each one of them turning slowly in the air, turning like the silent cogs of some great mechanical clock.

It is almost forty years since I last saw Arthur. He has kept his word, even after all this time. No letters, no notes. Instead he has sent me this message in a book, a message that only I could de-cipher. The doors, which have been closed for so many years, are now open again.

Pressing my finger on the hamsa, I think about the past, my past, but most of all I think about new stories that have not been written by anyone yet.

I get out of bed and put on my dressing gown. In the sitting room I sit at my piano and stare at the yellowing keys. A minute passes, then another. I bring my hands up from my lap and start to play Reynaldo Hahn's *L'heure exquise*. I play it slowly, pressing down the keys with careful precision, sending each note out into the night.

When I finish I play the same piece again, one more time. Then I close the piano and go out into the garden.

The night is vast and still. My breaths hang in the air like clouds of moondust. I lift my face, searching out the familiar patterns sequined into the night sky. For a long time I stand there in that great hall of the temple of stars. I should go back to sleep, I tell myself. I have to get up early. There are many tasks to do in the coming days and weeks — travel arrangements to make, things to hold on to, and things to let go of.

But first there is a letter I must write and send, a letter to Arthur, waiting for me in the House of Doors.

Here, on the margins of the desert, it is just gone midnight, but as I turn towards the east, turning with the rotation of the earth, I know that, on an island on the other side of the world, it is already morning.

Acknowledgements

The House of Doors is a work of fiction; nonetheless, it features characters and events drawn from history. Ethel Proudlock's murder trial took place in 1911, but I have set it in 1910 to coincide with Sun Yat Sen's extended stay in Penang.

The following books were helpful to me in the writing of my novel:

A Writer's Notebook by W. Somerset Maugham (William Heinemann, 1949)

The Summing Up by W. Somerset Maugham (William Heinemann, 1938)

The Gentleman in the Parlour by W. Somerset Maugham (William Heinemann, 1930)

The Casuarina Tree by W. Somerset Maugham (William Heinemann, 1926)

The Secret Lives of Somerset Maugham by Selena Hastings (John Murray, 2009)

Willie: The Life of W. Somerset Maugham by Robert Calder (Heinemann, 1989)

Somerset and All the Maughams by Robin Maugham (The New American Library, 1966)

Conversations with Willie by Robin Maugham (W. H. Allen, 1978)

Somerset Maugham by Ted Morgan (Triad Granada, 1981)

Remembering Mr. Maugham by Garson Kanin (Bantam, 1973)

Murder on the Verandah by Eric Lawlor (HarperCollins, 1999)

Sun Yat-Sen by Marie-Claire Bergère (Stanford University Press, 1998)

The Unfinished Revolution: Sun Yat-Sen and the Struggle for Modern China by Tjio Kayloe (Marshall Cavendish, 2017)

Sun Yat Sen in Penang by Khoo Salma Nasution (Areca Books, 2008)

My deepest gratitude to the staff of the excellent National Archives of Singapore for their warm welcome and unstinting assistance. It was a pleasure to visit the archives to conduct my research.

And to Dr Patrick Tan: thank you for our long and entertaining conversations about Somerset Maugham, and for your friendship.

An interview between the author and Tom Sutcliffe, *Front Row*, BBC Radio 4

TTE: It was Dr Sun Yat Sen's story that started this whole journey of writing this novel. I heard of his name from my father when I was a young boy because my father grew up on the same street – Armenian Street – as Dr Sun Yat Sen's headquarters. So my father was always telling me, 'oh, we've got Dr Sun Yat Sen just a few doors away'. That gave me the idea to write a novel with Sun Yat Sen as a character. And also as a form of tribute to my father because he died in 2013.

TS: So, it's been ten years in the writing, this novel?

TTE: It has been but I wasn't writing it all the time. Originally, I was going to write another novel, a different story, but I had to go for a knee operation, which didn't end up well. So, that particular book I felt required too much work, too much research. I told myself, let's start on this story. That's right, *The House of Doors*, because it's going to be a small and easy story to write. But little did I know it wasn't!

TS: Before we find out how those other strands came in, just explain the House of Doors, because that's a very important location in the novel.

TTE: Well, the House of Doors is what we call the shop house on Armenian Street, which is just a few doors away from Sun Yat Sen's headquarters as well on the same street. And it's the house where Lesley Hamlyn — one of the characters in my novel — finds a form of sanctuary and liberation from her life. It's where she discovers herself and gives full rein to her feelings and emotions.

TS: And it's called the House of Doors not just because, like all of these shop houses, it has these very distinctive carved doors at the entrance to it. But the man who owns it is collecting them because they're obviously fading away from the architecture and he wants to preserve them.

TTE: That's very right. He buys up all these doors from homes, shop houses, temples and clan buildings that are about to be demolished, and he collects them and displays them in this house. He hangs them from the rafters. He hangs them on the walls. So, that's why it's called the House of Doors.

TS: So you've got Sun Yat Sen. How did Somerset Maugham arrive and Elizabeth (Ethel) Proudlock, who is this woman who was tried for murder?

TTE: I felt Sun Yat Sen alone wasn't enough for the novel. I didn't want to write an entire novel about him because then I felt it would entail too much research again, and I've always been a fan of Somerset Maugham. I've been looking for a way to write about him without resorting to a biography as well. So I had this idea of bringing him to Malaya and discovering how he heard about Ethel Proudlock's trial. Now in reality, my research showed that he heard about the trial from Ethel's lawyer in Singapore but I've taken some artistic licence and let Lesley tell him about the story.

TS: Your epigraph for the novel is from Somerset Maugham: 'Fact and fiction are so intermingled in my work that now, looking back,

I can hardly distinguish one from the other.' Is that a kind of permission slip from your subject to sort of play with fact and fiction?

TTE: It is. You see because I saw these various real-life characters and the trial as mirrors. They're reflecting each other all the time and it's like a kaleidoscope where the slightest shift in position or in perception changes how you look at the whole pattern. That's what I'm hoping the readers will experience. That every time they read *The House of Doors* or they read something by Maugham or about Sun Yat Sen, it changes their perception of the book and of the characters as well.

TS: Well, as you say it, it's got multiple overlapping plot lines. It's also got two narrators who are sometimes at odds with each other in how they're telling the story. How did you keep track of it all in the writing of it?

TTE: It was much easier because of the different voices. Lesley's chapters are in the first person and Maugham's chapters are in the third person. Originally, every chapter was in the first person and I found that style confusing to me. I had to change that to different first person and third person and it worked out well because there's a lot of information in the Somerset Maugham chapters which I had to convey to the reader.

TS: And you can't do that through Lesley.

TTE: And Lesley's chapters are all from her point of view, which is what I wanted as well, because it shows how restricted and confined her world is.

TS: And indeed, her attitudes at times. She's very shocked that Somerset Maugham turns up with his secretary, Gerald, who was also his lifetime companion.

TTE: Yes, she wasn't happy with that. It's the attitudes of those days that she was reflecting.

TS: It's a book very much preoccupied with being remembered and the possibility that you might be entirely forgotten. I mean, almost the first line of the book is this . . . is this line of poetry: 'A story, like a bird of the mountain, can carry a name beyond the clouds, beyond even time itself.' That recurs again and again.

TTE: It's intentional. I suppose I don't have any children, my books are my children and I have this obsession – my friends would say – of being remembered after I'm dead. My books are the only way I can try and achieve that. And with Lesley, I try to give her that same anxiety about being forgotten.

TS: The interesting thing for Lesley, of course, is that she's not being remembered for having written a book, but potentially for having been *in* a book, and there's a lot of discussion about how Somerset Maugham actually *did* use real people as the beginnings of his stories and, very often, not much changed.

TTE: Sometimes he couldn't even be bothered to change the character's name. For instance, with Sadie Thompson in 'Rain', he used her name.

TS: What's your feeling on that? Lesley sort of challenges him at one point and says this is wrong. You shouldn't be doing it. You're stealing people's lives. What's your feeling on that?

TTE: I think it's morally questionable. But you know Somerset Maugham, in one of his journals, wrote that people were upset when they couldn't recognise themselves in his books!

TS: You said you admired Somerset Maugham. I mean now, of course, he might be accused of appropriation in a different way, of having colonially appropriated and written as a tourist. Do you think he gets these places right?

TTE: He wasn't in any place for long. He caught the atmosphere of the locations well. But I suspect that he wouldn't be much of an

TS: So what is it you admire about him as a writer?

TTE: He caught the emotional and human honesty. Well, that's his strength. He captures human weaknesses very sharply and very clearly. And he doesn't judge them. He's written about murderers and adulterers and cowards, and he doesn't judge them because to him, the greatest sin is hypocrisy.

TS: Which is slightly ironic given his life — that he had to lead it in concealment.

TTE: Yes, he had to lead it . . . But you know he tried to break away. Eventually he left his wife and he set up his house in the South of France. So, in a way, he tried . . . but we're all prisoners of our time, aren't we?

TS: In Malaysia, what are the kind of feelings about that colonial period?

TTE: I don't think many of us look back that far. We're very much living in the present moment. For Malaysians, history . . . Well, I can't say for every Malaysian but the general feeling is that it's the past. So let's live in the present and let's move on and make money and be successful!

TS: There's a very striking line in that story 'Rain' which lots of people in the novel refer to. It's referred to more than once in the novel because at the time it was a rather shocking story, and it caused something of a scandal. There's a line, it must be the shortest Somerset Maugham ever wrote: 'Desire is sad.' Do you agree with that?

TTE: I think unfulfilled desire is sad. Desire is empowering if it's fulfilled. But for Maugham, for much of his life, his desires were never fulfilled. That's one of the reasons I think that that line is there.

TS: And you have him replying to it in the book because you have him saying no story that lodges in the mind is not about love, at some level.

TTE: Yes. That was my epiphany as well when I was writing that scene. It suddenly struck me that all the great novels that we remember are all about love.

TS: And there are love stories here that are unexpected. I mean, Lesley has a love story that you tease us with in a certain direction. And you're leading us up the garden path a little bit. But also her husband has a love story.

TTE: Yes.

TS: Why was it important to have that kind of mirroring of her experience too?

TTE: I wanted to show Lesley and her husband as mirrors of Somerset Maugham's marriage to Syrie. We read a lot about Somerset Maugham having the freedom to be what he wanted to be. But for his wife there wasn't that option. With *The House of Doors*, I tried to show it from the wife's point of view. What happens when the situation is similar to that? To show that it was a very unfair time for women. That she couldn't have the freedom to love whoever she wanted. It's a mirror situation.

TS: Did you write some of it in Penang?

TTE: No.

TS: No? It was just memory, was it?

TTE: It was memory and I put myself in a trance when I write through music. I usually listen to one or two of the same pieces of music and it's on an endless loop writing that book.

TS: What is the piece of music that you play?

TTE: With this, it was Reynaldo Hahn's 'The Exquisite Hour' which is referenced in the book.

Interview first broadcast on BBC Radio 4's *Front Row* on 15 May 2023. Presented by Tom Sutcliffe and produced by Kirsty McQuire and Julian May for BBC Audio.

Listen to the interview on BBC Sounds: bbc.co.uk/programmes/moo1lyhk